ELSEWHERE

Eleven-year-old Billy Clegg and his big sister Peggy disappear from their home in Leeds after a suspicious fire in a local mill. The owner says the children caused it by lighting fireworks on Mischief Night. Their widowed mother Betty, badly injured in the incident, doesn't know if her children are alive or dead. She prefers to think of them as being *elsewhere*. Following various adventures, the resourceful duo find themselves a long way away from bleak post-war Britain. Though successful, both of them are haunted by memories of the fire and the possibility that they caused their own mother's death. When the family is finally reunited, the repercussions continue...

ELSEWHERE

ELSEWHERE

by

Ken McCoy

Magna Large Print Books
Gargrave, North Yorkshire,
BD23 3SE, England.

British Library Cataloguing in Publication Data.

A catalogue record of this book is
available from the British Library

ISBN   978-0-7505-4729-1

First published in Great Britain in 2018 by Piatkus

Copyright © 2018 by Ken McCoy

Cover illustration © Mary Wethey/Arcangel by arrangement with
Arcangel Images Ltd.

The moral right of the author has been asserted

Published in Large Print 2019 by arrangement with
Little, Brown Book Group

Magna Large Print is an imprint of Library Magna Books Ltd.

Printed and bound in Great Britain by
T.J. (International) Ltd., Cornwall, PL28 8RW

To Valerie Elisabeth Mary Gill
(as was, before she married me)

Chapter 1

Leeds, 4 November 1946

The light had gone from the day and it was now Mischief Night when otherwise well-behaved children roamed the streets, bent on causing mischief. Garden gates would be removed and swapped with neighbours' gates; dustbins removed and left in the middle of nearby roads; doors would be knocked upon with the callers then running away (a simple hoax for the more infantile mischief-makers); rival bonfire stacks would be set on fire a day earlier than the proper date – 5 November, Bonfire Night – a serious piece of mischief, this. The rival stack would have been created by many weeks of 'chumping' or collecting wood for the bonfire. To have all that hard work destroyed a day early was seriously annoying and always provoked retaliation from the victims; but it was all good, traditional fun, with the same stunts being passed down through the generations, with little variation.

On the odd occasion the miscreants would be caught and given a thick ear for their trouble, but it was worth the risk and these summary punishments were never reported to parents, and certainly not to the police by parents who had been no better behaved in their youth.

Bonfire Night was thus named because on 5

November 1605, Robert Catesby and his gang of dissident fellow Catholics, including Guy Fawkes, were planning to blow up Protestant King James I who, two years prior to that, had succeeded Queen Elizabeth I as the English monarch. Way before that, in 1567, at the age of thirteen months, he had assumed the crown formerly belonging to his mother, Mary Queen of Scots, becoming King James VI of Scotland. Even once he was over forty, the Scots didn't have much time for him, believing him to be tainted by his mother's Catholicism, though his regents and advisers had taken pains to bring him up in the Protestant tradition.

It seemed James was unpopular with Catholics too, for not making a stand and adopting his mother's faith once he reached his majority. This led them to take matters into their own hands. Early one November morning in the second year of James's rule over England, prompted by an anonymous letter, guards searched the cellars of Parliament and found Guy Fawkes standing guard over thirty-six barrels of gunpowder. When asked by his interrogators why he was in possession of so much explosive material, his reply was: 'To blow you Scotch buggers back to your native mountains!'

Perhaps he thought this reply might endear him to his monarch, who was constantly having trouble with the Scottish branch of his kingdom, but it earned Guy, or Guido Fawkes as he was known back then, no clemency whatsoever. He was sentenced to be hanged, drawn and quartered: a punishment designed to strike terror into the hearts of anyone even contemplating such a heinous act of treason. He was to be 'put to death halfway between Heaven and Earth, as he was unworthy of both'.

And so it was that on 31 January 1606 Fawkes was dragged on a hurdle to receive this terrible punishment, prior to which he had been tortured mercilessly on the rack. However, while he was hoisting his broken body on to the scaffold, he decided he'd had enough of this torment and would make his own way to heaven, if that indeed was where he was bound. He flung himself, head first, from the ladder and broke his neck, dying instantly and thereby denying the executioners their moment of grisly retribution. This also ensured, by personal order of the king, that henceforth Fawkes's fellow Catholics were denied the right to vote, and in fact declared to be traitors, especially the Jesuit priests. Fawkes's remains were vengefully quartered, and his butchered body parts put on display around the kingdom, with his head on a spike on London Bridge, along with those of his fellow Gunpowder Plot conspirators.

King James also ordered that throughout the villages, towns and cities of England bonfires should be lit on 5 November ever afterwards to celebrate his survival. He was an unmanly monarch and those who knew him best referred to him as Queen James, though not to his face.

Four hundred and some years later, the passage of time had left people wondering if they lit their bonfires as a reminder of this act of treachery or as a way of celebrating the courageous men who once tried to remove a tyrannical government. Countless fires were lit in celebration or commemoration; countless properties put at risk in consequence. This particular story begins on 4 November 1946, and the building in danger was not the Houses of Parliament but Blainey Brothers' clothing factory in Leeds.

The factory was five storeys high, built of Victorian brick, and had six stacks pointing a total of twenty-four smoking chimney pots at the Leeds sky – a sky which already held its fair share of soot. The skyline was also dominated by the gleaming white clock tower of Leeds University's Parkinson Building, completed ten years previously. This was the scene being contemplated from a nearby hill by two boys and a girl.

'That's Leeds University, that is,' said Peggy Clegg, the girl. 'You two might be goin' there if you pass your scholarships. They give you a degree and then you can be a teacher or a doctor or summat.'

'Who wants to be a teacher?' said her brother Billy. 'I wanna be a Spitfire pilot.'

'What? So the Germans can shoot you down?'

'The Germans have lost again – that's two nil to us. So they can't shoot anyone down. All I'll have ter do is fly around at five hundred miles an hour. I bet it's great fun.'

'Me as well,' said David, who'd been instantly converted to the idea of being a fighter pilot with no one to fight.

The three children were unaware of the concealed peril threatening the peaceful scene below. They didn't have thirty-six barrels of gunpowder, they just had a few tuppenny fireworks, and they definitely weren't planning on blowing up the factory. But someone else was.

'Our mam works in there,' said twelve-year-old Peggy. Her actual Christian names were Margaret Mary. She was a bright girl, pretty enough, albeit somewhat gawky in build and not particularly athletic, unlike her younger brother Billy who was matchstick thin but very lively, and forever in trouble both at school and at home, although he wasn't a bad lad at heart. When Peggy was with him she kept him in check, as she could easily beat him up and Billy knew it. In fact, she could beat up most boys of her own age.

'It looks a right mucky 'ole,' said David.

The three of them stared solemnly down at the 'mucky 'ole', which was coming to the end of its useful life. A quarter of its windows were un-glazed, giving it the appearance of a dark and dirty monster with twenty sightless eyes. The rest of the unwashed windows either reflected the sparse lighting from the gas lamps below or were illuminated by a murky yellow light from within.

'It is a right mucky 'ole,' said Billy. 'Our mam gets her cards and coppers this week.'

'What does that mean?'

'It means they're layin' off workers – sackin' them all. Cards is what they give yer when yer leave and coppers is yer wages. When our mam loses her job, we'll be looking at the workhouse. Our dad got himself killed in Germany so he's no help. Mind you, when he were here, he was as much use as a chocolate fireguard was our dad.'

'Chocolate fireguard ... that's a good 'un,' said David, laughing.

'You shouldn't say that, Billy,' chided his sister.

'I don't see why not. I thought it were right good news when our mam got that telegram. I didn't see her cryin' like Raymond Lubble's mam did. Ray said his mam didn't stop cryin' for a fortnight. Our mam never even started.'

'I never liked Raymond Lubble,' commented Peggy. 'He never blew his nose.'

Billy and David recited together: 'Here comes trouble, Raymond Lubble/ Four foot six and a big snot bubble.'

'It's not right to be glad our dad's dead,' said Peggy, returning to the subject. 'You shouldn't speak ill of the dead. Mam says that.'

'Give over, Peg. Our dad used ter beat us black an' blue when he came home from the pub. He beat our mam as well. He spent all his wages in t'pub while we lived on bread an' drippin'. Then he came home an' knocked seven bells out of all of us.'

'There aren't no workhouses no more,' said David, who was not related to the brother and sister, just a friend. 'My mam reckons me dad died in one o' them camps in Germany, with him bein' a Jew. They'd have got us as well only me uncle Eli sneaked us out under some rags on his 'orse an' cart an' handed us over to some kind French people who looked after us. Then we got sent here.'

'Are you a Jew?' asked Billy. 'Is that why yer've got a big nose?'

'Dunno. Mam says it's best not ter be, so we're nowt really. Anyroad your nose is bigger than mine.'

16

'We're Catholics.'

'I know. D'yer go ter Confession an' tell the priest all yer sins an' stuff?'

'Yeah, yer've got to if yer a Catholic, else yer won't go to Heaven.'

'Won't I go to Heaven then?'

'No.'

'Where will I go?'

'No idea. Where d'yer wanna go?'

'Bridlington.'

'What's wrong with Scarborough?'

'Nowt, but I've been ter Bridlington before with me mam an' it's all right.'

'We've been ter Blackpool.'

'I know.'

'What about your dad?' asked David. 'D'yer think he went to Heaven?'

'Doubt it.'

'Well, I reckon my dad went to Heaven,' David said. 'He were a real good bloke, me dad. Never got drunk nor nowt. I reckon he's in Heaven.'

'So what?'

'How d'yer mean, so what? Me dad were a Jew and I bet he's in Heaven, an' your dad were a Catholic and he's most prob'ly in Hell, so there's not only Catholics go to Heaven.'

'No, I 'spect not,' conceded Billy.

The three of them trudged down the hill to-wards the factory, their conversation stifled by the profundity of the subject they'd chanced upon. Both David and Billy inwardly vowed never to talk about religion again as none of it made much sense, although Billy was mulling over in his mind the prospects of Bridlington versus Heaven. He'd

17

never given any thought to there being a choice.

'What fireworks have yer got?' he asked David, having now expunged all thoughts of Jews and Catholics and Bridlington and Heaven.

The conversation was back on familiar ground. Fireworks beat religion into a cocked hat as far as the boys were concerned. David grinned. 'Six Little Demons, two rockets and two jumpin' crackers.'

'I've got nine Little Demons.'

'I've got three Roman candles and a rainbow fountain,' said Peggy. 'Why do you only ever buy bangers? All they do is go bang.'

'I got nine for a shilling,' said Billy, 'an' they're usually tuppence each, which makes one and six, so I saved sixpence. And bangers are always best for Mischief Night.'

'I think Mischief Night's daft,' said Peggy, but she was a girl so she was ignored. Fireworks was boys' stuff.

'I bet I can fire one of my rockets straight through one o' them ground-floor winders,' said David.

'Bet yer can't,' said Billy.

'How much?'

'I bet yer two of me bangers – that's fourpence. How much did yer rockets cost?'

'Fourpence each.'

Billy spat on his hand and held it out to seal the bet. David took it, shook it and wiped his hand on his coat as Peggy looked on in disgust.

The trio reached the bottom of the hill and entered the factory yard through a hole in the wire fence. A loose strand caught on a tear in Billy's

18

coat and extended it by three inches. He didn't notice. Torn garments were always a mystery to him, in pretty much the same way as scabs on knees and scuffed shoes were. To their left, lights were on in four of the five storeys, but in front of them, and to their right, there was no sign of life. Billy pointed left, up to the second floor of illuminated windows.

'Our mam works up there. It's a cuttin' room. She's a cutter.'

'What's she cut?' David asked.

'Cloth for clothes and stuff. She uses right big scissors called shears. Sometimes she brings stuff home to make clothes for us. We've got a Singer sewing machine. Auntie Dot gave it to us. Mam made our Peg's dress.' David looked at Peggy's dress, mostly hidden by her coat which, unlike her brother's, had no tears. Not knowing a good dress from a bad one, he made no comment. Instead he picked up a loose brick from the ground.

'Watcha gonna do with that?' Billy asked.

'Well, I'm allowin' fer gravity.'

'Why?'

'Because everythin's affected by the first law of gravity,' said David, hoping not to be questioned too deeply.

'What's that when it's at home?'

'What goes up must come down.'

'And that's a law, is it?'

'Yep. If you jump up in the air, yer don't just stay there. Yer come back down.'

'I suppose I do. Didn't know it was a law though.'

'If I prop the front end of a rocket on a brick,'

19

said David, 'so it's pointing up a bit, gravity'll bring it down and then it'll go straight through that winder.'

'Nah, I think yer'll need two bricks on top of each other,' said Billy – to whom the success of the venture was more important than winning the bet.

David set the rocket on one brick and bent down to the ground to trace its line of travel before conceding that Billy might be right. He found another brick nearby, stood it on top of the first, and bent down again to assess its new line of flight.

'I think that should do it,' he said, taking care to point the rocket in exactly the right direction.

Billy was by now as keen as David that the experiment should be a success. They were just boys and still young enough to put the spirit of adventure first. Billy stood behind the rocket as David lit the blue touch-paper.

The rocket fizzed into life, made a clumsy take-off and rose no more than three feet before hitting the factory wall and bursting into a mass of coloured sparks.

'Yer need another brick at least,' suggested Billy, 'mebbe even two more.'

'I think three should do it,' said David, setting up his second rocket on three bricks. He turned to Billy. 'Same bet again? Double or nowt?'

After the dismal failure of the first attempt Billy was surprised his friend was still up for a bet.

'Okay,' he said. 'Double or nowt.'

Lester Blainey was in the cellar beneath the

working half of his factory. At that time in the evening the workers should all have left, but he'd overlooked the fact that a few of them would still be hard at work, finishing jobs already started that would be needed first thing tomorrow. Although the factory was due to close down, the female workers took pride in their jobs and to them the prospect of imminent redundancy was no excuse for shoddy workmanship. If a job was worth doing, it was worth doing well. Anyway, they all clocked in and out and would be paid for any overtime – even if it were self-inflicted.

Lester Blainey often overlooked the obvious in the running of his factory, which was why it was running out of business. He owned the place after 'buying' his late brother's share from his sister-in-law, failing to pay her properly in an act of financial chicanery that had left her all but destitute. His younger brother Jack had always been the driving force in the business but he was dead now, the victim of cancer, unlike the many men killed in the recent war that Lester Blainey had avoided due to his advancing years. He was fifty-seven years old and way past his best – although even his best had never been all that impressive. His only other sibling was his sister, Jean, who was a senior police officer with the West Yorkshire Police. She wouldn't have been so pleased had she known what he was up to.

The clothing factory had been losing orders steadily. The following Friday, Lester Blainey had intended to close the place down and sell up, but right now he'd decided to set fire to the place and claim the insurance money, which should leave him considerably better off.

The cellar housed several boilers, originally coal-fired but now gas-fired after Jack had had them all converted before the war. The installers had warned them at the time about the danger of explosions caused by gas leaks. They'd be strong enough to bring the whole factory down apparently. Jack had taken careful note of this and imposed a strict safety regime for anyone having cause to enter the cellars, whereas Lester had seen a distinct advantage in having an easy means to hand of destroying the building. This was the reason that had brought him here tonight. The mains gas supply to the unoccupied part of the factory had been turned off. Lester Blainey was in the cellars beneath the working half. There were four separate boilers in four cellars and he knew the locations of all the large locking nuts which, when loosened, would release gas from the mains. All the task required was a large spanner that he had with him, and a certain amount of elbow grease. He knew not to open the nuts fully, just enough to ease open a joint and allow a slow build-up of gas throughout the basement. He did the job methodically, one cellar at a time. The last nut proved to be the most awkward – seemingly a fraction too large for the spanner – but he needed the gas to escape from here too so as to carry out his plan. This was the fourth and largest cellar. He would then place a lighted candle in the doorway at the far side, about fifty feet from the gas leak. After that he'd run out of the cellar door, which was just adjacent to the overall exit from the building.

'Shit!'

He cursed aloud as he tried to jam the spanner on to an unforgiving nut. Among his bag of tools Blainey found a lump hammer with which he hammered the spanner until it fitted around the locking nut. Then he heaved on it with both hands until it made a full turn and he could smell gas escaping. Time to make his own escape. Fifty feet away, in the doorway, he placed the lighted candle, then ran as fast as he could up the steps and out into the factory yard.

He wasn't sure how long it would take. He knew the candle wouldn't go out for hours but guessed the gas would reach it within minutes, if not seconds. His second guess was a lot nearer.

David lit the touch-paper of his second rocket and stood back, hoping for success this time. Failure would mean losing four of his six Little Demons to Billy. Peggy lit her rainbow fountain and stood back as it sparked into life. David's rocket fizzed, took off and went straight through the target window, hitting something inside and disintegrating in an explosion of noise and colour. His jubilation was cut short by another explosion that was a thousand times louder. It blew out the bottom of the factory wall fifty yards to their left. Out of the dust and debris a man came running towards them. He stopped and looked at the window through which David's rocket had gone. It was still firing out the sparks that should have formed its aerial display. Then he looked at Peggy's rainbow fountain that was still going from colour to colour with sparks flying all over. For once, Blainey thought on his feet and saw the advantage to himself in this unexpected turn of events. He stopped in his tracks, despite the imminent collapse of the building and the flames issuing from behind him, and screamed at the children.

'What the hell are you buggers up to? Throwing fireworks at my factory... Just look what yer've done! Blown the whole bloody place up!'

'It weren't us, mister,' said David. 'It were only a fourpenny rocket an' it went off in there.' He pointed at the dark window on the ground floor, a good fifty yards from the inferno.

'I don't care where it went off. Sparks travel. It were you lot what did this – I'm getting the police! And don't think I don't know who you are.' The furious man peered hard at Peggy. 'You're Betty Clegg's lass.' Then he looked back at the blazing building and suddenly realised it still had a few occupants.

'She's in there, yer know. Yer mam's in there!'

'What?'

'Yer mam's working up there with the other cutters.'

The four of them looked up at the second-floor cutting room, which by now had flames shooting out of all the windows.

'Will she have got out?' asked Billy.

'How the hell could she have got out?' said the man, scathingly. 'The lower floors are even worse.'

Billy ran towards the blaze but was stopped by Peggy, who ran after him and grabbed his arm.

'It's no use, Billy. We can't do anything.'

'But our mam's in there!'

He screamed at the flames.

'MAAAAM!'

His sister joined in, although she knew their cries would go unheard. They screamed until they were both hoarse and in floods of tears, staring up, open-mouthed, at the roaring inferno that even now was taking their mother's life. It was an appalling sensation, haunting their memories for many years afterwards; a searing combination of heat, smoke and abject misery that sent them backing away from the fire. Watching it was too much for them to bear. An optimistic thought struck Peggy then. Optimism was all she had left.

'Mam might not be in there,' she said to Billy. 'She usually finishes work at five or half-past at the latest. It must be half-past six now.'

'Do you think so, Peg? I never thought of that.'

'I'm just saying what I know, that's all.'

'You're right. She's always home before half-five. I bet she's not in there at all.'

'Come on, Billy. We'd better go home and see what's what.'

Peggy turned and trudged away. Despite her optimistic words her head hung low in misery. Billy followed her in like manner, as did David, who hadn't lost his mother in the fire but was moved to tears by the sorrow of his closest friends.

Blainey called out after them: 'Hey, you lot! Don't you go running away. I know who you are... I know where yer live!'

He walked as far as the factory gates and turned back to admire his handiwork, pleased that he'd taken advantage of those daft kids messing about with their fireworks. A factory burning down on

25

Mischief Night – the police would have to believe it was kids to blame. In a couple of weeks Lester Blainey's money worries would be well and truly over. He gave no thought to his innocent employees, who had perished in the blaze. The blame for that would be heaped on the kids.

By now the three children were running as fast as they could back up the hill. None of them looked at the scene of devastation below them. Tears streamed down all three faces. Finally, when they ran out of breath, they stood still.

'What shall we do?' Billy asked his sister.

'I don't know. I s'pose we'd best go home an' see if our mam's there.'

'What if she isn't?'

'I don't know, Billy.'

'Yer might have ter run away,' David advised. 'It weren't us what caused all that, but if that feller says it was, they'll believe him, not us.'

'Rotten fireworks!' cursed Billy, taking his from his pockets and throwing them over a nearby wall. The others did the same, as if ridding themselves of the accursed objects might ease their anguish. The three children lived close to each other in Ashton Place, a short, cobbled street of terraced houses. They were old, down-at-heel dwellings, enlivened only by their inhabitants who took pride in their homes and kept the street neat and tidy. Every step was scoured with a donkey stone; every yard was kept clean, as was every window, and every door and gate looked to have been recently painted – and probably had been. Whenever a visiting horse left droppings on the cobbles, a watchful resident would insist that the driver of the cart should remove the nuisance immediately, and such instructions were always obeyed; it was a rule of the street. Washing lines were strung across it from side to side but carried no washing because today was Thursday and washday was Monday. It was the accepted, if unwritten, rule.

They parted company in silence. Peggy and Billy opened the gate to their yard, hoping against hope a light might be on in the back room; but no such luck. Peggy unhooked a key hanging from a nail in the outside lavatory and they went inside. She switched on the light.

'Mam!' she shouted. 'Mam... There's been a fire at the factory.'

No answer.

Their optimism waned. Billy shouted as well. They went through to the front room, always kept for best, then up the narrow stairs to the two first-floor bedrooms. Still no sign of Mam. Billy climbed another flight of stairs to his own attic bedroom, knowing she wouldn't be there either. Why would she be? But it was his last remaining hope. Of course she was nowhere to be seen. He sat down on his bed and burst into tears. Their mam wasn't in, which was where she definitely would be if she were still alive. Peggy, also in tears, came slowly up the stairs to join him. She sat beside her brother and put an arm around him.

'I don't think we've got a mam any more,' said Billy.

Peggy said nothing. Her young brain was trying to think of something to do; something to help their situation. No point going to the police; they'd only lock up Billy and her for burning down the factory. Their mam wouldn't have been the only one to have died in the fire. No point going to any of the neighbours for help either. Both children felt terribly sick in the face of this devastating and momentous loss. Peggy tried to overcome it by thinking of a plan.

'I ... I wonder if David's told his mam what happened?' She voiced her thoughts out loud. 'If he has, there'll be someone knocking on our door any minute.'

'Is ... is there any money in the house?' Billy asked, after several minutes spent sobbing. He knew his sister was trying to do her best for them both, so he tried to help. Their nearest relatives were Uncle Joe and Auntie Freda in Nuneaton. No aunts or uncles close enough to help them, in fact no one at all to turn to, given the enormity of their problem. What happened now was entirely up to the two of them and no one else.

They were on their own.

'It's Thursday ... there should be rent money and some gas-meter money in the box on the mantelpiece,' said Peggy.

'How much is that?'

'About fifteen shillings altogether, why?'

'If we're gonna run away, we might as well take it. We'll need money to run away with.'

'Where would we run to?'

'Blackpool,' said Billy. 'I like Blackpool and we know our way around there.'

'We know the Tower and the Pleasure Beach, that's all.'

28

'It's more than we know of anywhere else.'

Peggy wiped away a tear because her younger brother was right. Their mam had taken them on a two-day trip to Blackpool last summer. It was the only holiday they'd ever had.

'Mebbe we should pack a case with our stuff,' suggested Billy, warming to his own idea. Making a plan would help take his mind off the horror of their plight. 'It won't take much of a case to hold my stuff – a pair of socks, a shirt, me best pull-over and me raincoat.'

'Me too. There's a case in Mam's room. We'll get all our things in that easy.'

'Shall I take me banjo?' asked Billy.

For his age he was a good banjo player.

'Nay, Billy, we'll have enough stuff to cart about without carrying that.'

'Okay,' he said, staring at his precious banjo case; inside it was the instrument his uncle Joe had given him after somehow bringing it back from the war, which was more than Billy's dad ever brought back, apart from a Hitler Youth knife the boy wasn't allowed even to touch. He found himself wishing it was his dad who'd been caught in the fire, not his mam. He mentioned this to Peggy, but she told him not to talk such horrible talk.

'Okay,' said Billy, wishing his sister wasn't always such a bloomin' Goody Two Shoes. He'd swap a dead dad for a live mam any day of the week.

Ten minutes later they were standing at the back door with the packed suitcase, looking round perhaps for the last time at the house that had been their home all their lives. Billy opened the door

29

and Peggy turned the light off. Her brother locked the door and put the key on the hook in the yard lavatory just in case their mam came home and needed it. He dearly hoped she would. In fact, he'd never hoped for anything more.

'Billy,' said his sister as they walked away, 'we're gonna need a lot more than fifteen bob. Have you any ideas?'

She knew Billy had done a bit of shoplifting in the past without being caught. She had remonstrated with him about it many times, but maybe it was a skill that could come in handy.

'I've never nicked no money, Peg, just sweets 'n' stuff.'

'I know. I was only wondering if you had any ideas.'

'Well, I've got one idea but I've never tried it. It were mainly David's idea but I always thought it was a good 'un.'

'What is it?'

'There's an off-licence shop on Compton Road that stays open late. It sells sweets and tobacco and beer and stuff.'

He outlined his plan to his sister as they headed for the shop in question. It was half a mile from their home and run by people who wouldn't know either of them. In accordance with the plan Peggy went in on her own. Her major problem was superseded by the immediate danger she was facing.

'Could I have two ounces of sherbet lemons, please?' she asked the elderly woman behind the counter, having first ascertained that the sherbet lemons were on the top shelf and it would require the stepladder to reach them.

'Just two ounces? That'll be threepence, you know.'

'That's okay,' said Peggy politely, placing a three-penny bit on the counter.

The woman went out of a back door and came back with the steps, which she propped up against the shelf. Once her back was turned, Billy darted in, went behind the counter, opened the till, took out all the notes and left, leaving the till open. He was in and out in seconds.

'Mrs!' called out Peggy.

'What's that, love?'

The shopkeeper climbed down the steps pre-cariously, holding the jar of sherbet lemons.

'When you went up for the sweets, a lad came in and took some money from your till.'

'He what?'

The woman spotted the open drawer and took a few steps towards it. 'Oh, no! He's taken all our notes. Who was he? Do you know him?'

'No, I'm not from round here. He was about fourteen, with ginger hair and a grey jumper.'

'I'd best tell the police immediately. Which way did he go?'

'I saw him run out of the shop and across the road.'

'Look, wait here. We have a telephone. I need to ring the police. Oh, dear, I could do without this. There's some young devils round here... Ginger hair, did you say?'

'Yes, he looked a proper rough sort ... a bit spotty too. Mrs, I need to go, me mam'll wonder where I am.'

'Oh, right.'

As the distraught woman went to ring the police Peggy left the shop and headed for the rendezvous she'd arranged with Billy, who was waiting by a stop for the tram that would take them into town. The two of them boarded it when it arrived and went upstairs, selecting two seats surrounded by empty ones.

'Did you get away all right?' Billy asked, conspiratorially.

'Yeah.'

'Did you shout and warn her that I'd been and gone?'

'I did.'

'And did you leave your sweet money on the counter?'

'I did – threepence – but I didn't get any sweets.'

'That should do it. If you left money and didn't pick up your sweets, they'll think you're daft but honest. They won't suspect you.'

'She thinks you're a fourteen-year-old lad with ginger hair and spots.' Billy was eleven and had dark hair and clear skin. 'How much did you get?' She kept her voice low.

He took a wad of ten-shilling and pound notes from his pocket and began to count them, silently. It was more money than either of them had ever seen in their lives before.

'Twenty-six pounds ten,' he whispered finally. 'That should keep us going for a bit.'

'Blimey! I feel sorry for the woman in the shop. She was really upset.'

'She's nowhere near as upset as us, Peg.'

'Yeah, I know.'

'In fact, I bet if she knew our problems, she'd have given us the money.'

'We've certainly got problems, Billy. So, we've got twenty-seven pounds five shillings altogether – that's a month's wages for most men.'

'I'll give you fourteen pounds and I'll look after the rest.'

'Okay,' said Peggy.

The uniformed police officer took off his helmet and placed it on the shop counter.

'This girl who came in, do you think she was part of it?'

'No, I wouldn't have thought so. In fact, she shouted to warn me that the lad had taken the money. If she'd been part of it, she'd have run off with him – and she left her own money on the counter without me serving her.'

'About fourteen with ginger hair, you say?'

'That's what the girl said. And I think she said he was wearing a grey jumper. Oh, heck! We've lost a full day's takings.'

'How much?'

'Near enough thirty pounds, I should think. I haven't checked it properly yet.'

'Lot of money,' said the constable.

'Money we can't afford to lose.'

'Are you insured against theft?'

'I don't know. I'll have to ask me husband. He's out at the Compton Club. Good God, he'll go mad when he comes in.'

'Well, he can't blame you. Seems to me that this lad knew just what he was doing. He needs catching before he does it again. Ginger hair and about fourteen… I'll ask down at the station. I bet someone down there knows him. Maybe we can get your money back for you.'

'Oh, I do hope you can.'

Chapter 2

Blainey's Clothing Factory, 6.14 p.m.

Betty Clegg put down her cutting shears and called out to her workmate Janice. 'I'm just going to the lav, then I'm away. I've been busting for five minutes but I like to finish a garment once I've started it. Though I don't know why I bother, with old Buggerlugs Blainey laying us all off on Friday.'

'You clocking out, then?'

'I am, yeah. The kids'll have got their own teas with a bit of luck. I can get meself fish and chips and put me feet up. Fish and two penn'orth of chips, nice cuppa and listen to the wireless – *Dick Barton's* on tonight and there's a play – *King Solomon's Mines.*'

'The kids might be out Mischievin', Betty.'

'Oh, damnation! I forgot about that. Our Peg'll keep Billy in check, though. See you tomorrow, Jan.'

'I'm not comin' in tomorrow, Betty. I'm going to Burton's. I've heard they're setting people on in their trouser room. Yer should come with me. We can go together as a job lot – a cutter and a machinist.'

'D'you know, I think I will. Bugger Blainey! That's what I say.'

'Aye, me an' all.'

Betty punched her card in the clock and went down four flights of stairs to the ground-floor lavatories. Ten minutes later she was on her way out of the building when the explosion blew her clean through a window, to land on a grassy area twenty yards away, completely unconscious. Flames roared through what remained of the window; brick rubble and debris poured down on her, almost burying her.

Jimmy Potter, Blainey's maintenance man, had left the factory just seconds before the blast. It flung him to the ground where he shielded his head from the falling debris using his hands and arms. The heat was searing the hair from his head as he picked himself up and staggered away. Jimmy had spent too much time being shelled over in Germany for this to be a complete shock to him, but he wasn't happy about losing his hair, which he patted fiercely with his hands, cursing loudly as he did so.

He saw an arm sticking out of a pile of broken bricks and his soldier's instinct sent him to investigate. He picked away the bricks and thought he recognised a woman from the cutting room.

'Betty... Betty Clegg? Is that you?'

He wasn't entirely certain, such was the state of her face, but it didn't matter who it was: Jimmy had to get her away from here before the whole factory came down on them. He scrabbled away all the dust and broken bricks under which she was buried, picked her up and slung her over his shoulder in a fireman's lift. Luckily wartime rations had kept her slim and she was no great weight to carry. With the front wall collapsing behind them onto the very spot where Betty had just lain, he staggered to the factory gate with her and laid her on the ground as gently as he could. Nearby he saw Lester Blainey, his boss, staring at the conflagration and looking none too worried about the situation. A thought struck Jimmy, who had no time for Blainey. He called across to him.

'This should turn out well for you, Mr Blainey.'

'What're you talking about?'

'Well, I imagine it's insured. Good timing for it to burn to the ground, just when you're closing down.'

This was a bit too near the mark for Blainey, who spat out his reply. 'Don't talk so damn stupid, man! This fire was caused by kids and their damn fireworks. I saw them. One of them was Betty Clegg's girl – not that her mother'll be worried. I reckon she's in there somewhere.'

He nodded towards the flames.

'You don't look too worried yourself,' muttered Jimmy. He chose not to enlighten Blainey that Betty Clegg was lying on the ground close by. In the distance he could hear the sound of fire engines.

'Did you call for an ambulance as well?' Jimmy asked his erstwhile boss.

'Of course I have.'

Within minutes one pulled up. Jimmy ran across and told them about Betty, who at that moment was probably the only accessible casualty. By the look of the mounting flames, all the other victims

36

would perish.

'We'll take her. There's other ambulances on the way,' the driver told him.

'Do you mind if I come along?' said Jimmy, who thought he needed to be around to tell Betty about Blainey's accusation.

'Yes, I think you should. That cut on your head needs stitching, which we can't do here, but we can put something on those burns right now.'

'Oh ... right,' said Jimmy, who'd been ignoring his own injuries up until then. He touched his scalp, very carefully. 'Bloody hell! All me soddin' hair's gone!'

'Hiya, Betty, how're you doing?'

Betty peered up at Jimmy from her bed in St James's casualty ward. Due to the sedatives she'd had, her voice was weak and barely audible.

'I'm told I've got a fractured skull and a broken pelvis, plus all sorts of other stuff. No one's told me what happened. T'last I knew I was in the lavatory. Do you know?'

'The factory blew up, Betty. There's nowt left of it now.'

'All I remember is going to the lav. After that ... well, waking up here.'

'I found you outside on the ground. It looks as though you were blown clean out of the building. What else is wrong with you? You look to be plastered up good and proper.'

'Well, apart from me fractured skull and pelvis, I've got a broken arm, three broken ribs, a broken shin bone and all sorts of other cuts and bruises.'

'Blimey! It'd have been quicker for you to tell

me what you haven't broken.'

'True. Mind you, it might have been a lot worse.'

'How's that?'

'I'm told someone picked me up and carried me to the gate before the factory wall fell down on where I landed. I'm guessing that was you.'

'It was, yeah. I saw your arm sticking out from the rubble.'

'You saved my life, Jimmy.'

'Well, it's a life worth saving. It wasn't much trouble. You're only a lightweight.'

She looked up at him with overwhelming gratitude. He was fortyish and carried a war wound in his leg that restricted him to working as an odd-job man.

'It means a lot to me, Jimmy.'

'Well, I could hardly leave you there.'

'There's them as would have, under the circumstances. Look, I know you've already done a lot for me but I need to get word to my kids, to tell them what's happened.'

'Okay. I can do that for you.'

'What exactly *did* happen, Jimmy?'

'I couldn't say exactly. All I know is there was a massive explosion, like a bomb dropping. Could have been gas leaking out, I suppose. The factory went up in flames. I'd only just left it myself. Then I saw an arm sticking out of the rubble ahead of me, and it was yours.'

'Jimmy, what happened to all the other girls up on the second floor? There were at least a dozen working late, my mate Janice Earnshaw among 'em. Were they caught up in it?'

He shook his head sadly. 'Peggy, I think everyone'll have been caught up in it.'

'Oh, heck! Who else have they brought in?'

He left it a few seconds before saying, quietly, 'Only you, as far as I know.'

'Oh.'

'It was really bad, Betty.'

'I hope Janice is all right. All I remember is going down to the lav...'

'Good job you weren't still sitting there when it happened.'

Betty tried to manage a smile but failed. Jimmy's face turned serious as he leaned towards her. 'Look, I've got to tell you this ... although I think it's rubbish meself. Blainey reckons it was kids what did it, messing about with fireworks. He reckons your Peggy were one of them.'

'Our Peggy! Give over, Jimmy. She'll have been out with Billy and his pal David.'

'I'm only telling you what Blainey said to me. But I reckon it were an insurance job, with him shutting up shop on Friday. I more or less told him so, and that's when he said the kids had caused it.'

'What? My kids burnt a factory down when their mam was inside it? I don't think so.'

'I know. That explosion were massive. It'd take more than a tuppenny cracker to do that.'

Betty closed her eyes as she weighed up everything that had been said. Jimmy stood by her, patiently, assuming she hadn't fallen asleep.

'What time is it?' she asked eventually.

He took out his pocket watch. 'Half-past midnight. They've been working on you for five hours near enough. I've been hanging around waiting for you to wake up.'

'Was that so's you could tell me what Blainey's been saying?'

He gave a brief nod. 'Yes, I thought it best coming from a friend who didn't believe a word of it.'

'Don't you have a wife to go home to?'

'No, I live on me own. My wife left me during the war. It happened to a lot of us. She reckons I came back half the man she married. To be fair I wasn't much of a catch, what with me game leg and sometimes not being right in me head ... although I'm a lot better than I was. When I first came back I was in a proper state – shell-shocked, psychologically damaged, and I could hardly walk or talk. No work prospects at all. She was off on her toes within days. Our divorce came through last month. I didn't contest it, no point. I didn't want her any more than she wanted me.'

'You look all right to me. Not exactly Errol Flynn, but you're not an ugly man.'

'How long do you think you'll be in here?'

'Quite a while, I should think. It'll be a few weeks before I can walk, even with a stick. Look, will you call at our house and tell the kids I'm okay and they can come and see me tomorrow? They'll be in bed, so you might have to knock loud.'

'They'll more than likely still be up, waiting for news of you,' he said.

'Oh my God! If they saw the factory go up in smoke, they'll think I'm dead.'

Jimmy shrugged. She was right.

'I hope no one's accused them of starting it. Their mam dead and them accused of it all... They won't know where to turn. I really need you

40

to go and see them for me, Jimmy.' She looked at his bandages and realised she was asking a lot of him.

'How are you anyway? How's your head?'

Jimmy grinned. 'Bald,' he said, and left to do her bidding, thinking the most likely place to find the children would be at the police station. In a cell probably, or maybe a locked room, with them being young. He decided to check the house first.

The desk sergeant seemed more interested in the ledger on his counter than in Jimmy, who stood patiently in front of him for a full minute before he spoke up.

'Well, it's a good job I'm not here to report a murder.'

The policeman looked up. Jimmy wasn't an impressive-looking man and he was still dressed in the work clothes that had been scorched by the flames. The policeman looked at his bandaged head and asked, 'What can I do for you, sir?'

'It's about the fire at Blainey's Mill. I assume you know about it?'

'Yes, I do.'

'Well, I work there and I was caught up in it.' He pointed to his head. 'That's how I came by this. Only just got out in time. I managed to help a lady to safety as well, which is why I'm here.'

'I'm afraid I don't deal in commendations for bravery, sir.'

This irked Jimmy. 'You don't seem to deal in politeness and good manners either. Is there someone intelligent I can speak to?'

'You only get to speak to me, I'm afraid.'

'Right. The lady's name is Betty Clegg. She's in St James's Hospital with serious injuries and her children appear to have gone missing. She's asked me to try and find them.'

'And you think they might be here, do you?'

'I don't know where they are. I'm here to ask for help.'

'In that case, you'd better come through. Inspector Dennison would like a word.'

'Right,' said Jimmy, puzzled by this sudden change of attitude.

The sergeant opened a flap in the counter and ushered Jimmy through a door, down a short corridor and into a small interview room.

'Take a seat. I'll get Inspector Dennison.'

A uniformed inspector arrived and sat down at the table opposite Jimmy. He opened a notebook.

'Could I have your full name, please?'

'James Albert Potter.'

'Well, Mr Potter, this is an informal interview. You're free to go, as and when you please.'

'I know that. And I didn't come here to be interviewed, I came here for help.'

'Yes, but a capital crime might well have been committed and I have to treat you as a material witness.'

'You mean, the fire? I was very nearly a material corpse! I'm here to try and find the children of a woman called Betty Clegg, who was badly injured in the explosion.'

'Badly injured? You mean, she didn't die in it?'

'No, she's in St James's Hospital. What makes you think she's dead?'

The Inspector looked at a file he'd brought in

with him. 'We were given information that she was in the building when it went up in flames. According to this there were no survivors.'

'Does it mention James Potter on that list too?'

'It does, yes.'

'Well, that's me and I'm not dead either. I don't know who gave you that information but both me and Betty Clegg survived the fire.' A thought struck Jimmy even as he spoke. 'Did the information come from Lester Blainey, by any chance? I've a feeling he started that fire for the insurance money.'

'That's a serious accusation, Mr Potter. Do you have anything with which to substantiate this?'

'Yeah – common sense. The firm was losing money hand over fist. He was planning to close it down this coming Friday. It's all just a bit too convenient, don't you think?'

'Mr Blainey tells us that children were seen playing with fireworks nearby when the fire started. In fact, he saw a firework alive and sparking inside the building. He also recognised one of the children as Betty Clegg's daughter.'

'Yes, that's what he told me.'

'Oh, you spoke to him at the scene, did you?'

'He were standing at the gate watching it all burn down just as I was carrying Betty away from danger. She'd been blown out of the building by the explosion, which wasn't a tuppenny firework going off, I can tell you. It was more like a ten-tonne bomb.'

'You know about bombs, do you?'

'I should do, yes. I was a sapper in the war.'

The policeman sat back in his chair. 'We have

fire inspectors looking for the seat of the blaze, but I'm told that the area where the fireworks were let off was being used as a storage place for highly combustible material. So any unguarded spark there might well have led to a serious blaze.'

'Look, no one knew that building better than I did and there was bugger-all combustible stuff stored in there! Without proper heating it were too damp to store stuff. I reckon it was a gas explosion.'

'So the spark from the firework might have transferred itself to where gas was leaking? That still means the children are culpable and certainly explains why they've run away from home.'

'Well, I spent a lot of time down in the cellars, including today, and I never smelt any gas leak. There were signs all over, warning people not to carry naked flames, and that included cigarettes.'

'And yet you believe it to have been a gas explosion?'

'I do, and I'll leave that one for you to work out, Inspector.' Jimmy got up from his seat. 'I take it you don't know where the children are then?'

'We don't, but if we find them, I'm afraid they'll be arrested and remanded in custody.'

'Well, if that happens their mother's in St James's. I'll leave my address as well, if you like.'

'Yes, please. The fire people will no doubt want a word with you, but I advise you to keep your suspicions about the cause of the blaze to yourself.'

Jimmy nodded, although he had no intention of complying.

Leeds City Station, earlier that evening

Billy and Peggy looked up at the destination boards. 'There's a train to Blackpool at half-past seven,' Billy said. 'Stops at Preston and gets into Blackpool at half-ten.'

'What do we do then? We can't just walk into a boarding house and ask to be put up – we're kids.'

'I've thought about that,' said Billy. 'Down near the Pleasure Beach there's a row of beach huts, do you remember? With its being November, I bet they'll all be empty. We could sleep in one of them.'

'They'll be locked up,' said Peggy.

'Mebbe, mebbe not. I bet we could soon prise a door open. Anyway it's only for tonight. Tomorrow we can think of something else to do.'

'I suppose you're right. We've had enough to think about today.'

'By the way, did you think to bring the ration books?'

'Oh, heck, no!'

'I did,' said Billy, who liked to keep one step ahead of his elder sister. 'I just hope Mam doesn't need them.'

'Well, I hope she flipping well does,' said Peggy. 'I hope she plays hell with us for nicking the ration books.'

'So do I,' said Billy, adding, 'I brought that photo of her off the mantelpiece as well.'

'So she'd be with us?'

'Yeah.'

At that late time of year Blackpool wasn't a popular destination and the children got a compartment to themselves. The three-hour journey went by mainly in silence and they spent it staring out of the window at the dark scenery passing by. Billy divided the money up and gave his sister the fourteen pounds he'd promised her.

'This way if one of us loses their share, we'll still have half left,' he explained.

'Well, I don't plan on losing mine.'

Chapter 3

On alighting from the train, their holiday memories guided them along to the promenade which, in the days so soon after the war, was without the famous Illuminations that had first been displayed twenty years before. The children walked down the promenade towards the Pleasure Beach currently lost in darkness, identifying itself only by the silhouette of the Big Dipper against the glare of distant street lights.

'I'm gonna go on that tomorrow,' Billy said, taking his turn to carry the suitcase.

'Billy, we're not going to spend our money on the Pleasure Beach,' said Peggy.

He said nothing, he knew she was right. It was exactly what their mam would have said. On their summer trip they'd each spent half-a-crown on rides and it hadn't gone far.

'I think this money should last us until after Christmas,' Peggy estimated.

'I wonder what we'll be doing on Christmas

Day?' Billy said.

Had he been able to foresee the answer to his question he'd have been perfectly astounded, but it was a remark to which Peggy had no answer; in fact it caused tears to well up in her eyes. Christmas Day was special in the Clegg household. Early-morning present opening was followed by nine o'clock Mass, which was always a carol service, with Peggy maybe singing a solo 'Adeste Fidelis'. Then back home and playing with presents before helping Mam prepare the Christmas dinner. There'd be none of that this year.

Billy spotted his sister's tears and said, 'Sorry, Peg.'

He shed tears of his own then. Grief kept them both quiet. They reached the part of the beach where the huts stood, twenty of them, all painted in bright colours and backing on to the stone sea wall, about fifty yards away from the high-water mark of the Irish Sea, which swished over the dark sand in cold breakers. There was a three-quarter moon which, glimpsed between clouds, cast a cold and dismal light over the beach. Billy and Peggy went along the row of huts trying all the doors, which were padlocked shut and would remain so until the new season began in the spring.

Billy paused when he found a lock with a faulty hasp – a steel strip attached to the wooden door-frame. In it was a slit through which a U-shaped staple protruded to which the padlock was fixed. It was next to a handle between the door and the frame but the screws had rusted and the whole hasp was rusty and loose under his fingers.

'Peg, this is faulty. We just need something to prise it free with ... something metal.'

'Metal? This is a beach, you don't find metal on a beach. Anyway it's dark. I can hardly see the huts, never mind find a piece of metal.'

Billy bent his head and walked up and down, squinting in the darkness and stamping his feet on the sand to try and locate something suitable. Peggy watched him and felt she ought to do the same, if only to placate him. It was she who trod on the toy spade. She picked it up and squinted at in in the dim moonlight.

'Is this any good? It's a kid's spade but the digging bit's made of metal.'

Billy took it and examined it in the dim light. The wooden handle might give him a bit of leverage if the thin metal of the spade held up. He rammed it as far down behind the hasp as he could and pulled on the handle. The hasp loosened its grip on the wooden doorframe, then the handle broke away from the metal spade.

'I've got it loose, Peg. Can you get your fingers into this gap? You're stronger than me.'

She put the fingers of her right hand into the gap between hasp and doorframe and pulled as hard as she could. The rusting metal dug into her flesh.

'It's moved a bit but it hurts like mad,' she said, taking her hand out and holding it up to her eyes, looking for blood. She felt rather than saw it.

'I'm bleeding.'

Billy gave this some thought then opened the suitcase. 'You put some hankies in here, didn't you?'

'Billy, this is no time to think about blowing your nose. You don't always blow your flipping nose at the best of times. Yer as bad as Raymond Lubble sometimes!'

'No, watch this.'

He wrapped a handkerchief around his hand, which he stuck into the gap. The handkerchief gave him some protection from the rusting metal. With a yank he pulled the hasp clean away from the doorframe.

'See,' he said, triumphantly.

'Clever clogs,' said Peggy, taking the hanky from him and wrapping it around her injured hand.

They opened the door and stepped inside the dark interior. It was a darkness they didn't want to have to get used to, especially when the door was shut. The musty smell was overpowering.

'Niffs a bit,' commented Peggy.

'Yeah, but it's got walls and a roof that'll keep the wind and rain off us,' Billy pointed out. He brought the suitcase inside.

'We're going to have to sleep on a hard floor,' said Peggy.

'We could make pillows out of our coats,' Billy suggested, 'and cover ourselves with all the rest of our stuff. Tomorrow we can buy a couple of sleeping bags or something.'

'We'll probably need to shut the door,' Peggy said, 'to give us some privacy.'

Billy took hold of the door and brought it shut, sending the hut into complete darkness.

'Billy, open it again, please,' said Peggy, quickly.

He kicked it open; he didn't need asking twice. 'Bit much that, wasn't it?'

49

'It was,' she said.

'I wish I was braver,' he said. 'I'm really scared of all this.'

'So am I, but I think we're doing all right for a couple of kids.'

'Are we?'

'We are, definitely. Tomorrow we should buy torches and stuff, maybe a proper oil light.'

'If we leave the door open all night it might not be as smelly in the morning,' suggested Billy.

'I s'pose so,' said Peggy, who wasn't warming to this adventure any more than her brother was. Thoughts of the tragedy they had suffered had been mercifully distracted by their endeavours, but now she remembered their mother once again and wondered if she might still be alive. Peggy put her hands together and knelt down on the wooden floor.

'Dear Father in Heaven, please let our mam still be alive.'

Billy knelt down and joined her. They repeated the prayer six times in unison. It gave them some comfort, but not much. In fact there wasn't much comfort of any kind to be had in the hut that night. Sleep didn't come easily to either of them.

'She might still be alive, you know,' said Billy. 'She might have been out looking for us. Maybe we should have waited for her.'

'Maybe,' said Peggy, but she wasn't at all con-vinced. Rather than have them come home to an empty house, their mother would have left them a note, definitely. But there was nothing to be gained from telling Billy that; Peggy was his big sister and therefore responsible for his welfare.

Chapter 4

The early sun was lighting the mud-grey sea when Billy woke up for the seventh time. Peggy was still asleep but he knew she'd had a bad night too so didn't wake her. He needed to go to the toilet and decided he had two choices: behind one of the beach huts or else a public convenience; but his need required privacy, so that ruled out the beach hut option. He was already dressed, having slept fully clothed, so he left the hut and made his way up to the promenade. He was greeted by screeching seagulls, diving at him and taunting him with their strident cries, hoping he had food about his person, something they could steal. On his previous trip he'd found this entertaining, but not this morning.

Across the road was the Pleasure Beach, which to his displeasure looked deserted. There was a clock that told him it was almost half-past seven and there was a sign at the entrance with the word 'Toilets' written on it and an arrow indicating their location. He crossed the road and followed the arrow, which took him inside the famous funfair. Nothing there even looked like opening. There was no music, no laughter or cries of fear and excitement coming from the various rides. Just a cold wind blowing discarded paper along the asphalt pathways between the amusements and stalls. Nor was the Laughing Policeman audible

51

inside his glass compartment, his infectious merriment provided by a popular record made by Charles Penrose many years previously. Normally a sixpence in the slot would have sent the model of a fat policeman into fits of loud laughter, but not today. He just stood there with glazed eyes and a frozen grin; not even a proper smile.

Men were beginning to arrive, carrying tool bags. Billy stopped a passing workman and asked, 'Is it all closed, mister?'

'It is, lad. Won't be open for four or five months ... that's if we can get our jobs done by then.'

'Are the toilets open?'

'They are, lad. That was our first job – always look after yer own conveniences. We're thankful we did or we'd be in a proper pickle working here. Free as well, for them as work here.'

'Well, I don't work here. How will they know?'

'They'll not be bothered, lad. You won't need no pennies for these bogs. Hot and cold running water as well. Our plumber's made sure of that.'

The conveniences were divided into Ladies and Gents and each had a dozen washbasins with both hot and cold water plus long rows of toilet cubicles. Billy thought how thankful Peggy would be to learn of all this. She was a real stickler for keeping herself clean. He tapped his trouser pocket to confirm his money was still there. It was. Maybe there was a shop nearby where he could buy them something for breakfast and perhaps a bar of soap – both of them had forgotten to bring that. Had their mam been around they wouldn't have left home without soap and a towel. This thought made him sad, as did all memories of his mam who might be dead, and he and Peggy blamed for it. He had his ration book in another pocket, which was something. They could buy soap, but they couldn't buy a ration book.

He settled for running his hands under a hot tap and wiping them dry on toilet paper. Good job they had some of that there, but it was Bronco, that shiny paper no one liked. After leaving the toilet he asked a workman if there were any cafés open nearby, and was given directions to one not far away. Five minutes later he was back at the beach hut, reporting all his findings to his sister.

'They've got hot and cold water, but no soap or towel and the toilet paper's Bronco.'

'So, we need soap and two towels and proper toilet paper. I think we've got enough to put up with without havin' ter use shiny lavvy paper that skids off your bum. We haven't got much, Billy, but we'll have proper lavvy paper from now on. How did you sleep?' she asked him.

'Not very well.'

'Nor me. I don't know how we're going to go on if we have to live all winter in here.'

'I've got an idea,' he said.

'You and your ideas. Go on…'

'Well, with us bein' Catholics,' said Billy, 'we could find a Catholic church and ask for sanctuary. They could maybe put us up and help us.'

'What, in the church?'

'No, in the presbytery, where the priest lives.'

'I know what a presbytery is and I think they'd just hand us over to the police.'

'Peg, they can't do that if you ask for sanctuary. It's against God's rules. I've read it in a book.'

'What would we tell them?'

'The truth. We didn't burn that factory down. How can a fourpenny rocket burn a huge brick building down so quick?'

'Why did that man say we did then?'

'I don't know, but he knew who you were. How did he know that?'

'I don't know, Billy, but he was coming away from where the explosion was. We were nowhere near it.'

'I can't stop wondering about Mam. Honest, do you think she's dead, Peg?'

'I don't know, Billy. I honestly don't. It was an awful fire, though.'

'We need to find out about her, Peg. She might be all right, and wondering what's happened to us.'

'Maybe a Catholic priest could find out for us.'

'I think he could, Peg.'

'Anyway, I need to go for a wee. Across the road, d'you say?'

'Yeah, there's a sign. I'll come and show you, then we can get some breakfast from a café.'

'I think you're right about that church, Billy.'

'I'd best bring the case, eh?'

'Yeah. I think we'd best keep it with us for now.'

They both had a full English breakfast of eggs, bacon, sausage, tomato, black pudding and fried bread. Billy sat back after drinking his second cup of tea.

'Well, I think that should do me 'til teatime.'

'And me. Maybe this is what we should do every day, have a really good breakfast. Put us up

54

for the day.'

'I wonder if there's anywhere that might put us up at night?' said Billy.

'I thought we were going to find a church and ask for sanctuary?'

'Yeah, I know.'

'You've gone off the idea, haven't you?'

'Well, it's a bit risky, Peg. If the priest finds out our mam's dead and we're on us own, he'll most likely call the police.'

'Or he might call Father O'Flaherty at St Augustine's. We should be thinking about Mam, not about us being blamed for the factory explosion.'

'I know. I keep thinking that meself, but I can't help being worried about gettin' locked up in jail.'

'Tell you what,' said Peggy, 'why don't we go to the train station? We can leave the case there all day for sixpence. Then we can take a good look round town and buy whatever else we need if we're going to spend any more time in that bloomin' hut.'

'Sleeping bags, blankets and a torch ... and another padlock,' suggested Billy.

'By the way,' said Peggy, 'if anyone asks why we're not at school, we just say we're on a day trip with our parents and we'll be back to school tomorrow. That's what we'll always say.'

'Yeah, we need to have answers ready for everything.'

'That's what Mam always said about you.'

'Did she?'

'She did. "Eee, our Billy's got an answer for

everything," she used to say – and you did.'

He forced a grin. 'We might have to think up some other answers. I wish I could think of one that'd get us into a boarding house. I'm not looking forward to living in that flipping hut.'

By mid-morning their total shopping amounted to two bars of chocolate and a bottle of dandelion and burdock. They were in a shopping area just behind the Tower when their fortunes changed, but whether for better or for worse would remain a moot point.

A well-preserved, middle-aged lady wearing a fur coat and hat stood staring into the window of a clothes shop near to where the children were standing, planning their next port-of-call. The lady was carrying a heavy handbag but, more importantly, a large purse was sticking out of the bag for all the world to see. She put it down on the ground to ease her burden for a few seconds. An idea formed in Billy's mind, one that needed acting upon very quickly.

'You know that fortune teller on the front,' he said to Peggy. 'Gypsy Petulengro?'

'Yeah, why?'

'I'll meet you there in a few minutes.'

With no further explanation Billy took off at high speed, barely breaking his stride as he bobbed down and whipped the purse from the lady's shopping bag, continuing on his way at full gallop before turning down a side street.

Totally unaware of what had happened, the lady picked up her handbag and went into the shop. A shocked Peggy turned and quickly headed in the direction of Gypsy Petulengro's premises. Billy was waiting there.

'Did she see me?'

'See you? She didn't even notice her purse was gone. She'll be in that shop now, wondering where it is.'

'She looked rich. I bet she could afford to lose it.'

'How much is in it?'

'Dunno. There's an ice-cream place next door, shall we go in there?'

It was a small ice-cream parlour, currently catering for the sparse winter trade with just two tables for anyone who needed to sit down. Apart from the children no one did, nor were there any customers queuing for ice creams. They were sitting at a table, each enjoying a sundae, a luxury they'd never been able to afford before. It was a cramped and shabby place, next to a noisy amusement arcade, with a picture of Blackpool Tower on the wall that seemed surplus to requirements as the real thing was on view through a high window. A youth came in and spoke to the vendor.

'Quiet today, Albert?'

'Yeah, well, apart from that bloody racket from next door.'

'I'd have thought yer'd be used ter that by now.'

'Well, me ears is gettin' older, so I don't hear it so loud nowadays. Anyway, I'm only opening for a few hours. There's always a bit o' passing trade from people comin' and goin' to t'amusements and the Tower – mainly to do a bit o' dancing. Worth its weight in gold ter me is that dance floor. Me and the missis used ter do a bit, yer know, before she passed on. Just ballroom stuff. None of that American jitterbug rubbish. Not proper dancing, that.'

Without making a purchase the youth sat at the children's table, took out a packet of Senior Service and lit one.

'Mind if I smoke?' he said.

'Why ask, you already are?' said Peggy, who knew something of the niceties of smoking in public places.

'Hey, I'll put it out if it bothers you.'

'Don't bother,' she retorted, wondering why he'd sat at their table and not the other one. They didn't like the look of him ... shifty, Peggy thought. He made both her and Billy feel uncomfortable. He looked at them and grinned.

'Pretty slick, that. Do you do it a lot?'

He spoke in a quiet voice so the ice-cream vendor wouldn't hear him.

'Do *what* a lot?' Peggy asked.

The youth craned his head towards Billy. '*You know what* – nick purses.'

Silence from the children, just the blare of music from next door. Billy was wondering if he was some sort of plain-clothes policeman, but surely he was too young – sixteen, seventeen maybe, any older and he'd have been called up for his War Service, even though the fighting was over.

'Who are you?' said Peggy eventually.

'Never mind who I am. Like I said, I saw you and I followed you here.'

'What yer gonna do?' asked Billy, perturbed.

The youth waved a hand at him dismissively. 'It's okay, I'm not gonna turn you in or nowt. I just like your style. You don't look like thieves, neither of you.'

'We're not,' said Peggy. 'We're runaways, if you must know.'

'What're you running away from?'

'That's our business.'

'Fair enough. D'yer have anywhere to stay?'

They answered simultaneously.

'Yes,' said Billy.

'Not really,' said Peggy.

'That means no,' said the youth. 'Who d'yer think's gonna take a couple of scruffy kids in without askin' questions?'

Neither of them had an answer to this.

'What's in the purse?' asked the youth.

'None of your business!' said Billy.

'And we're no scruffier than you,' added Peggy.

The youth's eyes flashed and Billy wondered if they'd been too brave for their own good. The youth smiled then took a deep drag on his cigarette.

'That's the right answer,' he said, tapping his cigarette into an ashtray. 'It isn't any of my business, but it might be, if I was on your side.'

'How d'you mean?' said Peggy.

The youth leant forward across the table and spoke, very confidentially, to Billy. 'Look, open the purse and take out whatever money's in there and stick it in your pocket. That's all yours. I don't want any of it. But these old women often keep valuables in their purses. I'm only interested if there are any valuables.'

'What valuables?' asked Peggy.

'Rings, jewels, stuff made of gold ... you know.

You wouldn't know what to do with anything like that, would you?'

'Prob'ly not.'

'Well, I would and I'd split the take with you. Go on, take the money out and let's see what else is in there.'

Scarcely taking his eyes off the youth, Billy took the purse from his pocket and unzipped it. Inside was a wad of notes, which he took out and stuck in his pocket. He looked to see what else was in there. There were a few coins including two half crowns, which he took out and added to the money in his pocket. Apart from that, just small change, a florin and four pennies.

'Two and fourpence,' Billy said.

'Let me see,' said the youth.

Billy handed the purse over, glad to be rid of this incriminating piece of evidence. The youth examined it more closely and stuck his fingers inside.

'There's a pocket in here,' he said, 'with something in it.'

He took out a gold ring with three diamonds in it and a pair of gold earrings and held them in the palm of his hand, carefully shielding it from two customers who had just arrived at the counter.

'I bet these are worth more than the money.'

'Why would she keep them in a purse?' said Billy.

'No idea. All I know is, it's what some women do. The safest place for a ring is on yer finger.'

'You can have them,' said Peggy.

'I *would* have had the lot if your brother hadn't beaten me to it.'

'How do you know he's my brother?'

'You look alike. He is, isn't he?'

'What if he is?'

'*You* were planning to nick it, were you?' said Billy.

'Yeah, I'd been following her for ten minutes when you two showed up. Don't get me wrong, I don't begrudge anyone their takings, but I was a bit put out.'

'You can have the jewels,' repeated Peggy.

'Oh, no, I can't. I'm going to give them back to you with my address so you can bring them to me.'

'Why would I do that?'

'Because I can fix you up with a nice place to stay and you can help me with my work.'

'What work do you do?'

'I'm a professional tea leaf.'

'A thief,' said Billy, who knew something about rhyming slang.

The youth handed the jewels back then took a pencil from his pocket and wrote an address and telephone number down on the back of a menu.

'That's me. George Golding, and that's my address. My friends call me Goldie. I'm always in at six o'clock for me tea.'

Peggy took the menu, folded it up and stuck it in her pocket, mainly to get rid of this person. Goldie got to his feet and left as quickly as he'd arrived.

'Phew!' said Billy. 'I didn't like him.'

'Nor me, but he could have taken the jewels. I wonder why he didn't?'

Billy shrugged. 'Because he wants us to go and

work for him, stealin' stuff, I s'pose.'

'Yeah, I think yer right,' said Peggy. 'How much money did you get?'

Billy took the money from his pocket. It included three fivers and a wad of ten-shilling notes. He counted it three times, as if he couldn't believe the total.

'Forty-two pounds!'

'What?'

Billy surreptitiously handed it over to her to check. She came to the same total. 'Blimey, Billy, she must have been a millionaire! We could live for months on all this.'

'That's if we had somewhere to live.'

'Maybe we should do the shopping we set out to do.'

At that moment the winter sun came out and turned the grey sea to a shade of deep purple. Light bounced off the windows of a passing tram, dazzling them. The children shared a smile. Since they were both eternal optimists, they took this for a sign that their grey and dismal days were over. They both thought of their mother then, but kept these thoughts to themselves.

After calling in at a café for afternoon tea they reclaimed the suitcase from the station and arrived back at the hut along with the case and a large rucksack containing two sleeping bags, two torches, spare batteries, and two woolly hats. They were hoping their second night here would be more comfortable. They closed the door and found it had a hook-and-eye type of fastener on the inside; just enough to keep it closed and stop it banging in the wind.

Their sleeping bags were warm and comfortable and they both fell asleep quickly and slept well. The next morning they awoke an hour after daylight and were alarmed by a rattling at the door. The various cracks in the hut's joints let in just enough light for them to see each other. When Billy opened his eyes he saw Peggy holding a forefinger to her lips and holding up her other hand to warn him to be quiet. They both held their breath, waiting for the door to open, with Billy preparing what he was going to say. Peggy knew he'd be the one doing the talking, so she made no such preparation. She'd just back up whatever nonsense he came out with. To their relief no one came in, or even opened the door. Eventually the noises stopped and they heard someone walking away through the sand and whistling tunelessly.

'Blimey, what was all that about?' said Billy.

'I think someone was repairing the lock,' guessed Peggy.

'Lock? There isn't a lock on the outside. I took it off.'

'I know, that's what's bothering me.' Peggy lifted up the hook and pushed at the door. It wouldn't open. Billy found his torch and switched it on. 'They've put another lock on the outside,' Peggy said. 'We're locked in.'

'Oh, heck, Peg! Maybe if we bang they might hear us and let us out.'

'And what if they get the police and we're searched and they find all the money and jewels?'

'Oh, heck!'

They both sat down to think. Billy was still holding his torch. He shone it all around their wooden prison, looking intently at its construction. It consisted of plywood panels set into wooden frames. The panels were different sizes and the biggest were about two feet square and at the back of the hut. Billy shone the torch at a panel next to the floor. He put on his shoes and placed his torch so that it was shining full at the panel, then sat on the floor with his feet braced against the wall.

'What are you doing?' Peggy asked.

'I'm gonna try and kick that panel out. I think if we both kick at it long enough we should be able to do it.'

A loud banging started up from a pile-driver over in the Pleasure Beach building site, which easily masked any noise Billy began to make as he kicked at the panel. At school he had a reputation for being the hardest kicker of a football in his year. Had he been more accurate he'd have played for the school team, but had never achieved such glory. Peggy watched intently.

'Hey, Billy, it's going. The bottom's coming away. Keep kicking!'

Billy was kicking with both feet as hard as he could. Eventually he lay back, exhausted.

'I'll have a go,' said Peggy.

With her third kick the panel flew out of its frame. 'There,' she said. 'It wasn't so hard.'

'Hey, I did all the donkey work!'

Within a minute they were both outside, having left their belongings within.

'What do we do now?' said Billy. They went around the front of the hut and examined the new padlock that had just been fitted.

'There were some padlocks like that in the shop where we got the sleeping bags,' he remembered. 'What we have to do is swap this with one of our own so we'll have a key and no one else will.'

'Yeah, but how do we get this lock off?'

'Smash it off with a hammer.'

'We haven't got a hammer.'

'We will have when we buy one.'

The two children were looking at the array of hammers in the shop when Billy spotted something that looked like a miniature crowbar in a display below. It was described as a pinch bar. It was about eighteen inches long and had a spike at one end and a hooked, flattened claw at the other.

'I bet that'd get that lock off,' he said. 'Stick that spiky end through the hook on the padlock and prise it off.'

Peggy, who was nowhere near as practically minded as her younger brother, shrugged. 'Get what you think. Get a hammer as well. You can buy both for seven and six.'

'Yeah, we might need a hammer to tap that panel back in.'

'Why would we do that?'

'So's no one can see it's loose. We can buy a new padlock and lock the front door and go in and out through the back. Then we can leave all our stuff in all day long.'

'Not the money,' Peggy said. 'We must keep that with us ... always.'

'Yeah, okay. I think I'll get a packet of nails as well.'

So, along with a pinch bar, a hammer, a packet

of nails and a new padlock, the children returned to the hut. The beach was deserted due to the steely sky and matching sea, the sun's glare just visible as it sank slowly below the western horizon. It took the resourceful Billy a matter of minutes to prise the padlock off, replace it with the new one, and try out the two keys, one of which he gave to Peggy.

'I know,' she said. 'If we lose one, we've still got one.'

Then they went around the back where Billy took out the loose panel and examined it by the light of his torch. It still had several, inch-and-a-half-long, rusting panel pins hanging from their nail holes He pulled out all but four, replaced the panel and secured it by knocking four new nails not quite all the way in. Then he scrabbled a hole in the sand at the back of the hut, placed the hammer and pinch bar in it, and covered it up with sand again.

'There,' he said. 'We can use the pinch bar to get in and out whenever we want. We'll have to keep a torch with us at all times.'

'And the money,' said Peggy.

'Yeah, we'd better split it again, just in case.'

'Trouble is, none of it's ours really,' said Peggy, thinking out loud, as she sometimes did. 'I wonder what Mam'd say if she knew we'd turned into thieves.'

It was enough to set Billy off. 'Blimey, Peg. We're in a proper mess, aren't we?'

With tears in their eyes, they headed for a tram that would take them up to the Tower, inside which was warmth, food, drink and various amusements. But that was all – no mam, which was all either of them wanted. The seagulls, un-aware of their misery, proceeded to taunt them with their screeching and swooping, causing Billy to curse at them.

'Gerraway, bloody seagulls!'

'Language, Billy.'

They each paid the sixpence fee to enter the Tower, omitting to buy the one-shilling tickets that would allow them to travel to the top in the lift.

'I'd like to go to the top one day,' Billy had said, 'I bet it's great up there.'

'Maybe another time,' said Peggy, 'let's just see what's down here, first.'

Down here was mainly the Tower Ballroom where Reginald Dixon was on the stage, playing the famous Wurlitzer organ. Billy and Peggy bought cups of tea and a cream bun each then sat and watched the patrons dancing to the amazing sounds coming from the Wurlitzer.

'Blimey, it sounds like a whole band up there,' said Billy.

'I know. It's the most famous organ in England,' Peggy told him. Then, 'Mam always listened to him on the wireless, don't you remember?'

'Blimey! Is that him?' Billy said, looking at the famous man with admiring eyes.

''Course it is – and I can do the waltz,' Peggy said, then added, 'they taught us that at youth club.'

'What's a waltz?'

'It's a dance you do when there's three beats to the bar in the music.'

'What're you talking about?'

'Well, this music's got four beats to the bar so it's either a foxtrot or a quickstep, I think.'

'Which one is this then?'

'Dunno. I only know the waltz.'

She tapped out four beats to the bar on the table.

'One, two, three, four, one, two, three, four...'

'I bet you can do that with any music,' said Billy.

'No, you can't, not to a waltz.'

'I bet you I can.'

He tapped his hand on his knee, following the rhythm of the music, and gave up after three tries. 'Okay, you're right, Mrs Clever-Clogs. Bet you can't do the dance.' Even as Billy spoke, Reginald Dixon changed the tune to 'The Blue Danube'.

'I can. Just you watch. This is a waltz,' said Peggy, and tapped the table in time to the music.

'One two three, one two three...'

She got up from the table. 'The steps are dead easy, see? Left, right, feet together, left, right, feet together... Come on, you try it.'

'No, it's daft.'

'No, it's not. It's good fun. That's why people do it.'

Billy, always one for a bit of fun, got to his feet and stood by his sister's side as she did the waltz step. After a couple of attempts he managed to match her.

'See,' said Peggy, 'you can do the waltz. Mind you, it's harder for a girl.'

'Why's that?'

'Because a girl has to do the same steps, only

68

backwards. Look, let's get on the floor and try it out. You've got to hold me like them men are holding their partners, though.'

'I can't hold you like that, you're me sister.'

'I'm not asking you to hug me tight, just hold on to me so that I can follow your steps. You being the man, you have to lead.'

'Man? I'm eleven.'

'That doesn't matter; you have to lead. We don't have to twirl around or do any fancy stuff. Just go in a straight line to the end of the floor.'

'Right.' Billy studied the other dancers then took her right hand in his left and slid his right hand, very tentatively, around her waist.

'Billy, you'll have to hold me tighter than that. It's your job to lead.'

'Lead you where?'

'Around the dance floor.'

'We're not going around the dance floor, we're just going to the far end.'

'All right, all right. Let's get going before the music stops.'

Their first few steps were quite clumsy but, with Peggy's guidance, Billy picked up the rhythm of the music and realised he was enjoying it. They travelled half the length of the enormous dance floor in a dead straight line.

As they came off the floor a thought struck him. 'Where do you keep your money?'

'In my coat.'

'Where's your coat?'

'Oh, heck!'

It took them just a few seconds to get back to their table where Peggy's coat was hanging on the back of a chair with the money still in an inside pocket.

'Whew!' she breathed in relief.

'I think if we want to do any more dancing,' said Billy, 'we'd better do it with our coats on. I've got my money in three different pockets. Ten quid and some change in each.'

'Why? Do you want to do some more dancing?'

'I wouldn't mind. I thought I'd got the hang of it. I need to learn how to turn, though.'

'Oh, that's easy.'

By the end of the afternoon Billy was waltzing his sister right round the famous dance floor. In between dances they waited patiently at their table for another waltz to be played. From a seat in the lower balcony Goldie glanced down at them then resumed examining the contents of a lady's hand-bag that he had concealed inside a brown-paper carrier bag. Eleven pounds ten and a packet of Mint Imperials. He stuck one in his mouth, re-moved the money and dropped the lady's bag to the floor where it would be found by cleaners and handed in to the lost property department, to be claimed by its very disappointed owner the next day. Goldie never gave a second thought to his victims; to him they were all mugs. The girl down there had been stupid, leaving her coat on the chair like that. He'd been tempted to nip down and empty the pockets, if only to give him some leverage when he asked them to join him once more.

The urgency with which they ran back to their table, and her obvious relief when she found the money intact, told him that she'd been careless.

Silly girl. If they did join him, she'd need to learn not to be so foolish.

Reginald Dixon and his Wurlitzer were descending from view through the stage floor as he played a quickstep to the Blackpool signature tune 'I Do Like To Be Beside The Seaside', when Goldie appeared beside the children's table.

'Have you found somewhere to stay yet?'

'We're still here, aren't we?' said Billy. 'What do you want?'

'Well, I've been watching you and I don't think it'll be too long before someone nicks all your money off you.' He looked at Peggy and snapped his fingers. 'I could have taken all the money in your coat as easy as that, but I didn't.'

'Why not?' she asked.

'Because I like you.'

'We're not joining your thieving gang,' said Billy. 'If we get caught we'll be done for a lot more than nicking handbags.'

'I haven't got a gang. There's just me and my granddad. I do all the thieving. He fences anything that needs fencing.'

'What's that mean?'

'It means any jewellery or valuables I lift, he knows where to sell them to get top dollar.'

'Do you ever get caught?'

'Yep. The last time was two years ago when I was very careless. I got fourteen days in a juvenile detention centre. The bed was a bit hard and the dormitory a bit smelly with the kid in the next bed farting all night, but the food was okay. Anyway, what's this major crime you've committed that they're going to bang you up for?'

71

'Nowt,' said Billy. 'We haven't done nowt – but the police'll think it were us.'

'What happened?'

'Nowt.'

'I think it was a lot more than that.'

'If you must know, a factory got burnt down!' Peggy told him.

'A factory? And they think you did it?'

'They do, yeah, but we didn't. We'd been playing with fireworks but we're sure it was nothing to do with us, only this bloke who was running away from the fire saw us and he'll have reported it to the police. He knew who I was.'

'Anybody hurt?'

'Yeah.'

'Dead?'

'Yeah.'

'Blimey, you're in a proper spot an' no mistake!'

'Prob'ly our ... our ... mam ... was killed,' blurted out Billy, trying to get his words spoken before the tears arrived. 'She ... she worked there and didn't come home after ... so ... so we ran away, didn't we, Peg?'

With the disappearance of Reginald Dixon, the dancers cleared the floor while he took a short break. Billy wiped away a flood of tears with his sleeve as Peggy continued the story. 'We think a lot of people might have died,' she said, relieved to be able to tell someone about this. Even if it was only Goldie.

'Whereabouts?'

'Leeds.'

'Blimey!' he said. 'I think I read about that in the papers. It was a massive blaze, wasn't it?'

'What did it say?'

'Well, that there were quite a few people missing presumed dead, but they didn't know how many.'

Billy was still sobbing. 'We think our mam was one of them.'

'But you don't know for sure?'

'No. We didn't really know who to ask without giving ourselves away,' said Peggy.

'Have you got a dad?'

'Our dad were killed in the war.'

'Bloody hell! Yer in a proper fix.'

Goldie sat down at the table and rubbed his chin thoughtfully. 'Well, I can see why yer don't wanna risk being caught by no coppers fer nicking any more handbags, but where are yer staying?'

'In a beach hut.'

'Aw, yer've got ter be jokin'!'

'Where else could we stay? We're a couple of kids.'

'How d'yer get in and out?'

'We put our own lock on it. We've got a key.'

'Hey, I like yer style, but yer can stay at our place, if yer like.'

'We're not doing any thieving,' said Peggy.

'I'm not asking yer to ... although maybe yer could do a bit o' distraction work for me.'

'We don't know what that is,' said Peggy.

'Tell yer what. You come back with me and we'll fix up a rate to cover yer full board. Granddad's a good cook and we have a room each for you. It's a big improvement on a beach hut.'

The children looked at each other. Having a proper roof over their heads was a big temptation.

'How much will you charge us?' Billy asked.

'Three pounds ten a week each – that's seven pounds a week full board for the two of you. How's that sound?'

'Dunno,' said Billy.

'Sounds about right,' said Peggy, who had been checking on rates charged by guest houses.

'What, three good meals a day and a roof over your heads? I should think it does sound about right.'

'Okay, we'll come, but we'll have to go back to the hut to get our stuff first.'

Goldie looked at his watch. 'It's ten to six. See me outside the front of the Tower in one hour.'

'We haven't got any watches,' said Peggy.

Goldie reached into a pocket and brought out a silver pocket watch, which he showed her. 'Tell yer what. I'll swap yer this watch for the ring yer've got in that purse. It's no good ter you, and this watch is proper silver ... and everybody needs a watch at some time.'

'Okay,' said Peggy.

Billy took the ring out of the purse and handed it to him in exchange for the watch. Goldie got up and vanished, as was his wont.

Billy said, 'Do we trust him, Peg?'

She shrugged as she looked at their new watch, checking the time with the ballroom clock. The watch told the same time and there was a second hand turning that told her it was working properly.

'Dunno. This watch is all right, though. I thought I saw sympathy in his eyes when we told him our story.'

'You saw more than I did then. I wonder what he means by distraction work?'

74

'I think he prob'ly wants us to create a distraction so's he can do a bit of thieving.'

'So long as we're not thieving it should be all right, shouldn't it?'

'I dunno, Billy. I think we'll have to be very careful to steer clear of the police. They've only got to ask us where we're from and what school we go to and we've had it.'

'I wish we could find out about Mam.'

'D'you know? I'm not sure I do,' said Peggy.

'How d'yer mean?'

'Well, maybe it's better us thinking she might be still alive.'

'Well, she might be.'

'That's what I mean. Come on, we can catch a tram down to the Pleasure Beach.'

Chapter 5

Leeds, 6 November

Inspector Dennison covered his mouth with a handkerchief as he stood among the charred debris of the factory and spoke to the fire inspector. The burnt and blackened ashes of five floors' worth of timbers filled the cellars beneath them.

'Bit of a nightmare all round,' the fireman was telling him. 'There's a gas supply that we had to turn off, first job, when we got here. It was feeding the blaze, which is why there's nothing left of the place. All the gas pipes under the building were

75

blown up. If there was a leak, the faulty pipe'll be in bits somewhere.'

'So you think it was caused by a gas leak?'

'Well, I can't see what else it could have been. It'd take a lot of gas running through those pipes to heat a building this size. The initial explosion was massive, typical of a build-up of gas finding a naked flame.'

'Or a spark from a firework?'

'Yes, I've heard about the children and that remains a possibility. With so many windows un-glazed, the building would be like a wind-tunnel. A firework spark might travel some distance from cellar to cellar. All it had to do was come into contact with a faint whiff of gas and the whole lot would go up, which is what seems to have happened. We know where the explosion occurred, do you know where the children were playing?'

'No, I'd need to ask Mr Blainey that.'

'Hmm, Mr Blainey,' said the fireman. 'Not too sure about him.'

'Why's that?'

'Well, I've been made aware that the factory was losing money and he intended closing it down.'

'Is there any evidence that the blaze was started deliberately?'

'No. Trouble is, there's no evidence to prove it wasn't. There's no evidence of any kind. When you get a big gas explosion all the evidence tends to destroy itself. The insurers sent a loss adjuster round. He just looked at the devastation and threw his hands up. What was he supposed to make of it? They have their suspicions, but they can't find any evidence of foul play and nor can we.'

'It's big news all over West Yorkshire,' said Dennison, gloomily. 'There's a lot of pressure on us to get to the bottom of it.'

'To be honest, it'll be easier just to pin it on the kids.'

'Do you think that's the most likely cause?'

'I think it's fifty-fifty ... but you've only got corroborating evidence for one scenario.'

'It certainly looks like we'll have to take the kids to court,' said the policeman, 'and see what a jury makes of it all. With twelve lives being lost, I'm not sure they'll have too much sympathy, kids or no kids. One way or another they're in deep trouble – or they will be, if ever we find them.'

'Well, they must think they caused it or why would they run away?' said the fireman.

'Who knows what goes on in a frightened child's mind under those circumstances?' said Inspector Dennison. 'I'd rather a jury made that decision.'

Betty recognised Jimmy's footsteps because of his limp. She'd been placed in a sitting position by a nurse and managed to turn her head far enough to see him approaching. He looked much smarter than he had the last time she saw him. He'd taken the bandages off his head and replaced them with a large plaster, which poked out from beneath his flat cap.

'Hello, Betty, excuse the cap – it's to hide me bald swede. Are you all right?'

She was in tears.

'What's up, love?'

'I think you know, Jimmy,' she sobbed. 'My kids have run away from home. The police have been

77

round there and there's no sign of them. They must have got scared and decided to make a run for it.'

He sat down on the bedside chair. 'Ah, yes. That's more or less what I've come to tell you. I called round last night and had a good look. I can't see any of their clothes and if you had a suitcase in the house, you haven't now – or any money for that matter.'

'There should have been some in a tin on the mantelpiece.'

'Yeah, I had a look in there – empty.'

Betty smiled through her tears. 'Well, I'm glad they took off with a bit of money in their pockets. God knows where they've gone, though.'

'Are there any relatives they might have decided to visit?'

'Not really. I have a sister in Nuneaton but they've never been there and they wouldn't know how to find her. I had Police Inspector Plod around just now. He tells me the kids know about Blainey accusing them of setting the place on fire. The inspector tells me when the police catch 'em, they'll be charged with it. Twelve people dead, did you know that?'

Jimmy nodded sorrowfully. 'It's been in all the papers.'

'Was there anything about me being brought out alive?'

'I ... er, no, not yet ... nor me for that matter, which makes it only ten people dead.'

'So the kids'll think I burnt to death and they're the cause of it? Oh, my God, Jimmy! What'll be going through their minds?'

78

'Betty, I don't think it was the kids' fault. That place blew up like a bomb had hit it.'

'What? You think Blainey planted a bomb?'

'No, but I think he caused a gas explosion. He was close enough to the kids to be talking to them – accusing them of starting it all. But what was he doing there at that hour? That's what I want to know.'

'No idea. He normally leaves bang on half-five, which is our usual clocking off time, only some of us had work to finish. First bit of overtime we've had for a month.'

'Yeah, I know that, with it being my job ter lock the factory up after yer've all gone. It were nearly half-six when the place went up.'

'Trouble is, Jimmy, it's not what you think that counts, it's what the police and the courts think. That copper reckons my kids'll be locked up for a long time for what they've done, whether it was an accident or not. No wonder they've run away.'

'How much money was in the house?'

'About fifteen bob.'

'Well, they can't last above a week on that. They'll have to come home sometime,' said Jimmy.

'Come home – to what? I've been racking my brains to think where they might have gone but I can't think of anywhere. Elsewhere is where they are, Jimmy, and I don't know where that is, do you?'

There was as much pleading in her eyes as in her voice. She knew it was impossible for him to answer her.

'I don't, Betty, but I'll do my best to try and

track them down.'

'Thanks, Jimmy. Right now I've no one else to turn to.'

'I only hope I can be of some help. Let me help you out with your rent, Betty, until you get back on your feet.'

'That'll be a couple of months at least.'

'You should get some sort of compensation from Blainey.'

'I'm not holding my breath on that one. Anyway, how can you afford to help me out? You'll be laid off as well.'

'Well, I get two wages. I play piano three times a week in pubs so I've got a bit put away. With my tips I earn more from that than I do at Blainey's. There's enough jobs out there for me to play every night in some pub or other, plus I get a war pension due to me disability.'

'Wounded in the war, weren't you?'

'Shrapnel wound, yes.'

'And you play the piano?'

'Yeah, I've been playing since I was a lad.'

'Blimey, Jimmy, there's a lot about you I didn't know.'

'Well, this is the first time we've ever really spoken. I've always kept meself to meself.'

'Best way, sometimes. Did you get married again?'

He grinned. 'Are you asking?'

She looked at him and saw a man who could bring humour into her life – a rare commodity up until now.

'Just wondering, Jimmy.'

'Not sure how much of a catch I am nowadays.

Me first wife didn't think I was up to much.'

'Strikes me she probably wasn't worth marrying then.'

'That's what my mother said.'

'Is she still alive, your mother?'

'No, she's dead, and so's me dad. There's just me. They left me the house, though. Three bed through-terrace in Crossgates.'

'Really? It's not too bad in Crossgates. You don't talk like a maintenance man.'

'Don't I? How's a maintenance man supposed to talk?'

'You sound educated.'

'Well, I learnt to read and write.'

'No, you can do more than read and write.'

'Okay, I confess. I went to university. I've a degree in maths.'

'Did you really get a degree?'

'I did, and I used to be a maths teacher, but when I came back from the war my mental state wouldn't allow me to take on anything but the most menial of jobs.'

'Is that what they call shell-shock?'

'That's what they call it now. In the first war I'd probably have been shot for cowardice.'

'You can't have been shell-shocked when you rescued me.'

'It was more than just reacting to the explosions. It had a lot to do with what I saw as well – all the vile stuff the Nazis did to the French Resistance people and the Jews. For a long time it made me cry, just thinking about it. We were sent to help out in the relief of a concentration camp...' He shuddered and added, 'That was no picnic.

They call it the horror of war but that doesn't nearly cover it. When I was demobbed I took meself to see a hypnotherapist who specialises in that sort of thing. It cost me a few quid but the alternative was a loony bin.'

'Did it cure you?'

'No, but it kept me out of the loony bin. I still have flashbacks to those things, you know, shed tears for no apparent reason, but they're happening less and less.'

'That's good.'

After this Betty looked at Jimmy in a new light. He was quite tall and slimly built, not strikingly handsome like her late husband but he had kind blue eyes, a pleasant face and a twinkling smile – a smile a woman could trust. His teeth were perhaps too white and even to be his own. She knew his bandaged head covered a scalp burnt bald of hair but assumed it would grow back to its original fullness, black hair neatly combed with just a few traces of grey in it. She found herself guessing at his age – mid-forties probably – ten years older than she was. He wore glasses and normally had a thin moustache that probably suited him, also burnt off by the heat, along with his eyebrows. Betty wasn't struck on moustaches – no doubt because her late husband had had one. He'd been good-looking but that had counted for nothing after the first infatuation. He'd been a pig of a man. When she got the telegram notifying her of his death she'd been slightly taken aback by the news, but that was all. She hadn't shed a single tear for him, although she had smiled when his back-pay and her war widow's pension came through. It was the only helpful thing he'd ever done for her.

'Will you get all your hair back?' she asked Jimmy.

'I hope so. I might have a few more grey hairs, though.'

'What about your moustache? Will you grow that back again?'

'Why, didn't you like it?'

'I've never liked moustaches.'

'How old do you think I am?'

'I don't know – about forty-five, maybe.'

'I'm thirty-six.'

'Sorry, I'm no good at ages.'

She let out a deep, tearful sigh. 'I wish my kids would come home, Jimmy. Never mind what the flaming police might do to 'em. I just want to know they're safe. Here's me, stuck in this damned bed, not able to move a muscle to help 'em even if they do return.'

'Like I said, Betty, I'll look everywhere ... and *elsewhere*, if I ever find out where that is.'

She looked up at him, helplessly. 'What can I do, Jimmy?'

Her plaintive plea had him at a loss. He was here because he'd always had a soft spot for her, despite hardly knowing her. In his opinion, with her blonde hair and blue eyes, Betty was the prettiest woman in the factory – out of his league probably – but she'd always had a smile for him.

'*We'll* do the best we can, Betty,' he said comfortingly. 'If there's some way of proving Blainey did it I'll find it, don't you worry about that. Trouble is, I've been out there talking to the

83

fire inspectors and the explosion did so much damage there's not much left to prove how it started.'

'That's what the copper said. Which is why they'll go after the kids instead of Blainey.'

'I can have an ask round, to see if anyone has a clue about the kids.'

'I'd love it if you would, Jimmy. Billy's got a pal called David who lives at number eleven on our street. He might know something. Keep coming to see me, won't you?'

'I will,' he said. As if anything could stop him. He'd already made up his mind not to grow his moustache back.

Chapter 6

David twirled his breakfast spoon in his corn-flakes, thinking about what might happen to him. Nothing good, he knew that. He was in tears again, wiping them away on his shirt-sleeve. Today he was due to take the scholarship exam that should by rights haul him out of Gipton School and into one the city's high schools. His teacher had been confident he would pass, but in the past week or so the boy had shown a defeated side that his mother had never seen in him before. Given a choice, David would like to go to Roundhay High School with its extensive playing fields rather than one of the inner-city schools; but this morning's exam couldn't have been further from his mind. He could think only of twelve dead people, including Mrs Clegg, Billy's mam. He was ninety-nine per cent certain the explosion hadn't been his fault but if the police found out what he'd done with that rocket, what he thought would count for nothing. He'd been in trouble with them before and he knew that would count against him. Billy wouldn't have given him away, nor would Peggy, but they were nowhere to be found. He missed not being able to share his fears with them.

Outside in the street the bin men were at work. He looked up to see one of them hoist a fully laden dustbin on to his shoulders and carry it out of the yard to empty it into the bin wagon. That'd be David in a few years if he didn't pass his scholarship exam. Emptying bins – and him built like a matchstick man!

His mother had gone to work at eight o'clock leaving him to fend for himself, which he usually did. David was a bright and capable lad of whom his mother was proud, but she also couldn't understand his recent moods.

'I hope yer in a better frame of mind when yer take yer scholarship exam. I should mebbe take you to the doctor's. See if he can give you something to perk you up. Yer do need building up, son. I wouldn't care, but you eat like a flamin' horse. You must have hollow legs.'

'I'll be okay, Mam.'

'Yer need ter be, son. Yer whole future depends on yer going to a high school and gettin' yer School Certificate.'

'I know that, Mam. It'll work out, don't worry.'

85

'It's a pity Billy's not at home ter take his. Mind you, I think him and Peggy's got enough on their plates ter worry about. Have you any idea where they are?'

''Course I haven't, Mam. I'd tell yer if I did.'

He'd been dying to tell her what had happened on the night of the factory blaze, but would she believe him when he told her he'd actually played no part in it – well, apart from firing a rocket through the factory window? There was no way he could make that sound innocent, even though he knew for certain that his rocket hadn't caused the explosion. Would his mam insist on him going to the police, to tell them his story? Knowing her, she definitely would.

Jimmy was sitting on the saddle of his parked bicycle. It was half-past eight that morning and he knew David would soon emerge from his house to walk up Ashton Place to Gipton School. Betty had given him the address. It was twenty to nine when the lad appeared from the house. Jimmy swung his leg from the saddle and walked his bike alongside the boy.

'Are you David?'

He asked it as cheerfully as he could so as not to alarm the boy.

'Er, David Rosenhead, yeah.'

'And you're a friend of Billy Clegg?'

'Yeah,' said David, guardedly.

'The reason I'm asking is because his mam wants to know where Billy and Peggy are.'

'I think his mam's dead. She died in that fire at Blainey's factory.'

'She isn't dead, David. She's in St James's Hospital.'

'I don't think so.'

'David, she got out of the factory because I helped her, but I don't think Billy and Peggy can know that.'

'Blimey! I don't think anybody knows. Me mam dunt know and she's a pal of Mrs Clegg's. Is Betty all right?'

'She's got a few broken bones and she won't be walking for a bit but she'll live. David, I'm wondering if you know where Billy and Peggy might have gone?'

'I don't know. I didn't know they'd run away until after they went.'

'Any idea where they might have headed for?'

'No. They've never been anywhere really, 'cept to Blackpool last summer and they don't know anybody there, or not that they've told me anyway.'

'Oh... And do you know anything at all about the fire?'

David walked on in a thoughtful silence, which Jimmy reckoned might become productive, as thoughtful silences often do.

'It weren't their fault,' the boy said, at last.

'No, I don't think it was either,' said Jimmy, encouragingly.

'No, it definitely wasn't.'

'How do you know?'

David turned to face Jimmy. 'Mister, yer've not to tell anyone, else I might get into proper bother.'

'I won't tell anyone, David. So, how do you know it wasn't their fault?'

The words tumbled out then as if they had been bursting to escape for some time. 'Because I was with 'em, mister, and if it were anyone's fault it were mine. It were me what fired a rocket through t'factory winder, but it were miles away from where that explosion was – and t'factory blew up no more than seconds after me rocket went through that winder into an empty room, and a spark's not gonna travel far in a few seconds. I went back and had a good look 'cos that part never got burnt as much as the other end. A spark'd have ter go through three brick walls to reach the place the explosion happened.'

'You know, David, you'd make a brilliant witness if Billy and Peggy ever end up in court.'

'I know, but I'd have ter say it were my rocket what landed in the factory. Peggy let off a firework as well, but it wasn't doing no harm.'

'David, I don't think you're the kind of lad who'll let them take the blame for something they didn't do,' said Jimmy. 'I think you'll want to help them and I bet if you went to court they'd let you all off.'

'I don't think so. I've already been up in juvenile court for setting fire to some mucky old lavvies in Florence Street. They were right smelly places what needed burning down. I just set fire to a pile of old papers and it burnt the whole lot. I got fined ten bob what me mam had ter pay at a shilling a week. I were told that if I did owt like that again, I'd end up in reform school.'

'Oh dear. No, I don't suppose such a record would help your credibility in this case. Is there anything else you can tell me?'

'There is something. When the factory blew up, I saw a bloke running towards us right from where it happened. He stopped and accused us of causing it, but he were a lot nearer to it than we ever were. In fact, it looked to me as if he'd been caught up in it.'

'Do you know who he was?'

'Yeah. He talked about it being his factory and afterwards I saw his picture in the papers. It were Mr Blainey.'

'Really? Yes, I saw him there that night too, standing at the gate. He was running away from the explosion, was he?'

'He was. Running like mad until he saw us then he stopped and played hell with us. He told Peggy he knew who she was and that her mother was in the factory burning to death. I thought that were a right rotten thing to say, but he said it and he didn't look a bit sorry neither.'

'Well, Betty Clegg wasn't burning to death in the factory. She'd been blown out of it, and luckily I saw her and got her to safety.'

'Billy and Peggy'll be dead pleased.'

'Yes. Pity we don't know where they are.'

'Honest, mister. I haven't the foggiest. What's gonna happen now? Will yer be tellin' the coppers?'

Jimmy studied the boy. 'Well, I made you a promise that I wouldn't, but it might be in everyone's interest if, at some stage, you come forward and tell what you know, just as you've told me. I believe you because it all sounds quite plausible, so I'm sure a jury'll think so too. Tell you what, I'll wait for you on a morning from

89

time to time, just to keep you up to date with what's happening. If you have any problems, I'll try and help you.'

'Who are you?'

'My name's Jimmy – Jimmy Potter. I used to work at the factory so I know Blainey and what he's capable of. I'll leave you to go to school now and I won't say anything to anybody without telling you first. And if you do decide to go to the police, I'll come with you ... okay?'

'Okay, Mr Potter.'

'Call me Jimmy.'

'I'm taking me scholarship exam today.'

'Are you? Best of luck.'

'I'll need it with all this goin' on in me head.'

Jimmy placed a hand on the boy's shoulder. It was a friendly gesture that David felt his own father would have made, had he been alive.

'David, you have to learn to compartmentalise your problems.'

'What's that mean?'

'It means deal with them one at a time. Your exam is today's problem, so you must look upon that as your only problem. The fire is a problem for another day and a problem I might be able to help you with. So you have to forget all about the fire today. Can you do that?'

'I can try.'

'Today you only think about passing this exam. Today that's the only thing you have to do. The factory's in another compartment to be dealt with at a later stage ... if at all.'

'I'll try that, mister.'

'Good lad. You know, if you end up in court as

a bright lad who's just passed his scholarship, the judge won't want to jeopardise your future by sending you away. It'll be his duty to make sure you get a good education. Trust me, I know about these things.'

Eleven-year-old David walked on to school, relieved at being able to share the heavy burden he'd been carrying on his own, and now determined to give the exam his best shot. Eleven-year-old Billy was having no such luck.

Chapter 7

Billy stepped off the tram and walked alongside his sister. 'Are you sure we can trust him, Peg? He might end up nicking all our money.'

'I don't know, but if we don't take the money to his house he can't nick it, can he?'

'So, where do we leave it? Hang on, I think I know.'

'Hmm, thought you might.'

Peggy followed him along the back of the beach huts until they came to theirs, which had been bright red in its heyday but was now a tired, peeling pink.

'We can't leave it in there, Billy.'

'I know, but what's to say we can't bury it in the sand? We put it in my rucksack that's waterproof and bury the whole lot in the sand at the back of our hut. It's a zillion to one chance anyone'll go digging back here. We make a note of exactly where it's buried and come back and get it when we need it.'

Peggy thought about this plan but could find no holes in it. 'Okay, we just take what money we need for, say, a week. That's seven pounds for our board, plus say another four for spends – two pounds each. So we take eleven quid out, that leaves forty-nine.'

'Blimey, soon goes, dunnit?' said Billy. 'Makes you wonder how Mam managed.'

'I wish she was here to manage us. Anyway, we should tell Goldie we've left it at the station.'

'I like my idea better, though,' said Billy. 'Goldie might search all our stuff for the locker key.'

'Okay, let's bury it.'

So the money was buried a foot deep in the sand behind their beach hut, leaving no evidence that anything was down there. At six o'clock they were standing in front of the Tower with the suitcase containing their meagre belongings. Goldie was already waiting.

'Don't tell me you've put your money in that,' he said.

'No, it's safely hidden away,' said Peggy.

'You could have left it in our safe,' said Goldie.

'It's safely buried,' said Billy, 'on the beach, and Blackpool beach is a big beach.'

Even as he said it, Billy knew it was a daft thing to tell Goldie, who grinned.

'It's definitely a big beach. No flies on you, young 'un... Come on.'

He led them around the back of the Tower to a maze of streets and eventually to one called George Street. Most of the houses had bright paintwork, polished door knockers, donkey-stoned steps and signs boasting the luxury of H&C running water in all rooms. These were guest houses currently displaying *Vacancy* signs in their windows. It was not unusual for November. Come the holiday season the signs would be taken down and replaced with *No Vacancy* signs. Eventually they came to a house with no sign at all in the window, not even a sign saying it was a guest house.

'This is it,' said Goldie, mounting the four steps to the front door. It looked a respectable enough place to the children, clean and recently painted. 'It's in better condition than most of the guest houses round here. In fact, we're forever turnin' folk away who think we *are* a guest house.'

'How many rooms have you got?' Peggy asked as they entered the hallway, which boasted wall-to-wall carpet and a white telephone, beside which was what looked like a money box.

'Six bedrooms. You and your brother can have one each up on the second floor. Me and me granddad sleep on the first floor. You get a bathroom to share between the two of you. If you want to use the phone you put money in that box – it's an honesty box. We're very big on honesty in this house.'

'Right.' Billy grinned.

'What are your names, by the way?'

'I'm Billy and she's Peggy – Billy and Peggy Clegg.'

'Right, Billy and Peggy Clegg, you'll be given proper rent books, so your tenancies here are all legal and above board.'

93

'Apart from us both being under-age,' Peggy pointed out.

'That's your problem, not ours. Me and my granddad know nothing about you being on the run from the police.'

'Actually, we don't know if we are on the run,' said Peggy. 'We just don't want to take any chances.'

'And I think you're very wise not to,' said Goldie. 'Right, I'll introduce you two outlaws to me grandfather.'

Goldie's granddad was a grey-haired man who looked to be around seventy, though he could have been a poorly preserved fifty-five. Goldie was only in his late teens. His grandfather was sitting in the living room, reading a newspaper, amidst a cloud of pipe-tobacco smoke.

'Granddad, these are the kids I was telling you about.'

Harry Golding got to his feet and turned to greet his new guests. He gave them a cracked smile and held out a hand that Peggy shook, awkwardly, because she hadn't quite arrived at the hand-shaking age yet. Billy followed suit.

'George calls me Granddad but you must call me Harry.'

'Hello, Harry,' said the children, more or less in unison.

He had wild grey hair and a large nose, a feature that had been passed down to his grandson, but his eyes twinkled and held humour, something Goldie hadn't inherited. Peggy also noticed this but reserved her opinion as to whether the humour was genuine or not. These people were professionally dishonest, and therefore not to be trusted. She would remind Billy of this.

'We never had a granddad,' her brother said, obviously taken with the old man.

'Well, that's a terrible shame. George has only got the one, and that's me. So you're to be our guests?'

'Yes,' said Peggy, 'but Goldie wants us to help him with his robbery business though we've told him we can't, due to our circumstances.'

'Ah, yes. I've had these circumstances more or less explained to me, and they're not very good circumstances for children to be in.'

'So, do we have to help him?'

'I've explained to them that I don't need them to steal for me, just to distract,' said Goldie.

Harry rubbed his chin. 'I don't think we should expect them to do anything right now, except settle in to their new home.'

'Fair enough,' said Goldie. 'I've told them the terms and they've agreed: seven pounds a week for the two of them.'

Peggy opened her bag and took out seven pounds, which she held out for Harry to take. 'This is our first week's rent.'

'Thank you, Peggy. It may be that you find yourselves staying here rent-free if you can see your way clear to helping George from time to time.'

'We can afford to pay our rent for a while,' she told him.

'And we don't want nicking by the police,' said Billy.

'For aiding and abetting,' added Peggy, who

had read about such things in the Public Library.

'My word, you do know some stuff about the law for one so young,' said Harry. 'I can see we're going to have to watch our steps.'

'We won't give you any trouble, mister,' said Billy.

'There is one question I'd like to ask you both,' said Harry.

'What's that?'

'What do you intend doing during the days? You obviously don't go to school.'

Billy and Peggy looked at each other. 'Our school's in Leeds,' Peggy said. 'We can't go back there or the police'll pick us up straight away.'

'I know that, so what's your answer? Is it your intention to educate yourselves?'

'How would we do that?' said Billy, baffled.

Goldie looked equally baffled.

'I could help you,' said Harry.

'Bit late for that,' said Billy. 'I was due to take my scholarship this week, missed it now.'

'Do you get another chance?'

'I do, yes. This week was my City scholarship, I'm due to take the exam for St Michael's in February.'

'Then that's the one you must study for. How about you, Peggy?'

'I'm in the second form at Notre Dame Girls' High School. I don't take any big exams until the fifth form.'

'So, you'll be studying half a dozen subjects: English, maths, geography, history, probably French and science, eh?'

'And art,' added Peggy, 'although I'm not much

good at it.'

'I had a good education. I could be of help to you,' said Harry.

'Clever bloke, my granddad,' put in Goldie.

'Are you offering to teach us?' asked Peggy.

'Well, I can lay my hands on all the textbooks you may need and I can steer you through them, and I can teach Billy enough about English and maths to get him through his scholarship exam. Are you a bright boy at school, Billy?'

'Yeah, top three in the class usually, but I don't see how I can take the exam, with us being on the run.'

'Were you a teacher once?' asked Peggy.

'No, but I wasted a very good education and I read a lot. Billy, you don't know what lies ahead for you in the future. If you get a chance to take the exam, you should at least be prepared. I will teach you for five pounds a week for the two of you.' He had a slightly mad smile that reminded Peggy of the wolf in Red Riding Hood.

'That means our money won't last as long,' she said.

'If it doesn't,' said Harry, 'you can always help George out from time to time.' It was what Peggy half-expected – method in his madness. 'That way you get free board and a good education,' he added.

'I'd say you've both fallen on your feet,' said Goldie.

'Maybe,' grunted Billy, who had been thinking that the only good part about them being on the run was not having to go to school. Peggy didn't trust either Goldie or his granddad but what had they to lose if she and Billy stood firm and refused to help with their robberies? Two months sleeping in a warm bed with three meals a day was too good to turn down – with or without the lessons. They had money enough to last them until after Christmas. Surely they could wing it until then – next year could look after itself. When you're twelve, short-term planning is all you can cope with.

'It's a deal,' she decided, holding out her hand for Harry to shake.

The only thing Billy was shaking was his head. He'd need to have a word with his big sister once he got her on his own.

'Good,' said Harry. 'George, show them up to their rooms while I make us all something to eat. Do you have any preferences?'

'We generally just eat what's put in front of us,' said Peggy. 'At home we could never afford to be choosy.'

Their rooms were single rooms, side by side, with the bathroom next to Peggy's room. Half an hour later the two children were sitting on her bed discussing their immediate future.

'Why are we letting him teach us? He's not even a proper teacher.'

'Well, even if you don't want to learn any more, I do!'

'It'll only be for a couple of months. What can we learn in a couple of months?'

'Enough for you to pass your scholarship.'

'How can I take it? I'm not even going to school.'

'Billy, how do we know what's going to happen

to us? For all we know we might not be in any trouble and our mam might still be alive.'

'Do you really think so?'

'I don't know what to think, but I know we're thinking the worst.'

'David'll know.'

'But how do we contact him? It's not as though he's on the telephone or anything.'

'We could write to him.'

'And how does he contact us, without us giving away our address? And you can bet that if he gets a mystery letter from Blackpool, his mam'll open it.'

'What do you think we should do then?'

'Nothing, for the time being. Then I think I might ring up Father O'Flaherty at the church and tell him about our fix. He'll know whether Mam's alive or not and if the police blame us for the factory blowing up.'

'Why don't you ring him now?'

'Why do you think?'

'I don't know.'

'It's because I'd be frightened of him telling me Mam's dead. I don't want to hear that.'

'We'll have to hear it sometime, Peg – and he might tell us she's alive.'

'Well, you can ring if you like.'

Billy frowned at the prospect and knew it would take more courage than he had right now to make such a call.

'Yeah, mebbe we should leave it for a bit,' he said. 'These rooms are okay, aren't they? Comfy beds.'

'Yeah. How much money have we got left?'

'There's forty-nine quid and the jewels in the rucksack and I've got two pounds on me. You should have some left after giving Harry seven.'

She looked in her purse and counted her money. 'Two pounds three and six.'

'That makes us near enough even,' said Billy. 'It's best that we're even.'

'Oh, yeah. Why do we have to be even? What's yours is mine and what's mine's yours. Besides, fifty quid's a lot o' money. Mam only earned about six pounds a week and she kept us going all right.'

'I bet it's more expensive in Blackpool,' Billy said, 'and we're having to pay for our schooling, which I think is a bit daft.'

'We need to keep up with our schooling or we'll be way behind when we get back.'

'That's if Harry knows what he's doing.'

'If he doesn't we'll just have to tell him we don't want to do it any more,' said Peggy.

'Fair enough. I wonder how much he'll give us for the jewels.'

'Maybe we should look in jewellers' shops and see what things cost.'

'Or maybe we could sell it to a jeweller.'

'What? A couple of scruffy kids selling expensive jewellery?' said his sister. 'I don't think so.'

'Yeah, probably a bad idea.'

'Yeah, and if we did try and sell it, I bet the cops will have told all the jewellers to watch out for it. Although I suppose we could go to Preston to sell it or even Manchester.'

''S'right,' said Billy, who stuck up a finger to indicate the arrival of a new idea. 'Hey! I tell you what we could do.'

'What's that?'

'We could go to Manchester and tell the jeweller that our granny left you the stuff in her will, but you'd rather have the money to give to our mam who's skint.'

'That's right ... and you could make up one of your weird stories that everyone believes for some reason.'

'They're not weird. If they were weird no one would believe them.'

Apart from this, Peggy could find no flaws in his idea. They spent the next half hour acting out the scene inside the shop as Peggy played on the jeweller's heartstrings with her tale of woe. Billy was impressed by his sister's acting.

'Blimey, Peg! Yer've nearly got *me* in tears here.'

Chapter 8

St James's Hospital, 7 November

Betty was sitting up in bed reading the *Yorkshire Evening Post* when Jimmy arrived to visit. It was seven in the evening and he was looking particularly cheerful.

'Lost a penny and found a shilling?' she asked him.

'Better than that. I've got a residency at the Queen's Hotel. Four nights a week, three pounds a night. I've already got work for the other two nights so I don't need a day job any more.'

101

'That's brilliant, Jimmy.'

'I've got some other good news, this time for you.'

'About my children?'

Jimmy's face dropped. 'Aw, no, sorry. It's about work.'

'Oh, right. What is it?'

'Well, with the factory not giving us any through no fault of ours, we're entitled to four weeks' redundancy pay.'

'Give over! I can't see Blainey going for that.'

'He'll have no option. Remember when Jack Blainey was still alive and he made us all sign contracts?'

'I do, but that was the union's doing, wasn't it?'

'Not all of it. Our union bloke talked through his backside most of the time. Jack Blainey was a fair man – him and his brother were chalk and cheese. Anyway he put a clause in our contracts that said we were entitled to four weeks' redundancy money if ever we were required to leave the company due to no fault of our own.'

'I don't think I read that clause.'

'Did you actually read the contract?'

'Probably not. I don't think we were given any option. It was either sign or the sack. Though actually ... yes, I think I remember it happening now.'

'Really?'

'Yeah. It was about eleven years ago, wasn't it?'

'Nineteen thirty-five, June. That's the date on my contract.'

'That's right. Our Billy was a month old.'

'So?' said Jimmy, perplexed.

'Jack had a brain tumour and he knew he hadn't long to live. He died in March 'thirty-six – March the seventh to be exact.'

'How come you know exactly?'

Betty's eyes began to mist over. She spoke, quietly, without looking at him.

'Jack and I were having an affair.'

'Whoah! I didn't see that one coming. What, you and Jack Blainey?'

She nodded. 'It was a proper love affair, if you must know. My husband was a pig of a man. I was glad when he got called up.' She paused then added, 'And even gladder when he was killed. Does that sound awful?'

'Not to me. When did you find out about his tumour?'

'About eight months before he died, so there was no point him leaving his wife at that late stage. She was very ill too, in fact, she died two months before him. It was a bad time for me. I was living with a pig I loathed and in love with a dying woman's husband, who was also dying.'

Jimmy sat down in the chair beside her bed and asked, 'So, what does this have to do with the contract?'

'Well, he didn't trust Lester to keep the company going after he died. In fact, he anticipated his brother running it into the ground so he stuck that clause in the contract just to give us all some protection, as and when the company went down. To be honest, I'd forgotten about it.'

'Did he leave you anything in his will?'

'Not in his will, no, but he ... erm ... he did leave me with something.'

'What was that?'

Betty hesitated for a while before saying, 'He left me with my Billy.'

'How do you mean?'

'I mean Jack was Billy's dad.'

'Bloody hell, Betty!'

She smiled. 'There's no mention of it in any will but he did leave both Billy and Peggy a legacy worth about two thousand each, to mature and be collected on their twenty-first birthdays.'

'Four grand?'

'Yeah, all invested – could be worth twice that now. It was never mentioned in Jack's will. It was just something he arranged through a lawyer. Lester never knew about it, nor did Jack's wife, who passed away never knowing about Jack and me. The documents are all with a solicitor and I have a copy. The money's in a bank. Jack arranged it all. It'll be enough to set them both up with a nice house when they get married, plus a good few quid in the bank, to quote Jack.'

'And your husband thought Billy was his?'

'Well, he assumed so and I didn't tell him any different. I must say, Jack loved Billy a lot more than my husband ever did. He doted on him, which is why he gave him the two grand. He gave Peggy the same to make it fair.'

'Do the kids know about this money?'

'Oh, no. That'd probably mean me telling Billy who his dad really is. Not that he'd mind, but there's a time and place for everything.'

'Yeah, I suppose there is. I just hope this business with the factory hasn't buggered up their lives.'

Betty looked up at him and murmured, 'It's up

to me to make sure it doesn't, Jimmy.'

'Up to *us*, you mean. Now I'm mixed up in it, I want to see it through to the end.'

'Thanks, Jimmy, but where do we start?'

'Well, I suppose job number one is to find 'em.'

Chapter 9

Blackpool, 7 November

'Shepherd's pie,' called out Harry from the kitchen. 'Do you both like shepherd's pie?'

'Yes,' replied Billy, wallowing in the delicious aroma. 'Smells good, Peg.'

Peggy was still nodding her agreement as Goldie came into the room. 'I've an idea how I can find out about your mam,' he said.

'Oh, heck!' said Billy.

'What sort of idea?' Peggy asked.

Goldie hesitated for a while before he said, 'Well, I've got a pal who works on the *Yorkshire Evening Post* in Leeds. He's only a junior reporter, but with the fire being big news, I reckon the paper'll have a record somewhere of all the people who died or were injured in it.'

'Oh,' said Peggy, looking at her brother. She could see good and bad in this.

'He should be able to dig it out for me. Do you want me to try?'

The brother and sister looked at each other, then Peggy said, quietly, 'Well, I suppose we really ought to know how she is.'

'I'm not sure I do,' put in Billy.

'Billy, she's our mam. We really ought to know. If she's alive, we can go back.'

'We'll still get done for burning the factory down. Which means we'll get done for everyone who did die.'

Peggy shook her head. 'I don't know how they can blame us for burning it down. All I lit was a rainbow fountain and it was nowhere near the factory, and you didn't set any fireworks off at all.'

'You mean, we should let David take the blame?'

'Dunno. He might have already taken the blame,' Peggy said. 'He's the one who fired his rocket through the factory window, not us.'

'I don't see how a measly rocket could have started a massive fire like that.'

'No,' said Peggy, 'neither do I.'

Goldie stood there, patiently listening to the exchange between brother and sister. 'Are you saying there was someone else with you, who actually might have started the fire?'

'I don't think any of us did,' muttered Billy.

'Well,' Goldie said, 'what's it to be? Do you want me to ring this pal of mine or not?'

Peggy looked at Billy and said, 'At least we'll know exactly where we stand.'

'Okay,' said Billy, after some thought, 'mebbe yer right. In any case, if Goldie doesn't tell that bloke at the *Evening Post* that we're stayin' with him, how will the cops get to know?'

'So you want me to ring my pal?' Goldie said. 'I won't mention you're stayin' with me.'

'Please,' said Peggy.

'I'll ring him right now if you like. What's your mam's name?'

Peggy said nothing. She just looked at Billy, passing the responsibility on to him. They needed to do this together.

'Elizabeth Clegg,' said Billy, giving away his mother's name as if he were parting with a state secret.

At breakfast the next morning Peggy had been reluctantly impressed by the pristine white table-cloth and the meal in general. Typical Blackpool boarding house breakfast: eggs, bacon, tomatoes, mushrooms and a fried slice – a much better breakfast than the Kellogg's Cornflakes they'd had at home.

'This all looks very nice,' she said before they sat down.

'Thank you,' said Harry.

After this the four of them ate in a silence broken only by *Housewives' Choice* playing on the wireless. Both Billy and Peggy were wondering if Goldie had news of their mother, but neither wanted to broach the subject lest the news be bad.

Then he said, 'I rang that mate of mine on the *Yorkshire Evening Post* yesterday. He got back in touch last night.'

Both Peggy's and Billy's hearts skipped a beat as they looked at Goldie.

'What ... er ... what did he say?' asked Peggy. Her eyes and Billy's were now fixed on Goldie.

'I didn't tell yer last night because I thought I'd

let yer both have a good sleep first.'

'I don't think I like the sound of this,' said Billy. 'Is our mam all right?'

Goldie gave him a compassionate look and said, 'I'm afraid not, Billy. Elizabeth Clegg was listed among the people who died. There were eleven altogether and she was one of them. In fact, none of the people working in the mill survived, apart from one bloke who's a handyman or something. He left just before the place went up.'

Goldie's lie was actually a half-truth. He did have a friend who worked for the newspaper, which was how he knew about the handyman, although Betty's name was not among the list of dead. In fact, she had been named as a second survivor, but such news was of no use to Goldie, who needed the kids to work for him.

The children made no comment, such was their appalling grief at the awful finality of this news. Their mam was definitely dead No more pretending they would see her again. All such hope had been destroyed by this news. Billy put his knife and fork down, his appetite for breakfast deserting him.

'I b ... bet he d ... did it,' he stuttered, through his tears.

'Who?' asked Goldie, chewing on a piece of bacon.

'That handyman b ... bloke. If he l ... left just before the place went up. I b ... bet he set it on fire.'

'Could be,' said Goldie. 'He might have had a grudge against his boss and turned the gas on in the cellar, which is what happened apparently. They're saying it was a gas leak that was ignited, probably by the spark from a firework. The police are looking for three children who were seen playing with fireworks in the factory yard.'

'Well, that was us, but I bet we were nowhere near that leak,' said Peggy, morosely. Her knife and fork were also out of action. 'Anyway the place went up about three seconds after David's rocket went through the window.'

'The escaping gas might well have reached that part of the building,' put in Harry.

'That means it would have blown up right in front of us,' Billy pointed out, 'and it didn't.'

'Sharp lad, your brother,' Harry said to Peggy. 'He's definitely got a point.'

'Trouble is, a lot of folk have died and the police'll want to be blaming someone,' said Goldie.

'I'm sorry to hear about your mother,' added Harry, 'but you two appear to be the hot favourites. The point is, it was a tragic accident. You weren't to know there was a gas leak and you were hardly going to do something that might kill your mother. No one can seriously blame it on you.'

Harry didn't notice his grandson looking daggers at him.

'What'll happen to us?' Billy asked. Although, having just been told about his mam's death, he wasn't really bothered what happened to them. Nor was Peggy.

'Not sure,' said Harry, now taking note of Goldie's glare. 'The law's a funny thing.'

'I think we should go back and give ourselves up,' said Peggy. 'We should tell the police our side of the story.'

'What about David?' Billy asked her. 'Are we going to shop him to the police?'

'We'll have to, Billy. Mam would want us to tell the whole truth. David won't get into any more trouble than we do.'

Goldie and his granddad looked at each other. This definitely wasn't going the way they had planned. They needed the kids here with them, to help with their thieving. The winter season wasn't as lucrative as Goldie made it out to be, but with the kids' help he could still make good money.

'There was a similar incident in Preston a couple of years back,' Harry said, thinking quickly. 'Kids messing with matches and fireworks on a caravan site and some propane gas cylinders went off like bombs. Two killed and a few injured.'

'What happened to the kids?' Peggy asked.

'Well, there was a bit of a ter-do about it all. People standing outside court waving banners saying it weren't the kids' fault and others wanting them locking up.'

'And what happened to the children?'

He shook his head, sadly. 'Well, they were locked up if I remember rightly.'

'That's right,' put in Goldie, now ready to add to his granddad's work of fiction. 'Three years in juvenile detention and quite a few after that in a proper prison. Seven years, I think they have to do.'

'And that's for killing just two people,' said Harry. 'The kids were a bit older than you two, but I don't know if that'll make much difference. They can't let you off scot-free, that's for sure. If you get caught it'll be quite a few years before you breathe free air again.'

'So we'll most prob'ly get locked up,' said Billy. He looked at his sister. 'Maybe we deserve it if we killed our mam.'

'I think you might change your tune once you're banged up,' said Goldie. 'There's a lot of bullying goes on in them detention places.'

'How do you know?' asked Billy.

'Because I spent some time there meself when I was a kid – and I was a lot tougher than you two. Knew how to look after meself.'

Sammy Kaye came on the wireless singing 'Chickery Chick' – a cheerful song that didn't suit the mood of the moment.

'Turn that damned thing off,' said Harry.

Goldie got up to oblige, then he stood behind the chairs of the two downcast children and placed his arms around their shoulders. 'Look,' he said, 'you don't think it was anything to do with you, and if what you're telling us is right, neither do I. In fact, you can bet your boots the police aren't entirely satisfied it was you. So why don't you give it some time? You could always write a letter to the police, posted from Manchester or somewhere, giving them your side of the story. I bet that'll make them think again. You never know. They might come up with the real culprits.'

'Good idea,' said Harry. 'If the coppers can't track you down, they'll try and track some other bugger down.'

'I suppose we could do that,' said Peggy.

'It sounds better than gettin' locked up,' said Billy. 'I wish we could write a letter to our mam, though.'

Peggy shook her head sorrowfully. 'Too late for that, Billy. It's just you and me now.'

'And us,' said Goldie.

'And we're taking a hell of a risk on your behalf,' said Harry. 'Harbouring fugitives from the law.'

'How're you supposed to know we're fugitives?' said Peggy. 'All you say is that we haven't told you anything, and we'll back you up. We've got nothing to lose.'

'You really are a sharp girl,' said Harry, 'but with you being kids, the police would wonder why we've taken you in without notifying them. We'd be hauled in for questioning at least.'

'And you've both got police records.'

He shrugged and smiled. 'Like I said, you're a sharp girl.'

'Blimey!' said Billy. 'I never thought I'd be a fugitive. Wait 'til I tell 'em at school.'

'What school would that be?' said Peggy.

'Sharp girl, your sister,' Harry repeated.

After breakfast Billy and Peggy went out for a walk on the sea front. They automatically headed south, in the direction of the huts and their hidden loot.

'I wish Mam could come back for ten minutes,' Billy said, looking up at the Tower. 'She'd tell us what to do.'

'Yeah, it's a shame people can't do that when they go suddenly,' said Peggy. 'Come back for ten minutes, just to sort things out.'

'You'd think God'd arrange that sort of thing,' Billy added, 'especially when they go unexpectedly, like Mam did.' He looked at his sister and asked, 'What do you think she'd say?'

'I bet she'd say not to trust Goldie or his grand-dad. I bet she'd tell us to go back home and give ourselves up.'

'No, she'd wouldn't say that if she knew we'd be locked up.'

'She deffo wouldn't be too pleased with us for nicking stuff,' said Peggy.

'How would we manage without the money we've nicked? I bet Mam couldn't answer that one.'

'We wouldn't have to nick anything if we gave ourselves up, Billy. We'd be looked after.'

'You mean, they'd stick us in jail.'

'Maybe, maybe not. Harry said what happened was an accident so we might not be blamed for it. They'd put us in a home.'

'I don't wanna go in no home,' said Billy.

'No, nor me.'

Billy looked out across the Irish Sea. A brilliant rainbow was arching across the sky, contrasting with the background of grey clouds and tailing off into the distant mist.

'Ireland's over there somewhere, innit?' he said, gesturing out to sea.

'Yeah.'

'That's where the crock of gold is, then. End of the rainbow.'

Peggy nodded towards the north. 'It might be at this end,' she said. 'Mos' prob'ly in Morecambe.'

'Or maybe there's a crock of gold at each end. Is Ireland a foreign country?'

'I suppose so,' said Peggy.

'But they speak English?'

'Think so. There's Irish nuns at our school and

113

they speak English.'

'S'pposin' we went over to Ireland? I bet we could get on a ship that'd take us over there and then we could look for the crock of gold.'

'It's all a fairy story, is this crock of gold.'

'I thought it might be...' said Billy, disappointed.

'Well, we're Catholics and we talk their language so we'd fit in all right,' said Peggy.

She looked to the west at the gloomy silhouette of a ship sailing south, probably the Dublin/Anglesey ferry. The low sky was as grey as the sea. The only cheerful thing about the view was the now-fading rainbow.

'Not sure I fancy going across that lot,' she said.

Billy pulled a face. 'I bet we've got enough money to pay the fare.'

'Yeah, but we'd have none left for when we got over there. We could get a tram up to Morecambe ... tanner each, I would think. You could look for your crock of gold up there while I have a cup of tea in a café.'

Billy looked up and shouted at the sky: 'What do you think, Mam? What shall we do?'

Passers-by looked at him, embarrassing Peggy. 'Billy, don't do that. People will think you're a loony.'

He grinned and walked on. It wasn't the first time he'd been called a loony. His mam had called him that from time to time. He looked up at the northern end of the rainbow and wondered about the merit of taking a tram to Morecambe. The people up there wouldn't know they were sitting under the end of a rainbow on top of a crock of gold just waiting to be found.

'What does a crock of gold look like?' he asked his sister.

'It doesn't look like anything, Billy. There's no such thing.'

Chapter 10

Harry gathered most of the breakfast dishes up with practised hands and carried them into the kitchen.

'You know the main problem with them kids,' he said to his grandson, who was following in his wake carrying the rest of the dishes.

'What's that?'

'They've turned up at the wrong time of year. Bang out of season. If the Illuminations hadn't closed down for the war they might have been useful now, but it'll be Easter before the crowds come back. No decent picking this time of year, George.'

'I don't know, I'm not doing so bad. There's plenty of locals out and about, and people coming into town for the dancing and weekends away.' He added, slyly, 'There's one thing you've forgotten, Granddad.'

'What's that?'

'Two things, actually. One is that in winter all the competition leaves town. Right now I might well be the only half-decent thief working Blackpool. And number two, people won't be on their guard so much. You don't see any posters around at this time of year telling people to beware of pickpockets. On top of that, the police won't be on the lookout quite as much as usual, and with the kids for distraction I should be able to make us a lot more money.'

'Aye, yer might have a point, lad. So, are yer gonna train the young 'uns up?'

'I think so. Just a couple of harmless jobs at first where I don't hardly need 'em, and work up from there.'

'Softly softly catchee monkey, eh? I like yer style, lad.'

Chapter 11

'Why have we come to Preston?' Billy asked. The three of them were sitting on a park bench there having travelled by bus the seventeen miles inland from Blackpool.

By way of an answer Goldie nodded in the direction of a bookmaker's shop at the other side of the road, in clear view from where they were sitting.

'We're here because it's not Blackpool,' he said. 'In my business I have to spread my work far and wide to avoid being picked up. And even if I am pinched it'll be for just the one job. The coppers won't have a clue about the others I did in Blackpool or Fleetwood or St Annes. Or anywhere else for that matter.'

'You get about a lot then,' commented Billy.

'I do. I've even worked in Manchester when things are a bit slow around Blacky.'

'What's so special about that bookie's?'

'I know a bloke who works in there.' Goldie took a gun-metal grey box from his pocket. 'He's on the other end of this.'

'What's that?' Billy asked.

'It's a walkie-talkie I bought from an army surplus shop. Me and Roy have pulled this scam before when he worked in a bookie's in Blackpool. Works a treat. When a punter comes out after drawing big winnings, Roy'll know how much, and what pocket he's got it in. With a bit of help from you it'll soon be in *my* pocket. Whatever it is, I keep half and split the rest between you and Roy.'

'You can do that, can you?'

'Yep, I can do that. It's a bit more difficult if it's in an inside pocket but I can still do it.'

'So you're a pickpocket as well,' said Peggy.

'I am. And a very good one, although I says so meself. Every man has to have a trade.' He took out his pocket watch and checked the time. 'Right, the three-thirty at Kempton should be over now. They'll be queuing up at the paying-out window. I'm hoping there's a big player in there.'

A minute later a voice came through his handset: 'Calling Goldie, calling Goldie...'

'Goldie speaking.'

'Man in a beige raincoat and brown trilby picked up a ton. He's just laid a pony on Jester's Lad in the three-forty-five at Haydock.'

'What odds?' Goldie enquired.

'Seven to two ... second favourite. Knowing him, it'll be his last bet.'

'Thanks, Roy, keep me posted.'

'Will do ... over and out.'

Goldie grinned and explained the situation to the children. 'A punter's just won a hundred quid and then laid twenty-five of it on a horse that's running in ten minutes. If he wins, he'll be coming out with the best part of two hundred pounds on him.'

'What do we do?' Billy asked.

'I want you to be already over there when he comes out, acting like you're playing a game of Tig. I'll be a bit higher up the road, looking in a shop window and listening to this.' He indicated the handset he was carrying. 'When I get word he's leaving I'll raise my arm, which means he'll be out in a couple of seconds. At this point you're only a few yards away so that when he does come out one of you bumps straight into him. He won't be expecting it and you'll be shouting "sorry, mister", and carrying on with your game, running off. In the meantime I'll have bumped into him from the other side and lifted his wallet. All I do is walk on after apologising to him myself, then I turn the corner and leg it, just like you'll be doing. We'll meet back at the bus stop where we got off.' He looked at them sternly and added, 'You should remember where that is because I told you to.'

'We remember,' said Peggy. 'We're not daft.'

Fifteen minutes later all three of them were in position, with the children playing a game of Tig while keeping most of their attention on Goldie. When his arm went up Billy set off towards the bookie's, pausing momentarily for the door to open. He checked that the man leaving followed the description given by Goldie then took off again, running straight into the punter at speed, so much so that he fell down on the pavement. Peggy, still playing her part, ran up to her fallen brother, touched him on his shoulder and shouted 'Tig!' before she ran off. Billy looked up to see Goldie apologising to the man for bumping into him, and the man looking down at Billy and calling him a stupid bloody kid.

Billy, after examining a graze to his knee, got to his feet, called out, 'Sorry, mister,' and went off in chase of his sister. Five minutes later they were both at the bus stop. A minute after that Goldie joined them. Blood from Billy's grazed knee was running into his sock. Goldie glanced at it, took a handkerchief from his pocket and handed it to him to dab away the blood.

'Good ruse, getting yourself injured like that. Took his mind right off the possibility of being robbed.'

'I didn't do it on purpose,' Billy told him, forming the handkerchief into a bandage and tying it around his knee. 'He was a big bloke. I just bounced off him.'

'Yeah, he was a bit of a size. Look, here comes a bus. It's going to Fleetwood but we'll need to get on it just to get away from here.'

An hour later they were back in the house with Goldie counting the money in the man's purloined wallet. It amounted to one hundred and forty-two pounds.

'I thought you said there'd be nearly two hundred,' said Billy.

'At best, Billy. His second horse came in third so they paid out quarter odds. This is his winnings from that plus earlier from Kempton plus whatever he had in the first place. Not a bad pick up. I get a half, you two take a quarter and so does Roy. That's thirty-five pounds ten shillings for you. Tell you what, to make up for your injury I'll make it up to thirty-five pounds fifteen. That's five bob injury money... Okay?'

'Okay,' said Peggy.

Billy was examining his knee to see if it was worth five shillings. He looked up at Goldie and said, 'I think this is worth at least ten bob.'

Goldie laughed, as did his granddad. 'Okay, young 'un. Thirty-six quid it is, and I'll throw in a sticking plaster for good measure.'

It was late afternoon three days later. Peggy, Billy and Goldie were in Lytham St Annes, Blackpool's next-door neighbour just a few miles to the south. It was a smart seaside town, popular with retired people with plenty of money to spare. The three young people were standing outside a somewhat upmarket café with a mouth-watering menu displayed in the window.

'Look at this,' Billy was saying, 'roast topside of beef with new and mashed potatoes, carrots, cabbage and peas and Yorkshire pudding ... and you get apple pie and a pot of tea, which means you can have at least two cups, all for five bob.'

'It's too much, Billy,' said Peggy. 'If we start eating like that we'll be skint by Christmas.'

'Maybe not,' said Goldie. 'There's ways and means of dining out when there are two of you.'

As they walked away from the café he proceeded to tell them how it was done, with Billy listening in great admiration and Peggy shaking her head.

'What if we get caught?' she said, after Goldie had outlined his plan.

'What're they gonna get you for? It's not as though yer doin' a runner.'

'And if it all goes wrong we can always pay,' added Billy. 'C'mon, Peg, it'll be a proper wheeze.'

She shook her head and gave in. 'Okay. I suppose I go in first, then you come in and pretend you don't know me.'

'I know how it works, Peg.'

'So long as you do.'

Without another word to either of them she turned and headed back to the café where she sat at a corner table and ordered the roast beef meal her brother had been drooling over. She was half-way through hers when Billy came in, made a show of looking around for a vacant place then made his way over to his sister's table and ordered a cup of tea and a doughnut, priced at sixpence on the menu. Peggy glanced at him as she would any stranger sitting at her table and continued with her meal without saying anything. She finished at approximately the same time as her brother and asked for the bill. Billy took the opportunity to do the same and the waitress returned with two bills that she placed beside their respective plates. Peggy picked up Billy's bill and took it to the till where she paid with a two-shilling piece.

Five minutes after she left Billy approached the woman at the till and thrust his bill under her nose. 'This can't be right,' he said. 'I had a cup of tea and a doughnut and you've charged me five bob.'

'Cup of tea and a doughnut? Are you sure?'

''Course I'm sure. Ask that lady what served me.'

The waitress was summoned and confirmed that Billy had only had a cup of tea and a doughnut. 'I think he must have picked up the wrong bill,' she said, looking across at the now-empty table.

'It was the only bill there,' said Billy, taking sixpence from his pocket. 'I think my bill should be a tanner.'

'That's right,' said the cashier, taking his money. 'There's obviously been a mix-up, sorry about that.'

A few minutes later he joined his sister and Goldie who were checking out a café on the sea front. Peggy turned with a look of concern on her face.

'Did it work?'

Billy gave a broad grin. ''Course it worked, they thought it was all their fault. Right, what's on the menu for me?'

An hour later, with the stomachs of both children fuller than they'd been for weeks, they were watching the woman Goldie was now referring to as 'the mark'. She was looking in a fashion shop window. Two minutes earlier he had been standing beside her, not that she'd spared him so much as a glance, which suited Goldie. She was a well-dressed, well-preserved woman in her sixties and Goldie was the type of young man she always chose to ignore ... a ne'er-do-well. She had a handbag slung in the crook of her left arm because her left hand was otherwise engaged with a cigarette holder. Her right hand was thrust deep in her coat pocket since the day was cold. Goldie was now fifty yards away, talking to Peggy and Billy.

'There'll be rich pickings in that handbag,' he said.

'How d'you know?' Billy asked.

'Because I've taken a dekko at the rings on her fingers. Real massive diamonds on two of 'em. Proper diamonds as well, none of yer imitation jobs.'

'How can you tell?' asked Peggy.

'From the settings.'

'So, what d'you want us to do?' said Billy.

'I want you two to stand beside her and look at the stuff in the winder. Start makin' jokes that she can hear. I need you to distract her attention long enough fer me ter nick her bag. She's not gripping it in her hand, it's just loose around her arm. As soon as I grab it I'll have it off her in a flash, and then I'll be gone.'

'What do we do after?' asked Peggy. 'We're not hanging around 'til the coppers come.'

'No, we're not,' said Billy.

'You just walk away in the opposite direction from me, which is back this way. She'll be looking to see which way I ran. Then you turn down that side street and leg it to the nearest tram stop. I'll see you back at the Tower front door.'

'So all we do is look in the window and make daft remarks about the dresses and stuff?' said Billy.

'That's exactly what you do, but loud enough for her to hear. Billy, you stand with yer back to her and make sure she can't see Peggy because you're in the way.'

'Why?' asked Peggy.

'Because I don't want her describing you to the police.'

'You mean the police'll know we were in on it?'

'Mebbe, mebbe not. No point taking unnecessary risks. Okay, off you go. I'll be one minute behind yer.'

Satisfied that their part in the crime didn't involve them doing anything illegal, Billy and Peggy made their way cautiously towards the fashion shop where the woman was staring fixedly at a fur coat. They went and stood beside her. Peggy pointed to a print dress that was marked at 5 guineas.

'Blimey!' said Billy. 'Have yer seen how much that dress costs.'

'Never mind the dress,' said Peggy, who could see that the woman's interest was taken up by a fur coat. 'See how much that coat is? Twenty guineas. Who's gonna be daft enough to pay that much for a flipping coat?'

The woman, now annoyed, glanced their way, but only saw Billy's back, which was shielding her view of Peggy's face. She was thus distracted when Goldie arrived on the scene. He snatched at the woman's handbag with both hands and took off with it, but not before pulling her to the ground where she screamed with rage. A hundred yards away an approaching police car saw the whole incident and accelerated in chase of

Goldie. The children looked down at the woman on the ground, screaming at the disappearing thief. They headed in the opposite direction and were passed by the police car, which by now had its siren blaring.

'Don't run, Billy!' warned Peggy. 'We're not running away from anything.'

He slowed down to a fast walk. They turned down a side street where they both took to their heels and didn't stop until they reached the main road. A tram was approaching from the south. They crossed the road, went to a stop and waved the tram down. Twenty minutes later they were alighting outside Blackpool Tower.

'No sign of Goldie,' observed Billy, looking across the road at the Tower's front doors.

'He'll be along,' said Peggy. 'No fear of that. I doubt if the coppers'll catch Goldie.'

'Yeah, he is a bit slippery, isn't he? That ruse of his in the café worked brilliantly. We could do that again in Blackpool. I wonder where he is?'

'I bet he's on the next tram.'

They both stood on the steps outside the Tower's doors and made themselves conspicuous for anyone looking their way. But Goldie wasn't on the next tram, nor the one after that. In fact ten trams and an hour went by with no sign of him.

'Maybe he went straight to the house,' guessed Billy.

'Maybe he did, but he definitely said he'd meet us at the Tower.'

'I think we should go to the house. If he gets back here and we've gone, that's where he'll go.'

'Okay,' said Peggy.

The children were in the lounge, listening to *The Robinson Family* on the wireless, when the doorbell rang. Goldie still wasn't home and Harry was worried that the police might have caught him. Billy and Peggy were worried that it was the police at the door. They listened at the lounge door and heard the front door open, then a low murmur of what sounded like police voices. Peggy opened the door a crack so that they could hear more clearly.

'It's about your grandson, Mr Golding.'

'How do you know who I am?'

Peggy opened the door a little wider so that she could see who it was, then closed it quickly and quietly.

'It's the police,' she whispered, opening the door just a crack once again. 'They don't sound official or anything.'

'Is that good?'

''Course it is. If they've come to arrest someone they sound very official. Anyway ... shhh, let's listen.'

'Your grandson told us where to find you,' a voice was saying.

'I ... er ... why would he need to do that?'

Billy and Peggy were wondering the same thing.

'He's been in an accident in Lytham St Annes.'

'What sort of accident?'

One of the two policemen cleared his throat, nervously, and explained. 'Well, we were in a patrol car when we saw him steal a lady's handbag.'

126

'That doesn't sound like my grandson. He's a good lad.'

'Mr Golding, we know he's got a criminal record for such things.'

Harry conceded this point immediately. 'Oh, right.'

'Anyway we gave chase in the car but lost him when he ran down a narrow alley. As far as we can ascertain he came out into a street where he saw a bicycle in the driveway of a private house. He took the bicycle, presumably to speed up his escape from us. What he obviously hadn't realised was that the brakes on the bicycle were non-existent. The owner was mending them and had removed the worn brake blocks to replace them with new.'

'So he had an accident. What exactly happened?'

'He was obviously cycling as fast as he could but when he arrived at the main road junction he couldn't stop and went straight out into heavy traffic.' The officer paused and added sorrowfully, 'He, erm, was hit by a bus, Mr Golding. We arrived on the scene soon afterwards and rang for an ambulance.'

'An ambulance? Which hospital is he in?'

'He was taken to Victoria Hospital here in Blackpool. I went with him in the ambulance. It was there that he managed to give me your name and address. He was badly injured and knew I'd need to contact you.'

'How do you mean, *managed?* How badly injured is he?'

There was a long pause then, 'Mr Golding, I'm sorry to inform you that when we got to the hospital your grandson George was declared dead on arrival.'

Harry let out a long, low howl of grief and sank to his knees with his hands clutched together as if in prayer. Then he went quiet for half a minute, watched in awkward silence by the policemen. He got to his feet and vented his pent-up anguish on them.

'You murderin' bastards! I reckon it were your fault for chasin' him.'

'I'm really sorry, Mr Golding, but we were only doing our jobs as police officers. The lady who had her bag stolen was injured when he dragged her to the ground.'

'Injured? Oh bloody dear. My lad's dead and I'm supposed to have sympathy for this woman who was only injured!'

The second policeman spoke now. 'No, Mr Golding. We're just trying to put you fully in the picture as to how it all came about. It would appear from the woman's statement that he might have been working in conjunction with two children. Would you know anything about them, Mr Golding?'

Peggy whispered in Billy's ear, 'Out the back door, quick. Grab all yer stuff.'

Billy needed no second bidding. Within two minutes they were both walking quickly up the back street, carrying as many possessions as they had to hand, and putting as much distance between them and the Goldings' house as they could. Ten minutes later they were in Blackpool Tower ballroom, their only sanctuary. Reginald Dixon was playing the Wurlitzer and the dance floor was full of mainly aging couples enjoying their afternoon dance. Billy and Peggy weren't enjoying their day at all, but Goldie's reported death hadn't had the same devastating effect on them as their mother's had. They bought cups of tea and sat down at a table.

'Do you think we might be to blame?' Billy asked his sister.

'I don't see how.'

'No, nor me. I'm sorry Goldie's dead though. At least he gave us a place to live.'

'We can't go back there, Billy.'

'Yeah, I know.'

'And we've got that thirty-six quid. Have you got your half on you?'

''Course I have,' Billy assured her. 'Plus we've got the money and stuff back behind the beach hut.'

'Yeah. Good job we didn't take that to the house.'

'Fancy nicking a bike that had no brakes. I thought Goldie was smarter than that.'

'There was some good in him,' Peggy said. 'I think he genuinely tried to help us.'

'Help us to help him more like,' said Billy, who was quite cynical for one so young.

His sister shook her head. 'When we first met him,' she said, 'just after he saw you take that woman's bag, he could have easily taken it off us if he'd wanted to. We couldn't have stopped him.'

'No, I suppose not.'

There was a brief silence between them. 'It could be,' Peggy said, after some thought, 'that this might have been bad for Goldie but a good thing for us.'

'How d'you work that out?'

'Well, I think if we'd stayed with him, the police would have caught the three of us before much longer. I mean, we went on two jobs with him and neither of them went exactly smoothly.'

Billy looked down at his knee that still had the plaster on – the plaster Goldie had put on for him. 'That's right. I'm sorry he's dead, though – he never did us any harm. I suppose old Harry was a good bloke deep down.'

'Maybe, maybe not. Pity we had to be assistant thieves to pay our way. Ah, well, we'd better go and see if the rest of our money's still under the sand.'

'It's not really *our* money, though, is it?'

'Billy, it's as much ours as the money you nicked from that shop in Leeds. It's either steal or starve for us.'

'I suppose so,' he said, morosely. 'Anyway, it looks like we'll be spending one more night in the hut.'

'At least,' said Peggy.

They awoke late the following morning after a poor night's sleep. Both of them were still fully clothed but more comfortable than the first night they'd slept there. They had divided the money from the bookie's job and each carried eighteen pounds about their person. Billy kept his share inside the lining of his jacket sleeve, accessed via a tear he'd deliberately made in the shoulder seam some time previously. Most small boys needed private places about their person for secreting items of contraband they might acquire from time to time, and Billy was no exception. Peggy planned on keeping hers in a pocket in her knickers.

'Mam made it special for me, ter nick bread buns from the school dinners. Didn't yer know?'

'No. I did wonder where them buns came from, though. I wouldn't have eaten them if I'd known they'd been in yer knickers. I thought they tasted a bit funny.'

'They were all right toasted,' said his sister.

'Yeah, I reckon it took out all the smelly-knicker smell.'

'I've been thinking about Harry,' said Peggy.

'Yer mean, whether he told the police about us?'

'No, not that. I've been wondering how he's going on, with Goldie being dead.'

'He'll not be so suited,' said Billy. 'I reckon he thought the world of Goldie.'

'I know. I hope he's okay. Maybe I should ring him. When Goldie gave me the address he put a phone number on it.'

'I don't s'ppose it'll do any harm to ring. Shall we go for some breakfast and ring him after?'

'Yeah, I think I'll do that. It'll be handy to know what he told the police about us. We might need to leave Blackpool.'

It had turned nine o'clock when they made their way to the phone box, wanting to get this job over with. Both of them kept a wary eye out for any policemen who might wonder why they weren't in school. Just another worry they had to live with.

'Hello.'

131

Harry's voice sounded low and dejected.

'It's Peggy, Harry. Me and Billy were listening when the police came yesterday. We're really, really sorry about Goldie ... er ... George. We ran off when the police asked about the two children.'

'And yer want ter know if I shopped yer. Is that it?'

'No, we knew you wouldn't do that. We were just worried about how you are.'

'I'm not so good, not so good at all. I never expected to be left on me own at my age. In fact, I've no idea how I'll go on wi' no money comin' in. He were a young devil were George but he kept me on me feet.' Harry gave a brief, sad laugh as he remembered his grandson.

'We'd come and see you, but we're a bit worried about the police.'

'There's no need ter worry, lass. I told 'em I knew nowt about no children. Force of habit wi' me and t'police – never tell 'em nowt. Bastards! It were them what killed him, chasin' him like he were a London gangster. I bet they had their lights flashin' and their bloody bells ringin'. He were just a lad tryin' ter scrape a few bob together for him and his granddad. Anyroad I told 'em what I think of 'em and I don't suppose they'll be in a hurry ter come back. So if you an' Billy want ter come an' see me yer'll be welcome, lass. I'll be in all day, feelin' sorry for meself.'

'I think we might do that, Harry.'

She came out of the telephone box to where Billy was waiting. 'He told the police he knew nothing about any children.'

'That's good. Do you believe him?'

132

'I do. I don't think he was in much of a mood for lying to me. I told him we might go round to see him today, but if we do we can't stay long just in case the police get wind of us being there.'

'I think we should go in the back door,' Billy suggested. 'That street was empty when we came out. When we get near we should ring him and tell him to leave it unlocked.'

'Yer a right crafty monkey, you are, Billy Clegg.'

Billy just grinned. He'd been called a lot worse. 'We could go up to our rooms and get the rest of our stuff we left behind. I think I'd like to check on that buried rucksack before we do anything else,' he said.

'Well, I can't see that anyone's found it and dug it up,' said Peggy. The look on Billy's face had her adding, 'Oh, go on, I'll come with you.'

Billy led the way around the back of the beach hut and measured out four shoe lengths from the corner of the hut to where the rucksack was buried, then he knelt down and scooped away the sand with his hands, helped by Peggy. They got to a depth of eighteen inches without finding anything.

'We didn't bury it any deeper than this,' Peggy said. 'Are you sure we're looking in the right place?'

'Yeah, it was exactly four footsteps from the edge of the hut. You saw me do it. It's definitely down here.'

'Well, we'd best make the hole a bit bigger. And when we do find it we'll make sure we know exactly where it is.'

They extended both the length and the width

133

and depth of the hole until it became apparent that the rucksack was not there. It had simply gone.

'How can it not be here?' said Billy, almost in tears after the appalling run of bad luck they'd both had. 'Who's taken it? Do you think someone saw us bury it?'

'No ... no one can have seen us bury it,' Peggy said. 'Not around the back of these huts. Who can see over here?'

'I don't know, Peg, but it's not fair. We do our best and people steal from us.'

'I suppose the people we stole from might be saying the same thing,' said his sister, philosophically.

'I don't care, it's not fair, doing it to us. We're just kids, tryin' to stay alive.'

'We'll live, Billy,' said Peggy, putting an arm around his shoulders. 'Even if we have to go back to Leeds to face the music.'

'Face the music – what does that mean?'

'It means take whatever punishment's coming to us.'

'Don't fancy that, Peg.'

But his sister had walked away, deep in thought. After a while she reappeared, saying, 'I think we should go see Harry ... tell him what's happened.'

'Why?'

'Because ... and I know it's not a nice thing to say about a dead person ... I think the only person who could have worked out where we hid the rucksack was Goldie. I think he took it.'

'How would he know?'

'Because you told him we'd buried it on the

beach, so he put two and two together and figured out that in the whole of Blackpool beach we'd have to bury it where we could find it easily, and that place would be near this hut. So all he had to do was find the right hut and he knew he'd be near the buried treasure.'

'How would he find the right hut?'

'He'd look for a hut with a new lock. He knew we had a key to the hut and we could only have a key if we'd fitted a new lock.'

'But there's a lot of beach in front of the hut. How come he knew to dig around the back?'

'Same reason as we buried it there. There's a lot of beach in front of the hut but not much behind, and he knew we'd bury it where no one could see us.'

'You think so?'

'I do. We buried it near enough to the hut so that we'd always be able to find it. A smart bloke like Goldie'd poke about with a stick and find it in ten minutes.'

'Blimey, you're right, Peg! I bet it's at Harry's house.'

'Trouble is, how do we go in there and tell him Goldie was stealing off us and can we have our stuff back?'

'I don't fancy asking him that.'

'Maybe we should go back and just have a look in Goldie's room for ourselves.'

'Yeah, maybe we should,' said Billy, brightening now at the prospect of recovering the stolen loot which, to his mind, was rightfully theirs.

Chapter 12

As the children approached the corner that led into Harry's street it was obvious something was amiss. A crowd of people were standing at the end of it, some of them gesticulating animatedly. From the street itself they heard loud engine noises and men shouting. Smoke was billowing over the rooftops.

'Blimey! It's a fire,' said Billy.

They both stopped in their tracks. The last fire they'd witnessed had meant trouble for them.

'Oh, heck! I hope it's nothing to do with Harry,' said Peggy.

'We'd best go look.'

They continued around the corner and saw a fire crew aiming hoses at flames billowing out of a house about fifty yards down the street.

'I think it's Harry's,' said Billy.

'It might not be.'

'I think it is.'

They walked down the street to identify the house.

Neighbours were out in force to watch the drama. 'Oh, no, it is his house! I hope he's not in there.'

'He's not,' said Billy. 'I just hope our rucksack's all right.'

'How do you know Harry's not inside?'

'Because he's over there, sitting on that wall.'

Peggy followed her brother's pointing finger to where Harry was sitting on a low wall opposite his blazing house. He was smoking a cigarette and didn't look the least bit upset to see his house burning down. The children approached him.

'Harry!' shouted Billy 'What's happened?'

'Me house is on fire. What's it bloody look like?'

'I was wondering how it happened.'

'So am I, lad,' said Harry when Billy approached more closely, 'and I need to get me story straight when the police and insurance people come asking their nosy bloody questions.'

'How d'yer mean?' Billy asked.

'I think he means he set fire to it himself,' said Peggy in a low voice that only Harry and Billy could hear.

'Hey, don't you go spreading that around!' Harry said, forcefully. 'I never said owt of the sort. That bloody house is a part of my life I'd rather forget. It wasn't exactly a happy place, and our George dying put the bloody tin hat on it.'

'Yeah, we're really sorry about George.'

'I fell asleep by the fire without putting the fireguard up. When I woke up the whole room was on fire. All I could do was run out to save meself.' He looked at the children. 'How does that sound?'

'Sounds all right to me,' said Billy, conspiratorially.

'So you did start it?' said Peggy, in a low voice.

'Hey! I never said that, but it was definitely started with a piece of coal from the fire setting fire to the rug what set fire to me favourite chair what set fire ter me. It burnt me trousers, look.' He showed them a charred trouser leg. 'I just got out before the whole room went up.'

'Did it burn your leg?' Peggy enquired.

'Not really. I managed to put it out before it spread right through. Good thick khaki trousers, these. I got 'em from the Army and Navy Stores. Saved me a scorched arse today.'

'What are you going to do now?' Billy asked. 'Where are you going to live?'

'Oh, I've got a pal who'll put me up 'til I get on me feet. After that I'm goin' back to sea.'

'To sea?'

'Yeah. I were ship's cook for nigh on twenty-five years. Mind you, I signed off twenty year ago but I've still got me papers. The war took a lot of good seamen and there's a shortage right now so I should be OK, even at my age. I reckon I've ten good years left in me.'

It sounded to Peggy as though he'd been planning this for some time, although she chose not to mention it.

'Did you manage to rescue any stuff from the house?' Billy asked.

'Like our George's stuff, yer mean?'

'Yeah. We, er, think he might have had a rucksack that belonged to us.'

'Did he now? Well, if he did, it's still in there.' Harry nodded towards the house, the interior of which was blazing fiercely now. 'If it were dodgy stuff, I wouldn't ask too many questions about it.'

'Right.'

'We'll forget all about it then,' said Peggy.

Harry patted a haversack by his side. 'I just managed ter bring this bag out with all my stuff in ... pension book, bank book, a nice few quid I had stashed away, stuff like that. I always have it packed ready and handy, just in case of an emergency.'

'Right,' said Billy.

'In fact, it'd do no harm if you could take it off me hands for a bit. I wouldn't want the coppers ter think I'd planned all this in advance – and me havin' this bag all packed and ready, it might look a bit suspicious. Better for me if they think I've lost everything.'

'Okay,' said Billy, much to his sister's disapproval.

'This pal who's putting me up,' said Harry, jabbing a thumb over his shoulder, 'lives in the next street back there, number forty-six. If you could take this bag and bring it to me at his place in the morning, I'd be really obliged. His name's Charlie Dickinson.'

A police car rounded the corner. Harry spotted it immediately as though he'd been waiting for such a vehicle to arrive. 'I should take the bag and be on your way right now,' he said, urgently.

The children did as he asked and were well away from him by the time the police car stopped and three uniformed constables emerged. They went over to the fire engine and enquired who was in charge. Eventually they went over to where Harry had put his cigarette out and was watching his house burn down with a shocked expression on his face.

'We're told this is your house, sir.'

Harry nodded as though words were beyond him.

'Could you tell us how it started?'

'I don't rightly know. I was asleep and when I woke up the room was on fire. So was I, for that matter.'

He shook his head in despair. 'I don't know what's gonna happen ter me next. Me grandson gets killed by a bus then me bloody house burns down. I didn't have much, but everything I did have were in that house.'

'We're sorry about that, sir.'

'I don't know. It might have been my fault it started. I fell asleep and I suppose a spark jumped out of the fire. That bloody coal we get nowadays is real sparky stuff.'

'Did you have a fireguard up?'

Harry shook his head. 'I don't know ... prob'ly not. I suppose it makes it my fault, does it? I reckon the insurance people'll say it was.'

'Your fault or not, it was an accident, sir. It's Mr Golding, isn't it?'

Harry looked up at the policeman. 'That's right. How d'yer know?'

'It was me who came to tell you about your grandson's accident.'

Harry wasn't sure if this was in his favour or not. 'You, was it? Well, I think I might have been a bit rude to yer. If so, I'm sorry. It set me back did that ... and now this. God knows what I'm gonna do. I'm sitting here without a penny ter scratch me arse with. I've got nothin' and nobody.'

'Well, if you're insured you should be okay.'

'That's if they pay out, with me havin' caused it, and even then it could be weeks if not months.

I think I might as well go and throw meself under a bleedin' bus too.'

'Do you have any relatives you can go to?'

'No, me son died in the war and his wife got married again. I've got a few friends, I suppose.'

'Well, we can put you in touch with people who'll take care of you until you get back on your feet.'

Harry gave a humourless laugh. 'Get back on me feet? I'm seventy years old. How can I get back on me bleedin' feet?'

To his relief the policemen left him then and went to do the job they'd come to do. Harry lit another cigarette and pondered his immediate future, which would include organising his grandson's funeral. He'd give George a good send-off no matter how much it cost. In fact, George could pay for his own send-off with some of the money and jewellery in Harry's haversack, much of which had come from George's room.

As they left the scene of the blaze, threading their way through the many onlookers Peggy chastised Billy, who had the haversack slung over his shoulder. 'You shouldn't have said we'd take that bag. If Harry gets done for setting his house on fire and we're caught with that bag, we could get done as well.'

'How can they do him for setting his own house on fire? It's his.'

'If he claims it was an accident he can get a lot of money from the insurance company. If he did it on purpose, it's a crime and he could get locked up for it.'

'I didn't know that.'

141

They trudged on in the general direction of the Tower. It was a bright day for November, without the usual Blackpool breeze blowing in from off-shore. 'I wonder,' said Billy, 'if that's how the fire at the factory started? With someone wanting to claim money from the insurance.'

'Dunno.'

'It might have been that bloke we saw running away from it. Do you know who he was?'

'No idea, but he knew who I was, and he knew who Mam was.'

'I wonder how he knew that? Maybe he was the boss.'

'Maybe.'

'And if he was the boss, he'd be able to claim off the insurance. I know they were sacking everyone, including Mam.'

'Billy, talk sense. Why would he do that and kill people as well? That's murder that is. All he had to do was sell it if he wanted the money – better than getting hung for murder.'

'Grown-ups do daft stuff all the time. They like to kill each other like they did in the war. What was all that about?'

'That was all about a madman called Hitler,' said Peggy. 'If it was that bloke at the factory, he killed our mam and he should be hanged for it.'

'Maybe that's what people are thinking about us,' muttered Billy. Then he brightened, saying, 'I think we ought to take a look inside this bag before we give it back to Harry. Our rucksack stuff might be in it.'

'So we take it out and then tell Harry what we've done?'

'Don't see why not,' said Billy, 'it's our stuff.'

'Or maybe we take it out and don't tell him. Do you think he'll know?'

'Dunno, don't care. It's our stuff. Anyway, a lot of kids'd just take the whole bag and never see Harry again.'

'You're right there, Billy. Good job for him that we're honest. I think we should get a tram down to the hut and do it there.'

'It's all here, Peg, all the jewels and stuff.'

'What about our forty-nine quid?'

'Well, there's a load of money. If the jewels are here, I bet our money's part of it too. We should just take out forty-nine quid and the jewels we recognise.'

'And then take the haversack to Harry? What do you think he'll say to that?'

'Dunno, don't care. We give him the bag and tell him we've taken our stuff out of it. If he doesn't like it, we just scarper.'

'So we don't go in the house, we stand on the doorstep, ready to run?'

'Yeah. If that other feller comes to the door, we ask him to give this to Harry then we scarper.'

'We should put a note inside telling him what's missing and why.'

'That's a good idea, Peg.'

'I'll make it a nice note, so it sounds as if we didn't think too badly of Goldie.'

'George,' corrected Billy.

It was Charlie Dickinson who answered Peggy's knock. 'Is Harry staying here?' Billy asked, politely.

Charlie looked down at the children standing on his doorstep and grinned. 'You'll be the kids Harry thought wouldn't turn up with his bag.'

'Well, we've brought it,' said Peggy.

'Harry!' Charlie shouted. 'Someone here to see you.'

Harry appeared and grinned over Charlie's shoulder. 'So, you've brought it, have you?'

'Most of it,' said Billy. 'We've taken out what was ours.'

'Have you now? Well, I can't say as I blame yer.'

The children looked at each other, happy that he'd said this.

'Charlie,' said Harry, 'can I have a few private minutes with these two?'

''Course yer can. I'll make us all a brew in the kitchen. Gimme me a shout when yer ready.'

Charlie was a much younger man than Harry, maybe in his mid-forties, with a cheerful face that the children took to instantly. Harry led the children through into a large, comfortably furnished lounge where the three of them sat down. Billy plonked the haversack on the floor but Harry made no move to pick it up.

'There's a note inside saying what we took and why,' said Peggy. 'Just our stuff, nothing else.'

'Okay.' Harry nodded, approvingly. 'George's funeral's on Friday,' he said. 'You're welcome to come but I'll understand if you can't make it. There won't be too many there.'

'We'll do our best,' said Peggy. 'We've never been to a funeral before, have we, Billy?'

'No.'

'Then on Saturday,' added Harry, 'I'm taking

144

me combination down to Liverpool to see if I can't get work.'

'What's a combination?' Billy asked.

'It's me motorbike and sidecar. It's called a combination. There's a liner called the *Britannic* leaving for New York on Monday. I'm applying for work on that as a ship's cook. Charlie tells me there's always work in Liverpool for experienced galley crew.'

'Does Charlie work on the ships?' asked Billy.

'Used to, before he bought this place. Never settled down properly, though. Not many sailors do. It gets into yer blood does the sea and the travellin'.'

'I wouldn't mind going to New York,' said Billy. 'We'd be out of the clutches of the coppers over there.'

'We can't afford it, Billy, and what would we do in New York? We don't have any passports or anything.'

'Dunno. I bet it's better than here, though.'

'Yer can come to Liverpool with me if you like,' offered Harry. 'You might find someone there who'll put you up, especially with you havin' a few quid. By the way, the jewellery you had in that haversack ... if yer like, I'll buy it off yer. I could get a nice few dollars for that in New York.'

'How much?'

'Seventy-five quid. How's that sound?'

'Not as good as a hundred,' said Billy.

'Oh, trying to haggle with me, eh? I like yer style, Billy. The most I'll go to is eighty-five. Add that to the forty-nine you took from my bag and that's ... erm ... a hundred and thirty-four quid.'

'We've got the other thirty-six too. Would that buy us tickets to New York?' asked the boy.

Harry shrugged. 'I'm not well up on fares, but if it does, yer'll be arrivin' in America without a penny ter scratch yer arses with – on the streets from Day One. That's if they let you in, two foreign kids with no passports. It's doubtful.'

Peggy knew that the money they currently had would keep them off the streets back home for some months.

'I don't want to go to New York,' she said.

'Can we stay here until you go?' Billy asked Harry.

To the boy, going to Liverpool was just the first step in them going to New York but he wasn't going to tell Peggy that. Although she knew him well enough to pretty much read his mind.

'I should think so,' said Harry, 'I'll ask Charlie.'

Peggy whispered in her brother's ear: 'Listen, you. If you manage to get on that bloomin' ship, I'm going back to Leeds to face the music on my own!'

'Why?'

'Because we just can't live like this, Billy.'

'I'm not sure what your sister's telling you, Billy,' said Harry, 'but I'm guessing she's trying to drill some common sense into you.'

Billy grinned and said, 'She's been trying to do that all me life. Will you still give us a ride to Liverpool?'

'If that's what you both want.'

Chapter 13

Betty managed to sit up in her hospital bed to greet her friend Jimmy.

'Hiya, Betty. I've just had a letter from Blainey's accountants. We were right about our contracts. Everyone who signed one is entitled to a calendar month's redundancy money.'

Betty managed a smile. 'Blimey! I bet Lester's not too pleased about that.'

She had been in hospital for over a week and was recovering well. Her broken bones had healed to the stage where they itched under the pot they were encased in. 'Did you bring me that scratching stick I asked you for?'

'I did. Well, it's a drumstick I got off a pal of mine, but it should do the job.'

Betty took the drumstick and forced it inside the plaster encasing her leg, rubbing it up and down. 'Ooh ... yes, that's better. Can you give my back a scratch, Jimmy?'

'Lean forward if you can. Is that all right?'

'Bit lower, left a bit. Ooh! That's it. Give me a good scratch. Aah ... that'll do. I wonder how much we'll be getting?'

'Well, it's based on a basic forty-hour week and there's four and a bit weeks in a month so I reckon it's our hourly rate times about a hundred and sixty-eight.'

'Well, I was on two and six an hour,' said Betty.

'Hey, same as me. Eight half crowns to a pound, so it's hundred and sixty-eight divided by eight ... that's twenty-one pounds – better than a slap in the face with a wet fish. Mind you, I doubt we'll get it before the insurance is paid out.'

'He must have had some money lying around. He needed to pay us our last week's wages,' said Betty. 'And yer know, the more I think, the more convinced I am Lester set it up himself. Could he do that?'

'I've been thinking the same thing,' said Jimmy. 'He could have set the gas to leak and set a flame for it to find. Where the kids were playing was a bit too far away to my mind.'

'How do you know where they were playing?'

Jimmy thought about his promise to David and knew if he told Betty, her first thought would be for her own children, which meant she'd tell the police about David, whose involvement in the incident she currently knew nothing about.

'I was there and when I was carrying you I saw a firework on the ground, still burning – one of them Roman candle type things.'

'Oh, heck. Our Peggy bought a Roman candle. Billy just bought bangers.'

'Anyway the firework I saw was a good fifty yards away from where the factory blew up, maybe more. In fact, I think I'll go back there and see if that part of the building's badly damaged, which it should be if that's where the spark caught the gas. If it isn't then it can't have been the kids and I'll tell the police as much.'

Having thought of that as an excuse, he privately decided to take David back to the place

148

where they'd set the fireworks and see what the damage was like there.

'It'd settle my mind a lot if you could do that, Jimmy. I don't like to think my kids were responsible for killing all them girls – they were good pals of mine.' Tears began to trickle at the thought, then Betty pictured her children and the trickle became a flood.

'I do wish I knew where my babies were. Why haven't they come home, Jimmy?'

'I don't know, Betty, but I'll do my damnedest to find them.'

'I know you will, but I don't see how you can. Maybe we should advertise in the papers. Tell 'em their mam's alive, they can come home with nothing to worry about. Shouldn't cost me too much, should it?'

'You know, that is not a bad idea, Betty. In fact, I doubt we'll need to pay to advertise. There's a good story in this. I bet we could get the papers to print it for nothing. Trouble is, would we be telling a lie, saying there's nothing for them to worry about? Maybe we should make sure of that before we do anything.'

'I just want them back, Jimmy. I want to know they're safe and well.'

'Maybe we should say you're alive and would they contact you to tell you how they are?'

'That'd be something, Jimmy. I'd feel so much better if I could just hear from them.'

Jimmy had intercepted David on his way to school and arranged for the two of them to visit the ruins of the factory the following Saturday.

The two of them arrived at the hole in the fence that was still there, as of course was the fence itself, still intact to a distance of some fifty yards to their left, where it was destroyed and covered with brick rubble.

'Are you sure it was here that you stood?' Jimmy asked the boy.

'Oh, yeah. We came through this hole and I tried to fire a rocket through that window over there.' He pointed to a ground-floor window directly in front of them, which was still intact, with the exception of its glass.

'And did your rocket go through the window?'

'Yeah. Well, the second one did. Peggy lit a rainbow fountain over there.' He pointed to where the spent firework still lay on the ground.

Jimmy went over to the factory and looked inside the building, which was still standing at this point. He saw the carcass of a spent rocket lying on the concrete floor inside. There was no hint of fire damage in the room, nor of any explosion.

'And how long after you sent the rocket did the building blow up?'

'Couple of seconds, that's all.'

David counted 'one, two' and clapped his hands to demonstrate the short passage of time.

'Hmm,' said Jimmy, 'a spark from your rocket would take a lot longer than that to reach where the gas was leaking. So the gas would have to travel up to the spark and not the other way round, and if that happened this bit of the building would have blown up, which it hasn't.'

'The wind wasn't blowing in that direction,'

David told him. 'I remember because I had to shade the match from the wind to light the touch-paper. The wind wasn't blowing from where we were to the explosion.'

'So the wind would have taken the sparks further away from any leaking gas?'

'I suppose so.'

'Then in my opinion you didn't cause it. The question is, what or *who* did? The hot favourite's Lester Blainey.'

'If you tell the police all this, will I have to go with you?'

'Of course. It's your story but it's a very believable one. I reckon the firemen will be able to remember which direction the wind was blowing that night, and the fact that this part of the building is still intact tells its own story. You kids should be in the clear, David. So why are you looking so worried?'

'Mr Potter,' pointed out David, 'I'm already in the clear. The police aren't looking for me, only for Billy and Peggy.'

'But surely you want to help them.'

'I do, but I don't know what's happened to them. They've been gone a long time and no one's heard from them. Suppose they never come back?'

'Of course they'll come back. How on earth will they live?'

'I don't know, but Billy and Peggy are really good at doing stuff – I think they'll be able to manage somehow. They think they've killed their mam and all sorts of other people. They'll be feeling dead rotten, even worse than I do. In their shoes, I wouldn't want to come back.'

Jimmy gave the matter some thought as he stared at the ruined factory. The boy definitely had a point. Billy and Peggy would be feeling dead rotten, no question about that. But how would they survive? They were just kids.

'Well, David,' Jimmy said, eventually, 'without you to back up what I say, it means me going to the police with only half a story, apparently based on guesswork, and I don't want to do that. All I can hope for is that Billy and Peggy come back and I can take them to the police with the proper story. Whether you come or not will be up to you.'

'Oh, I'd definitely come if they were here.'

'Okay, David, I'll leave you to it. How did you go on in your scholarship exam by the way?'

'I think I did all right, Mr Potter.'

'Good lad.'

Jimmy left David by the factory ruins and went on his way. David, purely out of juvenile curiosity, went rummaging through the ruins to see if he could find anything of value. He was just about to go home when he came across a huge spanner. It probably wasn't much use because it had a large nut jammed in the end but he picked it up anyway and tucked it through a belt loop in his trousers, to carry around like a sword. He might be able to get the nut out at home and sell the spanner to someone. Then he came across a real treasure trove – a scattering of broken cast-iron gas pipes. Now this was great. Scrap iron was what all scrappers wanted. If he could somehow acquire a wheelbarrow he could load it up and sell it for a nice few bob at the scrap merchant's up Meanwood Road.

David went home and made enquiries about a wheelbarrow, without success. This was where he missed his best pal. Billy would have found a barrow from somewhere. Then he and his mate would have made at least half a dozen trips to the scrapper's and made a nice few bob, as Billy would say. As David stared at his valuable find he got to thinking about what Jimmy had said about him and his two friends not being responsible for the explosion. Maybe he should tell his mam what had happened, and Jimmy's version of who and what had caused the blast. He could go to the police with her and Jimmy and sleep easy after that.

Then it occurred to him what would happen if Jimmy was wrong, and it stopped him from telling his mother. David would most likely be locked up if the police remained unconvinced, especially with his record for setting fire to the toilets on Florence Street. No, best not to say anything to anyone. Right now the police weren't after him for anything. Let it stay that way.

Chapter 14

The journey from Blackpool to Liverpool was uneventful if you ignored the discomfort of the two passengers in the side car which, mercifully, had a hood to keep out most of the driving Lancashire rain that pursued them throughout the whole journey.

The twenty-five-mile trip took them just under an hour, with Harry taking a pre-planned circuitous route that would keep him clear of nosy traffic policemen who might wonder about the absence of a tax disc or ask him for his insurance details. He dropped them off near the dock gates, bade them farewell and good luck, and gave them directions to a youth hostel that might provide accommodation. The children chose instead to roam the streets and familiarise themselves with this city-by-the-sea.

The bomb damage to Liverpool had occurred mainly five years ago but the evidence was still there. Much of the debris had been cleared away but the job of rebuilding had only just started as builders had quickly found it frustrating to have their fine work destroyed within days of them completing it. Now the war was well and truly over and the Luftwaffe no longer a problem, rebuilding had begun.

Of Liverpool's many buildings the Liver Building, home of the Royal Liver Insurance Company since its construction in 1911, was one of the tallest in the city and situated at the Pier Head along with the imposing Cunard and Port of Liverpool buildings. Hitler's bombs had failed to dislodge either of the two famous emblems of this powerful, mercantile city – the eighteen foot high Liver Birds sitting atop the Liver Building's twin clock towers. Despite the destructive efforts of the Luftwaffe the birds had sat there, motionless and defiant amidst all the destruction surrounding them, as the clocks ticked steadily on, never losing or gaining a single minute. Perhaps it was this that gave Liverpudlians the confidence that the war could never be won by an enemy airforce so useless as not to be able to knock down two of the country's most vulnerable sitting ducks.

Harry had dropped the children off with a feeling of regret. He'd miss them, but he wasn't going to play any part in an attempt to stow them away; that would only serve to jeopardise his own chances.

Down by the docks the buildings were huge and imposing, far grander than anything they remembered from Leeds, with many of the larger buildings down near the waterfront, which was where the children spent most of their time. It was very much a cosmopolitan city, especially near the docks, with men of many nationalities walking around speaking languages the kids couldn't understand. The sea air had its own unique aroma, much different from Blackpool, maybe due to the proximity of so many ships, bringing in cargo from all over the world. They got as near as they could to the sea to watch the big ships coming and going and this only served to reinforce Billy's determination to stow away on one of those ships and sail to America.

'I wonder if one of them's the *Britannic?*' he said.

'According to Harry that doesn't sail till two o'clock,' said Peggy, looking at the clocks on the Liver Building. 'It's only half past eleven.'

Hope sprang within Billy. That meant they had time to find the *Britannic* and stow away. Surely that couldn't be too hard for a couple of smart kids such as them? He had a lot of confidence in his ability to fool authority.

Across a road Billy noticed an old lady with a full shopping bag into which she put her purse. There was enough of it on display for him to remove it and be away before she could even shout for help.

'Billy, don't even think about it,' warned Peggy, who had been following the direction of his gaze. 'She's an old lady who doesn't look as if she's got much money.'

'I wasn't thinking about it,' returned her brother. 'But *he* is.' He nodded towards a youth of around eighteen, standing just a few yards away from the old lady. It was crossing Peggy's mind to shout out a warning when the youth sprang into action. He darted towards his target at high speed and whipped the purse from her bag with a practised snatch. The old lady was aware of what had happened but was too late to do anything about it, and probably too late to offer the police a description of the thief. She stood there, looking at him disappearing down the street in great strides. The old lady was shivering with shock and checking her bag, realising what was missing. The children felt sorry for her.

'I wouldn't have done that to her,' said Billy, in his own defence. 'That woman I nicked a purse off was a lot richer. Mos' prob'ly didn't even know how much she had in it.'

'I bet that woman does,' said his sister. 'Right down to the last penny – and I bet that's what he took.'

The two of them crossed the road where Peggy

put her arm around the old lady. 'We saw what happened, missis,' she said, 'if you want to tell the police.'

The old lady shook her head. Her accent was strong Scouse. 'I'll not bother them useless sods. He were off like a rocket were that lad. The bobbies round here couldn't catch a bleedin' cold. Anyway, that's me pension gone for the week.'

The children left her bemoaning her loss and headed in the direction they'd seen the thief take.

'Where would you go if you'd done it?' Peggy asked her brother.

'Nearest bus stop,' he said without hesitation. 'Unless I'd got a bike or something to get away on. Especially a bike with brakes that worked.'

Peggy pointed in the direction the thief had taken. 'Let's go down there and find a bus stop. See if we can spot him.'

'Then what? He looked a big lad to me.'

'We're not going to fight him, we're going to frighten him. What would you do if someone saw you nick a purse and challenged you about it?'

'Challenge him? Is that what we're gonna do? Don't fancy it much.'

'Let's just find him first,' said Peggy. 'If that old lady had her pension book in her bag, it'll have her address on it.'

Billy, who had been making mental notes of the streets in the area, pointed forward and said, 'There's buses running up and down over there. It's a main road. I bet that's where he went. He might have already got on a bus,' he added, hopefully.

'Yeah, and he might not. He'll be looking out to

see if that old lady appears, which she won't. She's given up and pretty soon he'll know that.'

They arrived at a main road, at that moment devoid of any buses, and looked to right and left. 'He's over there,' said Peggy, much to Billy's disappointment.

They headed in the direction of a lone youth standing at a bus stop. When they reached him Peggy called out, 'We saw you steal our grandma's purse, you'd better give it back.'

The youth was nonplussed by this challenge. 'I haven't stolen nothin'.'

'Yes, you have,' said Billy. 'She's our grandma and if you don't give it back we'll tell the police.'

'Behave, will yer. I don't see no scuffers.'

'If there's no police we'll get on the bus with you and tell the conductor and everyone on the bus what you've done,' threatened Peggy.

'She will, yer know,' added Billy. 'She hasn't got much money has our grandma and you stole her pension. How's she gonna go on without any money?'

The youth stared at them, knowing the contents of the purse couldn't be worth all this aggravation. After a moment's consideration he stuck his hand in his pocket, brought out the purse and tossed it to Billy, who caught it expertly and examined its contents as if he might know if anything was missing.

As they turned to head back the way they'd come a uniformed constable appeared, walking towards them. To the youth's consternation, the children approached the officer and handed him the purse. 'We found this on the pavement,' Peggy said. 'I think it must belong to an old lady because there's a pension book inside. It's got her address in it.'

The policeman smiled at them. 'That's very honest of you. Not a lot of that round here. Perhaps if you give me your address there might be a reward in it for you.'

Peggy shook her head. 'I don't think there's enough in that purse for her to be rewarding us. All we did was pick it up.'

'Well, thank you on the owner's behalf. I'll see she gets it.'

The policeman stuck the purse in his tunic pocket and went on his way, which was right past the youth, who was in two minds whether to take to his heels or not, but he hadn't seen the children pointing at him so chose to stay where he was and look innocent. When the policeman was a safe distance away he ran over to where the children stood.

'Hey, you two. I thought yer said it were yer granny's purse. Wotcha give it ter that copper for?'

''Cos we were lying,' said Billy, stoutly.

''Cos we don't like thieves who steal from poor old ladies,' added Peggy caustically.

'Who are you anyway?'

'No one. That's who we are.'

'Yer not from round here, are yer? I can tell by the way yer talk. Yer from bloody Yorkshire, aren't yer?'

'We are,' admitted Billy. 'And it's not a mucky 'ole like it is round here.'

'If it's a mucky 'ole why have yer come to the Pool? Yer look as if yer lost ter me.'

'None of your business,' said Billy, and as he spoke a thought struck him.

'We're looking for the docks.'

'Bloody hell! The docks? All yer have ter do is follow yer nose. I can smell the sea from here. Come on, I'll take yer, for yer cheek.'

'Don't think yer can steal owt off us,' said Billy, more than aware of the money they had about their persons. 'We're skint, us.'

'Poor but bleedin' honest, eh? Yer'll never get nowhere bein' poor but honest.'

'You don't look like no millionaire ter me,' said Billy.

'Well, I'll have yer know I don't nick off old women normally. It's special circumstances today.'

'What special circumstances?' asked Peggy.

'The circumstances are I'm gonna try and get aboard a ship an' bugger off out this country. The coppers have been giving me too much grief, it's just not safe for me round here.'

'You mean, stow away?' Peggy asked him. Billy's eyes lit up with interest. The subject hadn't been discussed between them since his sister had rejected the idea back in Blackpool.

'Do I look like a paying passenger?' said the youth.

The children both shook their heads. 'Have you done it before?' Billy asked.

'Only to Dublin and back. There's bugger-all pickings in Dublin. This time I fancy New York.'

'So do I!' blurted Billy.

'Not me,' said Peggy.

'There's a ship called the *Britannic* sailing for New York soon,' said Billy.

160

'How do you know that?'

'We know someone who's sailing on it,' said Peggy.

'He gave us a lift down here from Blackpool,' added Billy.

'So,' deduced the youth, 'you two are on yer own, are yer?'

'We are ... brother and sister. My name's Billy, I'm her brother. She's Peggy.'

'Pleased ter meet yer, Billy an' Peggy. My name's Spider. It's not me proper name but it's all I'll ever answer to. They call me Spider because of me legs.'

'Yeah, we saw you running.'

Spider grinned. 'I can shift, can't I?'

'You can,' said Billy.

'How come yer on yer own?'

'It's a long story, but we've been accused of something we didn't do and we don't want to go back to Leeds.'

'Leeds, eh? I've been there ... and you say Liverpool's a mucky 'ole? You've got no room ter talk.'

Billy grinned. He was beginning to like this Liverpool thief. Peggy was more wary, after the ones they'd befriended in Blackpool. She felt there was a lot more to Spider than met the eye.

'I don't s'pose yer've got five quid yer don't need, have yer?' he asked them.

'We haven't got any money we don't need,' said Peggy. 'Why do you want five quid?'

'Well, if yer wanted ter get away to New York, I reckon it could get yer into the docks and right up ter that ship yer on about. In fact, I think I might give it a go meself. Is it a big ship?'

'No idea,' said Billy.

161

'I s'pose it must be to go right across the Atlantic
– takes over a week, yer know. Which means yer
got ter take enough food and water ter last yer.'

'I never thought of that,' said Billy.

'Sounds ter me as if yer haven't thought this
through.'

'That's because we're not going to stow away,'
said Peggy.

Spider help his hands up. 'All right. I were just
tryin' to help, that's all. Any kid who's runnin'
away in this country'll get caught before long.
New York's a massive place, there's loads of places
for kids to live. No one ever bothers 'em there. The
New York coppers have enough ter deal with
without chasing round after bits of kids like you.'

Billy looked at his sister. 'He's right, yer know.
I've heard that meself.'

'Oh, yeah, and where have you heard it?'

'Harry told me.'

'I didn't hear him.'

'You weren't there when he told me. The
Bowery's the place to hide, that's what he said. Is
that right, Spider?'

'It's where I'm heading, if I get there.'

'That's where the Bowery Boys come from,' said
Billy. 'They're great, the Bowery Boys. We could
be Bowery Boys too.'

'They're not real, Billy. They're only on at the
pictures, and in case you hadn't noticed, I'm not
a boy.'

'I think we should give it a try,' Billy said, 'better
than being dragged back to Leeds and locked up
for life.'

'Locked up for life?' exclaimed Spider. 'Bloody

162

hell! What have you done?'

'We didn't actually do anything,' said Peggy. 'We just happened to be playing with fireworks when a factory blew up. It wasn't us, but they're after us for it.'

'Our mam was in it,' said Billy, 'she was killed – so were lot of other people.'

'Bloody hell! If y'ask me, you need ter get ter New York and right out of the way o' that lot.'

'He's right, Peg,' said Billy. 'What's this five quid for, Spider?'

'To bribe the bloke on the dock gates. I know him – I used ter work there meself as a kid. He'll let all three of us in for a fiver.'

'I should think he will,' said Peggy. 'I bet that's more than he earns in three days.'

'Yer'll also need money to buy proper clothes,' said Spider.

'What's wrong with our clothes?'

'Nothin', 'cept it'll get pretty cold out in the mid-Atlantic this time of year. What yer need is a couple o' duffel coats with hoods. They sell 'em at the Army and Navy Stores, maybe six or seven quid a time. Tell yer what, there's a market near the docks what sells stuff like that. I reckon us three can nick all we need from there.'

'We don't need to steal it, we can buy it,' said Peggy.

Billy looked at her, questioningly. 'Look,' she said to him, 'we only steal when we have to. Right now we don't have to. Thieves take risks. We can't afford to take unnecessary risks.'

'Okay,' said Billy.

He knew Peggy was right, she often was.

163

'Sounds to me like you've got pots of money,' remarked Spider.

'We've got just enough to give you five quid and buy a couple of coats,' said Peggy. 'After that we're skint, so don't get any big ideas about nicking from us.'

'I wouldn't dream of it.'

'So,' said Billy to his sister, 'are we going to have a go at stowing away?'

'Oh, I suppose so,' said Peggy, who was now taken with the idea herself. 'We'd best get to this shop and buy our duffel coats, then we can stock up on food and water. We'll most probably need another rucksack. Have you got one, Spider?'

'Yep, and now that you're forking out the five quid I've got everything I need.'

With the *Britannic* leaving the Albert Dock at two o'clock the three of them arrived at the port gates an hour earlier. The entrance was through a set of what looked like six stadium turnstiles and Spider took some time to find out which entrance his man was working at. Eventually he called them over to one at the end of the row. The three of them lined up by the booth as Spider pushed a five-pound note towards his man.

'Three of us, just to have a look round, Dennis. Whereabouts is the Albert Dock?'

'Through that tunnel, turn right and keep goin' 'til yer come to a big sign what says Albert Dock – about five minutes' walk from here. I hope yer not thinkin' of stowin' away on yon liner. Yer'll get me sacked, you will.'

'Don't be daft, Dennis. We just want ter look at

it, that's all.'

'Well, it's a fine ship right enough. Due in New York early doors a week on Monday mornin'. That's nine days from now. If they catch yer stowin' away they'll not bring yer back. No, they'll hand you over to the port authorities in New York. God knows what *they'll* do with yer.'

It sounded as if Dennis strongly suspected what they were up to.

'Good job we're not stowin' away then,' said Spider. 'Come on, you two.'

He led them through the docks until they came to the signs indicating they'd arrived at the Albert Dock at which was moored a magnificent passenger liner.

'Big bugger, isn't she?' said Spider. 'Thirty thousand tonnes, I reckon.'

'How do we get on board?' asked Peggy.

'We hang about until we see a big group boarding then we join 'em, mingle with 'em until they don't know themselves whether or not we're with 'em.'

Three groups of people were currently making their way to the ship before ascending the companionway.

'Wait until they all bunch up together in one big group,' said Spider, 'then join 'em so they don't know who's with who. Up on top there'll be a bloke in uniform checking tickets and stuff. We just split up and attach ourselves to a group bein' checked and walk through with them as though we belong. I'll meet you up on the boat deck. It'll be signposted somewhere. If not, it's the one with all the lifeboats, two decks up.'

165

Billy and Peggy did as instructed and within a couple of minutes were safely on board the ship and making their way up a staircase towards the boat deck, still mingling with an adult group. They arrived at a landing with doors leading out on to the deck through which they could see lifeboats. 'It's through here,' Billy said, opening the door.

They had just stepped out on to the wooden planking when a familiar voice hailed them. The voice they expected to hear was Spider's but this was a much older one.

'What the hell are you doing here?'

It was Harry. He was wearing a blue-and-white-striped apron and carrying a large tin, presumably containing food. The sight of him stopped the children in their tracks.

'We're going to New York,' said Billy.

'Paid passage, is it?'

'Er, no. Not really.'

'Bloody hell! How did yer manage ter get on board?'

The children chose not to answer.

'Where are yer planning ter stay? In the boats?'

'Prob'ly,' said Billy. 'Will we get caught?'

Harry lowered his voice so as not to be overheard by a group of passengers wandering past. 'Not if yer careful. Look, I don't want you involving me in this. I've only just started here and I've got a good number – just what I need.'

'We won't involve you, Harry,' promised Peggy.

'Any advice on which boat to hide in?' Billy asked.

'See, yer involving me already! When you unfasten the rope to get under the canvas cover just make sure you fasten it tight behind you. It's loose ropes they look for.'

'How do we do that?'

'It can be done but it's up to you to work it out. I haven't got time ter show yer. I should pick a boat that's well away from the doors, and do yer comin' and goin' at mealtimes when everyone's mainly in the dining rooms. Lunch is twelve 'til two, dinner seven 'til about nine. Now yer know as much as I do.'

'Okay,' said Billy.

'Us workers don't mingle with the passengers. We have our own deck three down from here. I'm only up here carting beef *bourguignon* to the bridge for the officers.'

'Smells nice. We've only brought bread buns, sausage rolls, chocolate and water.'

'Well, I hope you don't think I'm serving you lot beef *bourguignon* in yer lifeboat.'

'That'd be nice,' said Billy. 'See you around, Harry.'

'Oh, Jesus! I hope not! I've only been here half a bloody hour.'

The children leant on the ship's rail immediately next to a lifeboat and studied the knots in the rope tying the canvas down.

'I don't know how we can tie a knot like that from inside,' Billy was saying.

'I do,' said a familiar voice behind him. They turned around. It was Spider.

'So, you've figured out how not to get caught hiding in a lifeboat, have you?'

'We know *what* to do,' said Peggy. 'We've now

167

got to work out how to do it.'

'Do you want me to tell you?'

'If you know, yes.'

Spider took a large Swiss Army knife from his rucksack. 'You use one of these. You slacken the knot to give you about six inches more rope, then cut it just where it goes into the boat, climb inside, pull the loose end in after you, tie a piece of string to the end of the rope really tight and tie the other end of the string around one of the seats in the boat, but pull the whole thing hard so it looks as though the canvas is tied down properly. All you have to do to get in and out of the boat is undo the string and make sure the knot looks good from the outside. I'll show you how to do it.'

'Well, it's all right for you but we haven't got a knife and we haven't got string,' Peggy pointed out.

'You will have when I get in the boat with you. There's loads of room for the three of us. All we have to do is keep quiet while we're in there. But most of the daytime we can be wandering around the ship as though we belong. There'll be nearly a thousand passengers on board and most probably over a hundred kids, so who's gonna notice a few extra? We all look the part, don't we? And the ship'll have shops so if we get really hungry we can buy hot dogs and stuff.'

'I've never had a hot dog,' said Billy.

'Ah, these Americans, that's all they eat, hot dogs and hamburgers.'

'What about drinks?' Peggy asked. 'Can we get cups of tea?'

'I imagine so although Americans drink mostly

coffee and there's loads of Yanks on board, I've noticed. Maybe we should practise talking with American accents. Are you any good at accents?'

'We can't do American,' said Peggy.

'We can learn,' said Billy. 'I bet I can learn to speak like Sach in the Bowery Boys.'

'No,' said Spider. 'He's Lower East Side New York. Them lads don't go sailing across the Atlantic on posh ships. You need to be talking Downtown Manhattan.'

'Bugger me!' said Billy. 'What's the difference?'

'The same as between Liverpool and London, I should think.'

'We can do posh English accents, can't we, Billy?' said Peggy. 'We've no need to be Americans.'

'What about if we need a wee ... or anything?' asked Billy.

'Good question. There's a toilet just inside that door, but what you must always do is go before you bed down for the night, whether you need to or not.'

'You say, "bed down",' said Peggy. 'What do we bed down on?'

Spider grinned. 'I never said it was going to be a cushy ride. We all bed down on the bottom of the boat. Make your coat into a pillow if you like. It won't be comfy but you'll get some sleep.'

'We slept okay in the beach hut,' Billy said.

'No, we didn't, not for one bloomin' night and that wasn't bobbin' up and down all night.'

'Anyway,' said Spider, 'right now everyone's gonna be in their cabins getting themselves settled so it's a good time ter sort out our lifeboat. This one's number fifteen. I won't forget it, even if you do.'

'Number fifteen it is then,' said Billy. 'And we won't forget it, it's our house number where we live.'

'Lived,' corrected Peggy. Billy's smile faded from his face when his sister added, 'God knows where we'll be living next.'

'Ah, but isn't this a great adventure?' said Spider. 'And great adventurers always come out on top.'

'That's true, Peg,' said Billy.

Spider added, 'In about an hour or so's time the ship's hooter'll sound and a band'll start playin' an' the ship'll start to move off and everyone'll crowd the decks so they can wave to the people what they're leaving behind on the quayside. We'd best get our skates on and sort out number fifteen before this deck gets too crowded. Oh, by the way, yer might have to have another think about goin' straight ter New York.'

'Why?'

'Because I've seen an itinerary and we're stoppin' off in Miami first, then sailin' up the east coast ter New York. We get to Miami on Saturday mornin' and New York on Monday.'

'Well, we shouldn't need duffel coats in Miami,' said Peggy.

'I know,' said Spider, 'but I've been thinkin' about another idea, if yer up for it.'

'What's that?' asked Billy.

'Well, I know a few lads who've done the Miami run and they all got out of the port on the backs of trucks. It's tricky gettin' out of New York port, but Miami's a doddle. What happens is that these

170

trucks come in fully loaded to supply the ships and go out empty. All we do is slip the driver a few dollars to turn a blind eye and climb in the back. He takes us out and drops us off in Downtown Miami.'

'We haven't got any dollars,' Peggy pointed out.

'I should have by the time we get there,' said Spider. 'I might even be able to change all your money into dollars, for a small fee.'

'I dread to think where you'll be getting your dollars from.'

Spider grinned but made no comment.

The three of them were safely hidden under the canvas cover of lifeboat fifteen when the ship's hooter gave a loud blast and the liner moved away from the quayside and headed out into the grey and choppy Irish Sea. A band struck up just as Spider had forecast. The deck around them was crowded with noisy passengers all waving arms and flags and bunting at the people they were leaving behind and might never see again. The three stowaways crouched silently in the semi-darkness and whispered to each other.

'I bet it gets pitch black in here at night,' Peggy said.

'I've brought a torch and loads of batteries,' said Spider. To prove it he took a cycle lamp from his rucksack, stood it on a seat and switched it on.

'Turn it off,' Billy said. 'People outside'll be able to see we've got a torch.'

'No, they won't. It's daylight outside and daylight's ten times brighter than this. At night the deck'll be all lit up so if a bright light's shining on the outside canvas, how will anyone know there's a dim light on the other side as well? So long as I always point it downwards no one will ever know. And we don't need it on all the time.'

Peggy said nothing as she wasn't entirely certain he was right.

'He's right, Peg,' said Billy.

This only served to annoy his sister. 'I'm hungry,' she said, 'I'm going to have a bar of chocolate.'

'Are we going to stay in Miami or are we going to New York?' asked Billy.

'Well, I'm going up to New York,' said Spider.

'I bet it's nice and warm in Miami,' said Peggy, who thought that getting off in Miami was a good way for getting rid of Spider who she didn't trust.

Four decks below them, in the galley, Harry was taking a break and reading a copy of yesterday's Daily Express. On page two was the story of the two children of Mrs Elizabeth Clegg, who had run away from home after allegedly setting fire to a factory with fireworks. The report said there was some doubt as to who had started the blaze but the missing children were still the hot favourites and could be in serious trouble as and when they were caught. However the main theme of the article was that the children might well be under the impression they were responsible for the death of their mother, who had been working in the factory at the time and might have perished in the blaze along with many others, and it was this terrible belief that was keeping them away from home. But their mother had escaped the blaze, having been rescued by the factory maintenance man, Jimmy Potter, and it was Mrs Clegg's dearest wish that this article would be read by her children, who might then decide to come home and be reunited with her.

'Bloody hell!' muttered Harry to himself. What to do now? His usual clear thinking was still clouded by the loss of his grandson. Should he show the kids the article or not? If he showed it to them, they could hardly turn around and go back home without being captured. One thing he could do was contact Mrs Clegg anonymously and tell her that her children were safe and well. That should put her mind at rest. But should he put the children's minds at rest too? Of course he should.

Or should he? It would saddle them with a big decision to make. A decision that might lead to their being locked up for something they probably hadn't done. At worst it was most likely a terrible accident.

Whatever happened, they would need to make their way home from America at some point, and to what? It seemed to him they were facing a very bleak future back in England. He stuck the paper in his locker, meaning to give the matter a whole lot of thought before he made his decision. Maybe it was because he'd just lost his own grandson that he now felt a sort of parental responsibility for these two kids. Bloody hell! It never rained but it poured.

Billy and Peggy were leaning on the rail at the stern of the ship watching the waves disappearing behind them, churned up by the giant propellers.

Flying fish were leaping about in the turbulence – a magical sight to children whose only prior experience of the sea was a few days in Blackpool, or a Saturday matinee at the Western Cinema on Florence Street, better known as The Bughutch. The ship had sailed in a south-westerly direction heading for Florida and warmer weather. The children had left their coats in the lifeboat and stood in their shirt-sleeves, pleasantly amazed at such good weather this late in the year.

'I think we're heading south,' observed Peggy.

Billy looked up at the position of the sun and corrected her. 'South-west,' he said. 'Dead straight for Miami.'

'How do you know where Miami is?'

'Because we do geography and I'm good at it. Miami is in Florida, which is a state in the south-east of North America. You should know that, you go to big school.'

'We haven't done America yet. We're still doing Australia.'

'He's right,' said a voice from behind them.

They both spun round and were confronted by the smiling face of a boy of a similar age to Billy. 'We're stopping at Nassau in the Bahamas and then going up to Miami. How come you don't know that? Don't your folks tell you anything?'

The brother and sister said nothing.

'I reckon you're stowaways,' said the boy.

'What makes you say that?'

'Well, I've seen you about the ship but you never turn up for meals ... and you live in a lifeboat.'

'So you've been spying on us,' said Billy, belligerently.

'I bet I could beat you in a fight,' said the boy.

'Mebbe you can,' said Billy, 'but I bet you can't beat her.'

The boy looked at Peggy, then grinned and shrugged. There was a disarming humour in his eyes. 'Hey, I don't want no trouble with you guys,' he said. 'I only said it because I'm good at fighting.'

'So's she,' said Billy.

'Mebbe so. I might even be able to help you both.'

'You're from London,' guessed Peggy, detecting his accent.

'That's right and you two are from the north.'

'Yorkshire. Common as muck us,' said Billy. 'London, eh? Are you a rich kid?'

'Far from it. We live in South London. West London is where the rich kids live. My dad's a theatrical. We're not rich. We're working our passage by doing shows in the ship's theatre.'

'What? You and who else?'

'Me, my dad, and my sister.'

'Not your mother?'

'No, she's at home in England. She didn't like the theatrical life, so when we left for this trip she stayed at home. My dad's American. He met her when he was working over there before the war. They're good people but they don't get on too well.'

'What do you do on the stage?'

'A bit of cabaret. Me and my sister, Maisie, are pretty slick at tap dancing and singing. We do a Fred and Ginger routine.'

Peggy gazed at this talented boy with new eyes.

175

'How old are you?' she asked him.

'I'm eleven, my sister's twelve – thirteen in May.'

'You're both the same ages as us,' said Peggy. 'What's your name?

'Ross Duggan Junior ... same name as my dad only he ain't a Junior. He's thirty-seven. What's your name?'

'Billy Clegg.'

'Peggy Clegg,' put in his sister before Billy could introduce her to this boy to whom she had taken a liking – this boy who had offered to help them. 'When you said you might be able to help us, what did you mean?'

'Well, I guess the grub you eat in the lifeboat ain't as good as the stuff we get in the restaurant. I could maybe sneak you some out. Where's the other kid I sometimes see you with?'

'Oh, that's Spider. He doesn't like to be out with us much in case we give the game away.'

'Why are you stowing away?'

'Well ... we've been blamed for something we didn't do,' said Billy, after some hesitation.

'Cops on your tail, huh?'

'Something like that.'

'So you thought you'd be safe in Miami?'

'We intended going to New York ... maybe we will.'

'If I were you, I'd wait out the winter in Miami. It's what we're doing. We go up to New York in the spring.'

'Will you go to school in Miami?' Peggy asked him.

'Yeah, worse luck. Then to a theatre school in New York. What will you do about school when

176

you get there?'

'We haven't thought that far ahead yet,' said Peggy. 'Maybe we'll make do with the schooling we've had so far. We can both read and write well enough, and we're not too bad at arithmetic.'

'The three Rs,' said Billy, 'reading, writing and reckoning up.'

Ross grinned as though he understood what Billy was talking about. Peggy angled her face up to the sun and welcomed its warmth.

'Do you like fruit?' Ross asked.

'Of course ... why?'

'Because there's always a supply of free fruit to take out of the restaurant. I'll bring you a bag of it, if you like.'

'What ... now?'

'Sure.'

Ten minutes later Billy and Peggy were eating oranges, after eating their first bananas ... ever.

'The first bananas I saw were in Tarzan pictures,' Billy told Ross.

'I guess that'll be because of the Atlantic Ocean,' Ross said, 'and the German U-boats.'

'Our dad was killed by the Germans,' Peggy told him. She wasn't asking for sympathy, it was just a fact of their lives.

'I'm really sorry to hear that. Dad was over in the States when the Japanese bombed Pearl Harbor, bringing the Americans into the war. He enlisted and was wounded on Omaha Beach on D-Day. Brought home without ever firing a shot at the Germans. He hates not having done that, after seeing what they did to hundreds of his comrades.' Ross gave their story some thought,

177

then added, 'Y'know, if I tell my dad about yours he might wanna help you both, to make up for what he couldn't do in the war. He's a good man, my dad. What about your mum?'

'She died in a fire just before we ran away,' said Billy.

Peggy frowned her brother to silence, so he didn't elaborate. It was more than enough that Ross should know they were orphans – enough, perhaps, for him to persuade his dad to help them.

'Ah, the stowaways.'

Billy and Peggy looked up at Mr Duggan with guilt in their eyes – a sentiment noticed by the man, who held up his hands palms facing out.

'It's okay, kids, I'm not gonna turn you in.'

'Thank you,' said Peggy politely.

Ross Duggan Senior was a handsome man with jet black hair slicked back from a centre-parting in the fashion of the day, along with an Errol Flynn moustache. His looks met with Peggy's approval; Billy looked upon him with mistrust. 'How do we know you won't give us up?'

'What's to give up? So far as I'm concerned you two are just a couple of kids befriended by my two. Children of passengers I haven't met.'

Billy frowned as he unravelled the logic of this. It seemed to make sense.

'If I turn you in, what do you think will happen to you?' added Mr Duggan. 'Will the captain make you walk the plank?'

Billy remembered what the man in Albert Dock had told them. 'We'll be handed over to the port authorities in America.'

'And then what?'

'Dunno, nothing good.'

'Then I suggest you both keep your heads down. Do not mention to anyone that I know about you, and leave the ship in Miami with the same stealth as you boarded it. Once you're clear of the port we'll be waiting for you to see how we can help. That's all I can say right now.'

'Why would you do that?' asked Peggy.

'Because it seems to me that you're a couple of good kids who've been dealt a bad hand. We theatricals have a different view of life from the mere mortals who find us entertaining.'

'Dad wasn't always a theatrical,' said Ross. 'He took it up after he was brought back to England from the war and says it's in his blood now. He used to be an English teacher. Can either of you sing?'

'Yes,' said Billy, 'as a matter of fact we both can. Our Peg sings in the Leeds Girls' Choir ... why?'

'Well,' said Mr Duggan, 'when we get up to New York we've all got jobs in an off-Broadway play called *Twist*. It's based on the book by Dickens. They'll be auditioning for kids to play London orphans, and with you two being English you're already halfway there.'

'We can bowf do cockney accents,' said Billy, in a hybrid approximation that drew a smile from Duggan Senior.

Their friendship with Ross and Maisie enabled them to feel more confident about exploring the ship. Neither had brought swimming costumes so the ship's pool was of no interest to them until the day their new friends turned up with costumes they could borrow. Using the toilets as a changing room, Billy and Peggy, both competent swimmers, were soon joining Ross and Maisie in the water.

There was a theatre with afternoon entertainment for children which they thoroughly enjoyed, plus a cinema and a games room with table tennis table. Billy found he had the beating of most opponents. His sister saw a possible problem with this.

'Billy, there's no need to win every flipping game. At this rate you're going to stand out and get yourself noticed as the ship's champion table tennis player and that's the last thing we want.'

'So, what do you want me to do?'

'Play other games.'

'I'm no good at the other games. Most of them are daft.'

'That's the idea.'

'Oh, all right.' She was probably right, she usually was, but it was a bit irritating for Billy. There weren't many sports he was any good at.

It was the cruise director who changed the immediate course of their lives when he walked towards Billy and Peggy on deck one day; up until then he hadn't met Ross and Maisie Duggan.

'Ah, you must be the Duggan children, aren't you?'

'Yes,' said Billy instinctively.

It was a risky lie that got them out of immediate trouble; repairing any damage it might cause was a job for another time. Owning up to the truth would have dropped them both right in it.

'Singers and dancers, so I understand. I haven't

caught any of your shows as yet, which is a bit remiss of me, but I always seem to be too busy looking after passengers.'

'We're more singers than dancers,' said Peggy, who saw no option other than to support her brother's lie.

'In that case might I borrow you for ten minutes? I was looking for your father but I suppose you two will do at a pinch.'

'To do what?' asked Billy.

'A turn. I assume you know a song or two, or perhaps a witty ditty, to fill in a ten-minute slot in this morning's entertainment in the theatre.'

'Er, yes,' said Peggy, at a loss for what else to say. It was at the back of her mind to run for it as soon as the man had gone, but on a ship where was there to run?

'I know some comic songs,' said Billy, 'and my sister can sing "Somewhere Over the Rainbow" better than that Judy Garland.'

'Excellent, come with me. There's a band-call starting about now.'

Billy had to whistle the tune to 'Lavender Trousers' to the pianist, who had never heard of the song. When he actually sang to the piano accompaniment the cruise director was delighted. 'Excellent! We must get wardrobe to fix you up with a pair of lavender trousers. I'm sure they can knock a pair together before you go on. Of course it won't matter a jot if they don't fit properly.'

The repercussions of this were racing through Peggy's brain as she stepped up to sing 'Somewhere Over the Rainbow'. Maybe her ongoing problem overwhelmed any stage fright she had, or maybe her troubles helped feed the emotion she put into it, for she sang it beautifully and without any show of nervousness.

Their job was to fill in a ten-minute slot between dancing and Bingo. They both took to the stage as worried beginners and walked off as stars, to enthusiastic applause. Ross Duggan Senior was waiting for them, looking blazing mad.

'What the hell are you playing at?'

'The man thought we were your children and asked us to do it,' explained Billy.

'We had no option really,' added Peggy.

Ross took them to his dressing room and sat down with his head in his hands. 'How am I supposed to get out of this without giving you away?'

'You could tell them the truth,' suggested Billy. 'You could say we're not your children and you don't know who we are.'

'That's right,' said Peggy. 'There's hundreds of kids on board, we could be anybody's.'

'We could be the Mystery Kids,' suggested Billy.

Ross Junior and Maisie came in then. Billy appraised them of the situation. Ross Junior found it highly amusing. His sister didn't. With Duggan Senior still sitting with his head in his hands, the four children devised a plan.

'Maisie and me haven't really done anything yet,' said Ross Junior. 'That's why Duggie Davis mistook you for us.'

'That's his name, is it?' said Billy.

'Yeah,' said Ross Jnr. 'I bet me and Maisie could keep our heads down until we get to Miami and you could do all our stuff for us.'

'We don't dance,' Billy pointed out.

'What can you do?' enquired Ross Senior in a weary voice.

'Pretty much what you've just seen,' said Peggy. 'I know a few songs and Billy's good at the comic ditties and he can play the banjo, only he hasn't brought it with him.'

'Actually, you were both very good,' admitted Duggan. 'But you don't know enough to take Ross and Maisie's place. They've rehearsed their routines for weeks. It's no good, I'm gonna have to tell Duggie the truth.'

'Why?' his son asked. 'He thinks Billy and Peggy are us.'

'That's right,' said Maisie. 'Who's going to ask questions apart from the passengers?'

'The band,' said their father. 'They know Billy and Peggy aren't you.'

'Okay,' said his son. 'Tell the band the truth. See what they say. If they want to give Billy and Peggy away, it's up to them. It's only a few days before we're all off the ship.'

'Our friend Spider says he knows a way to get us off and out of the port without being caught.'

'Who the hell is Spider?'

'He's with us and he's very good at this sort of thing.'

'Is he now? He'll need to be.'

Ross Senior found himself nodding agreement to the plan. Musicians were unconventional beings, maybe they'd favour keeping quiet about the kids.

Providence in the form of a timely illness came to

183

their rescue. Duggie Davis was stricken with sea-sickness, an ailment that was to herald the end of his career as a ship's cruise director. He was confined to his cabin for the rest of the journey and the ship's entertainment was organised by Ross Duggan Senior. His real son and daughter were taken out of the show and no further mention was ever made of the two talented kids who had entertained so ably at the dance and Bingo event.

Lifeboat fifteen continued to be their home, but shipboard living was made somewhat easier by the gifts of food and chocolate bars brought to them by their gang of co-conspirators, which now included the band's drummer, who brought them books to read and batteries for their torches.

Chapter 15

In Miami, Spider's plan for escaping the port without going through passport control was very much a 'wing and a prayer' job.

'Doing the unexpected is the key to all this,' he told them. 'What we have to do is keep an eye out for the main chance.'

'Doesn't sound like much of a plan,' observed Peggy, drily.

'We're sharp kids,' said Spider. 'These customs guys aren't expecting the likes of us. And let's face it, if *we* don't know what we're gonna do, how will they?'

His reasoning made Billy smile and Peggy scowl.

They joined the Duggan family in their descent of the companionway. Ross Duggan Senior put his hand on Peggy's shoulder and spoke close into her ear. 'Just outside the port there's a place called Jack and Benny's Diner. We'll wait there for about an hour before we head off. That should give you time enough to get out and find us. Do you know how you're going to manage it?'

'No idea,' said Peggy, 'but we'll be there.'

At the bottom of the gangway the passengers with passports and papers swung right, across to the customs sheds. Spider stopped a port worker and, in his version of an American accent, asked him where the nearest rest rooms were.

'Workers' cans down there, buddy.'

The man pointed in the opposite direction from the customs sheds. Spider asked another question.

'Is there a quick way out of here without having to queue at customs? It's okay, we ain't smugglers or nuthin', we just need to clear the port in a hurry. Some nasty people are after us.'

The man was carrying a brush and a bulging sack of what looked like rubbish. This told Spider he wasn't one of the port's highly paid employees; just a man who knew his way around the place; a man who knew stuff the higher-level workers didn't know. Such men were always willing to sell their low-level knowledge to supplement their low-level wages. As a school-leaver Spider had once held down such a job in Liverpool docks.

'We ain't got much dough but if you help us out it's worth ten bucks to us.'

He now had the man's attention. Ten dollars was a very tempting amount of dough and Spider knew it.

'Where you kids from?'

'Downtown Miami,' said Spider. 'We shouldn't be in here really.'

'Yer got that right, kid.'

Billy thought Spider's accent had improved but the man wasn't quite as impressed. 'You don't sound like no Miami kid to me.'

'Well, we've lived all over. I was born in Canada.'

'Ten bucks, eh?'

'Well, twenny bucks is the most we can manage.'

Spider knew it was now an irresistible bribe, probably over a week's wages for the man. He looked at his two young companions and said, 'That's about six bucks each ... okay?'

Two heads nodded dismally; frightened expressions on both faces as they looked round to check that the 'nasty people' hadn't followed them. Spider returned his attention to the dock worker.

'It's all we can afford, sir.'

He took two ten-dollar bills out of his pocket and showed them to the man. He knew from experience that the more visible the money, the more desirable it becomes. This man didn't want to see such riches going back into Spider's pocket. Without taking his eyes off the money he grunted and said, 'Okay, come with me.'

He led them around the toilet block and pointed to a heavy truck parked in front of a ten-foot-high steel gate. 'That's a garbage truck. When I throw this sack in it, you get in as well. It'll stink like hell but no one's gonna follow you in there. It's my job to open the gate. When it's through the gates it'll stop at lights in two minutes' time, which is when you climb out. Twenny bucks, you said.'

Spider handed him the money.

'Okay, here we go,' said the man. 'While there ain't no one else about.'

Within a minute the three of them were un-comfortably ensconced amid a pile of stinking rubbish. There was the sound of a gate creaking open. They heard their man call out to the driver.

'Okay, Burt. See ya next week.'

The truck began to move. A triumphant smile lit up Spider's face. Billy and Peggy were holding their noses and breath, looking through the back of the truck and up at the pristine blue sky be-yond; a stark contrast to the squalor of their im-mediate surroundings.

'Nice day,' muttered Billy, picking rotten leaves from his hair.

The truck picked up a little speed then came to a halt. It had barely stopped before the three of them jumped clear and casually strolled to the sidewalk. They carried rucksacks on their backs containing all their meagre possessions.

'Where did you get twenty dollars?' Billy asked as they ambled along, dusting themselves clean of clinging rubbish.

'Nicked it on the ship – easiest money I ever took.'

'We haven't any dollars to give you.'

'I don't want any. I got plenty of my own, but you'll need to change your quids for dollars. Whatcha gonna do now?'

'We need to find a place called Jack and Benny's Diner,' Peggy told him. 'It's where we're meeting the Duggans.'

'Ah, well, in that case I guess I'll be leaving you. I'm heading straight for New York. I got plans, y'see.'

'Oh,' said a disappointed Billy. Despite his innate dishonesty, Spider had been their leader, their adviser ... and their friend.

'We'd like to thank you for all the help you've given us,' said Peggy. 'I'm quite sure if you ever decided to go straight you'd be very successful.'

'Maybe I will at that. Look, I'm gonna find a bus or a train station. If I were you I'd ask someone where this Jack and Benny place is. Seems to me you might have fallen on your feet with this Duggan family.'

'We kind of fell on our feet with you,' said Billy.

Unused to any such compliments, Spider gave an embarrassed shrug and said, 'Hey, we did okay, us three.'

'Will we see you again?' asked Billy. 'We'll most prob'ly be going to New York in the spring.'

Spider shook his head. 'New York's a big city ... biggest city in the world, I've heard.'

'We might be in a theatre there, in a play called *Twist*,' said Peggy. 'It's what the Duggans are doing when they get there. They're all theatricals.'

'*Twist* as in *Oliver Twist*? Hey, I've heard of that. Yeah, I can see you two doing that. Well, maybe I'll look you up there.'

They parted company with Spider and asked a passerby for directions to Jack and Benny's. Peggy looked at her brother and queried the morose expression on his face.

'What's up?'

'I wish we'd managed to say goodbye to Harry.

188

I liked him. It doesn't seem right that we're clearing off without saying goodbye.'

'I bet that's because we never had the chance to say goodbye to Mam.'

Billy thought for a while and said, 'How do you know?'

'Because I'm the same.'

'It's not fair,' he muttered.

'What isn't?'

'Y'know ... stuff.'

Harry left Immigration frowning, passport in hand, weighed down with regret. His beloved grandson in the ground and his house destroyed along with the comfortable life he'd left behind in England. He now had an additional regret. He regretted not making a chance to tell Billy and Peggy that their mother was alive. He'd thought he had plenty of time, with them heading for New York as was he, but from a distance he'd seen them leaving the ship and they'd hardly risk just going to have a look round Miami. It was why he'd decided to follow them but he was way behind. If they'd been picked up by Immigration he'd still be able to get a message to them, which would ease things for them no doubt.

He adopted a jovial air and asked the man checking his passport: 'I heard yer'd picked up a couple of young stowaways tryin' to sneak ashore.'

'Not through here, man. Nuthin' or no one ever gets past us.'

'Are yer sure?'

'Absolutely.' The customs officer jerked a thumb over his shoulder. 'The calaboose back there ain't had a customer for a month and even then it was a drunk guy who didn't realise he'd left the ship. Mind you, he realised when he sobered up and found it had left without him. What've yer heard?'

'Ah, somethin' – prob'ly got the wrong end of the stick.'

The only thing he could do now was to have a good look around the streets, see if he could spot the kids before he went back on board to sail up to New York. Although how the hell the kids could get out of a closed port with no passports and papers was a mystery to him, but Harry somehow knew they would. They were exceptional kids. No question.

Jack and Benny's was a converted train carriage, standing back from the road and painted red, white and blue with a huge Confederate flag flying from a pole on its roof. They walked the full length of it, looking in through the windows to see if the Duggans were inside. They were, sitting at a table in the window and waving. Young Ross was wearing a Confederate cap and a big grin on his face. Maisie wore a ten-gallon cowboy hat.

Billy and Peggy had just joined them when a waitress plonked a cap on Billy and a cowboy hat on Peggy. The children looked around and realised that every kid in the place was wearing similar head gear.

'You don't get to keep them unless you pay through the nose,' said Ross Senior. 'It's the way they do things in the States. Most kids in here will nag their parents to buy them.'

'Not us,' said his son.

'Nor us,' added Peggy. 'I like it, though.'

'And me,' said Billy. 'How much are they?'

'Ten dollars each.'

'It's a rebel cap. I doubt you'd wanna wear it in New York,' said young Ross, 'unless you dyed it dark blue.'

Ross Senior looked at Billy. 'Are you planning on staying in Miami for the winter?'

Billy looked at Peggy then spoke for the two of them. 'We think so. We're told it's freezing in New York in winter.'

'And where are you planning to stay in Miami?'

'No idea, but with it being warm, at least we won't freeze at night.'

'And you two are the same ages as Ross and Maisie?'

'Yes, I'm twelve, Billy's eleven.'

'Hmm.'

Ross Senior lapsed deep into thought, rubbing his chin and looking from Billy to Peggy and then to his own children. It was Maisie who read his mind.

'Did our replacement passports come through, Dad?'

'They did, yes, just before we left.'

'And you've brought them?'

'Well, I know we found the others, but it does no harm to have a spare for all sorts of reasons. Although the passport people will have cancelled the originals.'

'If you gave them to Billy and Peggy they could become us.'

'They couldn't get through Customs as you, not without the new ones.'

191

'I wasn't thinking about Customs, I was thinking about those "all sorts of reasons".'

'You're reading my mind again, Maisie.'

'Why would we want to become you?' Billy asked.

'Because we want to go back to England to live with Mum,' explained Ross Junior. 'Neither of us wants to work in the theatre. We just want a normal life and to live in one place.' He avoided his father's eyes as he spoke, but his dad smiled.

'It's okay, son. I fully understand. You both love your mom and she loves you. Maybe when this production's run its course I could come over to England to be with you all.'

'Dad, Mum will never have you back until you give up this theatre job and go back to being a teacher.'

'Maisie, the job in New York pays three times what I was making in London. If I do well at it, I can bring my reputation back with me and make the same money over there. All these shows are seen by London agents.'

'One of the reasons they want him is because he's got two kids of the right age, with English accents,' said his son to Billy.

'No, no. It's not part of my contract, but having two English kids certainly did me no harm when I auditioned in London.'

'Which is why you'd like me and Billy to act like your children?' said Peggy.

Ross Senior held his hands up. 'Hey! Have I even suggested this to anyone here? Mind you, now you come to mention it, it sure sounds like a good idea of yours, Ross boy.'

Ross Junior grinned. 'Does this mean we can go back to Mum in England?'

'Well, we need to give it some thought...'

'That means yes,' said his son.

'Can I take your orders?' asked an arriving waitress.

'Jack and Benny Special cheeseburger,' said Billy, reading from a menu on the wall.

'Make that two,' added Peggy, offering Ross Senior one of her precious pounds. He waved the offer away. 'With fries.'

'That's chips,' whispered Maisie to Billy.

'Yes, please. Do you do scraps?'

'Billy Clegg! Behave!'

Chapter 16

Ross Senior had rented a three-bedroom ground-floor apartment about a mile from the coast. After stopping off at the rental agency to pick up the keys, they arrived mid-afternoon. It was a sparsely furnished place with marble floors as befitted the near-tropical climate Miami enjoyed. There was crockery and cutlery and chairs enough for all of them, a refrigerator, a modern-looking radio and even a cheerful painting of fishing boats on the wall. Billy and Peggy had been assured that there would be room for them all, and more room once Ross Junior and Maisie had left, which would be in about a week's time.

'We have some money, Mr Duggan,' Peggy told

him. 'We're not totally skint. Trouble is, it's in pounds not dollars.'

'Really? And how many of these troublesome pounds do you have?'

She looked at Billy. 'Not sure how much we have left exactly.'

'Over a hundred,' he said conservatively. He was keeping sixty pounds in reserve for him and Peggy.

'That sounds like four hundred dollars at today's exchange rate.'

Billy was now converting his reserve fund into two hundred and forty dollars. He gave Peggy a knowing wink.

'We'd feel better if you let us pay something for rent and food,' said his sister to Ross Senior. 'Would twenty dollars a week be okay?'

'Fifteen will be fine.'

'Well, it's fifteen more than we pay,' said Ross Junior, 'plus we get three dollars a week allowance. So, when we go, Dad's going to be twenty-one dollars a week better off.'

His father smiled. 'As and when they get to help me out with my cabaret act, they'll be paid accordingly. It should be more than enough to cover any rent money.'

'You've got work here?' said Peggy.

'I have – three months in a cabaret club. I've developed an amusing and entertaining act.'

'He sings and plays the piano,' Ross explained. 'He can do jazz and all that ragtime stuff.'

'Er, I was classically trained, young man. I only play jazz and ragtime to please the uneducated ear.'

'What will we do about school?'

This earnt Peggy a glare from Billy.

'Well, I've got Ross and Maisie fixed up with a local school so the best way would be for you to take their places.'

'I bet someone asks for identification,' said Billy, who wasn't going down without a fight.

'Which of course we have,' said Maisie, 'in duplicate.'

'Billy and Peggy don't look much like our passport photos,' pointed out Ross Junior, taking his pal Billy's side.

'I have work permits for them, which should suffice ... if I'm asked. I'm not trying to smuggle them out of the country.'

'This means we can't even start school,' said Maisie.

'Not here. The next schools you go to will be your old schools in England.'

'With all our old friends,' said Ross.

His father nodded. 'I'll go down to the shipping office in the morning and see if there's any way I can sign you on. Entertainers who just work for their passage are always welcome, no matter how good or bad they are.'

'Gee, thanks, Dad.'

'I didn't mean it like that. If the *Britannic's* going back to England you could be on your way home in a week or so. It'll be sailing up to New York tomorrow. Two nights there, then two days sailing back here for an overnighter. I'll wire your mum and tell her to meet you in Liverpool.'

'Dad,' said Ross, 'we can find our way home from Liverpool on our own. We leave the ship, taxi to Lime Street Station, find a London train, get off in Euston, get on a tube and get off at the stop near home. All we need is the money for fares.'

'But if Mum meets us in Liverpool, she pays our fare,' Maisie pointed out.

'Why not? Your mum's loaded. That grocer's shop of hers makes enough money to keep our family without me having to teach English to dumb kids. The trouble with your mom is that she never saw the artist in me!'

His children looked at each other with the words, *Oh, not this again,* trapped silently inside them.

There was a note of irritation in Ross Senior's voice that Peggy hadn't heard before. Billy didn't help when he said, 'I wish we had a mam to go home to. We'd *walk* from Liverpool to Leeds if we could see her for just ten minutes, wouldn't we, Peg?'

Peggy's shoulders shook as she tried to hold back the inevitable tears. Billy seemed to be about to join in. Ross Senior walked out of the room and took refuge in his bedroom, where he sat on the bed and, not for the first timed, assessed his ill-managed life. After they'd carried him off the blood-soaked shingle of Omaha Beach, they took him to a landing craft, which had just disembarked eighty men, most of them heading to their deaths. He was taken to a hospital ship, very seriously wounded and not expected to live. In his semi-conscious state he himself thought he'd never survive the major operation he needed as they wheeled him through to the operating theatre on board the ship. The last thought in his head before he submitted to the anaesthetic was that if he survived, he'd turn his whole life around. No more teaching or soldiering for him. He wasn't even a good teacher, and he'd probably been a worse soldier. Had he been any good he'd have dug himself into that godforsaken beach and avoided all the bullets heading his way, fired by men who would never know him.

He miraculously survived, picking up a disability pension and a Purple Heart, and was sent over to England to recuperate. This suited him as his wife was English and they made a home in the South London suburbs. He took up amateur theatricals to occupy himself while he convalesced. To his wife's dismay he turned out to be a very talented wheelchair actor and when he got back on his feet he successfully auditioned to join a professional company with an engagement at the Garrick Theatre in London, within commuting distance of his home. Ross knew this was it. This was what had been hiding at the back of his mind as he waited to go in for his operation. The theatre. He wasn't a teacher, he was an actor!

The war had ended with him still in England and married, the two children and himself doing piecemeal acting work in between helping out in his wife's shop. He supplemented this by playing piano with a local dance band, but this didn't suit his wife one bit. She had married a professional man, a high-school teacher no less, with a good education and good looks – and had ended up with a mostly out-of-work actor and part-time musician. Then along came a chance for him to audition for the lead in an off-Broadway production in New York City. Ross's audition was successful and he managed to persuade his wife and children to come to New York with him. He even got the kids cabaret work on the ship to cover their passage. It was almost at the last minute that his wife had cried off. Her shop was a real money-spinner and to leave it in the care of paid assistants for an unknown length of time was just too risky; supposing they came back to a failing business?

These and other memories spun through his head as he sat on the bed. His principal thought was that he missed his wife, but she didn't understand him. Jesus! That was such an old chestnut no one took it seriously any more, not even the kids, two of whom were now in tears – and those two weren't even his, and yet he was planning on illegally replacing his own with them. He lit a cigarette.

'How the hell did that happen?' he murmured out loud.

'How did what happen, Dad?'

Ross looked up and saw Maisie standing there.

'Nothing, just talking to myself.' He smiled at her. 'Anyway, you being a mind-reader, you shouldn't have to ask that.'

'Well, maybe I don't need to.' She was holding a file of papers at which she briefly glanced.

'What's that?'

'Well, I'm guessing it's what's on your mind, Dad. I'm guessing it's the story of how the hell that happened.'

'Really?'

'Yes. With you being my dad, it was my duty to

keep an eye on you when they brought you back from the war in pieces. I was warned you might die, probably so that your actual death wouldn't come as such a shock to me. This went on for a week – the worst week of my life. I prayed for you all the time. Not much of a prayer, just one I made up: "Dear God, please let my dad live." I taught it to Ross and he prayed too. Between us I reckon we said it ten thousand times.'

'Ten thousand? And here's me thinking somebody up there likes me. It was somebody down here after all.'

'We, er, read your story, Dad.'

'What story's that?'

'The one you wrote called "Ross's Resurrection". Ten thousand two hundred words. The one that tells the story of your war and how they brought you back to life and how you realised your deathbed dream and became an actor.'

'You read that?'

'I've read it at least six times. Especially the bits about how much you love me and Ross. We're your world, you said, and you also said your world would be complete if only certain people in your world would accept that you've got no vocation for teaching; by "people" I'm guessing you mean Mum, mainly.'

He looked at the file in her hand. 'Is that it?'

'Yes, well, this is a copy.'

'What? You had copies made ... why?'

'Because I think it's brilliant and so does Miss Veitch at school.'

'Oh my God! You showed it to your English teacher? I bared my soul in that piece. It was for my eyes only.'

'I showed it to her to see if she thought it was as good as I think it is. She has an Oxford degree in English Literature.'

'I have quite a good one myself, and...'

'I know. Apparently it shows in your work. She thought you should send it to literary agent.'

'Literary agents, what do they know?'

'They see the talent in your work.'

'You mean you've already sent it to an agent?'

'Yes. I was perfectly honest and told them the circumstances and that you didn't know I was sending it.'

'And?'

Maisie grinned. 'And they've asked for the first thirty thousand words of any book you care to start, whether it be fiction or non-fiction. This is the Byron Agency, one of the top agencies in London. They wouldn't ask to see your work if it wasn't brilliant.'

'They said it was brilliant, did they?'

'Not in so many words. According to Miss Veitch, agents never call a writer brilliant until they're trying to sell that writer's manuscripts.'

'And are these letters in that file?'

'Yes ... and there's someone else who will have seen your short story by now, and not before time, I must say.'

Ross knew immediately who she was talking about. 'Maisie, you should have asked me before you did that.'

'Dad, you should have shown it to her yourself. It's exactly what she needs to hear from you. It explains everything about you, with the message that you're not to be changed now you've found your true self.'

'You think your mom will understand?'

'I'm sure she will. I left a copy under her pillow before we left, with a note from me explaining I put it there, not you.'

'Good.'

'She'll have read it by now.'

'Not good. She'll think it's all self-pitying slush, which maybe it is.'

'No, it's not. It's a soul-searching work of truth according to the agent.'

'Is that what they said?'

'Yes.'

She handed him her file. He took it, dropped the manuscript on the bed and opened the agent's letter, reading it with eyebrows raised.

'Well, they don't hate it, that's for sure. Maybe I will do as they ask. Will your mother have seen a copy of his letter?'

'Yes. And if she thinks as I do she'll say your future isn't in acting, it's in writing.'

'Do you think I'm not a good actor?'

'When you were with the amateur people you were the best, but among professional actors you're good but nothing special … sorry.'

'Don't be sorry, you're quite right. I know my limitations.'

'Dad, I think your writing is really special and so will the agents when you send them what they've asked for. And you can work from home and be with Mum all the time, and maybe help out in the shop when you get that writer's block thing.'

They looked at each other for a while until Maisie said, 'And you could go home with me and Ross next week if you wanted.'

'Well, I'm wondering if your mom might write to me here? She has the address and she'll know we've arrived by now. If she does and she's okay about everything, I'll go back with you. If not I'll stay here then go up to New York with Billy and Peggy, if only to give my acting one last chance.'

'And to give Billy and Peggy a chance?'

'Yeah, I don't want to let them down. But, either way, I will be coming home to you and your mom in the not-too-distant future, be sure of that. We'll all be together again, one way or another.'

Ross Junior came into the room. 'Hey, there's a cellar with all sorts of stuff in it.'

'Such as?' asked Maisie.

'Such as two bikes, which should be handy with it being dead flat around here, and a typewriter that works. Doesn't look all that old either.'

Maisie looked at her father with a knowing grin and a tilted head. 'Maybe it's an omen, Dad?'

'Y'know, Maisie, I can't believe you're only twelve.'

'Thirteen in May, Dad.'

'God help me when you're eighteen.'

Without so much as a by-your-leave to Ross Senior it took the two boys no time at all to take the bikes out for a ride to the coast. Both were of the sit-up-and-beg design but this didn't deter the boys who virtually whizzed down the road to the coast, whooping all the way. It was the first lift in Billy's cheerless mood since the fire.

The Atlantic Ocean was a stark contrast to the grey sea of Blackpool: bright blue and shimmering under the reflection of a clear blue sky. People were swimming in the water and sun-bathing on the beach and it was November. Billy felt that he was living in a different world, but his preferred one was where his mother had been living, so this was a lesser place, for all its beautiful weather. Still, it had put a rare smile on his face and he told himself that he must bring Peggy here as soon as possible; she deserved to smile as well. Wherever his mam was, she'd be pleased he was in a warm place and not frozen silly in Yorkshire.

'We're okay, Mam,' he said to the sky.

'What?'

'Nothing, I was talking to my mam, that's all.'

'I bet you miss her.'

'We do, yeah.'

'We miss our mum and she's still alive.'

There was a silence between them as they both looked out to sea, then scanned their new surroundings.

'All Maisie and I want is to go back to our mum and I don't think I can wait three months to see her again. Trouble is, we don't want to let Dad down,' said Ross.

'Me and Peggy should be able to take your places.'

'I hope you can. Duggie Davis liked those acts you both did. Dad says it's because you've got good timing, and anyone with good timing can act.'

'Act? I wasn't planning on doing any acting.'

'What were you planning on doing?'

'I don't know. Just messing about in the background.'

'We were going to get lines in *Twist* and you're supposed to be us.'

'Oh, heck! Are you sure you don't fancy staying here for a bit? Me and you could have great fun in a place like this. On the beach every day.'

'Nah, I think we'll be off as soon as Dad can organise it. We can't mess him about too much.'

'Is he a good actor, your dad?'

'He's okay. Mum reckons that if the play is moved on to proper Broadway they won't take Dad with them, which means he'll have to come home.'

'Is that because he's not good enough?'

Ross shrugged. 'I dunno. That's what Mum thinks, but she's a bit biased against theatre work. To appear in a Broadway show you have to be really good. They don't carry passengers, is what she says, but don't you tell him that.'

'Well, if your dad has to go home, what about me and Peggy?'

'You'll have to go back sometime.'

'I don't see why. I think we might get to like it over here ... if they'll let us stay.'

'Might your mother still be alive?'

Billy shook his head. 'No. We're pretty sure Mam died in the fire. Someone checked for us.'

The memory of his dead mother seemed to dull the bright day and all its warmth turned cold for Billy.

'Mebbe we should get back,' he said. 'Can you remember the way?'

Ross jabbed a thumb over his shoulder. 'Yeah,

straight down that road. It's on the left just past the petrol station. We should have a few days together before me and Maisie leave.'

'Yeah, that'll be good. I hope your dad doesn't make us go to school here. I should have taken my scholarship after we ran away. Did you take yours?'

'Yeah, I think I did all right. If not, Mum'll send me to a private school so I get a good School Certificate, but I don't fancy going to a snobby private school.'

'Billy Bunter goes to a private school,' said Billy, 'I don't think he's a snob. Anyway, there's no chance of me going to one. I'll just stay on at St Oggy's ... in the seniors 'til I'm fifteen when I can leave and get a job sweeping up in a factory for a shilling an hour.'

'St Oggy's? Is that a school?'

'St Augustine's. It's a Catholic school. No chance of me getting a good School Certificate there – prob'ly won't even stay there long enough to get to take it. My mam'd have been disappointed. Our Peg passed her scholarship.' Billy turned his bicycle around and pointed it towards the way back.

'Hey!' protested Ross. 'We don't have to go back just yet, we've only just got here.'

But talk of his dead mother had pricked Billy's cheery balloon. 'I'm roasted, Ross. If I stay out with no cap on I'll get sunstroke. My mam always said not to go out in the sun with no cap on, and the sun in Leeds isn't the same as this.'

'Okay then. Maybe I'll come back here later with Maisie.'

Chapter 17

St James's Hospital, Leeds

The young detective sergeant approached Betty's bed with some trepidation. He knew she didn't take crap from anyone, least of all a young copper come to talk to her about her missing children. He saw she was sitting up in bed, reading *Woman's Own* and drinking a cup of tea with her good arm, despite still being heavily bandaged.

'Mrs Clegg?'

With him being in plain clothes she didn't immediately identify him as a policeman. He did that for himself.

'My name's Detective Sergeant Dunstan. I've come to talk to you about your children.'

Her eyes lit up. 'Have you found them?'

'Er, no. I just wondered if you'd heard from them.'

'In here? They don't even know I'm alive. How could I have heard from them?'

'You're able to receive post in hospital.'

'Well, I haven't heard from them – and even if they did write, I suspect your lot'll have made arrangements to intercept any letters I get. Do you still think they blew that factory up with a tuppenny firework?'

'It was an explosion, Mrs Clegg. We're just trying to ascertain what ignited the gas. According to a witness, your children were playing with fireworks only a few yards away.'

'By "witness" you mean Lester Blainey?'

Dunstan said nothing.

'How old are you?' she asked him.

'I'm twenty-eight.'

'Blimey, you look about eighteen. Of course it was Blainey. The bloke who pulled me out saw the kids and he says they were at least fifty yards away, with the wind blowing away from the explosion. He remembers it because he noticed the direction the sparks from the fireworks were blowing. The breeze would have taken them away from the gas leak. I bet the firemen could have told you that. They notice things like wind direction. Have the police asked them?'

'I don't know. We're simply aware that there must have been a gas leak and that children were playing with fireworks in the near vicinity. And we know that those children have since run away from home. Why would they run away if they thought they hadn't done anything wrong?'

'Because that bugger Blainey saw 'em and told 'em he was gonna report 'em to the police for causing the fire. Then they find out that loads of people have died, most likely including me. I mean, they're kids, what do you expect? They got scared and ran away. How do you think I feel about that, Sergeant?'

'I can't imagine, Mrs Clegg.'

'I feel I might as well be dead, Sergeant. I feel useless. I feel like me life's been taken away from me. And I'll tell yer what really bugs me: it's that bugger Blainey gettin' away scot-free by lying about where the kids were playing. He's the reason I feel like I do. He's the reason my pals died and my children have run away. That explosion was about half-past six and I've never known a day when Blainey didn't leave the factory at half-five on the dot, so what was he doing down there at that time? I'll tell you what he was doing – he was setting up the explosion. He was closing the factory down the next weekend because it was doing so badly. An insurance claim'd come in very handy, don't you think?'

'We have no proof of that, Mrs Clegg.'

'No, but I bet you'd find a bit of proof if his sister wasn't a top boss in the police force. What chance have my kids got against them two?'

Having said her piece Betty returned her attention to the magazine. The young policeman got to his feet and resolved to investigate Blainey's circumstances. He might also have a word with the firemen about wind direction that night. Trouble was, he was newly promoted and didn't want to create any waves that might adversely affect his career. Mrs Clegg was quite right about Blainey's sister. She was the chief superintendent in overall charge of the case, having been promoted to high office during the war, mainly due to a dearth of senior male officers after so many had volunteered for the services, despite the police being a reserved occupation. Under peace-time circumstances she might just have made inspector.

Dunstan and his colleagues had been warned not to treat her brother as a suspect; such an investigation would be far too messy, not to mention bad for morale, especially if it reached the newspapers. As far as the top brass were concerned the Clegg children were convenient scapegoats. It wouldn't be a murder charge, just a case of severe juvenile delinquency that would see them banged up for a good few years. Accident or not, a lot of lives had been lost and a significant punishment must be seen to be imposed.

'I'll say good day to you then, Mrs Clegg, and I hope you'll be well soon. Here's my card if you ever need to contact me.'

'Thank you.'

Betty sat and watched his gaberdine-raincoated figure disappearing down the ward. He didn't seem a bad sort; maybe if she ever needed police help he'd be the one to go to. She'd mention it to Jimmy. Winter rain lashed against the windows. She looked back down at her magazine but couldn't concentrate. All she could see through misty eyes were her children, and all she could ask was: *where are you?* Over two weeks now, with only fifteen bob between them. They couldn't survive on that. Who was looking after them? Someone must be. God! She hoped they were in good hands, keeping dry and warm in this awful weather.

The phone rang in Lester Blainey's hallway. He was hoping it might be the insurance people confirming that his grossly exaggerated claim of £84,300 had been approved. It would be more than enough for him to retire on in luxury. In fact, the call was from his sister Jean.

'Lester, I need to talk to you about the explosion.'

'What about it?'

'Is it not a fact that you always left work at five-thirty on the dot? I remember this from when Jack was alive.'

'Yes, it is a fact, so what?'

'Then why were you in the factory when it blew up at half-past six?'

'Oh, you think I blew it up, do you?'

'I'm fending off suspicions about you and I need to satisfy myself completely that you had nothing to do with it.'

'I had some paperwork to finish.'

'And you left the factory by a door near the seat of the explosion instead of the main door you usually used. You can see why I'm concerned, Lester.'

'I'd gone down there because someone had complained about a smell of gas coming from the cellar. They were right. As soon as I caught a whiff of it, I got out as quick as I could by the nearest door. Only just in time, as it happens.'

'Could you produce this person to confirm that?'

'Hardly, she died in the fire.'

'How come there was such a bad gas leak? Jack was always so careful about gas.'

'I don't know.'

'I understand the odd job man, whatever his name is, says there was no smell a couple of hours earlier when he'd been down there.'

'How do you know all this?'

'Because we're the police, we ask questions. Bloody hell, Lester! Were it not for me covering your back here we'd probably be charging you with murder by now. If you are ever taken to court over this these are questions you'll have to answer to the jury's satisfaction. A half-decent prosecuting counsel would destroy you. You definitely need to keep yourself out of court, but I can't perform miracles.'

'Jean, it had nothing to do with me. I know it looks bad, with me claiming on the insurance, but I didn't start the fire and kill all those women. You've got to believe me.'

There was a long silence while she considered her position. 'Lester, you're my only surviving brother. My other brother, the one with the brains, is dead. As your sister, I feel obliged to cover for you on this. God help us both if you're lying and we're found out! I'll be thrown to the wolves and you know what will happen to you.'

'I'm not lying, Jean. The kids' fireworks caused that fire ... please, you've got to believe that!'

His sister held the receiver away from her and looked at it with distaste. She knew her brother only too well. 'Lester, just shut up and put the phone down, you whining little shit!'

With a smirk on his face he put the phone down. Okay, she didn't believe him, but no way would his copper sister let him hang. Her job was too important to her for her to risk the scandal. Plus she had a ten per cent share in the business, so she'd be picking up around eight grand insurance money. His sister would never turn up her nose at that sort of money. Not with her expensive gambling habit.

Chapter 18

St James's Hospital, 21 December

The ward was decked out with Christmas decorations that had been in annual use since before the war. The only new decorations were the bunches of holly and an optimistic cluster of mistletoe hanging over the doorway. It was over six weeks since Betty's accident and the plaster was due to be removed from her arm and leg the next day. Her head injury was successfully healing itself as were her broken ribs, which were still strapped up but nowhere near as painful.

The only thing on Betty's troubled mind was her children and what sort of a Christmas they would be having. Where were they, and how were they even existing? Two kids, aged twelve and eleven, had disappeared off the face of the earth. How could that be unless someone was holding them against their will? These and other thoughts tormented her as she sat up in bed, staring into space. Jimmy arrived at visiting hour as usual, carrying a bag of grapes that he placed on her bed.

'Don't know how fresh these are. I got 'em from the market this morning. The bloke said they were newly over from somewhere hot.'

'Kirkgate Market?'

'Yeah.'

'They'll tell you owt. Still, they look all right.'

She put one in her mouth and gave a nod of approval. 'Taste all right as well.'

Betty's physical wounds were healing, but her emotions were heading in the opposite direction. It seemed to her that she might never see her children again and the worst part was the not knowing. The bloody police still seemed hell-bent on arresting them as soon as they showed up, and if the kids got wind of this they'd stay away forever if necessary – and who could blame them? But why hadn't they so much as written? Any letter sent to their home address would be sent on to her. As usual Betty answered her own question. They hadn't written because they thought she was dead, and probably that they were the cause of her death.

'Anything to report about the kids?' she asked Jimmy, even though she knew if he had anything he'd have already told her.

He shook his head. 'Sorry, nothing at all.'

'I haven't even bought them any Christmas presents, Jimmy. I'd saved up, y'know. First year ever without buying them presents.'

'You had no chance to do that, Betty. I thought we'd get some response from the thing they ran in the *Express* last month.'

'Well, they never read newspapers, and why would they look for something about the factory fire?'

'I don't know, maybe a list of the people who died.'

'I don't think papers ever do that, do they?'

'They mentioned you were alive in the *Express*.'

'Did they? Sorry, Jimmy. I know you're doing your best.'

'To be honest, Betty, I don't know what more I can do. If the police can't find them, what chance do we have?'

'I'm just hoping they'll come back. Everybody needs hope, Jimmy. I can't bear to think of them perhaps believing I'm gone for good. I saddled them with a useless dad, and now they'll think I've gone.'

Jimmy looked at this lovely woman to whom he was very much attracted. He had hopes of his own in her direction.

'I can go home on Christmas Eve,' she told him. 'Though I don't know how I'll manage on my own. My leg isn't up to going up and down stairs and our lavatory's in the back yard.'

Jimmy had already given this a lot of thought and saw it as a golden opportunity to make a suggestion.

'I, er ... you could come to stay in my house if you like. There's a room downstairs you could use as a bedroom and I have an inside toilet ... built it myself. There's no bathroom as such, the bath's under a pine board in the scullery, but you'd have all the privacy you want with the door shut.'

'Well, it certainly sounds better than my house – Crossgates, isn't it?'

'Yeah, it's not a bad area. Good for shops and stuff ... and there's a Catholic church not far away – St Theresa's.'

He noticed her face freeze for a moment.

'What is it?'

'Oh, nothing. I just thought about the kids coming back to an empty house with me moving out and them not knowing where I am.'

'Of course they'll know where you are. You can tell all the neighbours.'

'What? That I'm moving in with you?'

'Well, it'll be perfectly innocent – just for your convenience until you're fully recovered, that's all. Surely they'll understand.'

'Jimmy, you don't know my neighbours. I'll just tell them I'm moving in with a friend for the time being.'

They chatted about the pros and cons of her moving in with him and the pros won, hands down.

'That's settled, then. I'll order us a taxi for the morning,' said Jimmy.

'Look, I have to ask – do you have an ulterior motive here?' Betty enquired.

'Nothing I would ever force on you but if you wanted to make our friendship a bit more permanent, I wouldn't say no.'

'I see. Fancy me, do you?'

'I've always fancied you, Betty. What about you?'

'What about me?'

'Do you fancy me?'

She looked up at him. His hair was growing back and he no longer sported a moustache. In fact, in a good light, he was passably handsome, and he was an easy man to get along with; a man who could make her smile. But did she want him as a husband? That's what he was asking.

'Jimmy, my life is a horror story right now. For me to give you a proper answer to that question

215

I need to be thinking straight, and there's only one thing that can do that for me.'

'The kids coming home?'

'Yes.'

'Fair enough.'

He took one of the grapes and popped it into his mouth.

'Do you still do the piano playing?' Betty asked.

'I do, yes, but I might have to cut down on that a bit.'

'Not because of me, I hope.'

'Oh, no. I've actually applied to go back to teaching.'

'Teaching what?'

'Maths. Of course. I told you I had a degree, didn't I?'

'From a proper university?'

'Yeah, Manchester. I taught maths at secondary level for eight years before I was called up. No reason I can't pick up where I left off. I think my head's in the right place now. As it happens, helping you seems to be helping me quite a bit. Keeps me thinking straight.'

'Well,' said Betty, 'I'm pleased your head was in the wrong place because it meant that you were in the right place when I got blown out of the factory.'

Jimmy grinned. 'That's one way of looking at it.'

'And that's why you didn't go back to teaching when you got your demob?'

'Exactly. I scarcely knew what two and two added up to when I first came out of the army. That job at Blainey's suited me down to the

216

ground. I didn't have to think, and I've always been a bit of a handyman so I knew I could do the tasks well enough. You see, university teaches you many things, including how to learn. I'm currently studying the mechanics of gas supply to industrial buildings. Even now, if I had to go court as a defence witness, I'm sure I could baffle them with science that would favour the kids.'

'You mean an expert witness?'

'I'm qualified to do that, yes. In the army I was a lieutenant in the Royal Engineers, an explosives expert ... a sapper.'

'A proper officer and you came from that to being an odd job man?'

'It was a safe job, better than facing being blown up every day.'

'You mean you were one of those bomb disposal people?'

'Exactly. It's how I got the shrapnel in my leg. I was walking away from a bomb I thought I'd defused, only I hadn't ... well, obviously. It blew me fifty feet through the air. Lucky for me I was wearing full protective gear, including a really decent helmet, or I'd have been a goner.'

'Did you get a medal or anything that might impress the judge?'

'I did, actually. I was awarded a British Empire Medal for meritorious conduct. At the time I thought I might have got a roasting for not defusing it properly. As it turned out it wasn't my fault. The info we'd been given on that type of bomb was wrong.'

'Well, I'm impressed. I bet they don't give them away to just anybody.'

'Ah, but will the jury be impressed?'

'I imagine so. It's more impressive than someone who's got his qualifications in a schoolroom. You know about explosions because you've been blown up by one.'

'So have you.'

There was a short silence between them then she told him, 'Jimmy, I think Blainey did it, and I told a copper that.'

'I think you're right. All he had to do was loosen a joint to get the gas leaking and leave a lit candle or something. A decent naked flame like that would set off a massive explosion like the one we saw. I'm as sure as I can be that a dying spark from a tuppenny firework wouldn't have travelled fifty yards against the wind to ignite that gas leak. A spark from a cheap firework'd die out after ten yards max. That was a planned explosion. Whatever ignited that gas was alive and firing and already in the factory waiting for the gas to hit it.'

'How do we prove that?'

'Well, that's the police's job.'

'Yeah,' said Betty, 'and Blainey's sister's in charge of the investigation.'

'I know that, but I reckon somewhere he'll have slipped up. He's not the sharpest tool in the box isn't Blainey, which is why the factory went bust. Somewhere he'll have left evidence that proves he did it. I'm going to have a look through the wreckage to see what I can find. Trouble is, a lot of scrap-metal scavengers have been around. Hmm, you know, it could be that he spoke to someone about his plan.'

'Surely even Blainey wouldn't be that stupid.'

'Maybe he would.'

'You could have a word with that copper I spoke to – Detective Sergeant Dunstan. I think I got through to him when I told him what I suspected about who caused the blast. I think you should tell him all the technical stuff about why a firework spark couldn't have set off the explosion. I've got his card with a phone number on it.'

'Yes, I'll take that. I could tell him what I think and back it up with technical evidence. Maybe have a word with the firemen who were there. As I was one of the few people at the scene, I imagine they would do me the courtesy of listening to my opinion.'

'Don't forget to tell them you were an officer in the sappers in the army and that you know more than most about explosions, and that's why you think it was planned.'

Betty was smiling now. It was the first smile Jimmy had seen on her since the explosion. 'Hey! What's the prettiest thing that a woman can wear?' he asked her.

'Definitely not this hospital nightie.'

'A smile,' he said.

She smiled again, as did Jimmy.

Chapter 19

Billy looked at the thermometer in the living room: 68° Fahrenheit and it was only ten o'clock in the morning. He switched on the ceiling fan – an item unheard of back in Yorkshire. The blades were spinning smoothly when Ross Senior came through from the kitchen.

'I think maybe we'll need to hire a proper air-conditioning unit before the weather gets really warm in the spring.'

'I thought we were going to New York then.'

'The show opens in April. We'll be going up in mid-March for rehearsals.'

'I thought you knew the play.'

'Well, I've done it before but not the part I'm playing this time.'

'What about me and Peggy?' asked Billy. 'What do we do?'

'You both have small parts that are easy enough to learn. I can rehearse you here before we go. I have a script.'

'Okay.'

'Do you think you're up to it?'

'Why not? We do well enough in your cabaret act, don't we?'

'You do, but this is acting not singing.'

'We've been acting out being Ross and Maisie for a month.'

'Yes, you have. Is that much of a problem?'

'Not really. If anyone ever hears us get the names mixed up, we'll say we sometimes have different names for each other just for fun. Some kids do that.'

'Good thinking. Look, I'm guessing you two will be missing your mom more than ever on Christmas Day, so if there's anything I can do to help, just say the word.'

'She always made us a great Christmas dinner.' The voice was Peggy's. It came from behind Ross, who turned and smiled at her. 'Well, that's something we'll have to tackle together this year. I've already got a turkey in the ice-box but we need all the other stuff. How about we go food shopping today? I think we should get a tree as well.'

'Oh, yeah, we always had a tree at home.'

Half an hour later Billy and Peggy were trailing behind Ross down a shopping boulevard. He was striding along in the sunshine, wearing a cream-coloured topcoat and a Panama hat. Even off-stage he was theatrical-looking. The boulevard was wide and the sidewalk had a grass verge running down the centre with a line of high palm trees growing from it. Most of the buildings were white and built in the art deco style. Huge American cars were parked nose to tail all the way down the road. It was a sight never seen in Leeds, where very few people even had cars. Ross pointed out the Beachcomber Cotton Club which had a picture of Rudy Vallee outside.

'That's where I'll be doing my cabaret.'

'Do you know Rudy Vallee?' Peggy asked him.

'No, but I soon will. I'm one of his supporting

acts. Maybe you'll be as well.'

'Us? What can we do?'

'You'd be a novelty act – kids who can entertain. They won't expect too much of you. In fact I reckon you could give them a lot more than they expect.'

'And would we meet Rudy Vallee?' asked Peggy.

'I imagine so.'

'Who's Rudy Vallee?' asked Billy.

'He's a crooner and a musician,' said Ross. 'He'll probably be the band leader.'

'*Strangers in the Night...*' crooned Peggy.

'He might let you have a go at one of his numbers,' said Ross, impressed by her singing the opening few bars of one of Vallee's songs.

'Honestly? Blimey, Ross! I wouldn't dare.'

'Peggy when you're in show business you dare do anything. I bet Billy wouldn't be scared to do one of his banjo songs, would you, Billy? How about "Lavender Trousers"? I can just see you on stage in a pair of baggy lavender trousers. You'd bring the house down with that.'

'Well, I could, only I haven't got a banjo here.'

'I bet the band has one,' said Ross, grinning. 'If not they'll get one.' Without them realising, he'd enlisted them both in his act.

The children had paused at a toy shop and were looking at the display in the window.

'We could most prob'ly afford to buy each other Chrissy presents,' Billy was saying. 'What would you like, Peg?'

'I wouldn't mind that book of children's stories by Hans Andersen. How about you?'

'That rifle looks great. I think it's supposed to

be a Remington like they use in the cowboy films. It fires caps.'

'Typical. Anything that goes bang.'

It was at that moment Billy looked up towards Ross, who was still walking away from them. He was fifty yards away when an approaching youth stumbled into him. It was an action that was familiar to Billy, who nudged his sister.

'I think that lad's just nicked Ross's wallet.'

'Are you sure?'

'Positive and I bet I can get it back. Look, I'll walk in front and you follow me, then set off running and barge into me when I reach him.'

'Okay, I get it.'

Peggy, knowing the routine, followed her younger brother's instructions, which led to Billy stumbling into the approaching youth and apologising to him. 'Sorry, buddy ... stupid girl!'

He then ran after his sister as if to chastise her. The youth glanced round, momentarily, then tapped his pocket. He glanced round again to see Billy waving the wallet at him and grinning as he took it back to Ross, who was at that moment searching his own pockets.

'Hey!' he exclaimed. 'I've just been robbed.'

'I know,' said Billy. 'I saw it and I got your wallet back for you ... he took it.' He pointed back at the thief, who was now running away.

'You got it back, how?'

'Same way as he took it, although I had Peggy to help me.'

'What? You picked his pocket?'

'Yeah. I saw which pocket he'd put it in, so it was easy.'

Ross took his wallet back. 'Thanks. Er, where did you learn how to do this?'

Billy and Peggy looked at each other. Neither of them thought it a good idea to tell Ross about the dubious tuition Spider had given them as they passed the time away on the ship.

'From someone we knew who, er, does it as a stage act,' said Peggy. 'He taught us how to do it.'

'Really? So this is something you could do on-stage?'

'As well as our usual routines?'

'Yes.'

'Not really,' said Billy. 'We're not that good yet.'

'Good enough to get me my wallet back though. Thanks very much. Losing this would have ruined our Christmas.'

'You should always keep your wallet in a pocket that buttons up,' Billy told him. 'Dips have got no chance with a buttoned-up pocket.'

'Dips, eh? My word, you know some stuff, you two.'

Billy and Peggy smiled at each other. For a brief moment Ross had reminded them of Harry, and each of them wondered how he was getting on without his reprobate grandson. He was too old to be starting a new life on his own. They, too, were starting a new life, having lost someone they loved, but had the advantage of youth on their side.

'Was that a toy shop window you were looking in back there?' Ross enquired of them.

'It was, yes.'

'See anything you liked?'

'Well, I liked a book by Hans Andersen and Billy liked a cowboy rifle that fires caps.'

Peggy said it to illustrate her intellectual superiority over her brother but was shot down in flames when Billy said, 'I don't read fairy stories. I prefer proper books like *Treasure Island* and *Tom Sawyer.*'

'They're not fairy stories, they're classical children's–'

Here Peggy was interrupted by Ross, who knew better than to get caught up in this display of sibling rivalry.

'Here's a delicatessen,' he said. 'We should find a lot of what we need here.'

Back in Leeds their mother was on the verge of tears at the thought of what a cold and lonely Christmas her children must be having. She herself was looking around Jimmy's house. She'd just arrived, having been transported there from hospital by taxi. Her arm was still in a sling and she used a crutch to help her walk.

The front room, that was to be her bedroom, looked particularly luxurious with a fine wide bed, what felt like Axminster carpet underfoot, a kidney-shaped dressing table, a chest of drawers and a large wardrobe that would more than accommodate all her clothing. Betty was wondering where it all came from.

'Jimmy, have you been buying furniture in just for me?'

It was a question that required a white lie. 'Oh, no. I've had some stuff in storage for a while.'

He had spent every spare hour of the previous three days preparing for her arrival. Every item of furniture in the room had been bought from a reputable secondhand furniture dealer friend of

Jimmy's, at no small cost. It more than met with Betty's approval, but she wished it didn't, so that she could somehow share in her children's misfortune. Not that it would have done anyone any good. Jimmy had spent many hours dusting and cleaning prior to her inspection. In the living room there was a warm fire in the grate, a vase of white roses on the sideboard, a fully decorated Christmas tree and the smell of coffee coming from the scullery where he'd been busy brewing up as she looked round.

'What do you think?' he asked her.

'It's a palace compared to my place. I'd be daft to turn down the chance of living here until I get properly better.'

'Well, I've never thought you were daft, Betty. We can get a taxi back to your place later if you'd like to check your post and see if see if there's anything needs doing.'

'Well, there's probably stuff like bills to pay, but I think I can leave it all until after Christmas.'

'I'll help you with all that, Betty.'

'Thanks, but I think I've got enough money to cope … just. That redundancy payment from Blainey's helped a lot.'

'I know. I couldn't believe it came through so quickly. I reckon he's trying to keep us all on side to make it easier for him to cover up what he's done.'

'Yeah, I thought the same thing myself. Still, it's money we're entitled to, so I'll not feel guilty accepting it. God, I wish we could get the police to arrest him.'

'I rang that copper you told me about and I'm

meeting him after Christmas to tell him what I know.'

'How did he sound?'

'He definitely sounded interested. There's something else I've been meaning to tell you as well.'

'What's that?'

'Well, being blown up at work constitutes an industrial injury, no matter what caused it. A decent lawyer could claim thousands in compensation for you from Blainey.'

'I can't afford to pay a lawyer.'

'You might not need to. What about that solicitor who handled Jack's bequest to your son Billy? He might be able to help. Tell him what happened to you and, if he thinks you've got a good case, he might agree to take his pay out of whatever damages you win.'

'But Wooltorton can't be sure of winning,' said Betty.

'I know, but for him to win, would be a hell of a feather in his cap and do his reputation no harm at all, especially with the publicity it'll get, with it being you.'

'Blimey, Jimmy! I'm glad I've got you on my side. Thousands, do you say?'

'Well, if Blainey's done for blowing up his own factory he won't be paid any insurance money at all but there should still be enough money left for you to fleece him dry.'

'If he gets no insurance money, how can he pay me damages?'

'The land the factory's on will have a value and he'll have other assets such as the house he lives in.'

'You mean, we leave him with nothing?'

'Why not? When you're dangling on the end of a rope you're not too worried about your assets.'

Chapter 20

Christmas Day 1946

Billy and Peggy awoke in their respective bedrooms with no expectations at all. To them it was just another day. No Mam, no presents, just sunshine, which was a pretty good present in itself. Billy had thought they might go to the beach on their bikes before lunch. He looked at the silver pocket watch Peggy had passed on to him: 8.35. He knocked on her door.

'Peg!'

'What?'

'It's Christmas.'

The door opened and she stood there in the pyjamas she'd bought with her own money. If she was to live in someone else's home she needed to be able to walk about decently dressed at all times. Billy had done likewise, although he wasn't quite so bothered about how he looked.

'Billy, I know it's Christmas. So what?'

'So we've got Ross a present, maybe we should be there when he opens it.'

'Oh, all right.'

Under the tree were four parcels. One marked for Billy, two for Peggy and one for Ross. Peggy picked up her two, curiously. Ross had arrived downstairs, alerted by the noise his two guests were making.

He'd been lying in bed thinking about his own kids, back in England, who would have been awake for probably five hours by now, given the time difference. Well, they had their mom and all their old friends to pay them attention, which meant they were better off there than over here. He needed to keep telling himself this, and that his missing them was the price he must pay for their well-being, and that it was a price worth paying.

'Merry Christmas, you two,' he called out. 'And thanks for the present, whatever it is.'

'Hey, you don't thank us, you thank Father Christmas,' said Billy.

'He still believes, bless him,' said Peggy, 'and he'll never stop believing.'

'Good for Billy. I'm not sure I've actually stopped believing myself.'

Peggy picked up one parcel, which was obviously a book. It was the Hans Andersen volume she'd seen in the bookshop window. 'Hey, thanks, Santa,' she said to Ross.

Seconds later Billy was thanking Santa for a toy rifle. Peggy, wondering why she'd got two parcels, opened the second one. It contained a woman's watch, not new, not gold or silver, very pretty, but not in a box. Just wrapped in tissue paper. She looked at Billy.

'Is this from you?'

'No, it's from Santa.'

'Well, it's not from me,' said Ross, winking at Billy, 'so I guess it must be from Santa.'

He opened his own parcel under the watchful gaze of the children. It was a book of English music hall songs, complete with words and music.

'Hey, Santa, this is brilliant! You couldn't have given me anything better. I can use these in my cabaret act.'

Billy couldn't help but notice that his sister wasn't quite so delighted with her present from him as she might have been, so he decided he needed to get her on her own and talk to her.

'Ross, would you mind if me and Peggy took the bikes down to the beach for an hour?' he asked.

'Not at all. In fact, I was going to suggest it. The turkey doesn't need to go in the oven until around eleven o'clock so take two hours if you like, then it's all hands to the pumps to get the lunch ready.'

Peggy wasn't wearing her watch when they set off and Billy asked her why.

'Because it's not new. If it was it'd be in a box.'

'I know that. I couldn't afford a new one. The watch you passed on to me wasn't new.'

'That watch was stolen.'

'So?'

'Billy, have you been up to your old tricks again?'

'No. You can give me it back if you like and I can return it to the shop and get my money returned. They said I could if I kept the receipt.'

'So you've got a receipt?'

'Yep. If the watch is undamaged we can go to the shop and I can get my money back. I'm not lying to you, Peggy.'

'Maybe you stole some money and bought it with that.'

'When could I have done that? I've hardly been out of your sight since we came here. Peg, I bought it with the money we brought with us. My share of the money Ross changed into dollars for us.'

They cycled in silence until they reached the sea front. By now Billy was the more disgruntled of the two. They left their bikes and walked across the beach to the sea. The weather was warming up and the sun glinted off the breakers. People on the beach were wishing each other Merry Christmas as were bathers in the sea. It all seemed very strange to Billy, who found himself in tears. He took the silver pocket watch from his pocket and hurled it into the waves.

'That was stupid. What did you do that for?' said Peggy.

Billy wiped his eyes with his sleeve and sobbed, 'Because it was rotten!'

'Why was it rotten?'

'It's what stopped you trusting me. If you still think your watch is bought with stolen money you can throw it into the sea, but I'm telling you the truth! I bought it with my own money and you can talk to the man I bought it off. He'll remember me because I told him it was a Christmas present for my sister and he helped me choose it, with it being a girl's style.'

'I can't do that,' she protested.

'Oh, so you can accuse me of stealing it, but you can't do that? Peg, I haven't stolen anything since we left England. Why would I need to steal? We've still got loads of money and I don't like stealing. Mam wouldn't like it and it scares me every time I do it. I hope I never have to steal again.'

Tears tumbled down his cheeks almost as fast as the words left his lips, and Peggy had never taken him for a cry-baby. Her brother never cried without good reason. It seemed that her not believing him was good enough. Feeling guilty for causing him distress, she took the new watch from her pocket and, under Billy's tearful gaze, slipped it on to her wrist.

'Thanks, Billy,' she said. 'Thanks for my present and sorry for not believing you.'

She put her arm around his shoulders and squeezed him to her, making him feel uncomfortable.

'I'm okay now,' he said gruffly.

'I bet you're sorry you threw your watch into the sea. It was probably worth a hundred dollars.'

'I don't care if it was worth a million dollars. It's rotten what that watch did to us. I might tell lies when I have to, Peg, but I never lie to you. If you don't trust me, I might as well be on my own and I don't want that. With Mam being dead, you're all I've got left.'

'And you're all I've got, Billy, so I do trust you. Hey, I'm glad I didn't throw my Christmas watch into the sea. It's a lovely watch ... thank you.'

Chapter 21

It was an itchy leg that woke Betty that Christmas morning. Fortunately she needed no assistance to scratch it. The clock beside her bed told her it was ten-past eight, which meant she'd had a solid ten hours' sleep, the best night she'd had since the explosion and her first not spent in a hospital bed. There was a noise coming from the next room. Jimmy was singing 'God Rest Ye, Merry Gentlemen' along with the wireless, except he was singing the soldier's version: 'God Rest Ye, Gerry Mentalmen'.

His version made her smile, but the smile faded when her children came to mind. She squeezed her eyes shut, determined to put on a brave face for Jimmy, this day of all days. But a quick prayer would do no harm. She managed to kneel by the side of the bed, make the sign of the cross and put her hands together.

'Please Lord, keep my children from harm. Let them have a wonderful Christmas and return them to me soon and in good health. Keep them safe and warm and happy ... and tell them I'm alive.'

It was all she could do. Right now prayer was all she had, until Jimmy came up with something better. It seemed she was relying on him to perform a miracle and he was certainly giving it his best shot. He'd written out all the reasons why he thought the explosion had been planned and he'd had them typed out by woman from Blainey's typing pool, who had her own machine at home. He had also written out all the reasons why the evidence pointed directly to Lester Blainey as the perpetrator and no one else, giving means, method, opportunity and motive. It all looked very convincing to Jimmy. Only Blainey could be the culprit and it was ridiculous to blame the children and their fireworks. He intended giving this to Detective Sergeant Dunstan the day after Boxing Day when their meeting was to take place. Jimmy had also thought about giving a copy to the *Yorkshire Post*, to see if they dare print it. If not then he was sure one of the nationals that wasn't scared of fighting a libel action would publish the story. To him this was a form of guerrilla warfare: continually taking damaging pot shots at the enemy, to weaken him to the point where he couldn't take any more. He figured there was a limit to Blainey's resilience. He was also hoping that once the information was made public it might bring someone else out of the woodwork; someone to whom Blainey had been talking. Jimmy was pretty certain there was at least one person out there who could drop Blainey right in it, and he was hardly the charming type of man that such a person might feel they had to protect at all costs. Jimmy had thought this through in great detail, discussing it with Betty also, to give her hope that all would turn out well.

He wished her Merry Christmas as she came out of her room in her dressing gown and made for the scullery. 'I've put clean towels and decent soap and toothpaste out for you,' he added, as she passed him by.

'Thanks, Jimmy. And Merry Christmas to you.'

He'd looked briefly at her expression, to see if he could detect sadness in it, but saw nothing but a steely determination not to break down on Christmas Day. God, how he admired this woman – *loved* this woman was nearer to the truth. But he knew he couldn't burden her with his clumsy advances until he'd got her children back for her, and then she might not need him. In the meantime he'd do everything he could for her. It was the only way he knew of expressing his love, and he needed to do that.

Chapter 22

Miami, January 1947

Once Ross Junior and Maisie had gone back to England, Ross Senior had placed his bogus children in local schools. Billy had been assessed as qualifying to join a fifth grade class in a local elementary school, and Peggy had been given a place in Junior High. Their English accents weren't considered strange, as the real Ross and Maisie had been brought up in England.

In fact, the children were both looked upon as novelties at first. They soon settled in and made plenty of friends. The hardest part was answering to the names of Ross and Maisie Duggan. The lessons were strange at first, but both of them were bright enough to cope and even Billy realised the benefit this extra education would bring him.

'I bet I could pass my scholarship right now no trouble at all,' he boasted, after being given an A+ for his English work.

'What did you get for math?'

'You mean maths. It's a plural word really, which you'd know if you were any good at English.'

'Billy, we need to fit in. Here they say math. What did you get?'

'I got a C plus.'

'I got an A plus and a B for English.'

'All right, clever clogs. At least we're not dunces. Do you find it harder work than at home?'

'Not really. A bit different maybe. I just tell myself I'm still at Notre Dame but with new teachers and in a different class.'

'Are you taking music at your school?' Billy asked her.

'Yeah, I'm in the school choir. Why do you ask?'

'Because I think Ross'll want us in his act.'

'Doing what?' asked Peggy.

'What we did on the ship. Which means we become a permanent part of the company. Not sure we want that.'

'Well, it'll mean another school we'll have to get used to.'

This wasn't a problem for Peggy. 'At least,' she said, 'we'll be used to being Ross and Maisie when we get there. How do you feel about us joining him in his cabaret act?'

'Depends how much money they pay us.'

'Hey, I've worked out a good routine that'll fit

you into my act,' said Ross, who'd been listening at the door. 'We need to rehearse it with the band, though.'

'Have you been earwigging us?' said Billy.

'Yep. So what do you say. Are you in or not? You'll enjoy the experience.'

'We're in,' said Billy.

Chapter 23

One week later. Beachcomber Club, Miami … January 1947

Ross was playing the piano and singing British Music Hall songs. The audience were singing along enthusiastically, aided by the lyrics being projected on to a large screen on the stage.

Ross's piano was on the dance floor but no one was dancing. They preferred sitting at their tables and singing. There'd be a time for dancing when Rudy Vallee and his band came on. Ross came to the end of 'Down at the Old Bull and Bush', and swivelled round in his chair.

'Ladies and gentlemen,' he said. 'A young Englishman's applied for the job as my assistant, so I've brought him here to give him a try out. However he's very young and maybe a bit shy, so if you could put your hands together and show your appreciation for Banjo Billy Clegg!'

Billy came on carrying a banjo and dressed in bright lavender trousers. There was a single microphone set at his height in the centre of the dance floor with a second mike halfway down the stand to pick up his banjo playing. He gave a cheeky grin, waved to the audience and began to pick, expertly, at his banjo. The audience were impressed even before he opened his mouth to sing...

I know what you're lookin' at me for,

He gave the audience a challenging look before continuing...

Wotcha gotcha eyes on I can tell.
Oh it's this old pair of Lavender Trousers
Don't you wish you had a pair like them?
My grandfather gave them to me
So that I should look a toff
And he told me as long as ever I lived
I should never never take them off...

He had the audience laughing from beginning to end when Ross went over to him and asked, 'Is that it? Is that your act?'

Billy gave him a worried look. 'Er, yes, sir.'

'Well that was rubbish, wasn't it, ladies and gentlemen?'

'Noooo...!' came the response.

'This is a sophisticated club,' said Ross, shaking a finger at Billy, 'and you come on dressed like a clown in those trousers.'

The audience began to shout for more. Ross gave them a look of amazement, then turned to Billy.

'I don't believe this, they want more. Have you got any more?'

'Yes, I've brought me sister, Peggy.'

'Peggy. Where is she?'

Peggy walked out on to the stage in front of the stage curtain. She waved to the audience who waved back, highly amused at all this. Ross turned to look at her and asked Billy, 'What does she do?'

'She thinks she can sing.'

'And can she?'

'She's all right ... not as good as me.'

'I flippin' am,' called out Peggy. 'I can sing proper songs.'

'Such as,' asked Ross.

'Such as this.'

With that the curtain began to rise behind her, revealing the whole orchestra in place and playing the opening bars to *Stranger in the Night*. Ross waved them to a stop.

'Whoa, she can't sing that! It's one of Rudy Vallee's hit songs.'

Peggy and the band ignored him and Peggy began to sing.

Strangers in the night
Exchanging glances
Wondering in the night
What were the chances...

She had a beautiful voice and the audience loved her from the start. Even more so when she was halfway through the song and Rudee Vallee strode out alongside her and they sang it as a duet. Peggy was experienced enough to pick up on his voice

239

and harmonise with him. When the song came to an end, Rudy stood back and applauded her before turning to the audience, asking,

'Well, what do you think, folks? Shall we give these English kids a job?'

There was a resounding "yes" from the audience as Billy went up on stage to join his sister in a bow.

Back in the dressing room Rudy came in to talk to them. 'How long have you kids been doing this?'

'Just a few times on the ship coming over.'

'Really? Where did you learn harmony?' he asked Peggy.

'I used to sing in a choir. I find harmony quite easy.'

'A choir girl eh. That explains it. Look, can you do your act once a week on a Saturday night? You won't be kept here late.'

Billy was about to ask how much, but Peggy dug him in the ribs.

'I assume you've got more comic songs, young man?'

'Loads,' said Billy.

'In that case I'll give you a ten minute spot, for ten dollars.'

'Is that ten each?' asked Billy.

'It's ten for the act.'

Ross held out a hand. 'I'm their guardian, so it's a deal.'

After a while the act matured into Billy walking out on to the dance floor with his banjo, asking Ross for a job.

'What as?'

'I'm a musician.'

'What do you play?'

This was where Billy's natural comic timing came into play. He looked down at his banjo, than at Ross, then at the audience, then he did some expert banjo picking before saying,

'Trombone.'

'And is that your trombone?'

'Don't be daft. This isn't a trombone, this is me saxophone. One of the strings has broke on me trombone so I brought me saxophone.'

It was enough to endear the audience to his nonsense and to have them clapping when they realised he was an excellent banjo player and an amusing singer of comic songs. Peggy varied her song every night until she had a repertoire of twelve numbers to choose from. By the end of their time at the club they had a professional routine and had gained a lot of stage experience – and a raise to twenty dollars a night. It was good preparation for theatre work. Ross was happy with them and looked forward to the New York audition with growing confidence.

Chapter 24

Leeds, 29 January 1947

David Rosenhead looked through the classroom window and saw that it was snowing. Not just a light scattering but snowing more heavily than he'd ever known it do before. Later on, it would be recorded as the heaviest snowfall of the twentieth century. He was glad his mother had made him wear his wellies that morning as well as gloves, balaclava and a woollen scarf. He'd need them all for his walk home, which usually took no more than ten minutes but today would take nearer an hour, what with all the snowball fights and snowmen to build. Every child in the class had their eyes glued to the windows and there was a buzz of excitement in the room.

'Yes, it's snowing,' said the teacher, Miss Stephard, casting a disapproving glance outside, as if the snow was one more errant pupil. 'I hope you will all behave sensibly once you're out of school and go straight home. Snow can be very dangerous.'

'Yes, miss.'

The staggered response came from maybe twelve of the forty-four children in the class. The other thirty-two had plans to behave anything but sensibly and they included David, whose thoughts were on Billy Clegg, his best pal and someone with

242

whom he'd have had great fun in snow such as this. But Billy had not been seen since Mischief Night, over two months ago. Rumours abounded about the Clegg children. Some said they must have been kidnapped or even murdered and their bodies dumped in Roundhay Park Lake. Prayers had been offered at Billy's and Peggy's Catholic schools, just down the road from David's. A mass had been said for them and a reward of £100 offered by the *Yorkshire Evening Post* for information leading to them being found. But even this offer of ten weeks' good wages for most men had turned up nothing. Their mother had left hospital and was now a source of scurrilous gossip locally, what with her lodging with Jimmy Potter.

'Poor bairns! They haven't even got a home to come back to now, with her leavin' the house empty.'

'I know. What're the poor little beggars gonna think when they find she's not there?'

'She wants lockin' up does that damned woman!'

Betty Clegg wasn't there to hear those remarks but she knew what her busybody neighbours thought about her. She was a pretty war widow and the object of many a man's admiration, including some of the husbands who lived in the street, and this didn't sit too well with the wives, none of whom were admired half as much as Betty Clegg was.

Her own thoughts were of the children too, wondering how they could survive such awful weather. Billy especially was susceptible to colds in winter and this weather was as bad as she'd ever known it. She knew about the gossip and cared little for it, although anyone caught gossiping about her within her hearing would soon feel the sharp edge of her tongue. In an odd way, these angry exchanges helped her to survive, insofar as she felt she was fighting back against the cruel world that had done this to her. Betty's life was clouded by a deep sense of sadness. All she wanted was for her children to come home.

She and Jimmy were not in a romantic relationship, whatever the neighbours thought, but they were great friends. He had given Sergeant Dunstan a copy of his report illustrating why Blainey was the hot favourite to have set the explosion. The policeman had read it and had made no comment, but Jimmy knew that such persuasive evidence couldn't be ignored completely. The *Yorkshire Evening Post* declined to run his version of the story as did two nationals but at least Jimmy had alerted all three newspapers that Lester Blainey was an arsonist and killer and this was a real scoop, just waiting for someone to print it. All Jimmy needed now was a piece of concrete evidence to add credence to his theory.

In the pubs and hotels where he played piano he talked about the factory explosion to anyone who would listen, openly slandering Blainey but fearing no repercussions. For the factory owner to sue him would bring the whole story out into the open, and Blainey wouldn't want that if he was guilty. He'd want it talked about as little as possible, especially as his insurance claim had yet to be settled.

In fact, Lester Blainey was aware of the campaign Jimmy was waging against him, but felt confident there was no way anyone could prove him guilty. He had covered his tracks completely and received the unexpected bonus of being able to blame the children for the fire. But it was certainly inconvenient, having Potter air his opinions throughout the hostelries of the town. What he needed was to persuade Betty Clegg to call off her attack dog, and Blainey figured there was only one way to do that. It was why he knocked on Jimmy's front door the day after the snow started to fall. Jimmy answered the knock. He was about to fire off a stream of invective, but Blainey cut him off with: 'I don't think the children started the fire.'

It was still snowing heavily, as it had been all day. Blainey's cap and coat were already thickly encrusted in the time it had taken him to reach the house after parking his car outside a minute ago.

'What did you say?'

Blainey brushed away a snowflake that had landed on his nose. Had it been anyone else standing outside his house Jimmy would have invited him in, but not this bastard.

Undaunted, Blainey said, 'I believe I made a mistake in the heat of the moment.'

'And have you told the police that?'

'No. I want to have a word with Mrs Clegg before I do anything. I believe she's living here at the moment.'

'Yes, she is, but I doubt if she's in any mood to discuss anything with you.'

'I think what I have to say may be to our mutual advantage.'

Betty appeared behind Jimmy. 'In what way?' she said.

'I'd much prefer to come inside out of the snow rather than discuss this on the doorstep,' said Blainey.

'Oh, let him in, Jimmy. Let's hear what this liar has to say.'

'Thank you, but I'm not a liar, which is why I'm here.'

Blainey followed Jimmy and Betty through to the living room where he chose not to sit down. He took off his cap and stood facing the others, who had their arms folded in front of them ready for the confrontation.

'I'm aware,' said Blainey to Jimmy, 'that you've been telling people I started the fire deliberately, so as to make an insurance claim.'

'I've only been saying that because it's true.'

'Actually it's not. I have no idea what caused the explosion other than it was a gas leak, which had been reported to me a few minutes before the accident happened. I went down to the cellars to investigate and smelt the gas myself, which was why I went outside in a hurry. Since it was Mischief Night there were all sorts of sparks flying around from the fireworks the kids were setting off everywhere. I'm still of the opinion that a firework sparked off the explosion when it set fire to the leaking gas. In fact, a rocket came down just outside the factory door, still sparking, as I ran out. Your children, whom I saw, were much too far away for their fireworks to have caused it.'

'So why did you tell the police they were to blame?' demanded Betty.

'I have no reasonable answer for that, other than that the explosion and the sight of my ruined factory left me dazed and shocked ... not thinking straight. I saw your children playing with fireworks. I remembered the gas leak. I put two and two together and made five.'

'Right ... so you'll tell the police all this, will you?'

'I will, but I have a condition to make, and I suspect you know what that is.'

'Do we?' said Betty, looking at her companion.

'You want me to stop slagging you off,' said Jimmy.

'Exactly. You stop your campaign against me and I'll tell the police it was most probably a falling rocket set by a person or persons unknown that set off the factory explosion. There's no way I would endanger the lives of all those women just for an insurance claim. It shocks me deeply that anyone would think me capable of such a thing.'

'And I suppose this version of events would clear the way for your claim to be settled,' said Jimmy.

'Of course. That's why we paid the premiums for so many years, after all. I have a second condition that you may receive more favourably.'

'What's that?'

'As and when my insurance claim goes through, I'll give Mrs Clegg one thousand pounds to cover the injury and loss she has suffered.'

'Sounds like a bribe so I'll keep my mouth shut,' said Jimmy.

'Call it what you like. I'll give you it in writing

if you like.'

'And you'll definitely tell the police you don't think it was my children who caused the explosion?' Betty intervened.

'I will, and I think they'll take my word for it in view of the doubt that's being cast on the cause of the explosion. Your children are being blamed because a lot of people died, the police need a result and there's no one else to hang the blame on.'

'Do you honestly believe my children aren't to blame?'

'Yes, I honestly believe that, Mrs Clegg.'

Betty looked at Jimmy, who wasn't at all convinced about any of this. 'What do you think?' she asked him.

'It's really up to you, Betty. I'll only stop slagging him off if you ask me to.'

'I think I want you to.'

'How do we know you'll give her the money?' said Jimmy.

'We can do it legally if you like,' offered Blainey. 'I'll set a solicitor on to drawing up an agreement. We can read it together and I'll sign and have it witnessed in front of you. So ... do we have an agreement?'

'We do,' said Betty. 'But we'd like to come with you when you tell the police it wasn't my children's fault. Can we do this tomorrow?'

'We can do the whole thing tomorrow if you like, Mrs Clegg. First the solicitor and then the police, although you'll have to wait for the insurance claim to come through before you get your money. Our legal contract should reassure you that the one thousand pounds will be paid in time.'

'It's you telling the police the truth about the children that's the most important thing to me,' said Betty.

'That's not to say she'll let you off paying the money,' added Jimmy. 'Betty needs it to help her turn her life around.'

Chapter 25

Heavy snow was still falling the next day when Betty and Jimmy trudged up the Headrow towards the solicitor's offices in Park Square. Both of them were wearing wellingtons to keep the slush off their legs. Blainey was outside the door to the office when they arrived. He was stamping his feet to keep them warm.

'Is this the place?' called out Jimmy.

'It is, see the plate.'

'Cooke and Richardson,' read Betty, after wiping the snow off a brass nameplate fixed to the wall.

'Which one are we going to see?'

'Mr Richardson,' said Blainey. 'He's been our company solicitor for years.'

Inside the building they shook the snow off their garments on to the floor of a reception hall and were shown into a spacious office in which Mr Richardson waited. He was a bald, portly man in his fifties, sitting behind a desk cluttered with files, papers and two telephones. He got to his feet and bade them all sit down. A woman had followed them through, holding a secretary's notepad. Her hair was worn in a bun and she was severely clad in a two-piece business suit. Betty decided on sight she didn't like her.

'This is Mrs Maureen Henderson,' explained Richardson. 'She'll be taking notes and will type up any documents we require.'

Betty and Jimmy nodded at the secretary, who gave them both a bleak smile and sat down facing them.

'So,' said Richardson, settling himself behind the desk again and eyeing his female visitor. 'I assume you're Elizabeth Clegg?'

'I am, yes, though most people call me Betty.'

She was slightly nervous to find herself before such an important professional man.

Richardson gave her a benevolent smile. 'Then I shall call you Betty. Now I understand this meeting is to confirm that a payment of one thousand pounds will be made to you by Mr Blainey when he receives payment for the factory fire from his insurers.' He then turned his attention to Jimmy.

'And I assume you are James Potter?'

'That's right. People call me Jimmy.'

'And the other part of this agreement is that, in exchange for Mrs Clegg being paid one thousand pounds, you will refrain from slandering Mr Blainey with accusations that he caused the incident, providing he goes to the police and tells them that he made a mistake in accusing Mrs Clegg's children of starting the explosion with their fireworks.'

'That's correct, yes.'

'I asked you to confirm that, as it's this part of

the agreement that gives rise to concern.'

'It's been giving Betty concern since the fire,' said Jimmy.

Mrs Henderson was taking down every word in shorthand. Richardson asked her to read back what she'd written. She did so, absolutely verbatim, including the last remark by Jimmy.

'Excellent,' said the lawyer to Jimmy. 'So, you've told Mr Blainey that you'll stop slandering him in exchange for one thousand pounds paid to Mrs Clegg?'

'Yes,' said Jimmy, feeling slightly uncomfortable by now.

Richardson looked at Betty again. 'And you concur with this?'

'What?'

'Do you confirm that what Mr Potter says is why we're here today?'

'Oh, yes.'

Richardson looked at Maureen Henderson. 'And you're a witness to these statements, Mrs Henderson?'

'I am indeed.'

She duly recorded this latest question and her own answer. Richardson returned his attention to Betty and Jimmy. 'You see, as an officer of the court, I cannot condone such an agreement. When I introduced this lady as Maureen Henderson, I omitted to mention that she is in fact a police-woman – a detective constable – brought here to witness the fact that you're attempting to black-mail Mr Blainey out of a thousand pounds.'

Jimmy and Betty froze in horror at such an accusation. It was plain that Betty would be getting no

251

money now and nor would her children be exonerated by Blainey.

'It was his idea, not ours!' she protested. 'We just went along with the suggestion.'

'That's right,' said Jimmy. 'He's trying to screw us, just as he's trying to screw his insurance company. We didn't ask him for money. He came round to my house and offered it, and a thousand pounds is too much for Betty to turn down. Her children are missing since the fire and she's not long out of hospital.'

'I think that is for the courts to decide,' said Richardson, looking at the policewoman, who nodded and got her feet, first addressing Betty.

'Elizabeth Clegg, I am arresting you for attempting to extort money by the use of threats. You are not obliged to say anything unless you wish to do so, but whatever you say may be given in evidence against you.'

She turned to Jimmy and repeated the caution to him. Betty looked at Richardson, who had picked up a telephone. He dialled a number, spoke for a few seconds and handed the receiver to Henderson, who spoke into it.

'Yes, I've cautioned then both, Sarge. I need a car to bring them in ... thanks.'

Jimmy looked at Richardson with blazing eyes. 'When I prove I'm right about this murdering bastard, I'll make your name stink to high heaven. You're no better than he is. In fact, I reckon you must be in this insurance scam with him. He does the dirty work, you make sure the law doesn't catch up with him.'

As Jimmy spoke Betty spotted a fleeting expression of concern on Richardson's face. It gave her the courage to speak out with a calm that belied this worrying situation.

'He's right, isn't he, Mr Richardson?' she said, quietly.

Twenty-four hours later they were both released on bail, just in time to catch the first edition of the *Yorkshire Evening Post*, where they were headline news. A copy lay on the doormat as they entered Jimmy's house.

'Bloody hell! This is all we need. As if the gossips haven't already got enough ammunition to make my life miserable. Why did we fall for that, Jimmy?'

'I could give you a thousand reasons, Betty. He offered you three years' wages in your hand. He knew a woman in your position wouldn't be able to turn that money down. It's how these people get away with the harm they do.'

'I should have known it was too good to be true. What do we do now?'

'I think I'd like a word with Detective Sergeant Dunstan, to put him fully in the picture.'

'I imagine he'll already be fully in the picture,' said Betty.

'No, he won't. He'll only have Blainey's version, and he doesn't trust Blainey any more than we do.'

'I wonder if Dunstan has any doubts about Richardson? I do. When you told him you thought he was in it with Blainey, you really shook him.'

'It'll do no harm to ask. It could be Richardson's got himself involved in something he wishes he'd kept clear of.'

'Jimmy, I'm frightened to go back to my own house for fear of the neighbours and what they might be saying. It wouldn't surprise me if one of them's put a brick through my window.'

'Tell you what, Betty, I'll go over there and have a look round. If I see any neighbours, I'll set them straight about Blainey and what he's done to you.'

'They won't believe you.'

'Maybe not, but at least I'll give them something a lot more juicy to gossip about. The truth's a much better story than the rubbish they're talking, and if any damage has been done to your house I'll find out who did it and report it to Detective Sergeant Dunstan.'

'How will you find out?'

Jimmy tapped his nose with his forefinger and grinned. 'Well, you see, I have an informant in your street who's definitely on our side.'

Curtains twitched and doors opened a crack as Jimmy went into Betty's back yard. The lower back window was indeed broken as she had feared. As he opened the door a voice from behind him called out, 'Are you her fancy man?'

Jimmy turned around. A woman's head and shoulders were just visible above the back gate. He walked over to her, inviting confrontation, something nosy people like her didn't like.

'What do mean by that?' he challenged her.

'Yer know very well what I mean. If yer not her fancy man, how come yer've a key to her house?'

'It's not her house,' said Jimmy. 'It's Mr Murgatroyd's house, her landlord – and he owns every other house in this street. And she's up-to-date with her rent, which is more than I can say for some. What number do you live at?'

He'd made it seem as if he represented the landlord, which put her on her guard. It would certainly explain his having a key. She chose not to answer his question.

'I suppose yer know her kids are missing and she doesn't give a bugger?'

'Doesn't she? You've spoken to her about her children, have you?'

It was a question to which the woman had no answer. Jimmy knew she wouldn't. 'She's an innocent victim of a man called Lester Blainey,' he said, 'and after the factory blast that badly injured her, what Betty needed most was friendship and support. Did you, or anyone in this street, visit her in hospital?'

Her answer was a stuttered, 'I ... I ... I don't know.'

'Of course you don't. You only know what the other gossiping witches tell you. Well, I'm telling you the truth. Betty Clegg hasn't deserted her children. She's deserted this street because she knows it's full of evil crones like you, who only see the worst in people.'

'I'm not like that!'

'Then why did you tell me she doesn't give a bugger about her missing children, which is a wicked lie? She's in a right state about them.'

'Mrs Rosenhead's been to see her,' the woman said, sheepishly.

'That'll be Mrs Rosenhead from number eleven,' he said, remembering David's address

255

and thereby confirming in the woman's opinion that he knew enough for him to be from the landlord.

'Yes.'

Jimmy wagged his finger. 'So, just one friend in the whole street? That's disgraceful, don't you think? Where I live the neighbours are friendly people who help each other in hard times. I see her window's broken and it wouldn't surprise me to find a brick inside. If that's the case, I'll report it to the police and they'll question everyone in the street to find out who did it. Unless you're willing to tell me who it was.'

'How would I know?' She said it too guardedly.

'Because I think it was probably you. You were the first one to turn up and bad mouth her, so you're the hot favourite. Landlords don't like tenants who chuck bricks through their neighbour's windows.'

'You can't prove that.'

'Not sure I have to. My advice to you is to bring your rent up-to-date.'

The woman paled slightly, spun on her heel and marched off down the street. Jimmy stepped out through the gate to check which back yard she went into. She saw him do this.

'I know where you live,' he called out.

He went inside Betty's house and picked up the few letters that had come through the door. He then looked at the broken glass and wondered if he should tidy it up. No, it'd do no harm to let the police look at it first. Instead he pulled out a tape-measure and took measurements to make the window secure. He'd only repair it with plywood, not with glass that might get broken again. After that he'd tell DS Dunstan what had been happening, along with his new suspicions about Blainey. Then he went down the street to number eleven and knocked on the door. It was David who answered.

'Hiya, David. I've actually come to speak to your mother about a broken window at Mrs Clegg's.'

'It weren't me mam who broke it!'

'I know that, David, but I thought she might know who did.'

'She doesn't.'

'Oh, erm ... what about you then? Do you know? I could stop them damaging it again if you told me.'

'It were Mrs Newton at number seventeen. I know because I saw her do it.' He confirmed it was the woman Jimmy had just been talking to.

'Did she see you?'

'No.'

'That's good, because she won't know it was you who told on her.'

'Doesn't bother me. She's a right old witch.'

'And you haven't told your mother it was her?'

'No. Me mam'd kick up a right fuss and the police'd want ter speak ter me.'

'Would that be bad?'

'It might be. I nicked some scrap iron what had been blown up in that explosion.'

'So what? I don't suppose they'll be bothered about a bit of scrap.'

'The day after I found it, the police stuck notices up warning people that it was a crime scene and not to take anything away. But that was after I'd picked up the scrap.'

'They'll have done that because it was a gas explosion and they'd want to find out why.'

'Oh, heck,' said David, gloomily.

'Why do you say that?'

'Well, this massive spanner what I found had a nut stuck in it and I thought it might have had something to do with gas. It smells like it anyroad, if you hold it right up ter yer nose.'

'Have you still got it?'

'Yeah, it's down in t'coal cellar. D'yer want me ter get it?'

'Please. I could take it off your hands if you like.'

'Happen I would.'

With that, David went back into the house and returned two minutes later with the large spanner attached to an equally large nut. Without taking them from the boy Jimmy bent down and sniffed.

'D'yer know what it is?'

'Yes, David. I know exactly what it is, and it's a good job you found this and not the police, because to them it would have been just another piece of scrap metal.'

'What is it, then?'

'Oh, probably nothing, but maybe ... just maybe it's something very important. What I need to do is to carry it away in something so my fingerprints aren't on it.'

'It'll have my fingerprints on it. Will I get into trouble?'

'No, David. I can assure you that you won't. Quite the opposite.'

'There's a cardboard box in our cellar what it'll fit in.'

'That could be the very thing, David.'

Chapter 26

'I wish to speak to Detective Sergeant Dunstan on a matter of great importance.'

'And who shall I tell him wants to see him?'

'My name is Potter, James Potter. He'll know what it's in connection with.'

'Yes, I think we all know what it's in connection with, Mr Potter.'

'How would you know?'

'Your reputation precedes you with regards to your slander of Mr Blainey.'

'Slander, my eye!' said Jimmy heatedly. 'If it was slander he'd have reported it officially and you'd have charged me with it before now. Have the police ever wondered why Blainey hasn't made an official complaint? It's because he's frightened that the truth will out. All you have is second-hand hearsay.'

The desk officer rolled his eyes. The intelligence of Jimmy's words belied his appearance.

'I'll get Sergeant Dunstan for you.'

Dunstan arrived within a few minutes and took the place of the desk sergeant.

'What can I do for you, Mr Potter?'

Jimmy hoisted the cardboard box onto the desk. 'There's something in here that might well solve the mystery of the fire at Blainey's.'

'Oh, yes, what is it then?'

'A spanner and a nut.'

Dunstan leant over the counter and whispered, 'Jimmy, are you drunk?'

'Sober as the judge I hope will soon be trying that murdering bastard Lester Blainey!'

'You'd better explain yourself here.'

Jimmy shook out the spanner onto the desk. It was still attached to the nut. 'I'm trying not to put my prints on this, Sergeant. It already has the prints of the boy who found it in the ruins of Blainey's factory, plus those of the last person to handle it before then.'

'There were notices put up outside that factory informing the public that nothing must be taken away.'

'I'm aware of that, but the notices went up the day *after* this was found.'

'You found it, did you?'

'No, it was found by a young lad looking for scrap metal to sell.'

'Go on.'

'Well, as you know, I was a handyman at the factory and I spent a lot of time in the cellars, which is why I know exactly where this came from. I now have a good idea what started the gas leak.'

'And what was that?'

'This spanner. You see, the nut that's jammed into it is a locking nut that tightens a joint between two-inch-diameter gas supply pipes. It's vitally important that the nut be tightened to a point where the joint is completely sealed and no gas could ever leak out. You can check this with the North Eastern Gas Board. They'll confirm it. As you can see from the size of the spanner it takes a lot of leverage to screw down the nut on to a gasket until the joint is completely sealed. I can tell by the size of it that this nut belongs to a two-inch supply pipe. After the gas goes through the meter it divides into several smaller pipes. The NEGB regularly check all their supply-pipe joints and they're the only people to tighten them up because until the incoming gas is registered at the gas meter, it belongs to them.'

'So?' asked Dunstan.

'So there's no reason for a spanner ever to be left jammed onto a nut. The very fact that it was attached to the nut at the time of the explosion tells its own story. It means whoever was using the spanner left it there in a hurry, which you would if you were deliberately causing a gas leak so as to blow up the factory.

'I've checked with the man at the NEGB, who I know well, and he agrees that there is no reason whatsoever for any of their lads to have left a spanner like this.' Jimmy paused and looked Dunstan in the eye, then he said, 'We both know I've got my suspicions about Lester Blainey. If this spanner has his prints on it, it'll prove he used it to loosen the nut sufficiently for the gas to escape and build up to a point where it would catch a random spark and explode ... only I doubt it caught a random spark because Blainey wouldn't want to leave his plan to chance. I reckon he left a naked flame somewhere far enough away from the leak to allow him to get himself out of the place before it went

261

up, and he was definitely in the vicinity at the time of the explosion. I saw him there myself.'

'So, you think this spanner will have Blainey's prints on it?'

'I think whoever's prints they are belong to the person responsible for the explosion and I reckon that was Blainey. I believe he had to hammer the spanner onto the nut, with its being too tight a fit. I know the gas board lads had to do that sometimes. Once it was jammed onto the nut, with him being in a rush, he couldn't get the spanner off in time to take with him.'

'Okay, Jimmy,' said the detective sergeant, looking thoughtfully at the nut and spanner. 'I'll take these to forensics and follow it up. We'll need to be taking prints off the boy who found it, and Mr Blainey too.'

'I wouldn't tell Blainey why, if I were you.'

'Jimmy, I'm not an idiot. I'll tell him it's routine. Right, who's this boy and where does he live?'

'If it's all right by you, I'll bring him in myself. He's a bit nervous of the police.'

'Does he have reason to be?'

'I wouldn't have thought so.'

'Okay, give me a few days to get the forensics checked and bring him in this time the day after tomorrow when I'm back on shift.'

'Mrs Rosenhead?'

'Yes.'

'Ah, my name's Jimmy Potter. Has your son David mentioned me at all?'

'Not that I remember. What about?'

'Is he in now?'

262

Mrs Rosenhead turned round and shouted.

'David! It's a man wants ter talk to yer. I hope yer've not been up ter nowt stupid!'

He arrived behind his mother. His eyes widened in worry when he saw Jimmy.

'It's okay, David. If anything I've brought good news. May I come in, Mrs Rosenhead?'

'I think yer'd better.'

Jimmy walked into an untidy back room. As in Betty's house, the front room was kept for best. This room was for living in. It had a Yorkshire Range fireplace set with a good fire, a dining table and four chairs and a three-piece suite. The result was a cramped but lived-in room. The wireless was playing big band music which Mrs Rosenhead switched off before turning to face Jimmy with her arms folded, almost belligerently.

'Right, what's this good news yer might have fer us?'

Jimmy could see why David hadn't told his mother about his part in the factory fire. In fact, Jimmy was nerving himself up to break the news.

'It's to do with the factory fire, Mrs Rosenhead.'

'What about it?'

'Well, I assume you know Mrs Clegg survived the explosion?'

'Yes, I've been ter visit her. It were a while before we found out, though. I ought ter go see her more often but I've been a bit busy. I'm on me own, yer know, after my husband never came back from the war. I have a couple of little jobs ter keep us goin' but it's probably no excuse fer me not visitin' Betty so often. She's a good woman, yer see.'

'I do know that, Mrs Rosenhead, and I wish

263

more people up this street knew her better. I think she'd enjoy a visit from you. In fact, she's living with me at the moment while she convalesces.'

'Is she now?'

Jimmy spotted the unspoken inference in her words. 'Yes. It's all perfectly proper, Mrs Rosenhead. She's unable to cope on her own, much less earn the money to pay rent.'

'I see. So what's this got ter do with our David?'

'It's to do with a piece of scrap metal he found in the ruins of the factory.'

'My God! He's not in trouble over a piece o' soddin' scrap, is he?'

Jimmy grinned. 'On the contrary, Mrs Rosenhead. It's this soddin' scrap that might solve the riddle of how the fire started. But the police want to know exactly where David found it.'

'I told yer where I found it,' blurted the lad, who didn't like the direction this was going.

'I know you did, David, but the police want to hear you tell them.'

'Why's that?'

Jimmy looked at the woman and said, 'Because a man's future rests on what the police may find on a spanner picked up by your lad.'

'What are they looking for?'

'Fingerprints, Mrs Rosenhead. It might well have on it the fingerprints of the person who started the factory fire, and if that's the case the Clegg children will be declared innocent of any involvement in it. That's good news, isn't it, David?'

He did indeed think it was good news, for him as well as his two pals. In fact, he thought this an ideal time for him to come clean about being there along with Billy and Peggy. He looked up at his mother.

'I was with 'em, Mam,' he said, quietly.

'With who, where?'

'With Billy and Peggy when the factory went up. I'd set off a rocket just before it blew up.'

'Oh my God! And yer've kept it quiet all this time. Yer flamin' little monkey! Why didn't yer tell me?'

''Cos I knew yer'd go mad.'

''Course I'd go mad. This means the police want you an' all.'

'Mrs Rosenhead,' said Jimmy. 'All the police want is for David to tell them where he found the spanner. It's very likely that the evidence they've got so far will exonerate all three of the children and put the blame fairly and squarely on the man responsible.'

'I bet that were Blainey!'

'You'd win your bet, Mrs Rosenhead,' said Jimmy, who saw no reason to defend the arsonist's reputation.

'Mr Blainey were there, Mam. We saw him running away from the explosion. That's when he blamed us for the fire. He told us Mrs Clegg were caught inside, but he didn't seem all that worried.'

'You should tell the police that as well,' said Jimmy.

Chapter 27

Three days later

It was against DS Dunstan's better judgement that he allowed Jimmy to accompany him to Lester Blainey's home. There were also two uniformed constables. Dunstan knocked on the door. Jimmy stood at the back of the group, having been told not to interfere in any way.

Blainey didn't notice him at first when he opened the door. Jimmy put this right by waving and calling out, 'They've come to arrest you, yer murderin' bastard!'

His remark had Dunstan cursing under his breath but he controlled his anger enough to say, 'Lester Blainey, I'm arresting you for murder and arson. You do not have to say anything, but anything you do say may be taken down and used in evidence against you.'

Blainey visibly blanched. His mouth opened and closed, but no words came out. The only words spoken came from Jimmy, who was determined to revel in this murderer's downfall.

'Ten dead thanks to you, but not to worry, Lester lad, they can only hang yer once. No insurance money fer you, just the wrong end of a noose.'

'For God's sake, shut up, Jimmy!' snapped Dunstan.

'Sorry,' he said, 'but I hope yer'll be paying a visit ter that bent solicitor of his an' all. Him and Richardson set me and Betty up fer blackmail. Ask him! Go on, ask him if Richardson was in for a share of the insurance.'

'Jimmy! Just shut up and let me do my job, or I'll have you banged up for the night!'

'Bloody hell! It's me that's done the job for you up to now.'

Dunstan held up an index finger and wagged it at him. 'One more word, Jimmy ... one more bloody word and I'll arrest you for obstructing the police in the course of their duty.'

'Oh, just shut up, Jimmy,' murmured one of the constables.

It was 7.30 in the evening and Jimmy had just walked in through the door. Betty was sitting in a fireside chair, as she had been most of the day.

'Jimmy, where the hell were you? I've been on my own and it's been a damned struggle, I can tell you!'

'I'm sorry, Betty. Have you eaten?'

'Yes. I managed to boil myself a couple of eggs, but that's all.'

'Okay. I'll go to the chippy.'

'Where've you been? You've been really secretive these last few days. If you've got another woman in tow, you don't have to hide her from me, you know.'

'Don't I?'

''Course not. Is that what it is?'

'No, it's not what it is.'

There was relief in Betty's eyes, which he failed

to notice.

'If you must know, I don't want another woman. I've had some … er … business to attend to and I didn't want to tell you about it until it was settled.'

'What business?'

'Well, it's to do with the fire. Lester Blainey's been arrested for starting it and he'll have the devil's own job getting out of it.'

Her eyes lit up. 'Honestly?'

'Absolutely. He's banged up in the Town Hall Bridewell even as we speak. You should have seen the look on his face when Dunstan arrested him. In fact, he wasn't so pleased when I told him he'd hang for ten murders an' all. Dunstan wasn't pleased with me about that. He threatened to arrest me. Me … who did all the work! So we've no need to be worrying about this blackmail rubbish. Dunstan's going to have a word with Richardson and it's my guess that Blainey'll drop him right in it. No honour among thieves and all that.'

'And you had something to do with this, did you?'

Jimmy grinned and nodded. 'Betty, I had everything to do with it, which'll make Blainey as mad as hell when he hears the whole story. He'll wish he never tried to set us up. It was me who found the evidence that's got him locked up and I doubt if anyone else would even have known what it was.'

'What was it then?'

'Well, I tell a lie, it was actually young David Rosenhead who found it.'

'Found what?'

'A big spanner with a nut wedged in it.' Jimmy explained the significance of this and how he'd been able to identify the spanner and pipe as belonging to the gas board. 'But they'd never have left a spanner attached to a nut like that. No one would unless they'd been trying to cause a leak ... and that person's fingerprints would still be on the spanner. Guess whose prints they were?'

'So all them people dying was Blainey's doing?'

'Yes, for the insurance money, like we always thought. He very nearly got you ... and me as well.'

'And my kids have nothing to worry about?'

'Nothing to do with them, and they'll know that when they read about it in the papers, which I reckon they soon will.'

'We need to tell the papers to make it clear that I got out alive. Then the kids'll want to come home to me.'

'I'm sure we can do that.'

'Bloody hell, Jimmy! And this is why you've been sneaking around very quietly for the past few days?'

'I wanted everything to be in place before I got your hopes up.'

'Well, you've got my hopes up now, Jimmy Potter. Come here and give me a kiss.'

Jimmy obliged, but it was the polite kiss of a gentleman, not a lover. He didn't want to push things. To Betty there was warmth in his gentle kiss; a lover's warmth that had been missing from her life for a long time.

'I'll get us some fish and chips, shall I?' he said.

'Can you manage to put the kettle on?'

'Jimmy, right now I think I can manage any-thing.'

Detective Chief Superintendent Jean Blainey watched through her office window as her hand-cuffed brother was brought out of a police car and taken inside the station to the floor below. Al-though she wasn't her brother's keeper, she knew this would put a complete block on any ambitions she had for future promotion.

'You brainless bastard, Lester!' she muttered. 'You're going to hang, and if you expect any more help from me, you can forget it.'

Chapter 28

Richmond, Virginia, March 1947

Billy and Peggy, as the bogus 'Ross' and 'Maisie', had left their respective schools and were on the thirteen-hundred-mile train journey from Miami to New York. This would take two and a half days, allowing for prolonged halts in Jacksonville and Richmond. Billy and Peggy took advantage of both stops to explore these Southern towns. What fascinated Billy most were the American cars he saw parked in the city streets. His favourite was the huge 1930s Buick he saw just outside the train station in Richmond. It had a black bonnet, or 'hood' as Ross would correct him later, and a maroon roof, wide running-boards and twin head-lamps that looked as if they could light up the whole town. Billy tried the driver's door but it was locked. All he'd wanted to do was sit behind the steering wheel, but that wasn't what the car's owner thought. He collared the boy as he was walking away from it.

'Tryin' to steal my car, were yer, kid?'

'I wasn't, mister, honest! I can't even drive. I'm only eleven. I wanted to sit inside, that's all. Never seen a car as big as that before.'

'We're actually travelling to New York on the train,' called out Peggy.

The man picked up on their accents. 'Say, you two. Where're you from?'

'England,' said Billy. 'Our dad was killed in the war fighting the Germans.'

Their father was far more use to them in death than he had ever been while alive. The man looked as if he was reconsidering his attitude.

'Brother and sister, huh?'

'That's right.'

'Hey, I fought in Germany myself. Whereabouts in England?'

'Leeds,' said Billy, assuming that the man wouldn't know much about this northern city.

'Hey, I know Leeds. They had an ordnance factory there we were sent to visit. I was a tank driver myself.'

'Yeah, they made tanks at Barnbow.'

'Absolutely right. They fitted seventeen-pounder guns to our Shermans, which is what I was sent to see and advise upon.'

'They made Centurions as well,' said Billy,

271

who'd been told that by a boy at school whose dad had worked on them.

'Yeah, I saw one of those being built. Too late to take part in the war, though. Great tank, so it was a shame.'

The accusation of car theft seemed to have been shelved thanks to this mutual interest in tanks.

'Would you like to have a spin in the car?' asked the man.

'We've been told never to ride in a car belonging to someone we don't know,' said Peggy, to Billy's disappointment.

'Now that makes a whole lotta sense. I guess you British kids are taught how to stay safe, whereas our kids over here have never had to live with all the bombing and stuff that went on over there.'

Billy almost told him that Leeds didn't get bombed much, but that wouldn't win him much sympathy; better to be a gallant victim of German bombing.

'Yeah,' he said. 'We had to take a gas mask everywhere we went, even to school.'

'Well, I sure did admire your British stoicism back then. Look, if you wanna to sit behind the wheel, be my guest, son.'

Peggy frowned. Billy's eyes lit up.

'Can I?' he said.

'Sure thing.'

The man took a key from his pocket and opened the car door. 'Climb in, son.'

Peggy stood guard as Billy climbed into the driver's seat. He could barely see over the steering wheel, which he clutched with both hands while he made the engine noise of a car changing up

272

and down through the gears. The man grinned. Peggy was embarrassed by what she thought was the childish behaviour of her brother. The man spoke to her.

'New York, eh? What's a couple of English kids doing going to New York? Not on your own, surely.'

'No, our ... our stepdad's with us.'

She decided there and then to take on the mantle of Maisie and hoped her brother was listening so he could pick up on it. He was.

'I'm Ross and she's Maisie,' Billy called out. 'We're going to New York to be in a Broadway show.'

Peggy frowned. Her brother had only spoken once but he'd already given out too much information. 'What sort of show?'

'It's called *Twist*,' said Billy, 'which is from a book by Charles Dickens. With it being an English thing and us being English, we get to play two of the kids in Fagin's gang.'

Peggy was standing behind the man, shaking her head and hoping Billy would get the message to pipe down. 'Our stepdad's playing Bill Sykes,' he added.

'Bill Sykes? I guess that's one of the lead parts.'

'It is,' said Peggy. 'But it's not proper Broadway,' she hastened to add. 'It's what they call an *off-Broadway* theatre.'

'I know about those places. But I heard that if it's a good show it's only one step away from the Great White Way, which is what some people call Broadway. Though I guess you know that.'

'Yes,' said Peggy. 'It's because it was the first

273

street in America to be lit by electric lights.'

'You got it, young lady.'

Billy was as impressed by his sister's knowledge of Broadway as she'd been by his of the tank factory in Leeds. He saw her gesturing with her head for him to get out of the car.

'Ross, we need to get back to the train,' she called out. 'We don't want it going without us.'

'You sure don't want that to happen,' said the man. 'Anyway, my name's Cliff Robinson and I hope you have a good journey. Tell your stepdad I wish him every success. The next time I'm in New York, I'll look out for your show and come see you. So if you hear there's a guy at the stage door called Cliff Robinson who wants to see the stars, you'll know it's me.'

'We will! Bye, Cliff,' they both called out.

'What's stoicism?' asked Billy as they walked back to the train.

'I think it's what you need to help you cope when you've got a lot of problems, such as being bombed and stuff.'

'Or your mam dying in a factory fire what wasn't your fault, although everyone most prob'ly thinks it was.'

'Yeah.'

'Do you think we'll cope in New York?' Billy asked her.

'Don't see why not.'

'I reckon we'd cope a lot better if our mam was still alive. D'yer think she might be?'

'Billy, I think it's our duty to think she might be. I'm not sure I trust what Goldie told us about

274

her. I bet he only said that so we'd give up hope and stay with him and his granddad.'

'The rotten bugger!' said Billy. 'If that's true, I'm glad he's dead.'

'You mustn't swear, Billy. And why did you tell Cliff about our real dad?'

'To get him on our side. It worked as well. We'd have been in a real pickle if I'd been handed over to the police.'

Peggy gave his words some thought before she said, 'Blimey, Billy! For heaven's sake, think before you try anything stupid like that again. If the police get hold of either of us, we're absolutely done for. We've just had a near escape if you ask me. It should teach us both to be more careful in future.'

'Yeah, I know. Sorry, Peg.'

The next day, in Penn Station, New York, they followed Ross from the platform to the concourse and looked in amazement at the vaulted ceiling, a hundred and fifty feet above. From it was suspended a huge clock displaying Eastern Standard Time. They walked out onto 33rd Street and marvelled again at the dozens of Doric columns surrounding and supporting the whole station.

'Blimey!' said Billy. 'It's one of the wonders of the world.'

Ross smiled at the boy's enthusiasm. 'Well, it's a lot more wonderful than many of them, and yet there's talk of pulling it down and putting something more modern in its place.'

'Oh, that would be a terrible shame,' said Peggy.

'An act of vandalism, should it ever happen,'

Ross agreed. 'The New York philistines say it takes up too much space – and in this city you find a lot of philistines. People with more power than sensibility.'

'I thought America had a lot of space.'

'That's very true, Peggy – oops! Sorry, Maisie. We must remember who you are at all times, especially when we get to the theatre.'

'Are we far from it?' Billy asked.

'We're not actually far from anywhere right here – Central Park, Madison Square Garden, Empire State Building ... and the Cort Theatre, which is up on forty-eighth. Do you want to walk or take a cab?'

Billy and Peggy said 'walk' and 'cab' simultaneously, which made Ross smile. 'I think the young lady should take precedence in this case,' he said.

'So long as the young gentleman gets it next time,' said Billy.

'Right,' said Ross, 'we get a cab to the Cort and I've got an apartment arranged just two blocks away, so we can all walk there. That should make you both happy.'

Most of the cabs were yellow but Billy waved at a red and yellow De Soto because he liked the look of it. To his amazement the cab drew to a halt beside him. The boy looked up at Ross, seeking his approval or otherwise.

'Is this okay?'

'It had better be. You flagged him down – just like a real New Yorker.'

Billy failed to suppress a broad grin.

'Wow! Can I sit in the front then?'

'Why not? Look, when we get there you can

276

come in with me while I find out more about the auditions they're having for the kids' parts. They're expecting us today although the auditions are actually set for tomorrow, so maybe I can get you in before anyone else.'

'How many parts are there?' Peggy asked.

'Six.'

'How many girls' parts?'

'None, I think they're all boys' parts, but this is the theatre and you'll be auditioning for the part of a boy whose voice hasn't broken yet, which is much the case with all the boys' parts.'

'What about my hair?'

'Least of our worries. They'll cut it much shorter, that's all, and dress you in boy's clothes. Probably some sort of baker boy cap, I should think. You don't have a problem with that, do you? On the other hand, who's to say that Fagin didn't have a girl or two in his gang of thieves? It's only *based* on Dickens' book, they're allowed to use what they call artistic licence.'

Chapter 29

Both Billy and Peggy were successful in their auditions that day, although they were very nervous to be reading out the lines they'd been given on a real theatre stage, with the director and the scriptwriter watching, with critical eyes, from the front stalls.

Billy was more adept than Peggy at the cockney accent, but it was plain that she was English and not an American putting on an English accent. They stood there in apprehension after acting out their pieces, awaiting a reaction from the director, who said, 'Yeah, they've got real British accents, and they know how to deliver lines, and they got good timing. Where'd they learn that?'

'I do a cabaret act that they're a part of,' explained Ross. 'They're both used to performing in front of audiences.'

'Well, if they can perform in front of a cabaret crowd, they'll be able to perform in front of a theatre audience. Yeah, I guess we'll take them.'

'Thanks, mister,' called out Billy, with a broad smile on his face.

'You're welcome, son. In fact I'm wondering if you might be right for the part of the Artful Dodger.' The director turned to the scriptwriter.

'What d'you think, Henry?'

'I was thinking the same thing myself. He's certainly got a sassy way about him.'

'He's got that and no mistake. Okay, kid. I want you here tomorrow to audition for the part of the Artful Dodger. You'll need to pick up a casting script from the office.'

'Thanks, mister. By the way, my sister's got a great singing voice if you need someone to be Nancy.'

The director laughed. 'I believe you, son, but your sister's at least ten years too young to play Nancy.'

'Oh,' said Billy. 'Sorry.'

'Don't be sorry, son. It's good to know that your sister can sing. We need to know everything about our company. Maybe we can use her singing, maybe not, but it's there if we need it.'

'And my dad can play the piano.'

'Yeah, we already know that.'

'And I can play the banjo.'

'Ross!' called out Ross Senior from the wings in a loud whisper. 'They don't need a banjo player and they don't need a juggler either.'

'Oh,' said Billy, who was going to mention that he could juggle with four balls. This exchange amused the two men, who had already taken a liking to the kid.

Happy with the auditions, Ross and the children left the theatre carrying their suitcases and turned right down West 48th Street in the direction of 6th Avenue, where they turned left and headed south towards the block housing their apartment. Billy was mesmerised by the size of both the cars and the buildings all around him.

The footpaths, or sidewalks, as Ross corrected him, were wider than many of the roads in Leeds and the cast iron lamp posts were huge, ornate iron works of art, created mainly for show than for service. They walked past the Radio City Music hall building and a shoe-shine man polishing the shoes of a black American serviceman, who was wearing an army forage cap that was much admired by Billy. He was tempted to ask the man where he could get one for himself.

'Don't be silly,' scolded Peggy. 'You only get one if you're in the army.'

'Well, I bet they have an army-navy store here,' argued Billy.

A passer-by scolded the white shoe-shine man for polishing the shoes of a black man.

'Ain't you ashamed? A white man shinin' the shoes of a nigger?'

The man retorted angrily. 'This man fought in Germany for our country, as did many other black guys – a lot of them was killed, so why should I be ashamed to clean a hero's shoes? Your shoes is as dirty as your mouth, so don't you come to me to shine 'em ... asshole!'

The man walked on. Billy was impressed by the shoeshine man's wit. The man saw him laughing and looked down at Billy's shoes.

'You're next, son. I'm only charging kids fifty cents.'

Billy looked down at his shoes, which had several weeks of international grime on them, although they looked OK to him. Ross was giving the man fifty cents.

Billy sat in the chair as the man shined his black shoes to a state he'd hadn't seen them in since they were new.

'Blimey! I wish me mam could see these,' he said to Peggy. 'What d'yer think she'd say?'

'She'd tell you that's how they're supposed to look all the time.'

'Not on me, they're not. These'll last me for weeks before I get 'em mucky enough for another shine.'

'At fifty cents a time you should have them cleaned at least three times a week, Billy Clegg.'

'I think once might be enough,' retorted her brother.

'It'll be an improvement.'

'Are you here every day?' Billy asked the man.

'Every day when it ain't rainin', son.'

'I'll be back next week, then. Hey, Peg! This is a great place, I'm gonna like it, I can tell.'

His sister shrugged. 'I'm going to wait and see how things work out.'

Billy knew she was a bit miffed at the possibility of him getting a better part than she could hope for. In the cabaret act she had played a bigger part than her brother. He knew her well enough to figure this out.

'Are you fed up because I've got shinier shoes than you, or is it because I might be playing the Artful Dodger?'

Jealousy wasn't something that Peggy would ever admit. Plus they had a much bigger problem to cope with than sibling rivalry.

'I'm not so childish. It's just that if you get a big part and you're good, which you will be, it might set people asking awkward questions about you ... about both of us.'

'Blimey! Never thought of that,' said Billy.

'She does have a point,' said Ross, who also hadn't thought about it until now. 'If he is good, it's the sort of production where Billy might be looked upon as a child star. This means the trade papers will definitely want to know all about him, if not the regular papers. Is this what we want?'

'It wouldn't be so bad,' said Peggy, 'if we weren't wanted for something we didn't actually do.'

The three of them walked on in silence for a few minutes, their silence punctuated by the hum of passing conversations in New York accents, a whistling cyclist, the hooting of car horns and the shrill cry of a newspaper vendor selling the *Daily Nooz*.

Thinking about what Peggy had just said, Ross added, 'Look, it might not be a bad idea for us to find out if you are still in trouble at home. I could ring your local newspaper in Leeds on some pretext or other and ask about it.'

'Hello, *Daily News*.'

'Could you put me through to the news desk, please?' said Ross.

'Anyone in particular?'

'Erm, actually I was wondering if you might be able to help me. I'm after the telephone number of a newspaper in England. Would you have such a thing?'

'Depends on the paper.'

'It's called the *Yorkshire Post*.'

He pronounced the second syllable of Yorkshire as if it rhymed with 'higher', as did the girl at the other end of the line.

'It's the way they say it,' Ross whispered to the children.

'*Yorkshire Post*... Gimme a minute.'

A minute later Ross had the telephone number of the *Yorkshire Post*, which he was passing on to an operator to place a long-distance call for him. He'd prepared himself with twenty dollars in coins, five of which he was asked to pay immediately and await a call back from the operator. 'The phone booth was in a row of five so he wasn't too worried about anyone being kept waiting. In any case he stayed inside the booth until the call came.

'*Yorkshire Post*.'

'Hello. I'm ringing from New York City and I'd like to be put through to the newsroom ... anyone there will do.'

'Putting you through now, sir.'

'Hello, Jim Beasley speaking.'

'Hello, Mr Beasley. My name is Ross Duggan and I'm ringing from New York City.'

'How can I help you, Mr Duggan?'

'Well, I'm an actor in a Broadway show and I wondered if you might give me some information on a woman I know in Leeds who was involved in a factory fire last November.'

'Could I have her name, please?'

'Yes, her name is Elizabeth Clegg.'

'Ah, Betty Clegg. She's in the news again right now. Her kids were suspected of causing the fire but the factory owner has just been arrested for doing it himself.'

'So the children are no longer wanted by the police?'

'I wouldn't have thought so.'

'And what about Mrs Clegg. Was she killed in the fire?'

'Oh, no. She was rescued. Look, this isn't my story, would you like me to put you on to the man who's running with it?'

'So she's definitely alive?'

'Yes, she is... Hang on ... sorry, he's not here. Could you call back tomorrow at this time?'

'I can indeed,' said Ross, looking at his watch. 'Look, would you get word to their mother that her son and daughter are over here in America with me and they're perfectly safe.'

'What? The kids are in America? This sounds like a great story. Be sure to call back tomorrow at this same time. My colleague's name is Frank Smyth.'

'I will.'

Ross hung up and went back to their small apartment. It had two bedrooms, one for Ross and Billy and one for Peggy. He knew he was carrying the most brilliant news to them and was already forming the announcement in his head. He opened the door and they got up from their respective chairs, both ready for the worst but hoping for the best. Ross smiled at them.

'It's good news! Your mother is alive and...'

The rest of his announcement was drowned by screams of delight from the children.

'Honest? She wasn't killed in the fire?'

'No, she's alive. I've asked the newspaper man to tell her that you're both okay and over here with me...'

More screams of delight that he had to subdue in order to get the rest of his news out. He held up his hands to quieten them. 'Shhhh ... the other news is that the police have arrested the factory owner for starting the fire, so you're both in the clear.'

Billy let out a deafening cheer and flung his arms around his sister, who was weeping with happiness. They danced around the room, dragging Ross with them. Ten minutes later, after they'd calmed down, Peggy had a disturbing thought.

'Shouldn't we have found this out before now? Like when we were still in England. It would have saved Mam a lot of worry – and us for that matter.'

'According to the man at the *Yorkshire Post*,' Ross told them, 'this story has only just become news again. So, if you'd enquired from the newspapers, you wouldn't have learnt much.'

'Oh, that's good then.'

'Fortuitous is the word I'd use,' said Ross, who became thoughtful and added, 'Look, I, er, don't want to spoil the moment for you, but I need to know what you plan to do now.'

'How do you mean?' Billy asked.

'I mean, do you want to stay here and act in the play or do you want to go home to your mother? I fully understand if you want to go home.'

'Oh, blimey!' said Billy. 'This means we're not on the run any more and we don't have to worry about anyone checking up on us if I get the Artful Dodger part.'

'Not if you still want to do it, you don't,' said Ross.

Peggy, who was sobbing with emotion, said, 'If ... if we go back ... we'll be letting you down ... won't we? I mean, Ross and Maisie have already gone back, so...'

Ross put an arm around her. 'Peggy, right now you mustn't worry about letting me down. You've both had a terrible time and it seems you're about to come through it. One thing is certain though: you don't have to be Ross and Maisie any more. I can tell the theatre people the true story and they'll use it for publicity if you decide to stay. In fact, you two might well be famous before the show opens. Publicity is everything in this business.'

'Famous?' said Billy. 'Hey, I never thought I'd be famous one day. Will we get our pictures in the papers?'

'It's only a possibility,' said Ross. 'Don't let it go

285

to your head.'

'No chance of that not happening,' said Peggy, still weeping with immense relief at the good fortune that had just been bestowed upon her and Billy. She looked up at the ceiling and murmured, 'Thank you, God.'

'We've been praying for this,' Billy explained.

'And your prayers have been well and truly answered.'

'It's most prob'ly 'cos we're Catholics,' said Billy.

'Lucky you, eh?' said Ross. 'We non-Catholic heathens have no such luck.'

'You're not a heathen, you're a good man who's looked after us,' said Peggy.

'Peggy, it's been a pleasure making your acquaintance.'

'We can go back to school,' she said.

'Oh, heck!' said Billy, wondering why his sister just had to spoil a good moment.

'If you stay here the theatre people would take care of your education,' Ross told them. 'It's the law over here. There is one thing, though. I told the man at the *Yorkshire Post* that I'd ring him at the same time tomorrow, to speak to the reporter who's working on the factory story. I'll ask him if he can get hold of your mother, for you two to speak to her at a day and time we will arrange.'

Billy whooped with delight at such an idea. Speaking to his mother again had been a dream of his ever since they ran away. The spoiled moment was now good once again.

'Do you really think they'll do that for us?' Peggy asked.

'Peggy, this is a massive story. You two turning

up out of the blue will be like manna from heaven for any newspaperman. Believe me, they'll jump at anything we want.'

Chapter 30

It was late afternoon the following day when Betty heard the knock at the door. Jimmy was out shopping, after ensuring that she could cope without him.

'Jimmy,' she'd said to him, 'all I've got to do is sit in a chair and maybe get up to make myself a cuppa.'

'If anyone knocks,' he'd told her, 'look through the window to see who it is. If it's anyone you don't want to talk to, tell them to come back in an hour when I'm home.'

'All right. Jimmy ... stop fussing.'

It was a polite knock. She looked through the window and saw a young man in a belted raincoat and trilby hat. Ignoring Jimmy's advice she went to the door and was leaning heavily on her walking stick when she opened it. The young man smiled at her.

'Mrs Elizabeth Clegg?'

'Yes.'

'My name's Frank Smyth of the *Yorkshire Post*. I wonder if I can have a word with you. I believe I might have some good news about your children.'

Betty's eyes lit up. 'Oh, yes, please ... oh, do come in.'

She stood back to allow him through to the living room where he stood and waited for her to invite him to sit down, which she did.

'Good news you say? Are they alive?'

'Oh, yes, very much so.'

Her eyes misted over with tears of joy.

'Wh ... where are they?' she faltered.

'We received a telephone call from New York yesterday, from a man called Ross Duggan. He's an actor in a New York play. He says your children are quite well and are over there with him.'

Betty seemed stunned to hear this. 'What? My children are in New York?'

'Er, yes.'

'You mean, New York in America?'

'Yes.'

She wiped her eyes with her sleeve. 'Good grief! How on Earth did they end up there? Oh, sorry about this. I was almost convinced they were both dead.'

'No, they're alive and definitely in New York.'

'Well, that's definitely elsewhere – more elsewhere than I ever imagined.'

'I see,' said Smyth, who didn't see at all.

'How on earth did they get there?'

'I don't actually know, Mrs Clegg. But Mr Duggan will be ringing us back today and I wondered if you might want to be at our office to speak to him?'

'What? Oh, yes, please – will he have my children with him?'

'Once again, I don't know. It was a colleague who took the call, but since I've been working on your story he passed the information on to me.'

'Are you sure this is all true? I must say, it sounds a bit far-fetched.'

'Yes, I admit it's hard to believe, which is why I came in person to invite you down to our office for when the next call comes through.'

'*If* it comes through,' said Betty, who wanted to believe this but wasn't strong enough to endure the pain of disappointment.

'We checked with our switchboard girl who assures us that the original call came from New York, so if it's some sort of hoax it's a very elaborate one.'

'What time is he ringing back?'

The reporter looked at his watch. 'In about an hour, I should think. With the time difference, that would make it about noon over there. Look, there was no plan made for the children to be with him today, but he did ask if we could make another arrangement for them to speak to you.'

'If my kids are living anywhere near him and they know he's speaking to me, they'll make damned sure they're with him when he rings. If not I'll think this whole thing is a load of baloney.'

Smyth frowned. 'Well, let's hope he's got them with him then. I'm in a car, so if you want to come with me you'll be there in good time.'

'Oh, right. Well, you need to give me a few minutes to get ready. Can I make you a cup of tea while you're waiting?'

'Yes, I'd like that. I gather the news that someone's been arrested for starting the fire is welcome news for you.'

'Best thing I've heard since it happened. Well ... second best now. It was my friend Jimmy who got

289

Lester Blainey arrested, you know. This is Jimmy's house.'

'So I gather. I was directed here by your former neighbours.'

'Oh, I bet they had plenty to say about me living with Jimmy Potter.'

'Not to me they didn't.'

'It's all open and above board,' Betty assured him. 'Jimmy saved my life that night and he's looking after me while I get properly better. He's a top man is Jimmy. He was wounded in Germany and they gave him a bravery medal, but the trauma he suffered stops him working at his old teaching job.'

'Really? That sounds like a story in itself. I think I'd like a chat with him about all this.'

'Well, I doubt if he'll be back before we go, but you can always call again.'

'I can indeed. Tell him to expect me this evening.'

'Right, I'll put that kettle on and make meself look presentable.'

An hour later, in the newsroom, two pairs of eyes were fixed on the same telephone – the one on Frank's desk. The appointed time came and went, along with it Betty's hopes.

'It takes quite a few minutes to get a transatlantic call connected,' Smyth assured her. 'I only hope the caller thought to make it a reverse charges call, otherwise it'll cost an arm and a leg for a decent conversation.'

After a further three minutes the phone rang. Smyth picked it up.

'Frank Smyth.'

'This is the call you're expecting. He's made it a collect call, which means we pay. Is that okay?' asked the switchboard girl.

'That's fine... Hello, this is Frank Smyth, who am I speaking to?'

'Ross Duggan calling from New York.'

'Excellent! Mr Duggan, do you by any chance have Mrs Clegg's children with you?'

'Yes, they're both here.'

'Grand! I have their mother with me. She would very much like to speak to them.'

Frank handed the phone to Betty, who took it with shaking hands. When she spoke her voice was barely audible.

'Hello?'

'Mam, is that you?' said Peggy.

'Peggy! Oh, my lovely Peggy! Is that really you?'

''Course it is. Billy's here as well.'

'And are you both okay?'

'Mam, we've been living in Miami all winter. We're both as brown as berries.'

'Oh, lovely! I wish I could see you both. How on earth did you get over there?'

'On a ship. We stowed away. We thought the police would want us for setting the factory on fire. Mam, we thought you were dead.'

'Well, I'm not, love. A man called Jimmy Potter saved my life. I've been in hospital but I'm a lot better now. Can you put Billy on?'

'Okay.'

'Hiya, Mam.'

'Oh, Billy love. I so pleased to hear your voice. I gather you've had a bit of an adventure.'

'We have, yeah. Mam, we thought you'd died in the fire, that's why we ran away. Sorry about taking the money.'

'That's perfectly all right, love. I'm only glad there was some to take. I can't imagine how you've managed all this time.'

Billy knew an explanation was being asked for, but he wasn't ready to give her one right now. No way would she approve of all the thieving.

'We've just been very lucky, Mam.'

'What are you doing in New York?'

'Mam, we're going to be in a play on Broadway!'

'A what?'

'A play, in a theatre.'

'You mean, in a proper theatre?'

'Yeah.'

'Billy,' she said, 'er ... what on Earth do you know about being in a play?'

'Well, we know all the lines for a start and the people at the theatre think we're good enough. Ross Duggan's an actor and he's got us parts. It's about Oliver Twist and I'm playing the Artful Dodger. We get paid money and a place to stay and everything. In fact, they'll give us schooling too if we need it.'

Betty squeezed her eyes tight shut. Her life seemed to have turned itself on its head. One minute her children were lost, possibly dead, the next minute they were actors in a Broadway play in New York, thousands of miles away. But they were alive and doing well so it seemed. She took in a deep breath and sighed it out, slowly.

'Billy ... this is a lot to take in, put Peggy back on.'

'Hello, Mam.'

'Peggy, are you ... erm ... are you both happy over there?'

'We are now. We weren't happy anywhere when we thought you were dead. We've been really miserable, praying for you and everything. There's a massive Catholic church here called St Patrick's. They have masses all day long and we've been there and lit loads of candles for you. They cost twenty cents each and we've spent over ten dollars ... but it's been worth it.'

'For both of us it seems. So, what's this theatre business our Billy was on about?'

'Mam, it's not proper Broadway, it's what they call off-Broadway, but it's true and it's a lovely theatre. We've both had auditions and got jobs.'

'He said something about schooling.'

'Ross says we'll have to do lessons every day. He says it's the law over here for child performers.'

'Oh dear, Peggy, I'm in a bit of a daze and I don't know what to say for the best. You see, I'd love for you to come home, but you can't do both things, can you? And it seems you've been given a chance of something really good over there.'

'We'd love to come home, Mam, but I don't think we can afford it right now. We can't stow away again. We were dead lucky the last time.'

'I know. I'm trying to think of you, and not get in the way of your chance of happiness.'

'You being alive has stopped us being sad. Mam, this is the happiest we've been ... ever. Isn't it, Billy? He's nodding his head off, Mam. You know what he's like. He can't take the grin off his face. Us being without a mam was awful and we

293

don't care if you're thousands of miles away, all we care about is that you're not dead.'

Billy took the phone from his sister. 'Mam, why don't you come over here? That's only one fare. With us it'll be two.'

'Trust you to think of that, Billy. Well, at least I know it's definitely my boy I'm speaking to.'

Ross tapped Billy on the shoulder and took the receiver from him. 'Mrs Clegg, Ross Duggan here. Just a thought. It seems to me that this story is worth a lot of money to a newspaper. Why don't you offer to sell it for the price of your fare over here? You're in a newspaper office right now. Why not give it a try?'

'Oh, dear. I'm not sure if I can do that.'

'Is there a reporter nearby?'

'Yes. A man called Frank Smyth.'

'Put him on, would you?'

'Okay.'

'Mr Smyth, the children have been given a sensational chance over here. They'll both be appearing in a Broadway play, which makes this a very big story, I should think, after all they've been through. I know most of it and if I thought I had the right, I'd sell it to the highest bidder. But it's not my story, it's theirs. I'm sure you know a lot about the UK end of it – so, would your newspaper be prepared to buy the whole story for enough money to send Mrs Clegg over here to see her children?'

Smyth was taken unawares. 'Erm, it's not a decision I can make myself. I'd have to speak to my editor.'

'Of course. Should I ring back tomorrow for

your decision?'

'That would be good. About the same time?'

'Same time, yeah. Obviously if you can't do it I'll need to try other papers, probably some of the UK nationals. In fact, I imagine the New York papers would snap my hand off for a story like this.'

'We're only a regional newspaper. What sort of sum are you thinking of, Mr Duggan?'

'Well, now that you've given me the idea of selling it to the New York papers, I'm thinking two thousand pounds.'

'That's a lot of money,' said Smyth. 'You could buy a small house over here for that sort of money.'

'I think it's a lot of story: a major scoop. A story that might end with a man being hanged by the sound of it. I'll ring back tomorrow, then.'

'Yes, please do.'

'Good. I'll put Billy back on to talk to his mother.'

'Mam, have you seen David since the fire?'

'No, why?'

'Well, he was with us that night and we wondered if the police had got him.'

'I haven't seen him, but I know it was David who found the evidence that got Blainey locked up.'

'Was it? Good old David. I knew he wouldn't let us dow–'

A loud crackling on the line ended their conversation prematurely. Billy handed the receiver to Ross, who listened for a few seconds before putting it back on the rest.

'I'm afraid these calls only last as long as the

Atlantic allows,' he said.

'I don't care. That was the best thing ever,' said Billy.

24 hours later

'Mr Smyth?'

'Speaking.'

'Ross Duggan here, ringing from New York. Have you had a word with your boss regarding my suggestion?'

'Yes, I have, and it seems we're agreeable to your suggestion but on certain conditions.'

'Which are?'

'That we have worldwide syndication rights to the story.'

Ross knew they'd be able to recoup the two thousand dollars several times over by selling the story on to newspapers around the world.

'I imagine that makes my price of two thousand pounds quite doable.'

'It's acceptable. Obviously we need to speak directly to Mrs Clegg and get her to sign a contract.'

'That sounds fine. I'll tell her to have the contract checked by a solicitor if that's okay?'

'I expected no less from you, Mr Duggan. It seems that both Mrs Clegg and the children have a lot to thank you for.'

'They're great kids, Mr Smyth. Do you have Mrs Clegg there by any chance?'

'Yes, I do. I'll put her on.'

'Hi, Mrs Clegg. They've agreed to pay two

thousand pounds for your story, which we'll have to write together. They're drawing up a contract that you'll need to have checked by a solicitor. Do you have one?'

'Yes I have. He's called Geoffrey Wooltorton.'

'Excellent. If you could put me back on to Mr Smyth, I'll arrange to phone my copy through, then he can put both halves of the story together.'

'Thank you very much for your help, Mr Duggan. I hope to see you over there, along with the children, just as soon as I can.'

Back in the apartment Billy and Peggy had a lot to think about. This story-telling business wasn't as straightforward as it might seem. They were in Peggy's room, just the two of them. They needed to talk about this without Ross being there, as not even he knew the whole truth – a truth that might get them into a lot of trouble back in the UK, if it hit the newspapers.

'What do we say about all the thieving we did?' said Peggy.

'Why should we say anything?'

'Billy, it's what kept us alive. Someone's bound to ask us how we managed, especially Mam. We could say we went begging ... or busking.'

'Possibly. I don't suppose we can admit to being thieves, but I bet we could come up with a good story involving Goldie.'

'But he's dead,' said Peggy.

'I know, but he wouldn't mind us involving him in a lie. We could tell them how he and his grand-dad helped us a lot when we first got to Blackpool and let us live in their house.'

'Yeah, I don't suppose Goldie'd mind that,' agreed Peggy. 'It's kind of true, and all the best lies are based on truth, according to Mam. That's how Lord Haw Haw managed to frighten everyone in the war. I bet we could tell the truth about the day Goldie was killed and our part in it, which wasn't much.'

'Do we tell them about Harry burning his house down?'

'No, just about his house burning down the day after he found out his grandson had been killed. How would we know he set it on fire himself?'

'We wouldn't unless he told us,' said Billy, 'which I don't think he actually did ... did he?'

Their vivid imaginations were now flooding with ideas.

'We *could* say,' said Peggy, 'that Goldie had trusted us and given us a bagful of money to bury in the sand behind our beach hut for him. We used some of it to live on and, after he died, we kept all of it. I know it sounds as if we did a wrong thing, but it would explain how we managed to stay alive for all that time, and no one could say it was stealing. It was either that or starve.'

'Hey, Peg, I think we're getting somewhere here. Mam used to say it's easy to bend the truth into a lie.'

'Mam was right about a lot of stuff... Blimey, Billy! She's alive is our mam and she's coming over here to see us!'

This brought another whoop from him, to the amusement of his sister who gave an unladylike whoop of her own.

'We might as well tell the truth about us

298

stowing away,' she added. 'No harm in that.'

'Yeah, and meeting the Duggans.'

'We mustn't get Ross into trouble,' cautioned Peggy. 'I mean, where would we be without him?'

'Okay, we need to tell him our version of the story for when he tells it to the paper, so we can see what he thinks about it first. I don't suppose it's much of a crime, knowing someone's stowed away and not reporting it.'

'It might be if he'd helped us.'

'Peg, we say he *didn't* help us. That was Ross and Maisie and they're over in England.'

'That's true.'

'And we can tell the truth about working in that club in Miami. They can always check with Rudy Vallee on that, and about us swapping names with Ross and Maisie. In fact, there's loads of truth we can tell them that makes a great story.'

'Including the truth about us not setting the factory on fire.'

This had Billy nodding. 'Oh, yeah, that's the best bit, especially the story of how David got Blainey locked up. I wonder how he did that?'

'David got us out of trouble.'

'Blimey, Peg. We owe him a massive favour, don't we?'

'Maybe we should give him some of the money. Tell you what, next time we speak to Mam we can see what she thinks. David's mam's always skint.'

'Everyone's in our street's always skint.'

Peggy grinned. 'Everyone ... except our mam. The richest woman in our street is Mrs Betty Clegg.'

'And it's us running away that's made her rich.'

'Billy, you'd be as well not saying that to Mam.'

'Hey, they call me Billy, not Silly.'

He looked out of the apartment window at the traffic in the street below and the skyscrapers looming in the distance over the roofs of nearby buildings. There was a colossal magic about this city that he didn't understand. He just felt it.

'I really like it here, Peg. I'm glad Mam's coming over.'

'I doubt she'll want to stay, though. In fact, for us to stay we need to get visas and work permits and stuff.'

'I bet the theatre'll sort all that out for us.'

'Mebbe.'

''Course they will, Peg.'

'Not for Mam they won't. She won't be able to stay.'

'I bet she would if she got a job in the theatre. There's all sorts of jobs. You don't have to be on the stage. She could work in the costume department.'

'That's a good idea, Billy. Let's mention it to her.'

Then his face dropped. 'She won't want to stop here. She'll say she's too old to come and live in a different country. She wouldn't even move out of our street when our dad's money came through. I bet she'll want us to go back with her.'

'If she does then I'm going back, Billy! She's our mam, and we're the only family she's got. Just keep remembering how we felt when we thought she was dead. If she goes back and leaves us here, it'll be like we've lost her all over again.'

Billy gave this some thought and said, 'You're right, Peg. If she wants to go straight back, we'll both go with her.'

Chapter 31

The show opened at the Cort Theatre on Thursday 21 March to excellent reviews. The two children became instant favourites, mainly because the audience had already read about their escapades, which had made headlines in every New York newspaper as well as many in the UK. In the audience on the second night was Spider, who had already picked the pockets of three patrons to the tune of twenty-two dollars. The theatre, it seemed to him, was a rich and untried hunting ground for pickpockets, and it amused him that Billy was playing one in the show. It occurred to him to meet up with the boy and give him a few tips on how to make his part more realistic.

It was on the evening of that second show that Peggy tapped on the door of the dressing room Billy was sharing with three other boys, one of whom had peed himself on-stage. The other two had sneaked off-stage to the toilet and been seen by the director, who wasn't at all pleased with them.

'Don't turn up tomorrow, boys. I'm replacing you with stage dummies who don't drink beer before appearing on-stage.'

So it was a gloomy scene in the dressing room

when Peggy entered it. 'Billy, me and Ross are ready to leave. You coming with us?' she said.

'Hey, Peg. I just got a note from Spider. He's at the stage door waiting for us.'

Peggy hesitated for just a second before saying, 'I don't think we should get tangled up with him again.'

'I'm only going to say hello to him.'

'Okay, Billy, but don't get mixed up in any of his schemes.'

'I'm not that daft, Peg. He's all right is Spider ... better than that lying bugger Goldie.'

'Then me and Ross'll leave through the main door, so we don't have to bump into him.'

'See you back at the apartment, Peg.'

'Don't be late, Billy. Don't have us worrying.'

'No chance.'

So he bade farewell to the two of his stage buddies whom he'd probably never see again, and headed for the stage door. Spider was standing smoking a cigarette when Billy went outside. The young man's Scouse accent seemed strangely alien in his current surroundings.

'Hiya there, Billy Boy.'

'Hiya, Spider.'

'Hey, la. Yer purron a gear act there, Billy. Star o' the show, I'd say.'

'Give over. I wasn't in it much.'

'I know, but what yer did shone out like a tanner on a sweep's arse. I know yer got yer name in the papers.'

'About us being runaways, that's all.'

'No, I meant the show review. They gave you a

gear write-up. That's why I came ter see fer meself. I thought, surely that's not the same Billy Clegg wot I know.'

'Well, it's me all right. How're you doing, Spider?'

'I'm doin' awright, Billy. Pickin's is good around here.'

'Whereabouts are you living?'

'I got a place on Lafayette Street ... it's in the Bowery.'

'The Bowery, great! So you're a Bowery Boy?'

Spider flicked his spent cigarette across the street with practised ease. 'Hey, Billy, them Bowery Boys ain't nothin' compared ter the mob I'm with. Would yer like ter come and see where we hang out? It ain't nuthin' special, just a basement, but we all got rooms and beds and we live like kings, Billy Boy.'

'Yeah, I'd love to come, is it far?'

'We're down on the Lower East Side. Far enough fer us ter need a cab, but I got the dough, Billy. We hail us down one of them yeller boys an' we's there in ten minutes.'

'Spider, you're beginning to talk like a Bowery Boy – half Scouse, half Bowery.'

'So, are yer comin'?'

'Okay,' said Billy, excited by the prospect. 'I suppose I can get a cab back.'

'Sure yer can. There's a cab rank right outside our door. In fact, one of the drivers is a Bowery Boy like us, only we don't call ourselves that. We call ourselves the Real Deal.'

'The Real Deal? I like that, Spider. Do they still call you Spider?'

'Sure do, but I get mixed up with another guy called Skyler – easy mistake ter make. Now Skyler's a real pro. He calls himself the Master of the Dip. He's a pickpocket. Man, this guy could go on the Broadway stage with his act. He can take the shirt off yer back without yer knowing it. He's the kind o' guy yer need ter meet, ter get yer act perfected. Imagine doin' that on-stage! You'd bring the house down, Billy.'

'Yeah, I imagine I would, but I think it takes years of practice.'

'It sure does, Billy. Many years. Years you ain't got really.'

'True, we're going back home as soon as we can afford it.'

'Not stowin' away, then?'

'No, we think our faces might be too well known, especially to all the ship's crews who'll have read our story.'

'That's very true, Billy. A guy don't need no well-known face in my business. Hey! Here's a cab.'

Ten minutes later they were descending the steps into the basement rooms of 247 Lafayette Street. As they entered, Spider locked the door behind them. Like he'd said, it wasn't the height of luxury here; in fact Billy wouldn't have swapped the beach hut in Blackpool for it. Its only advantage was that it had electric light illegally diverted from the rooms above, and cold running water.

'Cor, it niffs a bit,' commented Billy.

'Yeah, that's Pongo and he's not even here. Pongo's gorran odour problem – and a gas problem. Makes him a bit of a loner, as you can imagine.'

'Yeah, I can. There was a kid in our class at school who never stopped farting. He didn't have many friends either. His nickname was Windy – Windy Weatherall. Do you all have nicknames?'

'We do. Then none of us can squeal to the cops. Yer can't squeal on someone whose proper name yer do not know.'

'That's not very trusting.'

'Why should we have ter be trustin'? The cops around here beat the livin' daylights out of us but they get nuthin' because we don't know nuthin'.'

'I bet they know where you live.'

'Yeah, they know that, but here ain't where we keep our stashes. Each guy keeps his stash somewhere he alone knows. I got two places. One place I can give to the cops, and one place where I keep all the good stuff. We all got fences who take our stuff. Mine is up in the Bronx, miles away from here.'

'So, you been beaten up by the cops, have you?'

'Yeah, twice so far. It weren't nuthin' I couldn't handle. I squealed pretty quickly before they got rough. Cried like a baby. That's the secret. Make them think yer a softie who can't take no punishment an'll mebbe run straight to hospital. Tough guys who can take punishment generally get hit bad. Don't be a tough guy, Billy. No future in bein' a tough guy.'

'In that case, I think I've got a good future.'

Spider grinned but the expression was soon wiped away when they heard feet clattering down the outside steps.

'Are these your friends?' asked Billy.

Spider shook his head, worried.

'Sorry, Billy Boy, these ain't no friends o' mine.' There was a loud banging on the door and a shout of 'Police, open this door!'

'Not bleedin' likely,' said Spider. 'C'mon, Billy. We need ter scarper, mate.'

Billy followed him through a back door that led to a long passageway and at the end of this another door that opened onto a yard. They burst through a yard door and onto the street. Spider looked both ways and ran to his left, followed by Billy who struggled to keep up. At the end of the street Spider was waiting for him in a doorway.

'What's happening?' asked Billy, out of breath.

'Not sure. The Dealers were out on some sort of caper tonight. They wouldn't tell me much 'cos I wasn't in on it. It's the way we work. If yer not involved, yer not told.'

A torch beam lit up the street followed by a shout of: 'There they are!'

The sound of feet rushing towards them had Spider galloping off, followed by his slower pal. Billy looked back and saw three uniformed policemen chasing them. The street lighting varied from electric to old-fashioned gas lamps. Spider chose to dash down an alley where the lighting was dim. The ground was paved with cobblestones, just like their street at home in Leeds. Billy followed at full pelt. Their pursuers were less than fifty yards away and shouting again.

'Armed police. Stop or we'll shoot!'

'They're going to shoot us, Spider!' called out Billy.

'No, they won't.'

As he said this a shot rang out and Spider fell

to the ground and let out a stream of curses, followed by, 'They got me in the leg, Billy! Yer'd better scram, quick!'

'Can you get up?'

Spider got to his knees and put an arm around Billy's shoulders. To their left was a narrow gap between buildings. In Yorkshire it would have been known as a ginnel. The two of them hobbled up it and came to a step, which led to a recess in the wall and thence to a door at the top of two more steps. By now Spider was exhausted and moaning with pain.

'Here, you can sit down for a bit.'

'Yeah, thanks. Jeez! It's me leg, Billy.'

Torchlight shone up the alley but they were out of sight.

'Try the door,' Spider hissed

Billy tried but it was locked. Gunfire sounded once more. Random shots to scare them into giving up. The bullets ricocheted off the walls in all directions; one of them hitting the door behind them. It was more than Billy could stand. He went to the corner of the alley and shouted as loud as he could.

'Why are you shooting at us? We haven't done nowt!'

'Come out where we can see you.'

'We can't. You've shot my pal. He needs an ambulance. We haven't done nowt, mister. I'm only eleven and I'm from England.'

He added the last bit in the hope that it might help. It didn't.

'Limey kid, eh?'

'Spider's wounded, mister.'

At this point Spider, mercifully, lost consciousness. 'He's knocked out, mister. I think you might have killed him.'

These words alarmed a cop, who approached and shone his torch on Billy, now shivering with fear and cold, then on Spider, slumped on the steps with his left leg soaked in blood.

'Get back to the car and call an ambulance,' said one of the officers. 'You one of them Real Deal punks?' he addressed Billy.

'No, I'm not anything. I work in the Cort Theatre on-stage.'

'Stage-hand at your age? Don't give me that, kid.'

'No, I'm an actor in a play.'

His voice was quaking with fear, exhaustion, and shock at being shot at. 'Me name's Billy Clegg. Is he dead, mister?'

'No, he's not. He's just hit in the leg. He'll be going to the hospital and you're coming to the Precinct with us.'

'I haven't done anything, mister.'

The door behind them opened and a woman in a dressing gown stood there. 'What the hell's going on here?' she demanded.

'We're just running down a couple of felons.'

'And you've put a hole in my door.'

'That will be repaired, ma'am.'

'You betcha goddamned life it will!'

She looked down at Billy, who was still shivering with cold and shock. 'Felons, huh? He don't look like no felon to me, and you were shooting at him, were you?'

Billy thought it a good idea to enlist this

woman's help.

'We haven't done anything, missis, and they started shooting at us. I'm only eleven. They shot my friend in his leg.'

The woman shook her head and said scathingly, 'So, New York's finest are out shooting young kids now, are they? My old pappy was NYPD when there wuz real bad guys on the streets. These kids ... wuz they shootin' back at yer?'

No answer.

'I guess that means "no". My pappy ... he'd have been real ashamed of you guys.'

Spider's eyes flickered open and he gave a loud moan. Cold rain started to fall. The woman went back inside and emerged with an umbrella, which she held over both Spider and Billy.

'What's that noise?' moaned Spider.

'It's the rain.'

'Rain? It's not raining.'

The woman took the umbrella away.

'Is it rainin' now, son?'

'Yeah.'

She replaced the umbrella. The rain stopped falling on Spider.

The three officers stood unprotected in damp, embarrassed silence, listening to the exchange between the two boys and the woman and not feeling best pleased with the situation. There was the clanging of an approaching ambulance. All three cops sighed with relief. Billy knelt down beside Spider.

'The ambulance has come. Yer gonna be all right, mate.'

'Thanks, Billy. Are the cops still here?'

'Yeah, but you're going to hospital.'

'Did you tell them we haven't done nothin'?'

'Yeah.'

'Good. Keep telling everyone that, because we haven't. It'll be the other Dealers they're after.'

'If you tell us where they are, we can mebbe go easy on you two,' said a policeman.

'I've never even met them,' said Billy.

'Go easy on them for what?' demanded the woman. 'And if you put handcuffs on that young boy I'll complain to your chief myself. He's too small for handcuffs.'

'We know that, lady.'

Billy was marginally disappointed not to be handcuffed by the New York cops, as such an exciting detail would add spice to the story he was planning to tell his pals once he got back to Leeds. Right then, getting back home was uppermost in his mind. A policeman led him to a large, black police car with a blue light on the top and *9th Precinct* written on the door in white letters.

'What sort of car is this?' asked Billy out of genuine curiosity. If he was to tell his story to his pals they'd definitely want to know such a detail.

'It's a Plymouth, son.'

'I bet it's not an ordinary Plymouth. I bet it's souped up. Is it bullet-proof? How fast can it go?'

No answer. The cop didn't intend to disgrace his uniform by being drawn into conversation with a probable felon. Even if he was pint-sized and eleven years old.

Chapter 32

'I think he's got himself into trouble,' said Peggy
to Ross, who was staring out of the window
looking for any sign of Billy. 'That Spider boy he
met is a wrong 'un. He's a thief, and if he's picked
up, it could be that Billy's been picked up as well.'

'Maybe I could ring around the Precincts,' said
Ross. 'See if they've got a boy called Billy Clegg
in custody.'

'What do we do if they say they have?'

'I go down there and get him out. I tell them
he's a juvenile actor in a Broadway play, who
somehow got lost on his way home through un-
familiar streets.'

'I think it's worth a try, Ross. There's a phone
downstairs in the lobby.'

'Maybe I'll give it half an hour, see if he comes
home. In the meantime I'll get the phone numbers
of the local Precincts.'

'He deserves a proper roasting when he does
come home,' said Peggy. 'He should have known
better than to go off with Spider. He's the one
who helped us stow away – and he helped us get
out of the port in Miami without any passports.'

'He sounds like a resourceful young man. Pity
he wasn't resourceful enough to get Billy home
safely.'

Peggy shook her head in dismay.

Billy was taken to the 9th Precinct where he was left in a holding room until the police decided what they should charge him with. There was a frantic buzz of activity all around and a sea of uniformed male and female officers. The police occupied the furnished two-thirds of the room, which had a worn parquet floor and walls painted in two shades of yellow. Their area was furnished with chairs, desks and cupboards. There were mug shots pinned on the walls. Billy was frogmarched to the other end of the space, unwelcoming with its concrete floor and scuffed and stained walls painted a dull grey.

Projecting into this end of the room was a large cell, fifteen feet square. It was barred on three sides, with a bare brick wall on the other, giving no privacy to the six men currently housed there, most of them in various stages of inebriation. It had a low bench along the brick wall but offered no other seating arrangements. One man was sitting on the bench, four on the floor and one leaning against the bars, smoking; in fact four of the men were smoking, and the others looked to be asleep. Billy was thrown in quite roughly, landing in a heap on the floor, much to the amusement of the drunken inmates. He got to his feet and distanced himself from them as best he could. He sat on the bench. A large black man came to sit beside him.

'My name's Winston,' he said. 'How old are you, kid?'

'Eleven.'

'Jezz! Wotcha doin' in here? Moider someone?'

'I haven't done nothing. I went with a pal to his

lodgings and the police came barging in. We ran off.'

'Why d'yer run?'

'My pal thought it was the best idea. He was right as well. They shot at us.'

'Yeah, that's what cops do. Hey, haven't I seen you somewhere before?'

'Mebbe in the paper. My name's Billy Clegg. Me and my sister stowed away on a ship from England. We've both got jobs now, acting in a play at the Cort Theatre.'

'Jesus, man! I know about you. You ran away because you wuz blamed for a big fire that killed people.'

'That's right. Only it's been proved that it wasn't our fault. In fact, it was just like tonight. We hadn't done anything then either but the police don't always ask the right questions, do they? They just shot the pal who stowed away with us.'

'Is he okay?'

'Dunno. They took him to hospital. I need to pee,' Billy murmured. 'Is there anywhere I can go in here or will they let me out?'

'There should be a facility in here,' said Winston, looking around. 'They don't want the likes of us contaminating their personal crappers.' There was a door-shaped space in the corner. He went over to it, disappeared from view and came back to report.

'You can take a pee through there,' he said. 'That pal of yours who was shot... Is he yo' brother?'

'No, I haven't got a brother, just a sister, like I told you.'

'See that big dude over there?'

313

Winston's gaze directed Billy to look across the cell at a large man leaning against the bars.

'Yeah. What about him?'

Winston spoke in a quiet voice, not looking at the man in question. 'His name's Duke and he has a rep for likin' boys.'

'So what?'

'Well, I don't mean in a good way, if ya catch my drift. Maybe you should keep an eye on him. Him very drunk.'

'Oh, right.'

Billy had been told about such men, but apart from schoolboy jokes, knew nothing about them. He went across the cell towards the toilet area. Duke made to follow him but Winston beat Duke across the cell to where Billy was relieving himself in a urinal that consisted of a tin trough sloping towards a circular hole in the wall. To the right was a washbasin, which Duke had warned Billy not to use.

'Some of 'em will have peed in it.'

Beside the basin was an odorous and doorless closet that Billy hoped he'd never have need to visit. He stood at the tin trough and attended to his needs. Winston stood behind him, facing back into the cell. Duke growled at him.

'Outa my way. I need to piss.'

'You can wait until my friend's finished.'

The man swore violently and told Winston he had no intention of waiting. Winston stood fast, mainly because he'd been pushed around all his life and had learnt to push back, but this brute wasn't going to be easily deterred. Duke took a step back, swung his fist and aimed a punch at

Winston that was virtually telegraphed. Winston saw it coming and easily brushed it away with his left forearm, at the same time hooking his left foot around the back of Duke's unsteady legs and catching him off balance with a shoulder charge. He went stumbling backwards, tripping over Winston's outstretched foot. Duke keeled over as rigid as a felled tree and smashed his head on the concrete floor. Billy had turned around just in time to see all this happening. They both looked down at Duke, hoping he wouldn't get up to retaliate, but the man lay as still as the solid floor beneath him, blood pooling around his shaved head. Winston looked around to see if anyone else might have witnessed the incident, but it had taken place out of sight of the others.

'Why did you do that?' Billy asked curiously.

'Didn't do nuthin'. He was comin' for yer, kid, and he just fell down, as you probably saw.'

'Yeah, that's what I saw,' lied Billy.

'Drunk most prob'ly. At the time he fell I was right beside you, taking a pee. I didn't lay a hand on him. Did I, Billy?'

'No, you didn't. Blimey! He looks dead ter me.'

Winston bent over the man and listened for breathing. There was none. He whispered to Billy.

'Remember what we said? I was right beside you.'

'Why?'

Winston spoke to the boy in a low voice. 'Billy, in the can you don't ask questions when another guy asks a simple favour, but I'll tell you anyway. That man's a very bad guy and he was coming to have some fun with you – fun you wouldn't have liked. I stopped him is all you need to know.'

He then called out through the bars to whoever might pay attention.

'There's a guy on the floor here. Looks like he fell. I think he might be dead.'

Winston knew this would spur someone into action. Deaths in custody always proved a major pain-in-the-ass for the police, and were very hard to explain away convincingly. A detective in plain clothes came over to the cell and looked over to where Winston was pointing.

'Musta fell over and banged his head on the floor.'

'Did you see him fall?'

'No. One minute he was standing up, drunk as a skunk, then while I'm taking a pee, I hear a bang and there he is on the floor, lying like someone chop him down with an axe. This young feller was next to me. I reckon he saw the same thing.'

The detective looked at Billy, who said, 'That's right. He just fell backwards.'

Three uniformed men came in to assist. They picked up Duke and carried him out of the cell. One of them called out to the desk sergeant.

'We'll stick him in the medic room. Better call a doc and an ambulance. He's not looking good.'

The three uniformed men returned and opened the cell again with guns at the ready, hustling the inmates into a corner, away from the blood that was already being cleaned up by a janitor with a mop and bucket.

'Might as well clean up all the puke as well,' called out an inmate.

The janitor looked at one of the policemen, who

316

nodded his agreement. The janitor proceeded with his task, adding disinfectant to the cloying combination of odours. Billy was sitting on the floor with the other inmates. He had never felt so desolate since he'd believed his mam had died in the fire. Tears were rolling down his cheeks and he wished she were here now. She'd give these bullying men what for. Winston spotted his distress and saw it could be used to their advantage. He went over to the bars and peered through them, looking for a sympathetic cop. Nearby were two female detectives in plain clothes, one sitting on a desk and the other behind it on a chair. They were drinking coffee and eating doughnuts, which meant they weren't otherwise busy. Winston spoke quietly into the boy's ear.

'Billy, if anyone asks, at any time, tell them I was at the show you wuz in tonight. Sittin' in the front stalls where you could see my big ugly face.'

'Why?'

'Billy, I've told you about asking why in a place like this.'

'Oh, right.'

Winston called across to the detectives as politely as he could. 'Excuse me, ladies ... c ... could I have a w ... word, please?'

His slight stammer was put on, to elicit sympathy. The woman sitting on the desk looked round. She was blonde and pretty. Winston put on the most appealing expression he could muster. His was a face that didn't lend itself too easily to appeal. It was enough to bring her over, but not enough for her to speak pleasantly.

'Whaddya want, punk?'

Winston knew the tone didn't match the expression on her face – her aggression was strictly for show. He maintained his good manners.

'It's not about me, I'm speaking for my young friend Billy Clegg here. Do you know who he is?'

She looked at Billy, who was still sobbing, apparently unaware of what was going on.

'Is he the cry-baby sitting in the corner?'

'Yeah, but he's not a baby, he's a great kid. There was a lot about him in the papers recently. He and his sister Peggy stowed away from England when they were wanted there for a fire they never did start.'

These words rang a vague bell with the woman, as he'd known they would. If he knew who Billy was, she most certainly would.

'A whole bunch of people died and Billy and his sister wuz blamed, only it's been proved now it wasn't them. They came over here and both become actors in a Broadway show. You must have read about them?'

The detective gave a brief nod. 'Maybe I have,' she conceded, 'but what's that got to do with anything?'

'That boy you just called a baby ... that's Billy Clegg and he hasn't done nuthin' apart from being in the wrong place at the wrong time, and not for the first time in his life. He's very well known. I mean, even you knew who he was.'

'Okay. So I know who Billy Clegg is, but how do I know that's him?'

'He was in the show tonight. I went to see it.'

'So whaddya want me to do about it?'

'Miss, you got yerselves an eleven-year-old

juvenile in this drunk tank along with a bunch of adult felons, including one known child molester, lyin' on the floor through there dead drunk if not dead. How do you think that's gonna look when it gets in the *Daily Nooz?* Especially with the juvenile being a pop'lar theatre actor who's done nuthin' wrong! It's bound to get into the noozpapers. He's a name in this town.'

She went over to the desk sergeant, obviously relaying Winston's words. The sergeant stared at Winston, then at Billy, mind ticking over with the implications of what he'd just been told. If it were true, such a story would do the 9th Precinct no good at all. He picked up the phone and asked the switchboard to get him the Cort Theatre.

'Hello my name is Sergeant Brownlow of the Ninth Precinct,' he told the assistant stage manager who answered the call. 'We have a youth in custody here – says his name is Billy Clegg and that he's an actor in the show you have on.'

'Well, there's certainly a Billy Clegg in the company. Could you describe him, please?'

The sergeant called out: 'Billy Clegg, on your feet and stand up to the bars where I can see you.'

Billy struggled to his feet and pushed his way through the straggle of adult legs.

'Y ... yes?' he said, with his frightened face pressed to the bars.

'How old are you?'

'Er ... eleven.'

'Skinny kid, brown hair, says he's eleven,' said the sergeant to the lady at the Cort.

'Could be him. Look, I've got his details here. They say his birthdate is May twentieth, nineteen thirty-five. If he knows that, it's got to be him.'

'Clegg, give me the date and year you were born?'

'May twentieth, nineteen thirty-five.'

'Yeah, I think this is him.'

'I know Billy. He's a real good kid. What are you holding him for?'

'So far, for keeping bad company.'

'How long has that been a crime, Sergeant?'

'It's not a crime, miss, more of a last-ditch attempt at keeping the peace in this god-forsaken precinct. Okay, I'm lettin' him go.'

'You mean, you're letting an eleven-year-old boy out onto the god-forsaken streets of your precinct, which are strange to him, late on a Saturday night? He's a very important member of the company, so be it on your own head if anything happens to him, Sergeant Brownlow. I would prefer it if you escorted him safely to his lodgings. He has a guardian there waiting for him. Worried to death, no doubt.'

'Okay, miss, we'll get him safely back there. If you could give me the address, please?'

The sergeant made a note of it and called out to Billy, 'Okay, Clegg. You're free to walk.'

'What about me?' Winston asked. 'I was at the show with him, only I wasn't on the stage. So this robbery yer got me for can't have happened when the show was on, which was between seven-thirty and ten.'

Winston knew very well what time the robbery had been committed, with him having done it.

'Billy remembers seeing me. I was down near the front. Great show it was. I recommend it.'

'Yes, I saw him,' confirmed Billy. 'I could hardy miss that big ugly face.'

Winston grinned. Another long sigh from the sergeant. Then: 'Okay, he's free to go as well. And mind this, fellas. I'm doing you both a big favour here, so don't you go telling no lies to no papers.'

'I won't,' said Billy, drying his eyes, 'and thank you very much, sir. We're very sorry to have been any trouble, aren't we, Winston?'

'Very sorry indeed,' Winston grunted as an officer unlocked the door and let them out.

'You get to ride in a cop car,' said the sergeant to Billy. 'We don't want you getting lost again.'

'I'm okay walking,' said Winston hastily.

'See you, Winston,' said Billy, 'and thanks.'

'For what?'

'Dunno.'

'Well, thank you for being the famous Billy Clegg and gettin' us both out of the tank.'

Billy was still grinning when the precinct phone rang and the sergeant picked up. It was Ross checking if Billy had showed up there.

'Yeah, we've had him in custody, sir, along with a low-life he says is a friend. They've just been released. If I were you, I'd make him choose his friends more carefully. We're sending him back to you in a car, so that he don't get into no more trouble.'

Ross put the receiver down with as much relief as he would if Billy were his own son.

'Yeah, he's there,' he told Peggy. 'The police are bringing him back. It seems he fell into bad company.'

'That'll be Spider. If Mam was here she'd box

Billy's ears when he gets back. I wish I could!'

She looked at Ross, who held up his hands to placate her. 'Hey, I'm only too glad he's coming back to us, no way will I chastise him. But if you want to give him a good roasting, be my guest. Mind you, if he's been banged up in a Saturday night cell, not knowing how or when he's getting out, it'll be a hard enough lesson for him.'

'Yeah, I suppose I should feel sorry for him.'

'But you don't?'

'Not one bit. Not now he's coming back to us in one piece.'

'That's the spirit! Give him a smile and ask him if he's okay.'

'Then what?'

'Then you can give him a roasting.'

'Good grief!'

It was the following Monday morning and Ross was reading the newspaper at the breakfast table.

'What?' asked Peggy.

'It says here a man died in custody in the Ninth Precinct on Saturday night. Did that happen when you were there, Billy?'

'A man was drunk and fell and banged his head, that's all I know. There was a lot of blood about.'

'That must have been awful for you,' said Peggy.

'I didn't see it. I was having a wee at the time, with my back to him, but I had to step over him afterwards. He was probably drunk and fell over. Most of them had been drinking. Some of them had been sick on the floor. The smell was awful.'

Billy's voice was faint and distant-sounding, as

if remembering a bad dream. Ross and Peggy exchanged glances.

'You've been acting strange ever since you got back, Billy,' said his sister.

'You'd be acting strange if you'd been locked up in that place,' he retorted. 'It was horrible.'

'Maybe it'll teach you a lesson.'

'What lesson's that then?'

'Never to do anything else that might get you locked up.'

'I didn't do anything that night.'

'You got mixed up with Spider.'

'He was all right was Spider. I'll tell you something, though.'

'What's that?'

'I don't want to be a Bowery Boy any more.'

'Do you want to stay here in New York?'

'Well, if New York was in Old Yorkshire it wouldn't be too bad.'

It was the following morning when news came through that Winston had been arrested. Ross read out the relevant piece of the article.

'Winston Moran, a negro known to the police, was arrested for causing the death of Duke Lorraine, the man who died in police custody on Saturday night. One of the inmates in the holding cell told police he had seen Moran tripping Lorraine, causing him to fall heavily on his back. Moran has denied this.'

'That's a lie!' said Billy. 'Where that man fell was out of sight of anyone in the cell.'

'Did you see him fall?' Ross asked.

'No, but I know where Winston was when the

man fell.'

'Where was he?'

'Right beside me, having a wee as well. When we turned round the big drunk man was already down on the floor. We were the first to see him.'

It was a lie, but one Winston had prepped him for, and it was only fair to go along with it. Billy didn't want Winston to be in trouble for causing the death of that horrible man who had been coming to get him. It was a lie he was willing to tell the police as well.

'Billy,' said Ross, 'if you're sure, you need to go to the police and tell them this, or your friend will end up in serious trouble, accused of something he didn't do. And you know what that's like.'

'He wasn't really a friend, just a bloke who helped get me out of that place.'

'I'll go with you if you like.'

'Thanks. I don't want to go in there on my own again.'

An hour later he and Ross entered the station house of the 9th Precinct. Ross asked to see a senior officer regarding the recent death in custody. A lieutenant was brought out to talk to him. Ross introduced both himself and Billy, then asked the boy to tell what he knew.

'Winston didn't trip him up. I don't know what happened but Winston was beside me. We were both taking a wee when the other man fell. I also don't see how anyone else in the cell could have seen what happened. They were all round the corner from the urinal.'

'You're sure of this?'

'Yes.'

'And would you be prepared to testify to this in court?'

'Yes,' said Billy.

The officer looked at Ross. 'I have to say, this tallies exactly with the story that Moran and one of the other inmates told me as well. Trouble is, they're both niggers and their word don't carry much weight around here, but your boy backing Moran up should do the trick. On top of which the man who says he saw Duke pushed over ain't the most reliable of witnesses. He was a crony of Duke Lorraine's and tarred with the same brush.'

'What brush is that?'

'Lorraine had a perverted liking for boys.'

'And you allowed a drunk paedophile to occupy a cell with an eleven-year-old? It appears to me,' said Ross, 'that it was a principled black man who stopped Billy from being assaulted by a pervert, while a roomful of police remained oblivious.'

'What do you mean by "stopped" him?'

'I mean he was there beside Billy when Lorraine made his move. That must have stopped Lorraine from trying anything. In any case, Billy shouldn't have been in there with grown men.'

'We have no cells here for juveniles,' said the lieutenant. 'Now, I'm relying on your boy to be telling the truth, which is why I'm releasing Winston Moran.'

'Did you hear that, Winston?' called out Billy. 'They're letting you go.'

'Billy,' said the lieutenant, 'I'm taking Mr Duggan into my office for a few minutes for a private conversation. Would you stay here?'

'Er, yeah.'

The lieutenant took Ross into a side office where they both sat down. 'I don't believe this story of how Lorraine died for one minute,' said the cop, 'but it suits my purpose.'

'How come?'

'Well, Lorraine was a public nuisance, in and out of here all the time. It's my belief he made a play for the boy and Moran knocked him down. If he'd actually gone for the boy there's not a man in that cell who wouldn't have attacked him. It would have been a bloodbath, which would have given us a lot of problems. As it stands, it looks like he died in a drunken fall, which is good for us.'

'Why are you telling me this?'

'Because the boy will be feeling guilty about telling such a lie and I want you to reassure him.'

They both went out into the main office where Billy was waiting.

'The biggest problem I have right now,' said the lieutenant, 'is you, young man.'

'Me? What have I done?'

'It's not what you've done, it's who you are. You're newsworthy. Any story involving you will bring out the fact that you were arrested for no good reason, and that will do the Ninth Precinct no good at all.'

'I don't suppose it'll do me much good either.'

'No, it definitely won't. No arrested person, no matter how innocent, is seen by the public as totally free from blame. An arrest will earn you an unwarranted reputation, and in view of your troubles in England I think this is a case where sleeping dogs should be left to lie.'

'I agree entirely,' said Ross. 'I brought Billy down here because he told me his story and I didn't think it fair on Moran that he should keep it to himself.'

'Well, he better keep it to himself from now on,' mumbled the lieutenant.

'I will, don't worry about that,' Billy assured him. 'Does this mean Winston can go free?'

'It does indeed. In fact, you can take him with you if you like.'

'I don't think that's a good idea,' said Ross, looking at Billy, who was giving an almost imperceptible shake of his head. 'As innocent as he is, I suspect he's not a good influence.'

The lieutenant smiled and said he fully understood. Billy was perfectly happy not to have to see Winston again.

'I think we'd be as well to take this back into my office,' said the lieutenant, looking across at the tank. It was heavily occupied by felons, all staring at them and trying to make out what was being said. 'This business ain't as simple as you might think.'

When they were in the lieutenant's office, he stared at them for a few seconds before saying to Ross: 'Have you ever heard of a man called Don Vito Genovese?'

'I think so. He's a Mafia boss, isn't he?'

'He is. Genovese and Lucky Luciano had this city tied up once.'

'I thought Luciano was in prison.'

'He was released last year for providing information that helped the war effort. He was deported

327

to Sicily. When Luciano was around, he and Genovese infiltrated the unions on the New Jersey waterfront; they handled all the drugs that were being traded in New York. Anyone going up against them, cop or criminal, ended up in a mortuary. They paid off people in power in the government, in the unions, police and the justice system, and made themselves very powerful men, which made our job well-nigh impossible.'

'I thought it was the FBI who handled the Mob,' said Ross.

'You're well informed, Mr Duggan, but we've got to handle the street-level mess they leave behind them.'

'Such as?'

'Such as the gangs they use to trade their drugs. Just punks who think they're big men because they have the Mob behind them. Some of them carry guns. The Mob aren't actually behind them, they only use them when it's convenient. In fact there aren't too many punk gangs that meet with the Mob's approval – maybe Jimmy Coonan's Westies or Ragen's Colts, but certainly never any no-account gangs like the Real Deal. These punk gangs are the weak links in the Mob's chain of command and they're how we'll get to nail the top men eventually.'

'So the Real Deal wasn't a proper gang?' said Billy.

'No, they were small-time Bowery Boys, who did small-time thieving – pickpockets, bag-snatchers and third-rate burglars. Nuisance gangs.'

'How is Spider?' Billy asked.

'He's going to be all right but he needs an alibi.

When he met you his gang were busy robbing an all-night drug store – an armed robbery. We picked most of them up. Lucky for Spider that none of them fingered him for being there.'

'That's because he wasn't. He was at the theatre. He'd gone to see me.'

'Yeah, that tallies with what he told us. He had a ticket stub in his pocket. So if you can give us a statement to that effect, he'll be free to go when he's discharged from hospital. You know, the small-time gang Spider got mixed up in was as big a nuisance to the Mob as it was to us. They don't like anyone operating on their patch without their permission in case it conflicts with one of their criminal operations, which is why they sent a team to tell Real Deal to disband. The team arrived at their place not long after you left with the police, which was lucky for you.'

'Lucky? Why?'

'Because the team they sent were all armed and they overstepped the mark. When the Real Dealers got back from their heist two of them ended up in the morgue and another three in hospital – with only two expected to live. That'll be three murders and two attempted we now have to solve.'

Ross put a hand on Billy's shoulder. 'My God! That could have been you.'

'Yeah, it could.'

This would all be added to the dare-devil tale he had to tell his friends back in Leeds. All the same Billy felt a shiver run up his spine at such a prospect. 'Does that mean Spider can't go back there?' he asked.

'There's nothing to go back to, Billy. The building was torched; the cellar they used and three floors above it were destroyed. Mobsters are unbelievably ruthless. Fortunately no one else was hurt in the fire. The Mafia like to send out a severe lesson to people who don't behave, but the day will come when they themselves have to answer to us.

'Meanwhile, so far as your friend Spider's concerned he'll be on his own – out on the streets which are dangerous for him right now. We'll release him but we can't protect him.'

'And you think we can?' queried Ross.

'No, I'm not saying that. But what you can do is persuade him to leave town. Going back to England would be his safest bet.'

'I think Spider might need somewhere to stay when he comes out of hospital,' said Billy, tentatively. He knew if he asked straight out for his friend to live with them, Ross would refuse. But a foot in the door, a temporary arrangement, might possibly extend into a refuge for his pal. Meanwhile he'd be sure to visit Spider in hospital.

Ross and the police lieutenant exchanged glances. Billy signed a witness statement to confirm his account of Duke's death and they were free to go.

Outside the apartment building Ross put a staying hand on Billy's shoulder. 'Before we go in, Billy, I want you to know I think you were lying in your statement so as to protect Winston. I can't say I blame you, in the circumstances, and neither does the lieutenant. He much prefers your version of events to what probably happened because it's a lot less trouble for him, so it's all wrapped up as far as he's concerned. You should put it out of your mind now. With regard to Spider, I've asked for him to be given our address and told we'll put him up for a couple of days while he makes up his mind whether to return home or not. You don't want the Mob catching up with him, do you?'

'No, of course not,' said Billy, making a mental note to add sheltering Spider from the New York Mob to his story. He must write all this stuff down some time lest he forget it. And he should write about Ross too, so that everyone knew what a generous man he was, totally incapable of turning his back on anyone who needed help.

So that was how Spider went to stay with Billy, Peggy and Ross. He remained holed up in the apartment for two days. On the third morning he made his announcement.

'There's an old lady up in the Bronx who I stayed with when I first came here. I replied to a notice she had in a shop winder and she hired me to do odd jobs around the house and garden and to fix her car and drive her places. She's gorra telephone, so I rang her last night and asked if I could stay with her for a while until I got meself fully recovered. I told her I was goin' back to England eventually. She's gorra room above the garage.'

'Is that true,' asked Peggy, 'about you going back to England?'

'Yeah, why wouldn't it be? This city's too dangerous for a scally like me. If I can get enough money together for the fare I'm goin' back to Liverpool. It says in the paper that the Real Deal guy who was seriously ill in hospital died yesterday. That was my room mate Pongo. Three dead altogether and one of them could've been me. There are too many people with guns here, and scuffers arrestin' people fer doin' nuthin'. I was real scared in that hospital – cried like a baby all night, thinkin' I was gonna lose me leg and then spend years in a New York prison hobblin' around on a crutch, an' I ain't no cry-baby.'

'I know that, and I wish you well, Spider,' said Ross. 'How is your leg, by the way?'

'Well, the bullet was a through-and-through and it didn't even clip me femoral artery. That would have made me bleed ter death before I got to hospital. So I'm one lucky boy.'

'I cried as well,' admitted Billy.

'Ah, but you're eleven. I'm eighteen now and supposed to be a man. If I go back to England I'll be called up for the army, which might not be a bad life if I sign on as a regular.'

'So how will you raise the money to get back?' Peggy asked.

'Dunno. If I can leave it until me leg gets better I might try and work me passage, but I've gorra stash at the old lady's place. If I can fence that, there should be enough for me ter travel back in style.'

'You mean stolen goods?' said Ross, looking disapproving.

'Was that really what I said?' Spider grinned.

'Well, not in so many words.'

'What I mean is, I have some *property* there,'

said Spider, 'which I may sell so's to pay me fare home and do me duty by king and country. I'm an honest lad now, and honest lads don't stow away. Not like some people I could mention.'

He grinned at Billy, who felt himself grinning back. Spider could always talk himself out of any situation, something they had in common.

Ross shook his head. 'I dread to think how you came by this *property.*'

'Mr Duggan, in Liverpool we call it wheeler-dealing. You start off with something worth a little bit, and end up with something worth a lot more.'

'Spider, I believe you. Thousands wouldn't.'

'Your good opinion is the only one that counts wid me, Mr Duggan.'

That same day Spider took a bus to the Bronx, where he had money and jewellery hidden in the spare wheel compartment of the old lady's car. Two days after that Billy received a card in the post.

I got me a passig home what I bort for when me leg gets better
Yor a real pal Billy Boy
New York is a scary place for old Spider
Tarra

It was a note Billy would always treasure. He'd had many pals in his time but never one quite like Spider.

Chapter 33

'Mr Richardson? ... Lester Blainey here ... I'm ringing with news that might be to our advantage.'

'Really? Well, that'll make a nice change. Right now I'm in danger of being booted out of the legal profession, thanks to you and that scam you tried to pull on Mrs Clegg. I should never have got myself involved!'

'You won't be booted out if I'm found not guilty. That's what I'm ringing you about.'

'What's this news that might be to my advantage then?'

'It's to do with my fingerprints being on the spanner that might well have caused the gas leak.'

'You mean the fingerprints that point to you being guilty of arson and killing all those women?'

'Yes. You see, none of the investigating officers bothered to ask me how my prints came to be on that spanner. In fact, when I was arrested I was so confused I'd forgotten myself. But I've remembered since.'

'Look,' said Richardson brusquely, 'I don't want to talk about this on the phone. I'll be in to see you tomorrow.'

The following morning they sat face-to-face in a prison interview room.

'Right,' said the solicitor, 'tell me about the spanner.'

Lester leant forward and spoke in a low voice that could not be heard by the policeman standing by the door.

'You see, I told the police I was in the cellar because someone had reported a smell of gas coming from down there, but what I never mentioned was that I tried to tighten up the joint I thought was leaking. I knew where the gas board's spanner was kept and used it to try and tighten the suspect nut. It seemed tight enough so I had a look round to where else the leak might be coming from but I couldn't find anything so I went outside, which is where I was when the place went up. And that's how my prints got to be on the spanner.'

'It's a pity you didn't tell the police that story straight away, before the spanner was ever found.'

'When I was arrested I was in such a state of shock that my brain wasn't working properly. It's only over the last couple of days that I've remembered.'

'Hmm. The police will say you made up the story to suit the known facts.'

'Is that what you think, Mr Richardson?'

'I don't know what to think. What I do know is that the Clegg children have now been found.'

'So I heard. They ran away to America, which in itself is suspicious. Why would they do that if they were innocent?'

'I don't know. What I do know is that their mother will make a hell of a fuss if the police drop their charges against you, as will the newspapers who are now very much on her side. I think the police will be very reluctant to let you go.'

'Yes, it's a pity that bloody woman wasn't killed

in the fire.'

Richardson moved his head and eyes to one side, indicating the policeman in the room.

'I'm only saying,' said Blainey.

'Okay. I'll pass your version of events on to your barrister, who'll be Mr McKnight, and see what he thinks.'

'He probably won't believe me either.'

'It's his job to seem to believe you – whether he really does or not.'

'Good. And you reckon my chances would be better if that bloody Clegg woman weren't around?'

'Yes, they would, but she is, so why are we even talking about her?'

Chapter 34

When Jimmy got home that evening from his job playing piano in a city-centre pub he was pleased to see that Betty's usually pale and anxious demeanour had changed for the better. In fact she was whistling as she put the kettle on – a talent he hadn't been aware she possessed.

'My word, what's cheered you up?'

'A cheque,' said Betty. 'Frank Smyth's been round to get me to sign a contract for the story.'

'I thought you'd already been paid for that.'

'This is for the follow-up story, which is even better than the first one if the show gets on to Broadway proper.'

'And Blainey strung up.'

'I suppose so.'

'No suppose about it, Betty. He killed a lot of your pals and if he'd killed you he'd have got away with it.'

'You mean because I involved you and it was you who... Blimey, Jimmy!'

'So you surviving did for him, and quite right too.'

'You're right. I never thought of it like that. Anyway there's a cheque in that envelope on the table. Paid in advance, in full.'

Jimmy picked up the envelope and took out the cheque.

'They're staying with that actor bloke, aren't they?'

'Ross Duggan, yeah.'

'Married, is he?'

'Yeah, but she's over here, looking after a business.'

'Have you got a passport?'

'No, just an application form. I've already got my passport photo, and don't ask to look at it ... it's horrible!'

'I can't imagine you taking a bad photo.'

'Jimmy Potter, you're a terrible old charmer! That's the nicest thing anyone's said to me in ages.'

'Surely your husband said nice things to you. I mean you had two children by him.'

'One.'

'Ah, yes ... what about Billy's dad then? I imagine he was pretty nice to you.'

'Oh, yes, Jack was lovely.'

'And you'll be off to see the Broadway actor when you get to New York.'

'Jimmy, I'm going to see my children. Like I said, he's married with two children of his own.'

'And you're a beautiful widow and he's probably a matinee idol living the life of a bachelor.'

'I don't know what he is. I've never seen him, but Peggy thinks he's quite good-looking. Mind you, she thinks Humphrey Bogart's good-looking ... and anyway, what difference does it make?'

'None, I suppose. Unless you're looking for another man who might love you.'

He held her gaze, hoping his message had got through to her. It had, but she wasn't prepared to show it. If he wanted to tell her he loved her he should say the words, although something inside her was hoping he wouldn't – she might not be able to handle it. Betty was a woman on the cusp of middle age and all this lovey-dovey dating stuff was far behind her.

And then she was asking herself: why not? Why was she so concerned about Jimmy's opinion of her? Was it because it might conflict with her opinion of him? Courage, she told herself. They should have this out right now. Get it sorted, one way or the other.

'What are you trying to say, Jimmy?'

'Just stating the obvious.'

Jimmy wasn't a bad-looking man, she decided. Not exactly a matinee idol, but he'd a pleasant face nevertheless. He was kind, thoughtful, gentle, generous, amusing ... and he was the man who'd got Blainey locked up for burning the factory down, and her children absolved of all blame. He had a certain charm that the other women at the factory had mentioned, although she'd never noticed it ... until he smiled at her. Yes, he had a charming way with him had Jimmy Potter. Oh, what the hell? One of them had to say something. She took the bit between her teeth and said it.

'Might you be that man, Jimmy?'

'What man?'

'The man who might love me.'

Jimmy's heart began to pound. She'd handed him a golden opportunity that shouldn't be wasted. An inner voice was urging him.

Go on, say it out loud, Jimmy Potter.

'There's no *might* about it, Betty,' was what he came up with.

'I'm not entirely sure what you mean by that.'

'I think you are.'

'Are you saying you love me?'

Say it, Potter!

It was the hardest thing he'd ever had to do.

'Yes.'

It was a short and simple word but it might well change both their lives. Her face broke into a broad smile.

'How do you know?' she asked.

'I just do. Might you love me, do you think?'

'Well ... I think I might, yes.'

They continued to stare at each other, both happy that the awkward preliminaries were over. What needed to be said, had been said. But what next?

'Maybe we should kiss,' suggested Betty, 'then we'll both know for certain.'

'Sounds like an idea to me.'

The kiss was far more passionate than their words had been, each spelling out to the other that they were in love, and each very happy with the outcome.

'That kind of settles it for me,' said Betty. 'We're definitely in love.'

'Boy! Am I glad you said that.'

'Jimmy, I'm not a boy.'

'I'm glad about that as well. So, we're officially in love then?'

'We are.'

He went down on one knee. 'Betty Clegg, will you marry me?'

'Bloody hell, Jimmy!'

'Question too difficult?'

'No ... I mean, yes. I'd love to marry you.'

'Good. That'll be one in the eye for the kids when we get there.'

'*We?*'

'Definitely. I'm not letting my fiancée out on her own where there's a handsome actor on the prowl, and you won't have to pay for me. I can afford the fare, even though I've just hooked myself a rich beauty.'

'Good. I'm going to give David's mam some of the newspaper money. A couple of hundred, what do you think?'

'I reckon it'll be more money than she's ever had in one go,' said Jimmy, approvingly.

'Now there's a feeling I know well.'

It was a week later when Betty received a letter from her solicitor asking her to contact him to arrange a meeting regarding Jack Blainey's will. It had been delivered to her own house and only arrived after being picked up by Jimmy, who called by there every other day to collect the post and check that everything was in order, especially that no more bricks had been thrown through her window. One of the neighbours had stopped him recently to ask after Betty's welfare.

'She's got a way to go yet, but she's doing okay ... and for the benefit of all those who think she's living in sin with me, you can tell them she's not. She's in no condition to be living in sin with anyone even if she wanted to, which she doesn't. You can also tell them that we're engaged to be married!'

His manner was more curt than he'd meant it to be. 'No need ter snap me head off!'

'Maybe not, but it strikes me that very few of her neighbours have had a good word to say about Betty.'

'Not me, love. I speak as I find and I've never found nowt wrong wi' Betty Clegg. My name's Robinson, Rachel Robinson. Tell her I've been askin' after her.'

'I'll do that – thanks, Mrs Robinson.'

Betty made arrangements to see her solicitor, Geoff Wooltorton, the day after she read the letter. Jimmy insisted he should go with her.

'I can manage on me own, Jimmy.'

'I know that, Betty, but from now on you don't have to manage on your own. We're a team.'

'I haven't asked you here to discuss the claim for injuries caused by the fire,' Wooltorton told them.

341

'It's best we don't pursue that. I'll explain why later. I've asked you here because, as far as I can see, your son Billy is one of Jack Blainey's two closest surviving relatives and, since he's a minor, I am speaking to you on his behalf. In the earlier bequest to Billy and Peggy, Jack clearly states that Billy is his son and must be treated as such.'

Wooltorton looked, belatedly, at Jimmy, to check that he wasn't revealing a secret.

'It's okay,' said Jimmy. 'I do know about Betty's affair with Jack.'

'Good. In that case, since Jack's wife was named in his will as sole beneficiary but she died before him, his will has been classed as *bona vacantia*, which is Latin for *ownerless goods*, or *unclaimed estate*. I could make a claim for it on Billy's behalf. Jack left a house and various other items including cash in his bank account and he clearly stated in his will that he was leaving nothing to his brother.

'The problem we face is that with Jack's wife out of the picture, his sister, Chief Superintendent Blainey, is now Jack's closest living relative along with Billy. It might be as well just to claim half of his estate and let her have the other half. It'd save a lot of trouble, if she makes a claim, and with Billy being illegitimate, she might have a good case.'

'Blimey! That's a bit of a setback for a copper, having your brother hanged for mass murder.'

'It won't do her career much good, that's for sure.'

'So, is this money worth chasing?' asked Betty.

'It's a tricky one. If she has any sense the sister would settle out of court with each party getting an equal share.'

'Would she agree to that?'

'She says she will if you drop any fire injuries claim from Lester's estate, which is why I'm suggesting we don't pursue that claim. It's possible you might end up with everything Lester managed to leave, but nothing from Jack's estate.'

'I don't want any of Lester's rotten money!'

Wooltorton smiled. 'That should certainly encourage the sister to make a fifty-fifty split.'

'What about the two thousand pound bequests Jack made to Billy and Peggy?'

'Oh, they're both safe, with the money in a bank account accruing interest. You'll need to apply to be their *guardian ad litem* until they come of age.'

'Do you lot use Latin to get one over on us uneducated peasants?' said Betty.

Jimmy laughed. 'No, they do it so you get power of attorney over Billy's inheritance until such time as he's old enough to manage it for himself.'

'I wouldn't waste my time trying to get one over on you, Mrs Clegg,' said Wooltorton. 'So, what do you want to do?'

Betty went quiet for a while, pondering things over as the two men looked on. She drew her breath in and blew it out as she came to a decision.

'I don't want anything that's not rightly mine,' she said. 'Nothing at all. I'm happy with what I've got.'

'Mrs Clegg. Am I hearing you correctly? The other party has agreed to a fifty-fifty split.'

'Well I haven't. I don't want any of their money. It wouldn't feel right. Jack's dead, his wife who would have inherited his house died before him and his brother's been hanged for mass murder.

Their sister can't be feeling too good about things as it stands, without the publicity of her fighting one of Lester's victims in court for Blainey family money that I was never entitled to. That would make me a gold-digger. What I am is alive, I've got my kids back, and I've got Jimmy out of all this. Let the families of the dead girls go after the Blainey money.'

'You have a point, Mrs Clegg, maybe I will offer to represent them.'

'I'll tell them, shall I?'

'If we tell the papers about this and mention your name I bet they'll need no telling,' suggested Jimmy. 'They'll be queueing up outside your office the next morning.'

'I don't want them making me into some sort of working-class hero,' said Betty. 'If Jack meant to leave me his house he'd have said so in his will, and I don't want to go against his wishes. He left the kids two thousand each and I think that was more than generous. If the kids want to get rich they'll have to do that for themselves. They've got a whole lifetime to do it in, and two thousand's a pretty good start.'

She looked at Jimmy. 'Blimey, Jimmy! This is a proper state of affairs. I've got rich kids and I'm just a clothes factory worker.'

'I can think of worse problems.'

'You mean like all that stuff the kids have just been through?'

'Not just the kids, I mean the stuff you've all been through,' said Jimmy. 'The kids would've swapped Buckingham Palace and the Crown Jewels to get you back, I know I would. You can never put a price on your mam.'

'Anyway,' said Wooltorton, 'that's the current situation. Am I right in assuming that you wish me to drop all claims.'

'Yeah, drop the lot,' said Betty. 'Let the dead girls' people have a chance at that money. I like to sleep at night and I got quite a lot of money from the papers.'

'I know and I'd hate for you to have that swallowed up in legal fees, especially if we lost our case.'

'Right now,' said Betty, 'I just want all this damned Blainey business to end. All I want is to get across to New York to see my children and introduce them to their stepfather-to-be.'

'I think you're probably wise,' said Wooltorton.

'Betty Clegg, you're a woman of real style!' said Jimmy.

At that very moment Lester was in an ambulance heading for Leeds Infirmary to be checked out for a severe pain in his head.

'I think it's most probably a tumour,' he'd told the doctor in prison. 'The pain gets so bad it makes me pass out and when I wake up I never know what's happened or where I am. It's a family thing. My dad died of a brain tumour and so did my brother.'

'We'll have you checked out,' said the doctor, who had little sympathy for a man who had caused the deaths of so many innocent people.

'If it's a tumour it'll probably get me before the hangman does.'

'Does this mean you're going to plead guilty?'

'I might as well. What have I got to lose?'

That was when the doctor decided to tell the people at the Infirmary that in his opinion Blainey was lying to get himself off being hanged. He was taken from the ambulance, strapped to a trolley and wheeled into the hospital. He had closed his eyes and was feigning either sleep or unconsciousness. There was a method in this insofar as he knew the hospital quite well. It was near the top of one of the flights of stairs that he decided to make his escape. The policeman accompanying the porter who was wheeling the patient was momentarily distracted by a passing doctor, who asked him to help deal with a disturbance in the A&E ward. Blainey, who had already undone the strap securing him, slipped off the trolley and went through a door leading to the service stairs. Then, instead of going down as might be expected, he went up to the next floor, where he twisted and turned down several corridors and eventually found a lift. A minute later he was on the ground floor, well away from the panic breaking out around his empty trolley. Luckily for him he was still in his day clothes and not wearing hospital garb, so could pass for a member of the public.

He made his way to the Great George Street entrance, a door little used by patients, and was soon making for the Headrow where he caught a bus heading for Beeston, in the opposite direction from where he lived and probably the last area the police would think to look for him; he had just enough loose change in his pocket to pay for a cheap bus fare. On the bus was one vacant seat where an elderly woman was sitting in the window seat with a shopping bag in her lap. He gave her a smile and asked if she minded him sitting next to her. It wasn't exactly a winning smile but it wasn't her bus so she had no option other than to say she didn't mind. In any case it turned out that she was getting off at the next stop. It was after she alighted that she realised her purse was missing. Blainey got off two stops later and checked the purse's contents. Three pound notes, a ten-shilling note and some change; enough for him to get by until he decided what to do next. He found another bus stop and caught a bus to Wakefield.

For years he had visited a woman called Gertrude there, a woman of easy virtue who had satisfied his carnal desires. She was a hefty woman with one glass eye that didn't match its real-life counterpart.

'Lester bleedin' Blainey!' was her inelegant greeting. 'I never expected ter see you again. Have they let you out?'

'I've let meself out.'

'Had it on yer toes, eh? You bein' here could get me into trouble, Lester.'

'Only if they find out about you, which they won't, and I won't be staying long.'

'So, yer thought yer'd come here fer a bit of the other, did yer?'

'Why not, if you're up for it?'

'I'm allus up for it. I bet yer'd like a nice drop o' whisky first, eh?'

'I wouldn't say no, Gertrude.'

'Hey. I've told you before. You call me Gert and leave out the rude bit. Have yer got any money?'

'Not on me, no, but I'll see you right. You know you can trust me to do that. Put me up for a week and there's twenty quid in it for you.'

'Fair enough, but if the coppers come sniffin' round, I know nowt about yer bein' a wanted man. I've got no telly and I can't read. I've only got me wireless.'

'That's fine by me.'

Now safely ensconced in Gertrude's house he made his plans, the most pressing of which was to take care of that meddling bitch Betty Clegg. With her out of the way and no longer making a strong case for her children being innocent, convicting him would be a lot more difficult. His reasoning was faulty, of course, but stupidity never cured a desperate killer of murderous intent. All he knew was that it would help his cause if Betty Clegg were dead, and he knew exactly where she was living; with that prat Jimmy Potter. Blainey knew exactly where he lived – and where Betty Clegg would die.

He knew that Jimmy Potter played piano in pubs around the town. All Lester had to do was knock on the door when he knew Potter wasn't in. She'd come to the door and the rest would be easy. *FIRE SURVIVOR BETTY CLEGG MURDERED* would be the headline. Killing wouldn't be a problem for him; he'd done it before and got away with it. It was a fond memory in his perverse mind; but a memory that needed refreshing, and this was a golden opportunity.

Lester had armed himself with an eight-inch-long kitchen knife. He intended to plunge it into Betty the instant she opened the door to him. He had disguised himself by wearing a flat cap, scruffy workman's clothing and a pair of glasses that weren't his. Gertrude had been to his house late at night to pick up the cash he had stashed there. He now had two hundred and fifty pounds, which would be of great help over in Ireland, his eventual destination, and perhaps take him to America from there, if he could wangle a visa. Twenty of this he'd given to Gertrude, which she took with little gratitude as she knew what he had planned, and it didn't include her.

Betty was dozing in front of the fire when he knocked on the door. It was 8.30 in the evening, an odd time for anyone to be calling. Lester was ready with the knife that he held behind his back as the door opened. He was swift to raise the arm in readiness, but so was the yard brush being wielded by Betty, which came at him with such force that it sent him staggering backwards. A second thrust had him down on the ground and being beaten soundly about the head with the business end of the brush, wielded by a screaming Betty. No one saw the fat wallet spill from his coat as he fell, nor did anyone see Betty pick it up and stick it her pinafore pocket before resuming her attack on him. Her screams alerted neighbours, who arrived to see what was going on. Betty shouted the explanation at the top of her voice.

'This is Lester Blainey! He's the one who burnt his factory down and killed all them girls. He's come here ter finish me off with that knife – look! Yer need ter call the police. They'll be looking for him.'

Lester still had the knife clutched in his hand. Three men entered the yard and between them pinned him to the ground. The skin on his face was dotted with specks of blood from where the stiff bristles had met it forcefully, and still were doing. Betty hadn't quite finished with him.

'I'll ring nine nine nine!' shouted one woman, who also had every reason to hate Blainey since her sister had died in the fire.

And so the drama unfolded with Betty still wielding the brush in case Lester tried to escape, the three burly men holding him down and the whole group surrounded by women.

'I was ready for the murderin' pig!' Betty explained to them.

There were many nods of approval. 'How did yer know it was him callin' on you?' someone asked.

'Jimmy fitted a little spy-hole in the door, just in case. I knew ter check everyone who came knockin'. He's tried ter disguise himself, but I could see his ugly mush through the spy-hole and I knew who it was. I hit him with this brush before he could stab me.'

'Good old Jimmy, eh?' remarked a man.

'Good old Betty, yer mean!' chorused the women.

'Not so much of the "old"!' said Betty.

'I bet that bugger'll think again before he attacks a woman armed with a brush!'

Betty knew that Jimmy's spy-hole had probably saved her life. She stamped on Blainey's hand until he let go of the knife he'd intended to kill her with. A Black Maria arrived to take him back to prison where he was locked up in solitary.

Jimmy was shocked by the story Betty related when he got home just before midnight.

'Blimey! I'll be scared ter leave you on yer own in future.'

'No need, Jimmy. There was only Blainey I had to worry about ... and there's something else.'

'What's that?'

'Well, when he fell down, he dropped this.'

She took the wallet from her pocket and handed it over. Jimmy looked inside and counted out the contents.

'Two hundred and thirty quid,' he said. 'That's six months' wages for me ... at least it would be if I had a reg'lar job.'

'I know. What I *don't* know is what to do with it. Nobody saw me pick it up and it goes against the grain to give a sum like this back to him.'

'What could *he* do with it?' said Jimmy, then answered his own question. 'He could hire a better lawyer for his trial.'

'Then maybe I should hang on to it until after his trial.'

'He'll tell the police it's missing.'

'Two hundred and thirty quid? Why would they believe him?'

'Well, they'll believe you before they believe him, and you know nothing about it. I think you should hang on to it and see what happens.'

'Yeah, that's what I'll do. It's the price he paid for attacking me. Trouble is, if the kids find out I've nicked it they'll be very disappointed in me. I've always taught them to be honest.'

'There'll be no need for them to find out, and let's face it, it's still poor reward for what Blainey put you through.'

'You're not kidding! I wouldn't go through that again for ten million quid, never mind two hundred and thirty. Might as well hang on to it for a rainy day.'

'And with a clear conscience, I would hope,' said Jimmy.

'I think I'd like you to look after it for me,' she said. 'Then I won't be tempted to go splashing it around.'

'Just give me two hundred and you splash the thirty. It'll be safe with me.'

'I know that, Jimmy.'

'There's one other thing I need to remind you of.'

'What's that?'

'That I proposed to you *before* I knew your family was due to become rich – I don't want you to think I'm a gold-digger.'

'Jimmy Potter. You saved my life by digging me out of the factory ruins, that's all I need to know about you and your digging.'

Two days later Jimmy received a written request for him and Betty to meet Inspector Dennison at the police station. It was a request that worried Betty.

'Do you think something's cropped up and I'm back in trouble?'

'No, it'll be ter do with old Buggerlugs Blainey trying ter kill yer.'

'I do hope so, Jimmy. I've been feeling a lot

better about the factory business lately.'

The following day they were shown into an interview room where they sat at a table side by side. Dennison came in carrying a buff folder, which he laid on the table and opened. He looked up at them and smiled to see the worried expression on Betty's face.

'This is nothing that need concern you, Mrs Clegg. It's to do with a defence Blainey's putting up to explain why his fingerprints were on the spanner. He's saying he was using it just before the explosion, to seal a gas leak.'

'That's rubbish,' said Jimmy. 'I was in that cellar about an hour before that and I'd have known if there was any leak, which there wasn't. A gas leak is the first thing I'm looking for when I go down there. The air was as fresh as it is in here, and I've never known Blainey do a job that required a bit of graft. He was not what you'd call a working man. If he sniffed gas down there he'd have called me in to fix it.'

'And that's exactly the evidence we'll need to hear you give in court,' said Dennison. 'Oh, and he was also complaining that he lost a wallet full of money during the altercation in your yard.'

'Altercation?' snapped Betty. 'Is that what it was? And here's me thinking he was out to kill me. Has he explained why he came visiting at night armed with a knife?'

'No, he hasn't, but I suspect he tried to stab you so you wouldn't be around to make a loud and angry noise about his lame excuse regarding the explosion. A woman who hated him so vehemently would jeopardise any slim chance he had of acquittal. A jury would be easily persuaded by a woman of your passionate conviction. Without wishing to appear rude, I'd say you're any defence counsel's worst nightmare.'

'So you think he tried to kill Betty to shut her up?' said Jimmy.

'I can only say what we suspect, Mr Potter. Blainey hasn't given us a reason as yet. As far as the attack on Mrs Clegg's concerned, he's not answering any questions.'

'You mean he hasn't thought of an excuse yet. We're gonna get married, you know, me and Betty, and that bastard's tried ter kill her!'

'In that case, congratulations, I'm sure you'll be very happy – which is more than I can say for Blainey. He's due to be interviewed again tomorrow, which is when we'll put it to him to plead guilty on both charges if he wants any chance of escaping the gallows in favour of a life sentence. The thought of being hanged makes many a murderer see the advantage in admitting guilt to the court.'

'You mean he might not hang for killing all those women?'

'I'm saying a guilty plea is his only chance of escaping the death sentence. I'm not saying how much of a chance it is.'

Betty looked at him, saying, 'By the look of you, he hasn't got much of one.'

Dennison smiled at her perspicacity. 'To be honest, Mrs Clegg, he lost any chance he had left when he tried to kill you. The reason I asked you here was to put you fully in the picture, in case you read somewhere that he might be escaping proper justice. He's in solitary confinement right now and won't see the light of day until he makes his first journey to court.'

Chapter 35

Betty and Jimmy were leaning against the bow rails of the SS *United States* as the horizon became blurred by the distant shore. It was a beautiful March day, with the sun glinting off the Atlantic breakers.

'I think that's our first sighting of America,' said Jimmy, pointing at the distant coast. 'Blimey! I feel like Christopher Columbus,' said Betty, 'only I think we got here a bit quicker.'

'It took him over two months; it took us five days.'

'By heck! You know some stuff, Jimmy Potter.'

'I learnt that in primary school when I was about nine.'

'Will we see the Statue of Liberty?'

'We will. I think we sail right past it. That's why it was put there: to send out a message to visitors from the free world.'

'It wouldn't have lasted long if Hitler had got over here.'

An hour later the Statue of Liberty came into view off the port bow as the ship steered north towards the Hudson River. An hour after that, Jimmy and Betty were in a yellow cab heading for the Cort Theatre on West 48th Street. Jimmy looked at his watch and asked the driver, 'What time do you have?'

'A quarter after six. I'm guessing your watch shows different.'

'Yeah, it shows we should be getting ready for bed – quarter-past eleven. Mind you, we got plenty of sleep on the ship. What time does the show start, Betty?'

'Seven-thirty.'

'Cort Theatre?' said the driver. 'That's that British show, isn't it?'

'Yes, it's called *Twist*, based on the book by Charles Dickens.'

'Well, I sure hope you've got tickets. I hear that show's been selling out every night.'

'We have. My son and daughter work there. They've left us two tickets at the box office,' Betty explained.

'Work there?' said the driver. 'What do they do? Something backstage?'

'No, in the show. My daughter's one of Fagin's gang and my son plays the Artful Dodger.'

'Hey! I've seen the show and it's really good. If that's your boy playing the Artful Dodger, I gotta tell you – he's really somethin' else. I wish he was my boy.'

Betty swelled with pride. 'That's my son,' she said, smiling.

'You mean Billy Clegg. And you're his mom?'

'Yes, Betty Clegg, that's me, and Billy's sister is called Peggy.'

'Gee, I know that. She sings this song about starving kids on the London streets in winter. Real tear-jerker... And are you their dad, sir?'

356

'No, he died in the war. I'm hoping to become their stepfather.'

'Hey, man, I know the whole story! You're talking about the two runaway kids. It was in all the papers. They're kinda famous in New York. I hear it's why that show's sold out every night. Everyone loves a kid who beats the system, which is what they did. Ain't you seen them since they got here?'

'I haven't seen them for over four months. They thought I was dead, and I thought *they* might be too,' Betty confessed.

'Aw, gee, lady! Wait till I tell 'em about this back at the cab office! I'm the guy who brought the Clegg kids' mom to the theatre. My wife will never believe me. She's a great fan of the show. She's seen it three times. Well, I sure am gonna take her again after this.'

'Is there a place near the theatre where we can get something decent to eat that won't break the bank?' asked Betty.

'There sure is, lady. I'll take you to a great place that me and the other cabbies all use. So do some of the theatre people – maybe even your boy. It's just around the corner from the theatre. I'll take you to the box office and then show you the way to Danny's Eaterie.'

Billy looked at his reflection in the make-up room mirror. He was wearing ragged clothes and a battered top hat that was way too big for him. He had a blacked-out tooth, white make-up on his face and dark shading around the eyes, to make him look like a starving waif. His reflection drew a grin from him. He'd been playing the part for two weeks now and knew the lines backwards, to the extent that he'd polished them with a comedic rhythm that both the audience and the director loved.

'If this show hits Broadway, that kid's gotta come with us,' the director said to the stage manager. 'He's got them eating out of his hand.'

'Well, he won't come without his sister.'

'I know that and it's a comfort that she's so good as well. I'm guessing they're both better than Ross's own kids. The advantage is that with the kids not being Ross's, we're not obliged to take him if we find someone better.'

'Well he sure sounds like a Limey which is how he's supposed to sound. You think an American actor can do better? I ain't so sure. The ladies seem to like him.'

'I guess maybe you're right. Who knows in this business? The Clegg kids'll be meeting their *real* mom after the show.'

'Has she come to take them back?'

'I don't know, which is why we need to treat her with kid-gloves – make her realise that her kids have a big future in the theatre, especially if this show moves over to Broadway.'

'You think that's on the cards, do you?'

'I do, but keep that to yourself. In this business, rumours have a habit of back-firing.'

'No problem. What about their schooling if they stay?'

'I'll get them into a good stage school that'll teach them as well as most kids are taught in nor-mal schools. After that I reckon the Julliard'll welcome a couple of young Broadway stars with open arms. In the meantime they could be a great asset to our company. I think Manny should get them under contract as soon as.'

Manny Simons was this show's producer and currently had another on Broadway. The word going round the company was that he was considering closing his Broadway show down and replacing it with *Twist*. He had two years of his contract with the Broadway theatre owners left to run and the first show just wasn't paying its way; better to swap it for a successful one than run it at a loss. Impresarios are businessmen first and showmen second.

There was a loud knock on the make-up room door. It was an assistant stage manager. One of the girls went to answer it.

'Five minutes to curtain for Billy Clegg. Is he still in there? I've rounded all the other kids up, which is a bit of a nightmare, I might add. Three of them were in wardrobe drinking beer.'

'I'll be there,' shouted Billy, who loved everything about the theatre, including all the backstage naughtiness. He'd had a taste of American beer and thought it as sour as the English stuff; how anyone could get addicted to it was beyond him. Peggy was already in the wings, sitting on a chair and running her opening line through her head, then softly singing her song through to get it fixed securely in her memory, despite having already sung it twenty times on-stage. Tonight was an important night for her and Billy. Tonight their mother was going to be in the audience. Peggy knew where Mam would be sitting, row six right in the centre – best seats in the house some would say. The nearer you got to the front, the more neck-ache you got from peering upwards at the stage. Row six was where the directors sat when watching rehearsals. It put you more or less on a level with the performers.

Apparently her mother would be accompanied by a gentleman friend from Leeds called Jimmy. Peggy was really hoping she and Billy would like Jimmy because a man wouldn't travel all those thousands of miles with a mother to see her lost children if he was only a casual friend.

'Do you think Mam might get married again?' Billy had asked his sister.

'Well, if she does, good luck to her.'

'What if we don't like him?'

'So long as he's not cruel to us and Mam and she loves him, then it's all right with me, and you should feel the same. Let's face it, not long ago we thought Mam was dead, so we should be happy that she's alive and over here to see us. I never thought that'd happen in a million years.'

'Nor me,' said Billy. 'I wonder where she got the money from to come over?'

'She won't have nicked it, that's for sure.'

'Oh, no! Not our mam,' said Billy. 'Are we going to tell her about the money we nicked?'

'Well, *I* didn't nick any money so that's up to you.'

'No, but you spent the money I nicked, which makes you just as bad. She'll want to know how we managed to feed ourselves for all this time and where did we stay and stuff.'

'We can tell her about Goldie befriending us

over in Blackpool. After that we went to Liverpool with Harry and stowed away. I think the less we tell her the better.'

Billy followed this with: 'Then we met Mr Duggan and Ross and Maisie and they looked after us and got us these stage jobs. All that's true.'

'Yeah,' agreed Peggy. 'It's what we miss out that's the lies. When we go back to Leeds I think we should give that woman in the shop her money back, though. I always felt bad about that.'

'Anonymously,' said Billy. 'As if it was sent back by that ginger-haired kid who nicked it.'

'Yeah ... good idea.'

Such thoughts were running through Peggy's mind when Ross came over and sat down beside her.

'Going through your opening lines?'

'Yeah, something like that, and thinking about my mother. She'll be in the audience tonight. I hope she recognises us. It's ages since she's seen us.'

'Oh, I shouldn't worry about that. She'll recognise you as easily as you recognise her. You both have unforgettable faces, and you have an unforgettable voice, young lady. And she's hardly not going to recognise Billy, once he gets the audience laughing.'

Peggy smiled. 'No, I suppose you're right. It's just that up to us running away we'd both spent every day of our lives with her, and now we've spent about hundred and fifty days without her.'

'Been counting, eh?'

'I have. And Billy will know the exact number too. We left Mam two tickets at the box office.

Row six centre.'

'Good seats. I'll keep an eye out for her.'

'She's blonde and very pretty ... and she has a gentleman friend with her. He came over from England specially.'

Peggy was wondering why she'd told him this. She looked at Ross and realised, not for the first time, just how handsome and charming he was. She was hoping that Jimmy was also handsome and charming, if her mam was to get to know Ross Duggan during her stay here. Oh, heck! What if she fell in love with him? That was a problem they didn't need. It was a thought that had never struck her brother, but he was a boy, and boys never think along such lines. *Pity*, thought Peggy, because she wouldn't have minded having a chat with Billy about that possibility.

As the curtain went up the director walked out to centre-stage to make an announcement:

'Ladies and gentlemen, as you probably know, two members of our cast are genuine English children: a boy called Billy Clegg, who will be playing the Artful Dodger, and his sister Peggy, who will be playing Rose, the girl who sings "The Cold, Cold Streets of London Town". I have singled them out of this excellent cast because, due to a series of unfortunate circumstances, these two wonderful kids have ended up thousands of miles away from their home in England, and away from their dear mother whom they haven't seen since early last November. I've identified them and their parts in the show so that their mother can recognise them behind their make-up. For she is indeed in the audience tonight and it will be on this stage that she gets her first sight of them since they were forced to run away from home months ago...'

'Oh, God,' hissed Betty to Jimmy. 'I just know what's going to happen next!'

'So do I.' He grinned at her. 'You're in show business now, Betty Clegg.'

'And so, ladies and gentlemen,' announced the director, 'I'd like Mrs Clegg to stand up and identify herself. She's sitting in row six centre.'

A spotlight picked Betty out with unerring accuracy, leaving her with no option but to stand up, and raise a hand to tumultuous applause from the audience. Billy and Peggy could hear all this from the wings.

'I'm going out there to see her,' he said.

'No, you can't,' said Peggy. 'It's not allowed!'

But the director was signalling for them both to come on-stage. Hand in hand, they walked on, shading their eyes from the stage lights so they could see their mam. Now on her feet, Betty waved at them. They waved back.

'Hiya, Mam!' shouted Billy, waving both hands.

As if they'd been rehearsed, the whole audience got to their feet and shouted back, almost in unison.

'Hiya, Billy!'

Peggy thought she'd have a go with, 'We love you, Mam!'

The audience responded. 'We love you, Peggy!'

The applause seemed as though it might go on forever, but the director came back on and took a good minute to wave them into silence. Billy and Peggy walked into the wings without taking their eyes off Betty, whose face was streaming with tears. She kept her hand clasped over her mouth. She would remember this as the most joyous moment of her entire life.

That evening the show went well, marred only perhaps by the disproportionate amount of applause given to Peggy's singing and Billy's amusing antics as the Artful Dodger. In fact, well after the curtain fell at the end of Peggy's one-and-only song, the audience were still applauding and she was aware that this was for reasons other than just her singing, which had been good but not that good. With the curtain safely down on the applause, she turned to her fellow artistes and apologised.

'I'm really sorry about this. I know I'm not that good. I'm sure this is only because of our mother coming tonight.'

The young actress who was playing Nancy took her by the hand. 'Listen, kid. You and your brother's escapades have filled this theatre every night since we opened. Because of you, we're in a goddamned hit show and we don't begrudge you nuthin'!'

'Thanks.'

Murmurs of agreement came from other members of the cast as they left the stage to return to their dressing rooms or regroup for their first positions in Act Two. Billy was among the latter.

'Did you see Mam?' he asked Peggy.

''Course I did.'

'She looks okay, doesn't she?'

'Why wouldn't she?'

'Because of the fire and stuff.'

'Oh, yeah. Well, she's had time to recover from that.'

'Did you see that bloke with her?'

'I did, yeah.'

'What do you think?'

'Billy, what am I supposed to say?'

'Did he look all right to you?'

'I suppose so. We'll be meeting him later, I'll tell you more then.'

After the final curtain fell and the company were taking their joint applause, the director stepped forward and spoke directly to Betty.

'Mrs Clegg, I wonder if you could make your way up on to the stage. There are two young people here who want to give you a big hug. That goes for your companion as well.'

'That's me and you up there then,' said Jimmy.

The departing audience, having heard this, now stopped and turned back to applaud Betty as she arrived on-stage to be hugged by Billy and Peggy, who had come front of the curtain to greet her. It was the moment all three of them had dreamt of since Bonfire Night, a dream come true ... although none of them had dreamt of their reunion being quite so public.

As they left the stage the director came over to them. 'I'm guessing you guys need some privacy so you can have the use of my office for a while before the kids go back to the dressing rooms. Afterwards I'd like a word with you, Mrs Clegg.'

Jimmy, who had hung back during the

emotional reunion on-stage, waited as the three Cleggs entered the director's office. He felt they needed to be alone for a while before any outsider interrupted their family celebration. But Betty came to the door and ushered him in.

'This is Jimmy Potter,' she told her children. 'He has every right to be here because if not for him I wouldn't be here tonight. He saved my life on the night of the explosion.'

'Wow!' said Billy. 'Hiya, Jimmy.'

'Hello,' said Peggy, politely proffering her hand for him to shake.

'He got me out just before the wall came down right where I'd been lying,' Betty explained to them. 'He's also the one who proved that you lot didn't cause the explosion.'

'Well, it was partly me, and partly your friend David.'

'We thought Mam was dead,' said Peggy. 'In fact, someone told us she was.'

'He was called Goldie,' added Billy. 'We thought he was our friend, but he wasn't really. He's dead now.'

'Oh, dear, I'm sorry,' said Betty.

'He was all right sometimes,' said Peggy, with a sidelong glance at her brother. 'We stayed with him and Harry, who was his granddad, in Black-pool for a bit, then Goldie was knocked down by a bus and killed. I think he told us you were dead because he didn't want us to go back to Leeds.'

'He was a robber,' said Billy, wanting to add a little spice to the story, 'and wanted us to distract people, so that he could rob them.'

'Oh, please tell me you didn't?' said Betty.

366

'We only did it once,' said Peggy, shooting a censorious glance at her brother, 'which was when he got knocked down by a bus while trying to get away from the police. So that taught us a lesson.'

'I imagine it did. Oh, you poor children. You must have had a terrible time. So how did you end up here?'

'Well, Harry was so upset about Goldie that he set his house on fire and went to Liverpool to work on a ship as a cook. We went with him and stowed away on the same ship, coming to America.'

'That's where we met Ross and his children. Ross plays Bill Sykes in this show.'

'Oh, I didn't like him at all,' said Betty.

'That's because he's a good actor,' said Peggy. 'He's really very nice. He got us our jobs in this show.'

'There's got to be a book in this story,' murmured Jimmy.

'There is,' said Peggy. 'Ross is writing it.'

'It was really his own children who were supposed to be playing our parts,' said Billy, 'but they've gone back to England to be with their mam.'

Betty was looking with astonishment from one to the other as their story unfolded, with her trying to fill in all the missing pieces, of which there must surely be many. Jimmy was grinning all over his face.

He'd taken an immediate liking to Betty's remarkable children.

'Are you listening to all this, Jimmy?' she said.

'I'm trying to keep up but I've never heard

anything like it. I'd love to hear the unexpurgated version one day.'

'It'll take more than a day,' said Peggy, knowing they'd have to dream up an acceptable version of their adventures, leaving out most of the crimes they'd committed.

'So you stowed away on a ship and came to New York?' said their mother.

'Er, no. We got off the ship in Miami to spend Christmas somewhere warm. Ross had rented a house there. It was lovely, wasn't it, Billy?'

'Scorching. We went on the beach on Christmas morning. We both had suntans on New Year's Day.'

'Oh, for goodness' sake! And there I was, worrying about you keeping warm. Did you know we've had the worst winter in living memory back home?'

'What? You've had a lot of snow?'

'Snow! I've never seen so much of it. Well over a foot deep up Harehills Road. The trams had to stop running. There's a pile six foot high in the middle of our street where everybody's shovelled it out of the yards and off the path. It's frozen solid. The kids have been having a great time tunnelling into it. I thought about you, Billy every time I watched them. You'd never have been out of them tunnels. I'd have had a right job getting you in for your tea.'

She wiped away a tear as she remembered how she'd missed him, then replaced it with a smile.

'Is it all still there?' Billy asked her.

'It was when we left, and showing no sign of melting. Roundhay Park Lake's frozen over –

people are skating on it.'

'Trust us to be miles away the minute we get some decent snow,' grumbled Billy. 'I bet it was great sledging in Roundhay Park.'

'I wouldn't know. I was in hospital so I didn't do much sledging.'

'Oh, sorry,' said Peggy. 'Here we are, talking about snow and sledging when you've been badly injured. Are you fully recovered now, Mam?'

'Pretty much – now I know you two are all right. You being missing was the worst part of it all.'

'We thought we'd get the blame for burning the factory down and killing all those people,' Peggy told her, 'so we couldn't write without giving ourselves away. We thought all your post might be intercepted by the police.'

'Actually, yes, I think it was.'

'We slept in a beach hut in Blackpool for a few nights then we met Goldie and went to live with him and Harry, his granddad.'

'I suppose you both went hungry, did you?'

'We did a bit,' said Billy, before Peggy could in-tervene with the truth about his stealing. 'Harry was a great cook. He made us proper breakfasts with bacon, egg, tomatoes and stuff, and he made us proper dinners ... nearly as good as yours, Mam.'

'Then his grandson was killed?'

'Yeah. We were both sad because he never did us any harm – except tell us you were dead. We didn't know you were really alive until we got to New York and Ross rang the papers and found out the truth.

'That was a great time for us,' he recalled, hug-

369

ging his mother tight. 'Best time ever, since we ran away – well, *second* best time,' he added after a moment's thought.

'I'm glad you had some good times,' said Betty. 'So, where are you staying?'

'With Ross. He's renting an apartment. I bet you could stay with us tonight. There are three bedrooms and Mam could share with Peggy.'

'I'd like that,' said Peggy.

'If there's a settee I could sleep on that,' volunteered Jimmy.

'Yeah, there's a big settee,' said Peggy, pleased by the delicate way he'd reassured them that his behaviour towards their mother would remain respectful. Billy too had already decided that Jimmy Potter looked like an all round good man – almost as good a man as Ross. He couldn't wait to see how Mam would get along with this bloke who had stepped in and saved them and given them this wonderful new life. His sister had different thoughts on that subject.

Chapter 36

Peggy was quite surprised by how crowded the apartment seemed with the addition of just two people. But to her it was just one person too many and that person was Ross, who dominated any room with his showman's personality, which she hadn't really noticed before. Perhaps it was because this was the first time she'd seen him in the company of other adults. She supposed that with children he didn't feel quite so compelled to be constantly entertaining.

He talked about the war with Jimmy and she was pleased that Mam's new friend more than held his own with comparable stories.

She was surprised to learn that Jimmy had a good degree in maths and had been a teacher before the war, though after it could only work as a handyman.

'Are you over it now?' Ross enquired.

'I think I might be, and if I am, a lot of it's down to this lady here. Looking out for her taught me to get my own life in perspective and not worry about the past too much. I very nearly died and saw a lot of nasty stuff in combat – but not as nasty as very nearly dying then losing two children, not knowing whether they were alive or dead – or even if they were going to be locked up for murder.'

Ross looked at Betty with sympathetic eyes. 'Gee, Betty, that must have been real tough for you, and yet here you are. You won the battle ... well done!'

They exchanged glances, noticed by both Peggy and Jimmy, and once again Peggy noticed just how handsome Ross was compared to Jimmy, who was okay but no matinee idol. His limp did him no favours either. She decided it might be worthwhile to discuss his limp, which had to be the result of a war wound, obviously something far more serious than Ross had suffered.

'How did you damage your leg, Jimmy?' she asked.

'It was a land mine I thought I'd defused. I was

371

walking away from it when it went off. It blew me fifty feet through the air and gave me a leg full of shrapnel.'

'That sounds like a very brave thing to have done. Did you get a medal or anything?'

'I did, actually. I was awarded a British Empire Medal for meritorious conduct – at least, that's what it says on the gong.'

'When you write letters, do you stick BEM after your name?' asked Billy. 'I know I would.'

'Well, I suppose I would if it was an MBE, which isn't a war medal. I settle for my BSc. It's enough to impress anyone I'm writing to. Tells them I'm not quite as thick as two short planks, which is what my CO said about me for making a mess of defusing the mine. He was probably right although he obviously didn't stand in the way of my award, which is more than he ever got.'

Peggy turned her attention to Ross. 'Did you win any medals in the war?'

'Just the Purple Heart they give you for being wounded in action.'

To Peggy, this was one up to Jimmy. She caught her mother giving her a warning glance that said, *Now that's enough, change the subject.* It was a censorious glance, but one that endeared her mother to her and made Peggy smile. Any such reminder of Betty's familiar ways set her daughter smiling. They were a family again, and it would do this family no harm to have Jimmy join them. She hadn't known him long but she was sure of that. But, by the same token, her mother hadn't known Ross very long. Had she made a good assessment of him?

In the apartment was an old, upright piano that Ross had bought to practise on. At Betty's insistence he sat down at it and played a piano concerto by Beethoven. Jimmy, being a piano player himself, appreciated the artistry in his playing.

'Classically trained man by the sound of you.'

'Well,' said Ross, 'I had a piano tutor who thought there was no other music. Do you play?'

'A bit,' said Jimmy, taking over the stool. He set the room alive with a medley of Rag Time tunes made popular by Scott Joplin and Jelly Roll Morton. All of which had Ross tapping his foot with a big smile on his face.

'Brilliant! The nearest I get to that is modern dance music,' he said. 'I don't suppose you know the "Maple Leaf Rag", do you?'

'My favourite,' said Jimmy, proceeding to play that very tune, much to the delight of Ross and everyone else in the room, especially Peggy who was happy that Jimmy could hold his own against any accomplishment Ross had to offer. Not that either man realised he was in a competition. Only Betty, and perhaps Billy, knew that besides Peggy. In her eyes Jimmy was ahead by one British Empire Medal, but then Ross caught up when Billy asked: 'Have you got your Purple Heart with you?'

'As a matter of fact, I have. Would you like to see it?'

'I would, yes.'

Peggy glared at her brother, who had now given Ross a one point lead since he had the actual medal to show around. Ross went up to his room and came down carrying a gold heart suspended from a purple ribbon. In the middle of the gold setting was a purple heart on which was the profile in gold of George Washington, who had established the award.

'Ross, it's really beautiful,' said Betty. Then to Jimmy, she said, 'What's your medal like?'

'It's a silver medal on a pink ribbon with white stripes, to denote that it's a military medal.'

Peggy was bursting to say something in defence of Jimmy, who didn't seem at all bothered about his rival's grandstanding.

'It's not the medal that counts, it's what they did to deserve them,' she said.

'That's true,' agreed Jimmy. 'The Victoria Cross isn't exactly a work of art, but it's worth a hundred of my medal. I only knew one bloke who got one, and it cost him his life.'

This made Peggy smile as she liked the modest heroism of the reply, but Ross was nodding in agreement too. 'That's so true. What's a piece of tin compared to a man's life?'

'Or a mother's,' said Peggy, looking at Betty, who smiled sweetly. She must have a word in private with her daughter, she decided. Although she had to admit to herself that Ross Duggan was a man she might have gone for had she not already committed herself to Jimmy.

Behave yourself, Betty Clegg! He's a married man, she thought.

'Well,' she said aloud, 'it's been a very long day. I wonder if I might go to bed?'

'Of course,' Ross told her. 'Peggy, take your

mom to your room and leave us menfolk in here to set the world to rights. Goodnight to you both. And, Peggy, well done in the show tonight. You excelled yourself.'

'Thanks, Ross,' she said, although she felt she didn't want his praise.

'I agree,' said Jimmy. 'One of the best parts of the show. You and Billy were the stars tonight and no mistake.'

'I thought Mam was the star,' said Billy. 'She got the most applause.'

'She did indeed,' said Ross. He and Betty shared a smile.

Peggy could have cursed her brother for setting up Ross with this pleasant exchange. Just whose side was her brother on? She'd have a word with him tomorrow.

Chapter 37

Ross put on the kettle to make tea for his English companions. Betty heard him moving around and went to join him out of curiosity – or was it a desire to get to know him better? She came into the kitchen and Ross greeted her with a broad smile.

'Good morning, Betty. I'm surprised to see you up so early.'

'Well, yesterday was a long day but I think I've slept all the tiredness out of me. Seeing the children after all this time seems to have given me back the energy I thought I'd lost for good.'

'Yes, I imagine it must have. They're great kids.'

'I understand you have children of a similar age.'

'I have, yes – Ross and Maisie, the same ages as your two, which was a convenient coincidence in Miami when your two took my children's places in school. It was somewhat illegal, but all in a good cause.'

'Really? I didn't know that. So my two have spent time at a school, have they?'

'They have indeed, and I believe they did very well.'

'It must have been a strange existence for them ... to be impersonating two other children at a school in a foreign country, while not knowing if their mother was dead or alive. How did they manage?'

'Surprisingly well, although they did shed a few tears whenever the subject of their mother came up. Had they known you were alive they'd have gone home long before now to face the police, I'm sure. They never believed that the fire was their fault.'

'No, nor did I.'

The whistling kettle began to boil 'Look,' said Ross, 'I'm not exactly a dab hand at making tea. Would you ... er...?'

'Of course.'

Betty brushed past him and lifted the kettle off the gas stove, making sure he felt the softness of her body beneath her borrowed robe.

'Look, the trick is always to take the teapot to the kettle so that the water is still boiling when it hits the leaves.'

She was wearing the dressing gown with nothing underneath. Whether she'd done this purposely she wasn't sure, except that she and Jimmy had never had sex, which meant it was a long time since Betty had been with a man. It was loosely tied at the front so it hung forward when she leant over to pour out the tea. Ross got an eyeful and it seemed to him this was no accident. She was a physically beautiful woman, in body as well as her face, and he was very much attracted to her. He suspected that this display wasn't accidental, so thought it would do no harm to check things out with her.

'Betty, you don't seem to be ... er ... wearing too much under that dressing gown.'

'I'm actually not wearing anything. Does that bother you?'

'On the contrary. But it's been ... well, quite a while for me.'

'More than a while for me,' said Betty, smiling at him. 'Many years, in fact.'

Ross sat down, picked up his cup, looked into her eyes and said, 'I feel there are signs being given out here. Am I reading them correctly?'

'You mean, am I trying to seduce you? Allowing you to see my breasts?'

'Well, they are beautiful – and totally wasted on a single woman.'

'Really? I have children in this house who might walk into this room at any second.'

'And what might they find us doing?'

'Well, that would be up to you.'

'Betty, they wouldn't *want* to find us doing anything.'

'True. It would spoil all this for them.'

'I'm guessing it would spoil things for Jimmy as well.'

'It would indeed. We're engaged, you know.'

'So, he's the right man for you, is he?'

Betty gave this some thought then admitted, 'He was until you turned up. He's been a tremendous support to me, apart from saving my life, but I'm not sure that there's any chemistry between us.'

'Ah, the elusive chemistry. Do you feel chemistry between us?'

She returned his gaze with one of her own as she thought of an answer. 'It's very early days. I sense there might be, but I hardly know you.'

'You know I'm a married man?'

'I know that, but I suspect your marriage isn't a bed of roses.'

'True. I think my wife and I lack chemistry too. She's a good woman, but she hates me being in the theatre.'

'You're an attractive man and I imagine the theatre leaves you open to all sorts of temptations.'

'Oh, not as many as you think, although I seem to be responding to temptation right now.'

'Naughty boy!'

Betty tightened the belt of her dressing gown so that she was revealing nothing. 'All I can tell you is that Jimmy is only staying for a week. He has regular bookings back home playing piano and doesn't want to lose any of them.'

'That's understandable ... and you?'

'I'm supposed to be going back with him, the

kids as well, but circumstances here aren't quite what we had imagined so I think I'll be staying on for a while to see how things work out for them. If they have a future in the theatre, I don't want to stand in their way.'

'I think,' said Ross, 'that if your kids want it badly enough, they definitely have a future. How will Jimmy feel if you stay on, with me in the picture?'

'He doesn't know you're in the picture. In fact, neither did I until a few minutes ago.'

'So you thought you'd try me out with a loose dressing gown?'

'That wasn't planned, I can assure you.'

'All the same, I'm glad it happened.'

Betty picked up her teacup and took a sip from it. Then she said, 'I don't know where this is leading but I don't think I can do this to Jimmy. He's more than saved my life. He proved that the kids weren't responsible for the fire and all sorts of other stuff ... all for my sake.'

'In that case, I think you and I had better leave this thing alone, whatever this thing is ... and it would probably be better if you went back with Jimmy and married the man right away. I'm not sure that I'm as good as he is. I'm much too selfish. I'm only here because I wanted my own way, regardless of my wife's wishes.'

'And you'd go back to her, would you?'

'If I go back to England, I'll be going back to her and our children. Leaving her would mean abandoning them. I don't think I could do that.' He gave a short laugh. 'What the hell are we talking about? Here we are, two confused adults acting like a couple of teenagers, worrying about something that won't happen.'

'I agree. I'll pour some tea out for Jimmy and the kids and take it in,' said Betty, getting to her feet. 'Do you have a tray?'

Ross was holding a finger to his lips and pointing to the door to the living room, where someone was moving about. The kitchen door opened and Billy came in.

'Did I hear someone say something about tea?' he asked, brightly.

'Have you been earwigging on us?' said Betty.

Billy now had a guilty look on his face. This worried both Betty and Ross. How much had he heard?

'Not really,' said Billy.

'What else did you hear?'

'I think I heard Ross say you should go back with Jimmy. Does that mean we have to go too?'

'No, it doesn't. Jimmy has to go back to do his piano playing jobs and I'm probably going with him. If you and Peggy want to stay, I won't give you any argument so long as Ross promises to keep an eye on you both and make sure you finish your educations.'

'I see no problem with that,' said Ross. 'We get on fine, us three.'

Billy gave his mother a wide beam and said, 'Our Peggy thinks you're going to marry Jimmy. Is that right?'

'He's asked me and I've said yes.'

'Does that mean he'll be our dad?'

'He'll be the nearest you've ever had to a dad,' said Betty, putting her arm around her son's shoulders. It occurred to her to tell him about his real dad, but maybe this wasn't the time.

'But don't forget your dear old mam back in England.'

'Mam, me and Peg can manage over here. We're really enjoying ourselves and it's loads better now we know you're alive.'

'And the show won't last forever,' Ross assured her. 'Then it's back to sunny Leeds for Billy and Peggy.'

'And back to your wife for you,' said Betty, hoping to reinforce, in Billy's mind, that there was nothing between her and Ross.

'Hey, Peg, I think Mam fancies Ross.'

Billy had gone straight to Peggy's room and was unloading his worries on to her.

'Give over, Billy, she hardly knows him. What makes yer say that?'

'I just heard 'em talkin', and it were *that* sort of talk, yer know? Like they fancy each other. Any-road, Mam says she's gonna marry Jimmy.'

'Billy, make sense. You mean she fancies Ross and she's marrying Jimmy? That's just daft, even for you.'

'If it's daft it's not my fault. They're grown-ups, and grown-ups don't always make sense.'

'Well, you're right there, but I bet Jimmy's not so suited if she fancies Ross.'

'He prob'ly doesn't even know.'

'Then it's not up to us to tell him.'

'Why not?'

'Because yer might have got hold of the wrong end of the stick, that's why not. It won't be the first time neither.'

'I hope I have, Peg.'

'So do I.'

Chapter 38

Two months later Ross and Betty were together, in the apartment. Betty was reading a letter that had just been delivered.

'It's from Jimmy. He's coming over. In fact he should be here within a week. Oh, heck, Ross. Do you think I should have written and told him about us before he decided to come?'

Ross scratched his head, saying, 'Probably, but you haven't and we'll have to brave it out. He'll be coming back hoping to marry you over here, or to take you back, and we're going to have to tell him we're engaged.'

'I know,' said Betty. 'For me to let Jimmy down after all he's done for me ... I feel really rotten about it.'

'How rotten would you feel if you married him and let me down?'

'I know, I know. Jimmy's lovely, but he's the wrong man for me. I knew that as soon as you came into the picture. I suppose I was comparing him to my husband when I said I'd marry him – Jimmy is so much nicer.'

'Do you want me to tell him?'

'Oh, no. It has to come from me. I mean, what's he going to do when he's over here? He can't stay with us, under the circumstances.'

'Hmm. I'll have a scout round for a single person's apartment on a short let.'

'Oh dear, Ross! I'm not looking forward to telling him, not one bit.'

'Well, so long as you don't change your mind about who you want to marry.'

'No, there's no chance of that. I just wish I hadn't accepted his proposal. At the time it just seemed so right. I was swapping a dead bad husband for a live good one.'

'Well, it would have been a good swap, I suppose.'

'It was when we started talking about chemistry between a man and a woman,' said Betty. 'It set me thinking.'

'And...?'

'And I didn't think the chemistry was right between me and Jimmy.'

'I wouldn't give him that as a reason for you marrying me and not him. He's a plain-speaking man and I imagine he's also a plain-thinking one.'

'So, what do I tell him – that I've fallen in love with you and I don't love him?'

'Well, that would be the truth but I think you should, er, soften the blow a little.'

'How?'

'I don't know, but it has to be done. Jimmy's in for a massive disappointment and he's a man we both like.'

'I wish I'd written to him,' said Betty. 'Things like that can be said so much more easily in a letter.'

Chapter 39

Jimmy was on a ship heading directly to New York. He was leaning on the rail, watching the sea churning under the propellers, leaving a long trail of disturbed water behind. To his right he could see whales appearing out of the water and the odd school of flying fish. It was a fine day but he wasn't feeling fine. There was a major problem he had to iron out with Betty once he got over there; a problem he could have resolved by letter, but he missed her and wanted to see how happy she was with her life over there. He also brought news from Wooltorton about Jack Blainey's money.

Lester Blainey had just been hanged in Strangeways prison for the deaths he'd caused that awful night and his insurers had refused to pay out insurance money to anyone on the grounds of the fire being arson caused by Lester. Wooltorton, on Betty's instruction, took no part in this claim, but he was suing Lester's personal estate for substantial damages on Betty's behalf. This included the value of the land on which the factory had stood plus Lester's own house, its contents and whatever money he had in his bank.

Wooltorton expected Betty to be reasonably compensated for her troubles. Jimmy was pleased that he'd saved her life and brought about a just resolution to her and the kids. No wonder she'd asked him to marry her, or did she fall for his charm and good looks? He smiled to himself at the nonsense of such a thought. *Now then, Potter, don't get big-headed.* The one thing he knew about Betty Clegg was that she'd make a great wife for any man.

He was expecting her to be meeting him at the port when he arrived and wondered what she'd think about him bringing Ross's wife back with him. He grimaced at the thought. She wouldn't be too pleased when he told her why he'd brought the woman back with him. Perhaps he should have mentioned it in a letter or telephone call first, but it was a last-minute decision by her to come along and it had been practically too late to warn them. If both Betty and Ross turned up to meet them it might make things a bit easier. Or would it? Probably not. There was no easy way to do this, Jimmy decided.

The ship docked at a Manhattan terminal at exactly 7 a.m. Jimmy and Laura had been on deck since five, not wanting to miss any of the dramatic arrival in New York. As night turned into day they'd seen the lights of Long Island and then the skyline of Manhattan, after which came the unforgettable sight of the Statue of Liberty. On docking he went to the ship's rail to see if he could spot Betty in the crowd down there but she wasn't visible among the welcoming horde. He thought she might spot him as he went down the companionway but there was still no sign of her. On the quayside he found an elevated platform from where he got a good view of everyone and they a good view of him, but still no sign of Betty. Laura was growing impatient so he jumped down off his perch and said, 'She can't be here. I know where they live. I'll get us a cab.'

Back at the apartment Betty was pacing up and down, watched by Ross. 'He'll have expected me to meet him off the ship.'

'Betty, he knows where we are. He'll be on his way here in a cab.' There was a knock on the door then. They looked at each other, as if wondering who should answer it. In the end it was Betty who went.

Jimmy was standing there with a big smile on his face. Behind him was a beautiful woman whom Betty didn't recognise. Jimmy stood to one side to introduce her.

'This is Laura Duggan, Ross's wife. She came with me.'

Betty's heart sank. This was going to be even worse than she'd expected – twice as bad. 'Oh, hello, Laura, I'm Betty. Ross is inside. Come on in, both of you.'

Laura and Jimmy followed her through to the living room where Ross was sitting. He got to his feet with a look of shock on his face when his wife walked in. She held up her hands to stem any outburst.

'Ross, before you say anything I'm here because Jimmy and I have something to tell you and it wasn't fair him having to tell you on his own.'

'And what exactly is this thing?' asked Ross. 'It must be important for you to travel three thousand miles to announce it. Have you sold your business and come here to live or something?'

'Nothing like that, but it's very important. You see, Jimmy's a good man who has always looked out for Betty's welfare. What's good for her is good enough for him, which was why he went back to England when he did.'

'Not sure I see the logic in any of this,' said Ross.

'Well, he was under the foolish impression,' said Laura, 'that Betty was falling for you, so he thought it a good idea to bring me back over here with him.' She looked directly at Betty and added, 'Jimmy wanted to give you time to make up your mind about who and what you wanted out of life. You've had over a month alone with Ross, so I reckon you should know by now. What we want know is: *Do you want my husband or not?*'

'Good God, Laura!' said Ross. 'Don't beat about the bush. Speak your mind, why don't you?'

'I just have. Jimmy's been worrying about this moment all the way here, haven't you, Jimmy?'

Jimmy nodded. 'It's, erm, like she says.' Then to Betty he added, 'Was I right about thinking you were falling for Ross, or was I being stupid?'

Betty stared at him. In her mind were all the wonderful things this man done for her and how ungrateful she would seem if she dumped him. She said nothing because she hadn't the words. Laura spoke for her.

'Betty, Jimmy's a fine man and I know how much you owe him, but that's no basis for marriage, is it?'

'Well, you're right about him being a fine man,' said Betty, 'and I wouldn't want to do anything to hurt him.'

Ross was looking at Betty now, wondering where all this was leading.

'Telling him the truth won't hurt him,' said Laura, who had now read the signs and knew exactly where this was going.

'How do you know?'

'I know...' said Laura, hesitating before adding, 'I know because we've spent a lot of time together and Jimmy wants to marry me.'

'He wants to *what?*' exclaimed Ross.

'And I've said yes.'

There was a stunned silence all round. Neither Ross nor Betty had expected this. Betty felt a heavy weight dropping from her shoulders. A smile appeared on her face.

'Is this true, Jimmy?'

He nodded, ruefully. 'I'm really sorry, Betty, but I think I proposed to you because of the awful mess you were in, and I felt marrying me might get you out of it.'

'You did help me get out of it, Jimmy, but you didn't have to go and marry me.'

'That's exactly what I thought,' said Laura. 'So, now you know, what do we all do?'

'We could make it a double wedding,' said Ross.

'Who with?' asked Jimmy.

'With us – me and Betty. We want to get married as well.'

'What? You and Betty?'

'Yep.'

'Well,' said Laura, 'you could have mentioned this a bit earlier.'

'When?' asked Ross.

'When I told you about me and Jimmy.'

'Ah, you mean like a minute earlier? I do apologise. I just wanted to hear what you had to say,' said Ross. 'To be honest, Betty and I hadn't a clue how to break it to you. Did we, Betty?'

'Not a clue. It's a weight off my mind, I can tell you.'

Jimmy flopped down in a chair. 'Do you know, we've been worrying all the way over about how to break it to you?'

'Tell me about it,' said Betty.

'So everything's all right, is it?'

'Right as rain, Jimmy.'

'Have you told the kids?' he asked.

'Not officially. You?'

'Sort of,' said Jimmy. 'They had their suspicions, so we came clean. It was the way we talked to each other that gave us away. Look, I've booked us a place to stay not far from here and I wouldn't mind us getting over there and settling in. I know your number so I can give you a bell later and tell you all about the money you're due.'

Betty blushed a little as she thought of Jack, her former lover. It was a blush of guilt rather than embarrassment. She looked from one to the other of them and said, 'Look, to stop you all wondering, I'd better tell you this. Jack Blainey and I were lovers, which is one of the reasons why he was generous about arranging for redundancy money. When he found out he was dying of a brain tumour he made provision for both Billy and Peggy in a bequest he made just after Billy was born.'

'The bequest still stands,' put in Jimmy. 'But Wooltorton saw no future in wasting time and money on claiming the insurance payout for the fire, with it being arson caused by Lester. In fact the insurance company has refused to payout anyone. The rest was quite complicated but I understand from Wooltorton that with Lester also dying intestate the law is quite vague about who should inherit Jack's property.'

'In that case it's a good job I don't want any of their money,' said Betty.

'As far as you're concerned that certainly closes the door on the whole Blainey business,' said Jimmy.

'Good,' said Betty. 'I hope I never hear that damned name again.'

Billy was standing at the door with his sister. His mother turned in alarm, saying, 'Billy Clegg, have you been earwigging on us again?'

'We've only just come down for breakfast,' Billy said. 'So why did this Blainey feller leave me all that money?'

'Billy, he hasn't left you any money.'

All eyes were now on Betty, including those of Peggy, who hadn't heard quite as much as her brother.

Betty put an arm around him and explained, gently. 'The dad you thought was killed in the army wasn't actually your real dad.'

'Wasn't he? I never liked him, Mam. Mebbe that's the reason. Who's my dad, then? Is he alive?'

'I'm afraid not. Your real dad was a good man called Jack Blainey, who was Lester Blainey's brother. He died.'

The circumstances of his conception were of no interest to Billy. 'So I've got two dead dads?'

'No, love, just the one. We only ever get one dad.'

'It looks like I'm gonna end up with three,' said Billy, looking at Ross. 'Am I rich?'

'You get two thousand when you're twenty-one,' said Betty. 'The rest of it was just pie-in-the-sky money that would have been more trouble than it was worth, and I've had enough Blainey trouble recently.'

'I agree with Mam,' said Peggy 'Last Christmas we'd have given anything to get our mam back – and us out of trouble.' She gave her brother an admonishing look and added, 'Wouldn't we, Billy Clegg?'

A defeated Billy shrugged and said, 'Yeah, we would ... does Peggy get anything?'

'Like I said, the money from Jack's will is to be held in trust for you until you're twenty-one,' said his mother. 'Peggy gets the same. Two thousand pounds for each of you. That's the only guaranteed money we get.'

'Blimey, Peg, we're both stinking rich.'

'And I've got some good news for you both,' said Ross.

'What's that?' asked Billy.

'In May our show's being moved onto Broadway proper. There's a show closing down and we're moving in. The producer told me yesterday. That'll make you both bona fide Broadway actors.'

'Is that the kids' doing?' asked Laura. 'I understand they were very good.'

'So was Ross,' said Betty. 'He apparently attracted quite a following among theatre-going women.'

'I think the kids helped secure my place,' admitted Ross. 'Without them I think I might well have been dropped.'

'Nonsense,' said Betty.

'I agree with Mam,' said Peggy. 'He was really scary as Bill Sykes.'

'Will we get more money?' said Billy.

'A lot more than you're getting now, I should imagine,' said Ross. 'Same for me, I hope.' He gave Laura a pointed look. She glanced away.

'Billy, don't be so flipping mercenary,' scolded Betty. 'You've got money on the brain. And talking of money, I've been meaning to ask how you two managed for so long and got over here on the fifteen bob you took from the house?'

'We became robbers,' said Billy.

Before his mother could react, he left the room and set off for his new school. Betty looked at Ross and Jimmy, and said, 'There's a smart-looking bar down the street. Why don't you two go for a drink or two and let us girls have a good old natter about you?'

'It's a bit early for drinking,' said Jimmy.

'I bet they make coffee.'

'In that case we should definitely go for some coffee and set the world to rights as these lovely women pull us both to pieces,' said Ross.

With that, the two of them left the women alone. Peggy stared at her mother, wondering if she had anything important to tell her that she didn't want the men to hear.

'Is there something you want to say to me, Mam? Is that why you got rid of them?'

'Well, maybe I want to ask your opinion of what's just gone on. You know – me now being with Ross and Jimmy with Laura.'

'It's an opinion I'd be interested to hear myself,' said Laura, looking at Peggy.

'Well,' said Peggy, 'I still don't know Jimmy that well but he seems a good man and I'm not a bit surprised you took to him, Mam.'

'Yes, but I've now dropped him and taken to Ross. What do you think about that?'

'Ross is very handsome and charming.'

'I know, love, and that's a bit of a worry. I've already had one handsome husband and he was a dead loss.'

'Well Ross isn't like that,' said Laura, very quickly. 'He's a very good man, but a man with ambitions for a career he's not qualified for.'

'You mean the theatre?'

'I do, yes. I'd have much preferred him to stick to teaching but he hated that job.'

'Yeah. I don't think Jimmy was too keen on teaching either.'

'Ross is a very good actor,' said Peggy, feeling that the absent men should have someone to speak for them.

'Yeah, and that's something else that might be a worry,' said her mother.

'Oh, you'll be able to trust Ross,' Laura assured her. 'I don't know you, Betty, but from what I've seen so far, you seem absolutely what Ross needs in a woman. So, what can you tell me about Jimmy?'

'He's a man you can trust with your life. I know he dropped me for you, but I can see why. What you see is what you get with Jimmy. He's a really lovely man.'

'Did you love him?'

'I thought I did, but at the back of my mind I kept comparing my love for him to the love I'd once had for another man. You need to have been properly in love at least once to know what love really feels like.'

'You mean Billy's father?'

'Yes. I never felt about Jimmy the way I felt about Jack. When Jimmy went back to England I didn't even miss him, which I should have, had I loved him. You know, when Ross told me he loved me and I realised I loved him I was worried that I might be splitting up his family – and with his children being such good friends with mine that would have been awful. But now I know they'll have a great stepdad in Jimmy it makes me feel a lot better about things.'

'Tell me, Betty, do you feel for Ross the way you felt about Jack?'

'As a matter of fact, I do ... and I believe he feels the same way about me. Sorry, Laura.'

'Don't be sorry. My feelings for Jimmy are way stronger than anything I ever felt for Ross. In fact, I realise I'd never been properly in love with anyone before I met him.'

'My word!' said Betty. 'This love business really takes some unravelling.'

'It does, and how lucky we are that fate threw the four of us together like this.'

'Does Jimmy get on well with your children?'

'Oh yes, very well,' said Laura.

'So do we with Ross,' chimed in Peggy, before adding, 'I wonder what Ross Junior and Maisie'll think when they find out what's happened.'

'It sounds to me as if they might have known it was in the offing,' said Laura.

Peggy smiled and said, 'Knowing them, I think you're right.'

'My word, listen to you,' said her mother. 'Talking to us two as if you're the same age.'

'I'm giving the opinion of a daughter. I'm also wondering what the men are talking about.'

'I bet it's nothing to do with us,' said Laura. 'Men don't discuss such things with each other.'

'True,' said Betty. 'Anyway, as long as they get on with each other, that'll do for me. Are you happy with all this, Laura?'

'As a matter of fact, I'm delighted. When Ross first left to come here I thought our marriage was over, but I never reckoned on it ending up like this.'

'Me too. When I got the telegram telling me my husband was dead I vowed never to marry again. Once bitten and all that...'

Peggy was listening intently, wondering if she might learn anything from all this. Betty smiled at her, saying, 'Don't take too much notice of us, darling. Just remember to take the greatest care when you decide to get married. It's supposed to be for life, so be careful who you choose.'

'Well, I've pretty much gathered that much already,' said Peggy.

Epilogue

In the bar, Jimmy was playing the piano and singing old British music-hall songs along with Ross. It had been a quiet morning hitherto, with the patrons enjoying coffee and conversation. The two of them brought the place to life. The manager listened for a while and went over to speak to Jimmy.

'Would you be able to play here nights now and again?'

'How much?' asked Ross, before Jimmy could reply.

'Thirty dollars a night.'

'I believe the going rate is forty,' said Ross. 'I'm his agent.'

'Okay, forty then.'

'It's a deal,' said Ross.

Jimmy confronted him afterwards. 'Ross, how can I play here? I live in England.'

'You could get a teaching job here. You've got a degree in math, haven't you?'

'We English call it maths. I thought you had a degree in English.'

Ross ignored this. 'And you've taught before?'

'I have, but I didn't have much of a vocation for teaching.'

'You only need a vocation for teaching the arts – you've got a science degree. You should walk into a decent teaching job over here. Wounded

British war hero with a math degree.'

'It's a British Empire Medal not a VC.'

'Doesn't matter, it's a bravery medal, and there's always piano work in the theatres and bars for someone as good as you. I can put your name about if you like. New York's not such a bad old place, is it? And forty dollars is ten quid English money. I'd take the job myself but I'm tied up in the theatre. Can you make that sort of money over there for a few hours piano playing?'

'No. Ten quid was more than two weeks' wages for me.'

'Then stay here.'

'Oh, I don't know yet,' said Jimmy, who was obviously tempted by the idea. 'I've only been here two minutes.'

'I think you'll get to like it here.'

'Do you think so?'

'I do, honest, and I know Betty likes it ... and so do the kids.'

'What about your kids?'

'All they want is for their mom and dad to be happy and both of us to be within their range.'

'But will they be happy if you're with Betty and Laura's with me?'

'Oh, yes. So long as they know we don't hate each other. Kids are amazingly flexible in that way. Besides, Laura and I won't be three thousand miles apart any more, and I reckon the four of us will have a lot of get-togethers.'

'Yes, I reckon we will.'

Ross had got Jimmy thinking that New York wasn't a bad old place, and if Laura and her kids wanted to settle there, he'd be happy enough to join them. In fact, he'd be more than happy to live anywhere with Laura Duggan providing she was happy to become Laura Potter. It was odd how things had turned out. A month ago, if anyone had told him he'd be giving up on marrying Betty Clegg he'd have told them they were mad, but love is a strange thing and he knew Laura was really the one for him, and if Betty was happier with Ross, then Jimmy was happy for them both.

Ross replaced him at the piano and struck up with 'Pack Up Your Troubles', which, to their surprise, the audience all knew and joined in with. When the tune ended Jimmy joined him on the piano stool and said, 'Tell me, Ross, out of the four of us, who do you think came off best?'

'Well, I'm pretty happy with my outcome, but do you think the ladies got as good a deal as we did?'

'Well, my lady did. I'm not too sure about yours.'

Ross grinned, knowing he'd get on with this man.

At school, Billy's mind wasn't on the lesson. He was still wondering how much trouble he was in for admitting to becoming a robber. He'd have been better off telling his mam they'd been earning money busking, with him on his banjo and Peggy singing, but she'd have known his banjo was still in the house in Leeds so she'd have known that was a lie. On the plus side, however, he'd become quite a celebrity at school for his role in the soon-to-be Broadway hit show.

When Billy had left the house for school that morning Betty had looked in amazement at the door closing behind him.

'Just so you know,' said Peggy, who started school later than her brother. 'I was never a robber.'

'As a matter of fact, I don't think for a minute that either of you were. He's gone off without any breakfast, which is not like him at all – and what on earth made him say a ridiculous thing like that? A robber, for heaven's sake. Robbers get themselves locked up. My Billy wouldn't last two minutes locked up! As if I'd believe that!'

The publishers hope that this book has given you enjoyable reading. Large Print Books are especially designed to be as easy to see and hold as possible. If you wish a catalogue please ask at your local library or write directly to:

Magna Large Print Books
Cawood House,
Asquith Industrial Estate,
Gargrave,
Nr Skipton, North Yorkshire.
BD23 3SE

This Large Print Book for the partially sighted, who cannot read normal print, is published under the auspices of

THE ULVERSCROFT FOUNDATION